AF226883

The First Book of the Shadowland Hexology

THE DOOR INTO SHADOW

Copyright © J. I. Thacker, 2019

All rights reserved.

ISBN: 978-1-913152-00-0

COVER AND DESIGN

@hazel.designs

THE DOOR INTO SHADOW

J. I. Thacker

ΘΛΘ

PART ONE

*

THE MONKEY

While yet a boy I sought for ghosts, and sped
Through many a listening chamber, cave and ruin,
And starlight wood, with fearful steps pursuing
Hopes of high talk with the departed dead.

Shelley

Chapter 1: Midnight in the Garden of Death

By bobbing, flickering torchlight two boys moved deeper into the cemetery, kicking through shin-deep drifts of dead wet leaves. Skeletal trees, each a grave mother with a clutch of mossy tombstones at her feet, loomed out of the gloom every few steps. Above, a fuzzy moon was dimly visible in cold haze, while at ground level, the fog was thicker, lapping around the gravestones like a ghostly sea.

"This doesn't look right," whispered the younger boy, David, catching his elder brother's arm. Without the thrashing sounds of their feet through the leaves, the cemetery was suddenly frighteningly quiet.

"I think we've come too far to the left," Nathan agreed calmly, striking off in a new direction.

"What is it with this fog?"

"There's probably a reasonable explanation for it. Maybe we're in a little depression here –"

"You can say that again," interrupted David.

"What's the matter with you?" joked Nathan. "You haven't lived until you've been to a cemetery at midnight."

"You haven't died either," said David darkly.

"Hush – I see it." Nathan led his brother towards a tall square stone monument, topped with a sculpted limestone urn, wreathed in stone ivy. "Chez Carraway," he said.

Mossy limestone chippings and a low, rusted iron railing surrounded the tomb. David played his torch along the face of the memorial that was nearest to him; there, carved in stone, were the names of two of his grandparents, and their dates of birth and death, and below that were the hopeful words 'together again.' He had never met them; his father, had he still been alive, would probably have told him all about them. As it was, the words 'Herbert

Carraway' and 'Jean Carraway' were little more to David than a collection of crevices for lichens to make their homes in.

To his left, Nathan was kneeling down, assembling some equipment. He had already lit two candles in jars, which were guttering badly even though the air was quite still. On that side of the monument some more words were carved. David highlighted his parents' names with his wavering torch beam; they were much fresher than the names of his grandparents, with only a few specks of encroaching lichen to soften their edges. Martin and Hope Carraway. These were names that he recognized, names that had faces, faces that smiled at him from the prison of memory. They may have been gone for six years, and he may only have been eight when they died, but David remembered his parents well. He recalled moments with his mother and father, their expressions, and some of their actions, as if they were fragments of a silent movie. He could remember that his parents loved him, but he could not recall how their voices sounded. He remembered them like a piece of himself that had long been cut away but could never be forgotten.

"Have you got the pad?" Nathan asked.

"What are we doing here?" asked David, but his question was a resigned one, asked in a way that did not offer a challenge to what was about to happen.

"You know why we're here."

"What do I have to do?"

"Come and kneel beside me – wait – do you smell that?" asked Nathan, interrupting himself. "It smells like something from the chemistry lab."

David tested the air. There was a scent there, one that he hadn't noticed before. It was faint, but definite. "What is it?" he asked.

Nathan was sniffing his rucksack. He shook his head. "I'm not sure. Ethyl acetate maybe. Some kind of organic solvent, that's for sure. Strange kind of smell for a graveyard – I mean, I could imagine rotting flesh, yes, but –"

"I don't like it," said David flatly.

"Do you want to know if they were murdered or not? By summoning their ghosts we can find out."

"There are such things as accidents…"

"But what about what they said to me a few days earlier? You were only eight at the time, you wouldn't remember that long ago. Mum said *'Nathan – don't forget. If anything happens to your father and me, it's up to you to look after Baby D.'* She made me promise."

"Baby D?"

"That's you, you prize peach. Don't you even remember that? That's what we used to call you."

"You sound like you're sixty, not sixteen."

"I'm older than you. So I remember Mum and Dad better than you. Now get your pen and paper ready. I'm going to read from the book, okay? Your bit comes in a minute." So saying, Nathan began to read by torchlight, tracing the words with his right forefinger, mumbling under his breath.

David looked around nervously. Down near the ground, the cold fog was suffocatingly thick. That strange aroma was still lingering in the air. A slow rain fell from the trees all around them, like poisonous thoughts dripping from their twisted fingers. David shivered.

"That's it," said Nathan suddenly. "They're here, if they're here, if you see what I mean. Right. Now here's what I want you to do. Let your hand move across the page – don't consciously try to write anything – and picture Mum and Dad, okay?"

David let his hand pass over the page. He looked down to see what he had made: a straight, perhaps slightly wavy, line.

"It's all right," encouraged Nathan. "Take your time, and go slow."

"Why do I have to do it?" objected David.

"Because the younger you are, the more receptive you are. That's what the book says. You're our best shot."

David drew his hand across the page again, more slowly this time. He felt his hand move up and down the page a little as it went from left to right.

"Nothing," said David, looking down.

"You're getting it," said Nathan. "Keep going."

"Rum?" asked Nathan. "Run? K-something?"

David tried again. Nathan gasped. David looked at what he had written:

"I didn't do it," whispered David.

"Ssh. I know you didn't. Keep going."

"Mum? Dad? Is it you?"

"Yes, it's me. Us. I've got David with me. We've come to find out what happened –"

what happened

"Yes, what happened? Was it an accident?"

miss you NOT gone

"Miss us? We miss you. I miss you. David misses you…"

Hovelworbyou home keeping

Not running sleepy lonely

"Can you repeat that?" asked Nathan.

David stared at what he had written. Was he really writing this? A nudge from Nathan reminded him that he should be doing the next line. Once again, he drew his pencil across the increasingly damp page. He could not help but notice that the solvent smell seemed to be getting stronger.

not BABY you pa car running away

coldrooms old lovely love dovey us NOT

"Not what?" asked Nathan. "This is gibberish," he said. "Don't stop – concentrate harder. I think we're getting a confused signal. There must be other spirits here…"

lovely cold davy an LOVE YOU, WE us Run

"Mum? What are you talking about?"

"I think they want us to run," said Nathan, standing up. He pulled David up with him. "Let's get out of here," he said, looking around nervously. He began to drag David along with him back the way they had come.

"What about the candles?" whispered David.

"Forget them," said Nathan. "Did you hear that?" he asked, freezing.

They looked in all directions, searching the silent gloom with their torches. Swirling fog, dripping trees and stone memorials surrounded them. Ten metres behind them, the two faint orange smudges of light of the candles were still visible. David shook his head. He could neither hear nor see anything. He *was* scared though. But it was not the ominous words on his pad, the creeping fog, the looming trees, or the deep darkness that were making him afraid; he could tell that Nathan, his big brother, was scared, and that meant that there really was something to be frightened of.

There was a noise, something like a shoe scuffing against stones, from somewhere near the Carraway family tomb. As the boys looked that way once more, the two specks of candlelight vanished, as if snuffed out by a ghostly breath.

At that, they ran for their lives. David soon fell behind his brother, first only a few steps, then twenty; soon he could barely see Nathan's bobbing torchlight ahead of him. His legs felt like rubber. He wanted to call his brother but didn't dare. He knew that someone was behind him, but he could hear nothing over the sounds of his own feet lashing through leaves and long grass, his thumping heart and harsh breathing, and he did not want to look back. He cut across a path he recognized – should he turn onto the path, or keep going cross-country? Which way had Nathan gone? With panic beginning to shake him, he realized that he could no longer see his brother's torchlight. He must have gone cross-country. He had to have done. It was the quickest way to the railings. David went that way, sprinting for all he was worth between the gravestones. Soon he could see the far-off gleam of streetlights and the glowing curtains of someone's front bedroom – he was nearly there.

Then he was falling. His tiring feet had snagged on a tussock of grass. The ground beneath him was soft and wet, his landing a painless one, and he was getting to his feet again almost before he realized that he had fallen.

That whiff of solvent had become a stink, a nose-rankling stink.

David could see the railings. He was almost home. And there – was that Nathan, waiting on the other side? It was. "Come on!" his brother shouted.

Then someone grabbed him from behind and he was being bundled over, his arms pinned to his sides. He desperately struggled to free himself, but he was too small, too weak. Quickly his attacker clamped a wet, reeking pad over his face. He tried not to breathe, but could not help himself, gulping a lungful of chemistry. Immediately he felt nausea, dizziness, and worst of all, an awful need to breathe again.

It should have been the end. But it wasn't.

Chapter 2: The Empty Coffin

There was a gaping hole in the Carraway plot. The limestone chips had been piled up, off to one side, and a large, rectangular slab of stone had been removed to reveal the secret void beneath. David was surprised to detect no smell emanating from the tomb. Partly hidden behind an old cypress tree, a fluorescent yellow JCB was trying hard to be unobtrusive but was not succeeding. Like a vulture in a butcher's shop, it had things it wanted to do, but had to hide and wait until it was alone before it could begin. David thought that they should have black diggers for the cemetery.

This was the closest David had been to his parents for seven years. If he wanted to, he could easily climb down into that darkness and touch them… their coffins, at least… he thought of what the coffins contained, and an uncontrollable shudder shook his whole body.

On a piece of plastic grass, a shiny new beechwood coffin was waiting to be lowered into the crypt. It was empty. The coffin-bearers had carried it with all due solemnity, but it had looked so light that they might all float off into the air at any moment. Nathan would enjoy this: a Huck Finn moment… or was it Tom Sawyer who had witnessed his own funeral service? Maybe both; David could not be sure, but he thought it was both.

Everything was quiet, save for the calling of an unseen crow. Every few seconds it laughed aloud at the scene it was witnessing.

Krra!

Krra!

A strong arm grabbed him around the shoulders, and a large shaven head moved in close to his ear. "This is a joke," whispered Uncle Charlie, apparently agreeing with the watching bird.

David nodded silently and even managed a half smile.

The cemetery was covered in a thin uneven coating of snow. The snowfall had been intermittent, each layer partially melting before the next came. It had left the ground a mosaic of greens and whites, from apple green through mint green to the purest snow white where deeper drifts had gathered in thicker vegetation. Heavy grey clouds hung low overhead, promising more weather for the mourners.

There was a good turnout for Nathan's pretend funeral. In fact, the only person missing was Nathan himself... unless like Huck and Tom he was watching nearby, waiting to make a grand entrance. David even glanced over his shoulder, scanning the uneven ranks of tombs... just in case.

One year had passed since Nathan's disappearance, and everybody had lost all hope that he would ever be seen again, at least everybody who was grown up, everybody who was not Nathan's brother, everybody, in other words, whose opinion mattered. So here they were, burying an empty coffin, with the object of laying David's hope to rest along with it.

The mourners included four of Nathan's mates from high school, and even the deputy head, Mr Hobbs. Hobbs was short (considerably overtopped by Nathan's friends), muscular, and had a permanently aggressive gleam in his eye. He had shaken David's hand warmly enough, his grip fierce. Generally he passed the younger Carraway in the corridors without so much as a glance.

There were two police officers present, standing together on the far side of the Carraway memorial: Detective Constable Kramer, and Police Constable Fi Childs. Kramer (who had never told David his first name) was responsible for investigating Nathan's disappearance, and David despised him for his abject failure to generate so much as a single lead. His suit was ill-fitting on his bony frame, all shoulders and no chest, giving him the hollow appearance of a scarecrow. His deep-pitted eyes and uneven teeth did nothing to dispel that impression. Fi, on the other hand, was a nice, cuddly but ineffectual type of person. She was a family liaison officer, and David had spent quite a lot of time with her in the few days immediately following Nathan's abduction. She had a friendly air, but not a very professional one; she was more like an aunt than a police officer.

Then there was David, of course, and beside him, Uncle Charlie. Skulking in the background, smoking a hand-rolled cigarette, was Teresa, David's current social worker. In many ways she was the worst of the several social workers David had known, but somewhat oddly, he liked her best of all. She was unsympathetic and straight-talking, where the others had been too sympathetic and patronising. The others hid behind professional masks, while she was at least real, even if she was hard. David watched her as she ground out her cigarette under her black DM boots. She was kind of cool, in a way.

Next in line as one looked around the circle of mourners came Guy and Rebecca, his foster parents, standing at three o'clock as he looked across the hole in the ground. David was aware of them continually trying to catch his eye, perhaps to offer moral support, but he kept his head down, looking at his feet and the yawning rectangle of night in front of them.

Lastly there was the priest, muttering about Nathan as if he'd been a favourite nephew, when in fact he'd never met him – that was another thing that was beginning to annoy David.

He was trapped: trapped in a world of adults controlling his life, organising ridiculous pantomimes like this one. If his life was his to lead, he would be gone now, racing off between the mossy headstones, darting this way and that like a mountain hare… just as he had done that very night, one year before. One year… he could hardly believe that twelve months had passed since he had lost Nathan. His brother had been kneeling not a yard from where he was standing now. And David's pen had spouted gibberish… or had he really been a conduit for the words of his parents? He had written 'run,' which suggested that whoever had been talking was at least on their side – but it might just as well have been his own subconscious desire to flee that had shaped those words…

Suddenly David realized that the priest had stopped speaking. Uncle Charlie gave his shoulders a squeeze. "Would you like to say anything, mate?" he asked.

David nodded, and looked up at last. A ring of faces stared at him expectantly. "I only want to say one thing," he said. His voice came out quietly, almost apologetically. He cleared his throat, took a deep breath, and started again. "I'm not giving up hope, just because everyone else is. If there was a way out, Nathan would have found it. My brother could do –" he corrected himself – "*can* do anything he put – *puts* – his mind to." An invisible mangle seemed to grip his head, then, and began to wring tears from his eyes: not because his brother was dead, but because he had said the wrong thing. All these trappings of death, the coffin, the priest, and all these mourners had half-convinced him that Nathan really was dead. The funeral bluff had almost worked: the embers of David's hope had almost been extinguished.

Uncle Charlie was gripping him even more tightly in one arm, ruffling his hair with the other. "Good stuff," he whispered.

David watched as the coffin-bearers lowered the empty box down. A bucket of potting compost was offered to him, in case he wanted to shower 'earth' on the coffin. He shook his head, still blinking away tears. The priest was speaking again: "...commend to Almighty God our brother Nathan..."

Suddenly an awful sensation swept over David. It felt as though a dagger of ice had been rammed into his heart. His balance went, and the strength in his legs evaporated. He would have fallen, perhaps into the crypt itself, if Uncle Charlie had not grabbed him and held him up. A ripple passed through the assembled mourners.

"...make his face to shine upon him..." the priest was saying.

"I'm all right," said David weakly, but in truth, he was not. He was dizzy, and badly needed to sit down. The ground seemed to move beneath his feet, to shimmer like sunlit water. Only Uncle Charlie's bear-like grip kept him upright. The next thing he knew was that people were leaving, saying goodbye: Nathan's friends shaking his hand silently, Mr Hobbs saying that Nathan was a good student, Fi the family liaison officer hugging him, the hollow DC Kramer muttering something equally hollow about not having given up either. Teresa clapped him on the shoulder and showed him her clenched fist. He got the message: be strong. Then Guy and Rebecca were telling him to come, telling him that it was time to go.

"I want to stay a little while," he told them. He watched them reluctantly walk away. Now the priest was shaking his hand too, and then there was only Uncle Charlie with him by the graveside. The JCB's crew, like the vulture in the butcher's shop, waited with poorly-disguised impatience for everyone to leave so that they could do what they needed to.

"How are you?" asked Uncle Charlie.

"I don't know. I think I'm okay – I just went a bit dizzy back there for a minute."

"I mean about Nathan."

"I'm okay."

"You're a tough kid," Uncle Charlie observed. "Tough on the inside. A lot of people are tough on the outside, but they're all soft underneath. You – you're a hard centre."

"People always choose the soft centres, though, don't they?"

Uncle Charlie smiled. "Do you really want to get eaten?"

They stood in silence for a while. Then Uncle Charlie asked: "Are you ready to go?"

David thought about it. "I'll stay a little while, if that's all right," he said.

"It is with me. I'll bet it won't be with the Reads. They'll be waiting in the car park... when they see me coming back without you, I'll be in trouble."

"You're hard enough to deal with it," teased David.

"Getting shot at in that little war of mine was a picnic compared to getting told off by Rebecca Read," smiled Uncle Charlie. "Anyway, you know where I am, if you need me. Come and visit soon. Okay?"

David watched his uncle limp away through the cemetery until he was lost from sight behind a cluster of holly trees. The two men with their JCB were pretending not to watch him. They hopped from foot to foot and hunched their shoulders. Their meaning was clear.

David walked away, striking off the path into the deeper snow between the memorials. He was retracing his steps of that night, one year earlier. As he walked he heard the JCB snarling into action behind him, sealing in his parents and the empty coffin of their eldest son.

He could not be sure of the precise path he had taken that night, but he knew, give or take a few metres, that he was on the right track. Soon he reached the path he had cut across. Perhaps he should have gone along the path... but even as he considered this, he realized that he had been right to carry on between the headstones, because the man would have found it easier going on the path, and would have pulled him down all the quicker. On the other side of the path he was even less sure of the route he had taken, but soon he could see the railings that marked the edge of the cemetery, and beyond them the house whose lights had been on but whose occupants had not come to the rescue.

Somewhere around here was where he had fallen, tripped by the treacherous grass. A short way further, the man had finally caught him up... he remembered falling, the chemical stink, the rough texture of the man's overcoat, and the reeking pad of poison clamped over his face. He remembered Nathan coming from nowhere, piling into the man with everything he had... so slight a boy, his strength desperate, but hopeless...

The shock of Nathan's charge broke the man's hold on David, and for a moment at least, he was free. Unsteadily he rose to his feet, ready to join the battle between man and boy...

"Run, David, get help!" Nathan shouted.

David bunched his fist, staring at the silent snowy spot where his brother had said the last words he had heard him speak. The imagined spectres of man and boy danced in a violent embrace. David knew that he should never have left Nathan. Together they might have won. Alone, Nathan stood no chance.

After shaking in silent rage for a few moments David turned and walked on, right up to the edge of the cemetery. He remembered clambering up the railings – easier from this side, with the trees to help. Nathan was not following. There was no sign of him, nothing. Not a word, not a sound. There was only the mist and the trees, silent, impassive witnesses. He touched once again those cold, rusted railings, and watched the memory of his year-ago self sprinting away towards the glowing windows of one of the houses opposite, hammering on the door, hammering on the door, hammering on the door.

David picked a smallish, nondescript tree and sank down with his back to its bole. He buried his head in his hands, heedless of the snow beneath him. He should not have abandoned Nathan. What kind of person leaves their brother like that? He should not have left. Just as Nathan had not left *him*. Guilt had long ago settled heavily on him – and not even the fear of the monstrous creature who had attacked him could outweigh it.

You did the right thing, something inside him said. The words seemed to have popped up from a hidden source deep within him. *NO!* he thought furiously, almost speaking the word aloud.

David was alone. The JCB must have completed its task of resetting the slab over the crypt, for its growling had faded to silence. There was nobody in this part of the cemetery. The only sound was the intermittent ridicule from the crow.

Krra!

The sound was closer now, and looking up he saw the bird on a prominent perch most of the way up a naked tree.

Weirdly, the crow was white, pure white, as white as the deepest drifts of snow in the cemetery.

Krra!

A plume of vapour jetted from the crow's beak, its breath condensing in the stillness. The crow was not laughing at him: its harsh voice was the only voice it could use, its song only a single word roughly spoken. In its own way it was beautiful.

Krra!

David lurched to his feet. It was time to get out of this place. He had begun to suspect that the crow had a message for him, but with only a repeated monosyllable to impart that message, he would never understand it.

A whisper: "David!"

He turned. There was no-one there. It was definitely time to go. But there was something strange about the voice he had heard... it had almost sounded like –

"Smart moves, hanging back on your own," came the voice again, louder this time.

"Who's there?" hissed David, turning in a complete circle. There was no-one to be seen in any direction.

"You can hear me!" the voice told him, excitedly.

David started to stumble away, holding his ears. *I am going insane*, he thought. As he moved he looked back... and caught a glimpse of something incredible out of the corner of his eye. He looked at it, and it was gone; he looked half-away, and there it was again. There was a clot of sparkling mist hovering under the skeletal trees, tenuous, yes, but definite, yes.

"Nice eulogy," came the voice again. "But you're wrong about one thing. I am dead. As a doornail."

It was Nathan's voice.

What do you do when you bump into the ghost of your brother? The first thing you do is to doubt your own senses. Maybe wanting something badly enough makes it seem real. But that doesn't mean it *is* real. That much was obvious to David even before he had picked himself off the snowy ground on which he had suddenly collapsed.

"Nathan?" he asked cautiously.

Nathan's sparkly, shimmery form, thin as drizzle, approached David and tried to hug him. The result was painful pins and needles and numbing cold in David's body – it was like being stung and frozen at the same moment.

David scrambled away.

"Keep back!" he said. "What are you, some kind of vampire?"

"I'm sorry… I'll stay away… I didn't know…" Nathan said.

But David noted that his brother was brighter than before, as if he had sucked out some of his living sibling's essence and made it his own. The reaction seemed to prove that Nathan's ghost was real. And if Nathan was a ghost, then –

Then Nathan was dead.

David was immediately taken back to that night a year before. He saw himself fleeing once again. He saw – and imagined – his brother overpowered.

"I'm sorry… I tried to get help… but by the time…"

"It's all right."

"He killed you then. The Solvent Man. I hoped… prayed… that maybe you were alive somewhere…"

There was no reply from Nathan.

"Nathan?"

"I – I don't remember. I think I was taken somewhere else…"

"Can you show me?"

"I don't know. I don't remember. I don't know where I've been all this time. It feels like a lifetime. You've changed. How long is it since…?"

"A year."

"I only remember moments after he – you know – and just now. I bumped into you by the open grave…"

"I felt that. I didn't know what it was, but I felt it." David tried to get to his feet, but he was still numbed by Nathan's touch.

"Are you all right?"

"I'm okay," David said. "Let's go home. And then we can talk about finding him."

"The Solvent Man…? I don't think that's such a good idea."

David clenched his fist. "I do."

Chapter 3: The Monkey

Spring warmth melted winter snow; summer heat burnt spring's green luxury to dry yellow straw; the merciless ageing of autumn withered leaves and snapped them one by one from the trees.

David was now almost as old as Nathan had been when The Solvent Man had killed him. In two months it would be two years since that night. But the Carraways had made no progress in finding the place Nathan had been taken to die.

The ghost seemed to increase in vigour for a time, almost as if his spirit was nurtured by spring's verdant energy. For a few months, he was visible to David whenever his younger brother looked at him. But by summer he had begun to fade, and as often as not, although David could hear his brother's voice, he could no longer see him.

At first the brothers took long winter walks around their city, Fairfield, hoping that something would jog Nathan's memory; but they found nothing, and as the weather warmed, and distractions grew – football, exams – their excursions became less and less frequent. Occasionally Nathan would see other ghosts: but they were faint, uncommunicative, and invisible to his brother. They seemed to be mindless automata, drifting about aimlessly, although some would appear in the same place at regular intervals almost as if reliving the bodily existence they had lost. The brothers thought that perhaps all ghosts other than Nathan were this way – until, that is, they first encountered the Monkey.

That day, David had been given a detention after some trouble with Robbie Drake. He had never known what Drake had against him, but the answer was probably nothing: he doled out his aggression at random and it just so happened that today was David's turn. Drake was in David's year, but bigger than him, burly, with gleaming hyena's eyes and a jaw set open as if ready to snap. He would be finishing year eleven with no exam passes and seemed to despise anyone around him who wanted to do better – in other words, everyone else. He was sullen and monosyllabic with teachers and had a reputation among the boys as the hardest kid in the school.

The generally recommended thing to do was to avoid Drake entirely, or, if that failed, to avoid catching his eye, or, if that failed, to flee. The thing not to do was to sit on a bench at break time with your nose in a book trying to measure the unfathomable depths of trigonometry and be completely unaware of Drake's presence until he was already standing over you.

"Well, if it isn't Carraway Junior."

David didn't bother to look up. He didn't have to. He recognized the throaty voice immediately and cursed his stupidity. With his gaze still lowered, he could deduce by the number of feet he could see that Drake's two chief cronies, Moxy and Clegg, were flanking him, as they usually did.

"What do you want, Drake?" asked David, still not looking up.

"I heard a rumour that you're going crazy. Someone saw you talking to your brother as if he was standing next to you. Your poor, dear, dead brother. Is that true?"

It was distinctly possible. Although David had vowed not to mention his brother's ghost to anybody, there was a good chance he had dropped his guard low enough over the summer to allow someone to see him chatting away with thin air.

"We think you need help, don't we Clegg?" Drake went on.

Clegg didn't answer. He tended to nod or shake his head in preference to talking. Presumably if he said the wrong thing, Drake wouldn't think twice about putting a fist into his face. David guessed that Clegg would be nodding at this point.

"Get lost, Drake," said David.

"Ooh!" laughed Drake. "He talks like his brother used to." His voice changed, deepening to its usual smoke-cracked register. "Well your brother isn't here. He's been dead for two years. And that must hurt. Really hurt. You must miss him real bad."

"Not really," David said, looking up at last. "He's standing behind you."

Nathan was not, actually, anywhere near. David had no idea where he was. But Drake automatically glanced over his shoulder, and David could not help but laugh.

"Carraway, you…!" Drake grabbed the scruff of David's coat and hauled him to his feet. "You know what they do with people like you?" asked Drake. "Straightjacket boys."

Moxy and Clegg pulled David's coat sleeves down his arms. He resisted, trying to push them off, but in no time at all he found himself with his coat on back to front, its sleeves tied together around his back, and with his hood up in his face so he couldn't see anything.

"Get back to the nuthouse where you belong," Drake said, with a barking laugh. Then the three boys started him spinning, around and around like a mad top, and pushed him out into the playground, where he spun and staggered and staggered and spun before toppling over and crashing to the wet ground. Before he could struggle out of his predicament, hands grabbed him once more and hauled him roughly to his feet. His hood was pulled down, but he found himself face to face not with Drake, but with Mr Hobbs, the deputy head. "What do you think you're doing lying on the ground?" demanded Hobbs, as if he was talking to an imbecile. He showed no sign of recognising David, despite having attended Nathan's mock funeral. Of Drake, Clegg and Moxy, there was no sign other than a torn-up exercise book in a puddle near the bench where David had been sitting. They must have shredded David's maths book and melted into the crowd as soon as they spotted Hobbs on his way towards them.

"Sorry," muttered David, the breath knocked out of him from the fall. "You couldn't untie me could you?"

Hobbs grimaced with disgust. Shaking his head, he stalked off, leaving David standing in the middle of the playground, looking like a gigantic penguin. Passers-by giggled at his predicament. "Hilarious," he snapped, as a group of girls sauntered past, stifling laughter. He tried to shuffle out of his coat like a snake shedding its skin. Eventually he managed to spin it around, so the zip was in front, then pull the zip down, and finally free himself.

He took the scraps of his exercise book to maths and the teacher, Mrs Stone, gave him a detention. His protestations that the damage was not his fault fell on deaf ears. The book, Stone said, was his responsibility, and anything that happened to it was his fault. So he stayed after school for an hour and copied all his old work into a new exercise book before binning the muddy shreds of the old one. Nathan turned up half way through, having taken that long to track him down. He interrogated his brother about what had happened, although David could only reply with nods and shrugs to Nathan's guesses.

It was four thirty when David was finally given his freedom. The autumn air was cold, but the rays of the golden sun were still warm, even as it slipped lower towards the horizon. The last few leaves were falling in ones and twos from the cherry trees outside the school. With Nathan at his side, he walked at a slow, solemn pace until he was officially on the public pavement. Then he started running, sprinting like a dog let off its lead, down into the deep shadows of the terraced houses outside the school, faster and faster, into a dank subway and out the other side, across the open space of some waste ground, and over a zebra crossing, narrowly dodging a car. He ran until his heart was pounding, his lungs were bursting, and his legs had turned to jelly, before finally slowing to a walk.

Then, still panting for breath, he snarled: "If he'd been on his own... if he wasn't bigger than me... if I only knew kung fu... what *is* his problem? He's wasted an hour of my life and I'm going to have to explain a muddy coat to the Reads."

"What happened?"

"Someone must have seen me talking to you and come to the rather unfair conclusion that I have fallen out of my tree. They told Drake, Drake gave me a straightjacket and tore my maths book up. No big deal. Another regular day at Meadows High."

"It must have happened at school. It would be best if I stay away from now on…"

"What for?" David asked. Then he hissed: "Look out!"

Nathan moved, but it was too late. A mother and her sleeping toddler in its pushchair walked straight through him, glancing at David, wondering why he was talking to himself. Nathan hated it when people walked through him. The closest he could come to explaining the sensation was of being caught in a sudden wind, like a half-second long hurricane. The living didn't enjoy it either – as David knew well from the time Nathan had drifted through him at the funeral. Sometimes a more gentle connection between the brothers was possible, indeed necessary: it was as if Nathan was a lamp that needed refuelling from time to time. When he seemed to be fading, David could provide him with energy when they shared the same space, at the cost of a cold, momentary weakness. The woman who had encountered Nathan shuddered visibly and her child woke up and set up a raucous bawling.

"What for?" asked David again, when the woman and her still-howling child were some distance away.

Nathan did not reply immediately. He was still brushing himself down and straightening his phantom clothes. To David, he appeared grey, semi-transparent, and, apart from his face, largely indistinct. At some angles, with the light shining from behind him, he would disappear altogether. But usually, looking at Nathan was like looking at an old black and white movie projected onto the real world, only in three dimensions. In the dark, he seemed to glow; his face shone, and shards of light stuck out through the seams in his coat and trousers, making David think of an animated mirror-ball. Nathan always wore the same clothes: a waterproof coat and a pair of jeans, the same clothes he had been wearing the night he went missing, now nearly two years before.

"I distract you, dipstick," said Nathan, and started walking. David hurried to catch up. "Cause trouble. If I wasn't there you couldn't possibly talk to me and no-one could erroneously come up with the impression that you are insane."

David had always liked the fact that his brother used unusual words like *erroneously*. They had always seemed natural in Nathan's voice, even if no other kid at Meadows would have used them. "Maybe you're right. Anyway – it's all over for another day. Shall we head over to Ziggy's?" It was by now seven minutes before five. There was no doubt hardly a spare terminal at the local favourite internet café, but the alternative was to head home. A passing man wearing a suit and a woollen overcoat gave David a sharp look, perhaps wondering if he had been invited on a date.

"Not really," replied Nathan. "Anyway, you know what that place is like. We'll be lucky to get a space. I'll end up standing *in* a computer…"

"Oh, yeah. That's true."

"We could go and see Uncle Charlie."

David hadn't seen Uncle Charlie in weeks. It was one of those things he always meant to do, yet hardly ever got around to. It was not just the long walk to Uncle Charlie's shop that put him off: seeing Uncle Charlie was often a painful experience, even though David loved him dearly. He was, after all, David's last surviving relative. If you didn't count Nathan, that was. "You're right," said David. "We haven't seen Charlie in ages. And he might give us something cool from the shop, like a clapped-out old computer."

"Yeah, well, if he does, you're the one who'll be carrying the damn thing home."

David said nothing. Lost in his own thoughts, he hardly heard what Nathan had said.

They walked along a little way in silence. It was past five now; schoolchildren had largely disappeared from the streets, to be replaced by home-going shopworkers and business people. Traffic was thickening. Then, suddenly, Nathan grabbed David's elbow – or tried to. His hand passed straight through his brother's arm. "Look at that," he hissed, and gestured at a large car that had just driven past in the direction they were walking. 'Large car' was perhaps underselling it: it was like calling a Tyrannosaurus a 'large reptile'. The machine was more like a small tank. It was a huge, army-green monstrosity with what looked like armour plating all around it. And yet it *was* a car: it had four wheels, not tank tracks, and the woman at the wheel wasn't in uniform.

David watched as the car growled away, gushing diesel smoke, his mouth agape.

"Well?" demanded Nathan. "What do you think of that? Cool or what? And it lives on our street."

"It does? What is it?"

"It's a Hummer."

"Sounds more like a growler to me. How come I've never seen it, if it lives on our street?" asked David.

"New neighbour," explained Nathan. "Single mother, a doctor, apparently. I overheard Mrs R talking to Mr R this morn–" Nathan stopped talking in mid-sentence, staring after the disappearing Hummer.

"Nathan?"

"Something's wrong," said Nathan quietly.

David followed Nathan's gaze. The Hummer was turning right at the end of the road; in a moment it had disappeared from view. Other cars drove past. Bicycles whizzed down the hill. Odd leaves still trickled from the trees in the waning sunlight. There was nothing out of the ordinary.

"I can feel it," said Nathan, turning to look at David at last. "There's something in that car. I can't explain it. But it stinks, reeks of evil, it's… disgusting. Oh no. I think I'm going to be –"

"You can't," said David, as Nathan doubled up beside him, and fell to his knees. "You haven't eaten anything for nearly two years."

For a moment it seemed as if David was wrong, that Nathan was going to be sick right there on the pavement; but eventually he stood up, straightening his rumpled coat. "Good job I haven't," he said. "Come on." Still looking decidedly nauseous, Nathan set off down the road.

David ran to keep up. "Where are we going?"

"If we run, we can get back home in time to see what comes out of that car."

"OK," panted David, "but no ralphing." After that he had to concentrate on running, because Nathan was setting an incredible pace, and was drawing ahead of him all the time. They turned right, down a cul-de-sac; at the end, an alleyway led them to another road, which Nathan crossed without checking for traffic – a manoeuvre which gained him yet more time over David, who had to slow down to let a couple of cars past – then they hurtled down another alley, and turned left in time to see the Hummer disappearing into their road, a hundred metres ahead.

"Come on," shouted Nathan. He was now gaining ground rapidly. But then, unlike David, he didn't have to breathe.

David trailed Nathan around the corner into Chapman Close. The Hummer was already parked up on the driveway of one of the houses opposite the Reads' place. As he approached, the driver's side door opened and a woman climbed out. Nathan had already stopped running, a little way from the woman's house. David skidded to a halt beside his brother.

Her attention drawn by the sudden movement, the woman turned to look at David. She was blonde, her long hair held out of her eyes by a pair of shining black clips. In fact, having first noticed the clips, David realized that *everything* she wore was black: she had on a black pullover, black combat trousers, and black shoes.

"Don't stare," said Nathan. "Keep walking."

"She may be all in black, but she doesn't look too evil to me," whispered David, doing as he was bidden, slowly walking along the path. "In fact, I think I'm going to change doctors. Which surgery did you say she was at? The Victoria Road one?"

"Ssh," Nathan told him. "Watch."

The woman had turned away and was opening the nearside passenger door of the Hummer. A boy clambered down. At this, Nathan flinched, and stepped behind David, out of the boy's sight. "It can see me!" he hissed.

"It? He's just a kid," whispered David, trying not to move his lips.

"No – there's something else there too. I can't look – I don't want to catch its eye."

David's slow walk had drifted to a stop. The woman noticed; the boy, on the other hand, ignored him, and ambled towards the front door of the house.

"Hello," said the woman, smiling. She slammed the back door of the car.

"Er, hi," said David, still panting. "You're new, aren't you?"

"Yes, we just moved in yesterday. I'm Anna. That's Michael." Michael was waiting by the front door, staring at his shoes. "What's your name? Do you live here too?"

"Oh. Yes. Number seventeen. David." David found himself pointing across the road to the Reads' house. He suddenly realized that Nathan wasn't behind him any more. Where *was* he?

"Well," said Anna, smiling faintly, "I hope you and Michael can be friends."

"Yes. I hope so," agreed David, still glancing around for Nathan. There was no sign of him. He watched as Anna opened the front door and went inside, ushering Michael along beside her. She closed the door quietly behind them, and David was left standing alone, wondering where Nathan had gone. Eventually he spotted his brother near where another alleyway cut through to Easter Street. David hurried to join him.

"I didn't see anything," he reported. "Michael's a bit odd, but he looked fairly alive to me."

"It *was* Michael," Nathan asserted. "Well, not Michael, but something that came with him. A passenger. It looks like a monkey – a hideous little monkey hanging around his neck."

"A ghost?"

"No," said Nathan softly. "At least, I don't think so. I've seen a lot of ghosts around town – but this is something different. The ghosts I've seen wandering around Fairfield are empty of thoughts, aimless, lost – just like I was before I bumped into you at the cemetery. They mean no harm to anyone. This – whatever it is – is different. It's intelligent, purposeful, and evil."

"Something other than a ghost? A demon?"

"I don't know. I don't want to think about it. I'm scared."

"What have you got to be scared of?" David asked him. "You're already dead."

"I don't know. But I can't help it. All I know is, we've got to stay away from that kid."

Chapter 4: Carraway Family Heirlooms

Uncle Charlie lived in the corner shop that he owned. In its heyday, it had been a bike shop – you could tell, because the words "Smith's Bicycles" were visible through the cracked layers of paint spelling out "CHARLIES" above the shop window. Nowadays the shop sold only junk.

When David walked into the shop, Uncle Charlie looked up from behind the counter, where he was stuffing some red cloth out of sight. "David! Hello. Come in – I was just – erm – thinking about you," he said, with a somewhat sheepish grin.

"How's the leg?" called David, picking his way forwards. What had once been aisles between the jumbled rubbish were now mere rabbit-runs, and it was all he could do to find places to put his feet as he walked. Crockery, pots and pans, electrical appliances, weird books, and broken parts of curious gizmos spilled onto the floor, threatening to obliterate it completely.

Uncle Charlie hobbled out from behind the counter and slapped David on the shoulder. "The leg? Never better! And how's my David?"

"Okay, I guess."

"Only okay?"

"A kid at school gave me a straightjacket because he heard I'd been talking to Nathan," explained David. Beside him, Nathan was standing, rather disturbingly, in the middle of a bookcase, with only bits of him showing.

"Straightjacket? I don't think we had that when I was at school."

David explained the operation of the straightjacket, to which his uncle winced. "Anyway, there's no harm in talking to your brother. None at all. I sometimes talk to your dad."

"You do?" asked David hopefully.

"Yeah. I tell him stuff, when I go to the graveyard. It helps."

David opened his mouth to try and explain, but before he could, Nathan spoke. "Let it go," he said.

"All right," said David automatically.

"Hey?" asked Uncle Charlie.

"I mean, you're right," said David quickly. "It helps."

"That's my lad. Probably best to make sure no-one's watching first, though. Anyway, come upstairs and have a cuppa. I've got something for you."

David and Nathan exchanged raised eyebrows as they went out of the back of the shop to where the stairs were. Charlie led the way up, limping heavily and hanging onto the stair-rail for support, his wide shoulders blocking out the light from above. "It's something that belonged to your parents, which they particularly wanted you to have. I know it's been a long while – since they went, I mean. I should have dug it up earlier, but you know what this place is like…"

"Yeah," agreed David. "What is it?" he asked, trying to conceal the excitement in his voice.

"I'll show you," Charlie told him. They had reached the first floor of the shop, which was the part of the building that Charlie lived in. Charlie went into the living room, then started looking around, scratching his head. "Now, as to what I have done with it…"

Charlie's living room had been invaded by a large quantity of overflow from the shop downstairs and the cellar below that. The space behind the settee had been stuffed with bundles of obsolete magazines, papers, and pamphlets, on top of which were ten or more exotic-looking earthenware jars, some with cork stoppers. The coffee table had been taken over by a dismantled motor unit, which was surrounded by unwashed coffee mugs crammed shoulder to shoulder, daring one another to leap off the edge.

David stifled a groan. Charlie would never find whatever it was in all this rubbish – it probably wasn't even *in* the living room. But just as David was thinking this, Charlie found what he was looking for on the mantelpiece. It was a small, black, wooden box.

"You might call it a family heirloom, but it's not really ours. It's loot," explained Charlie. "From when your gee-gee was fighting in the war — the big war I mean, not the little one I was in… should be a picture of him here somewhere…" he clicked his fingers a few times, eyes darting over the walls. There were over a hundred black and white photographs spread over all four walls in the living room, ranging from a montage of ancient passport-sized photographs to a foot-high portrait of Charlie's father, David's grandfather. "Here's one," he said, pointing. "Him and his mates took that thing from the body of an SS officer."

The photo he was indicating showed five soldiers, their shirt-sleeves rolled up, standing in triumph on the shattered body of a tank, its turret gaping lopsidedly, tracks strewed behind it like tickertape where it had subsided to a stop after the final shell-strike, its once-deadly gun twisted into a drooping curve. At the bottom of the photograph a strip of paper had been added, which bore a typewritten legend: *The lads bag a tiger. Rennes, August 1944.*

"That's your gee-gee. Second one from the left. Got a picture of him playing Alekhine at chess somewhere. Dig it out for you sometime. Nathan would have given him a good game… so would you, of course," added Charlie quickly. "Cup of tea? I was just going to make one."

"Can I open it?" asked David.

"Of course. It's yours now. I'll make that tea," Charlie said, and shuffled off into the kitchen.

David opened the box.

Inside, enveloped in a bed of crushed red velvet, was a thin disc of translucent crystal, which could have been a lens taken from a telescope but for the many unpolished facets around its edge and its slightly irregular shape. A small pentagonal area in the centre of the crystal had been finely polished and could be peered through. David held the crystal close to one of the photographs on the wall to see if it magnified the image. It did not. It simply distorted it and broke apart the monochrome into faint rainbows.

"That!" exclaimed Nathan. "They used to have that in their bedroom. D'you remember, Dave?"

"No." David looked from the lens to the photograph and back again. It was hard to believe that the crystal he was holding could have been in the pocket of the man in the picture, who seemed to come from a different world to the one he knew.

"Hey! Have you seen these?" asked Nathan, pointing at the pile of exotic-looking jars. "Aren't these the things you use to catch genies?"

"If you're thinking what I think you're thinking…" David was interrupted by a stifled sob from the kitchen. "Is Charlie all right?" he whispered to Nathan.

Nathan flitted next door, straight through the wall. In two seconds he was back, shaking his head. "No," he said. "You better get in there."

Somewhat hesitantly, David went through to the kitchen. Uncle Charlie was standing at the sink, washing up a cup, and crying. David went up behind him and hugged him.

"I wanted to look after you, you know," murmured Charlie, "after your parents died… maybe if I'd tidied this place up a bit more… you could have come to live with me…"

"It's not your fault," David said.

"No? Then whose is it?"

David said nothing. He couldn't think of an answer. For a few seconds the only sound was the fizzing of the kettle, then even that clicked off, and there was silence.

"I've done some things in my time… things nobody would be proud of…"

"Who hasn't?"

"You haven't, for one."

David had no answer to that.

"Tea, tea," muttered Charlie, wiping his eyes with his sleeve. He found two teabags and dropped them into the cups he had rinsed out. "Some uncle I turned out to be."

"You're a brilliant uncle," said David firmly.

"I can't imagine your mum and dad saying that. They'd say I was pathetic. Say it was my fault… and worse things besides."

"No they wouldn't."

"You don't know!" snapped Charlie, looking at David fiercely. After a second, he lowered his eyes, pulled away, got the kettle, and poured out the hot water. "Hey," said Charlie, brightening. "While I'm giving things away, how would you like one of your mum's paintings?"

"My mum was a painter?" asked David, incredulously.

"Aye. And a pretty fair one, too. Come this way young man." Charlie led the way back through the living room, to the bedroom beyond. Charlie's bedroom was as unruly as the rest of the place, but amid all the frayed paperback books and unwashed socks, the room held a treasure. The painting that Charlie showed David was a disturbing abstract consisting of sombre, shadowy smudges lost in a grainy, lamp-black background.

"My mum painted that?"

"If you like it, it's yours. I can't look at it any more. It makes me – think of your mum." Charlie paused. "Be careful with it. Sometimes when I look at it… I think I'm going a little crazy. Our minds seem geared up to see patterns, you know? Every time I stare at that thing, I see the same pattern – one that couldn't have been her intention when she painted it… the eye cannot be satisfied with a set of vague smudges – it has to make something out of them – do you know what I mean?"

David stayed a little longer, while Uncle Charlie, his bad leg propped up on the bed, told him about his mum's painting. When he left, Nathan stayed behind for a moment. What he saw then, and told David about once he had caught him up, worried them both.

As soon as David was out of the door, Uncle Charlie got up from the bed, washed his hands, and dried them. Then, he washed and dried them again.

Then he started crying again.

"Page," said Nathan.

David looked up from his own book to turn over and crease down the next page of the book that Nathan was reading. It was bedtime, or almost; there was just time for a chapter or two before lights out. David was reading a Willard Price book, and was enthralled by a battle between crocodiles and sharks in the sea. He was not too enthralled, though, to keep glancing up now and then at his room's newest decoration – his mother's painting, propped up on the bookshelf, its faint daubs of grey just visible against the darker background. There *was* something odd about the painting – something that entranced him, that fixed his glance and made it a stare. It was as if the smudges of paint were in different places each time he looked, which was of course impossible. Nevertheless, it was a disturbing effect –

"Page," said Nathan.

"Page?" asked David. "You read like a train."

"I didn't know trains could read."

"You know what I mean."

"We could read the same book if you like," said Nathan.

"Yeah," agreed David. "But you'll be whingeing about how slow I am the whole time. *'Haven't you finished yet? You must have read it by now.'* "

"If it's too much trouble, don't bother," said Nathan testily.

"It isn't," said David, and reached out to turn Nathan's page.

The two boys read for a while. Or at least, Nathan read, while David stared at the page, concentration broken. His mind was wandering now, remembering films he had seen of ghostly goings-on where all manner of household items got thrown around. "How come you can't turn pages anyway? Poltergeists can throw chairs and things around in films."

"In films," agreed Nathan. "And anyway, maybe I'm not a poltergeist."

"Who says?" demanded David. "I mean, why not? Who decides what kind of ghost you are? Maybe you are a poltergeist, and just don't know it."

"I can't touch things. I lack a physical presence."

"Then how come I can see you?"

There was a pause while Nathan considered this.

"Got you there, haven't I?" asked David.

"Well," said Nathan at last, "it's something I've thought about a lot. It's obvious that you can see me because you're my brother. No-one else can; which means one of two things."

"Which are?"

"Either I don't exist, and you really do talk to yourself, or else your mind is sensitive to electromagnetic resonance that no-one else's senses can detect – a vibration or wavelength unique to the residual presence that I represent."

"I think I prefer the first option. At least I understand that."

"Maybe it has something to do with the solar neutrinos. I've often wondered about that."

"What sort of music do they make?" asked David, only half joking. He had no idea what a neutrino was.

"A neutrino is an elementary particle, emitted by the sun along with things like photons – light, in other words – but neutrinos pass straight through the Earth and out the other side without even noticing that we're here."

"But that's impossible," argued David, who knew at least that the Earth was pretty huge, and full of molten nickel and iron in the middle, which would pretty much absorb anything that was thrown at it. He tried to imagine something shining its way through the centre of the earth like light through a window pane, but couldn't quite believe it. A battle between sharks and crocodiles, no problem. He could buy that. But a magic bullet that could pass straight through the Earth's core – no.

"There are as many neutrinos hitting you now, at night, as hit you in the daytime. Millions of them. Passing straight through you without you even being aware of them."

"I still don't see what this has to do with turning the pages on your own book," objected David, trying to turn the conversation away from particle physics to matters of practicality.

"Okay, okay," muttered Nathan. "I'll give it a go." He focussed on the book in front of him, reaching out a ghostly hand. After a few seconds' concentration, the page began to flutter. Nathan gritted his teeth. A few seconds more, and the page stopped moving, Nathan relaxed, gave up. "I think I nearly had it there," he said at last. "But it was like trying to pick up a house."

"Maybe you'll be better if you keep practising," mused David. "Hey! Think what we could do if you got good at it. You could tackle people for me in footy. Knock the ball out of the keeper's hands. I could finally make it onto the football team… you could do my essays for me – you always were brainier than me."

"No way," said Nathan adamantly. "Not even if I could."

"Why not?" demanded David. "Don't tell me. Because it wouldn't be right."

"Look. Whatever I'm here for, it isn't to do your essays. Maybe that monkey-thing. Maybe that's why I'm hanging around. We can beat it. Free that kid."

"Michael," supplied David.

"Exactly. Those spirit jars of Uncle Charlie's. We just get one of them…"

"Yes?"

"Well, obviously I haven't worked out the specifics yet. There must be books about getting rid of ghosts and things. Exorcisms. All we need to do is get down to the library."

"Yeah. I'll turn the pages and you can read. First you don't want to go anywhere near it, now you want to grab it and stuff it in a jar."

"I never used the words *grab* and *stuff*."

David shrugged and picked up his book once more. He had barely opened it when Nathan spoke again: "Page."

David threw Willard Price down with an expressive sigh and turned Nathan's page. Instead of going back to his book, he picked up the black wooden box. David took the crystal out and turned it over in his hands, enjoying its weight, examining its varied facets. Some surfaces were polished, as smooth as melting ice; some were misted like ground glass; still others were polished and smooth but permeated by a network of fine cracks. The crystal itself was disc-shaped, and in the centre of each side there was a definite five-sided polished facet. It was like a lens pulled out of a dragon's eye. David peered through it. He could see a slightly shrunken, circular view of the world, fringed with rainbows. Slowly he panned around the bedroom… there was somebody sitting on the bed with him. Surprised, he almost dropped the crystal. But it was only Nathan, as tenuous as a breath in the cold. He looked through the crystal again. Nathan was still there – but David could no longer see through his brother. Nathan was somehow more real when viewed through the lens.

David excitedly told Nathan about this, and held up the crystal for his brother to peer through at him.

"I see nothing," Nathan said. "Only my own reflection in darkness."

"But what do you think it *means?*"

The loud voice of David's foster father, Guy, floated up the stairs. "David!

Time to put that light out."

"Okay," called David aloud. Then he repeated his question, this time in a whisper.

"Maybe there was more to our parents than we knew," Nathan replied. "Maybe it means nothing, since unless they had ghosts hanging around them they may not have known that the crystal could do that. We'll have to try to find out which. But you heard Guy – it's bed time."

David stowed the crystal away carefully. "Tell me something Nath. What do you get up to while I'm asleep?"

Nathan looked down at David with a serious expression. "I would have thought it should be obvious."

"This is me we're dealing with here –"

"All right," Nathan interrupted. "I haven't given up. I still go looking for our friend."

"What happens if you find him? Do I go to the cops, or..."

"That is a bridge we will cross when we get there."

"Well. All right. But be careful." David settled down to sleep, and turned off the bedside lamp.

Nathan stood up, automatically reaching out to close his book and put it away; his hand passed straight through it. He stood next to the bed for a few minutes, until he was sure that David was asleep. Then he reached forward to touch his brother's forehead. For a moment he concentrated, gritting his teeth as before; then, with a supreme effort, he managed to ruffle a few of David's hairs.

"I don't need to be careful," said Nathan. "I'm already dead, remember?" With that, he backed away from the bed and flitted straight through the wall, into the night.

Chapter 5: The Road to Nowhere

David's Saturday lunch often doubled up as breakfast and that particular Saturday was no exception. Mr and Mrs Read had already sat down, having probably been up for five hours and long since forgotten about breakfast. They were arguing about something. David didn't find out what, because as he appeared in the doorway, the conversation stopped dead.

"Back in the land of the living, eh?" asked Mr Read, running the palm of his right hand over the smooth top of his head.

David nodded, and quietly settled into his chair. Nathan followed David in and took station some distance behind the Reads. Everyone ate in silence for a while, until Mrs Read asked: "Guy, do you *have* to go back to work this afternoon?"

Mr Read threw down his knife and fork and sighed heavily. "I have no choice, Rebecca. Blasted surveyors. I've got to drag them into this place. They just don't want to go in. Reckon it's creepy, or some such rubbish. You'd think they didn't want the work. I need options on this development, and I need them fast. Every day that passes is another day we're paying money to the bank for the privilege of owning an empty shell... we need to get moving on this if it isn't going to cost us a damn fortune... haunted! They're just work shy if you ask me. Well, if they can't, or won't, do their work, I'll just have to get in another firm...they reckon I may have to go out of town because word has already got around about this blasted place... reluctant as I may be to do that for obvious reasons..."

"Did you say haunted?" interrupted David, unable to restrain himself any longer.

Mr Read glared at him, but, seemingly happy to have someone to complain to, answered the question. "That's what I said, didn't I? That's what *they* said, rather. Don't want to go back in the place. Too creepy. Of course it's creepy – it's been empty for fifty years! What place wouldn't be creepy after being empty for that length of time? And it smells. Big deal! So what if it smells? Solvents. Some sort of solvents they reckon – I told them that anything like that left behind would have evaporated years ago – but will they listen? All I want to know is, can we build on the existing structure, or are we going to have to knock it all down and start from scratch? And will anybody tell me?"

"Where is it?" blurted David. The word 'solvent' had brought back a foul memory. The stench of the cloth that had been clamped to his face two years before seemed to fill his nostrils again...

"Raglan Road. It's what used to be Tipler's Textile Co. Work went abroad, you see, so the factory became redundant. Sat there for decades minding its own business. Now with the property boom we're having, it's going to become luxury flats. Why? Why are you interested?"

David shrugged, trying to look casual. "Oh. No reason. Just curious."

"What's the point?" asked Nathan later. "There are ghosts all over the place. I don't have to wander half-way across town to find one. Maybe there is a ghost at this Tipler factory or whatever it's called, but I don't see what business it is of ours."

"What about the solvent?" pressed David. It was still early afternoon, and the late autumn sun was pleasantly warm. He had set off walking towards town out of sheer habit but had randomly diverted his course to the abandoned boatyards of the lower reaches of the River Fair. The idea to investigate the haunted factory had only just occurred to him, and picking his way back upstream through the abandoned shipyards that lined the river was proving painfully slow going. For Nathan, of course, such a journey could be accomplished in minutes, but the ghost of his brother was inexplicably reluctant to race ahead.

"Solvent? So Guy mentioned solvents. So what? There are solvents in the shed at the bottom of the garden, but you're not suggesting *he's* there, are you?"

"You heard what he said. There shouldn't be any, not after all this time…"

"Of course there *shouldn't* be. But there are enough kids abusing the stuff that every deserted building in this city is probably half-full of empty cans."

"Well, if you don't want to go, that's fine. I'll go myself. I still don't see why not."

"Why not?" echoed Nathan. "What has Guy ever done for you?"

"It wouldn't be *for* Guy," David said. He found it hard to express exactly why he thought they should at least check the place out. He had to admit that a connection between two whiffs of solvent in a large city was probably coincidence. Nevertheless, in a year's searching Nathan had found nothing – so surely this property of Guy's was worth a look? He said as much to Nathan, who with a show of reluctance agreed that David had a point, and flew off to the west in a rapidly diminishing blur.

David had promised to wait where he was, but he didn't. He followed slowly, wandering in and out of abandoned waterfront shells, then down along the muddy shore until a sturdy fence blocked his path and he was forced to turn inland once more. He walked until his feet ached, stopping only for a fizzy drink and a chocolate bar at a newsagent's shop. Before he knew it, the temperature was plummeting and it was almost dark. Fairfield was a different place at night. People you would have happily smiled at in passing suddenly became menacing presences, moving fast, hunched in a defensive posture against the weather and strangers. At dusk the thoughts of gangs of youths turned from fun to mischief.

But out here, in the rotten heart of Fairfield, David was alone. He crossed an area of weed-infested waste ground, passing between and sometimes through a series of vast concrete sheds. Then he had to return to the shore to make further progress, because his path was blocked by what everyone called "the TV factory." David didn't know if the factory had ever made TVs; peering through a smashed window revealed only a mysterious gloomy interior dotted with rusted machines. At the shoreward end of the TV factory was a quay, which was accessible by ducking under a fence. On this side, one of the doors to the factory had been forced open, offering a chance to explore the interior; but he skirted past it and carried on. Beyond the quay, the shore reverted to a gradual, muddy slope, dotted with slime-draped tyres, shopping trolleys, and old paint tins. Here a little-used footpath wound along the strandline, terminating in a small patch of green that apparently, to judge by the presence of two ancient cannon, marked the spot of a former military emplacement. He crossed the green, walked inland up Staithe Road a hundred metres or so, and found himself at the junction of Raglan Road.

Raglan Road was a narrow, empty dead end, flanked on both sides by chain link fences, three-metre-high brick walls and long-dead street lights. David might have hoped at this point that his quest for the Tipler factory was over, but there were several factories to choose from, at least two of which were hidden behind the crumbling walls. He looked for the presence of Guy Read's company in the form of a billboard advertising redevelopment; seeing nothing, he moved on down the road towards the setting sun.

The dead end of Raglan Road was surrounded by three more factories, one of them walled off and the other two protected by a combination of a chain link fence and strand board sheets. All three were marked as "Acquired for Development," and one – the one with the wall – bore the logo of Guy Read's company. David backed away to get a better view over the high wall; he could see little more than the top row of the factory's windows, all broken to varying degrees, and what looked in the gloom to be a crumbling roof.

David was still staring over the wall when Nathan arrived.

"I've been looking everywhere! I thought you were going to wait?"

David shrugged. "Got tired of waiting…"

"Got tired of waiting? I was only away ten minutes and I've been searching for you ever since. Anyway, never mind that now. You can't hang around here – Drake's on his way."

"Drake? What's he doing here?"

"What does it matter? Anyway, it's not just Drake. Moxy and Clegg are with him and another two I don't recognize. If he finds you here…" Nathan's voice trailed off, leaving an ominous silence.

"He'll what? He's not that bad."

"You don't know he's capable of!" said Nathan fiercely, his faint outline almost sparking in anger. "That kid's an animal. If you had an ounce of sense you'd already be running by now."

"Where are they?"

"Staithe Road. There's no time to get to the corner without them seeing you."

"Okay then Einstein. Which way *should* I run?"

David could almost hear the cogs whirring as his brother considered the problem: Raglan Road was a road to nowhere.

"Wait here," Nathan said, and fled, disappearing from sight through one of the walls.

David decided not to wait. He would have to climb one of the walls, even though they were too tall to leap and grab the top. It would be easier in the corner where two walls met. He was just lining up for a running jump when Nathan reappeared.

"I said wait! You can hide back up here. There's a way into the factory next door. Where the flattened fence is. Move!"

David's first thought was that if the factory he was being pointed to turned out to be Drake's gang's secret den, then he was completely sunk. Nevertheless, he obeyed his brother's order. The building was a grey concrete monstrosity with few openings at ground level. There was though a loading bay with a wide door formed of rusted corrugated steel sheeting, which had been bent back at the bottom left corner to reveal a triangle of darkness. David approached, passing between the steel posts of the trampled fence, each post set in a clump of yellowed grass and casting a shadow that with the sun so low seemed to stretch to eternity. He ducked low to enter the factory, trusting his brother that there were no hazards within. Inside, the light had almost gone but gleamed on here and there where the sun still reached through broken windows, deep copper glows showing up in the black like fires of torture in the nighted mines of Hell. He could vaguely make out a stairwell to his left, but the rising concrete steps quickly vanished into absolute darkness. Ahead, an enormous doorway led to the main factory floor. In the factory's eerie light, David got the weird impression that beyond the great inner doors was a miniature indoor forest.

"Come on. You'd better go up in case they come in…" Nathan told him. His brother, standing beside him, was glowing faintly in the blackness.

David began to feel his way up, happy to find that a railing was still in place. The steps turned anticlockwise at a small landing, half way to the first floor. As he crossed this patch of flat ground, there was a hollow crunch as his shoe crushed something – and David recognized the familiar sickening sensation of accidentally standing on a snail in the aftermath of night-time rain. The old factory seemed a strange place for a snail to make its home, but any thoughts that it might be a stray individual were dismissed two steps later when another snail cracked beneath his shoe. He found that his right hand, which was tracing the wall as his left followed the railing, was now sliding a disgusting path over wet slime. At least there was a little more light up on the first floor, either that or his eyes were beginning to adjust – he saw to his right beads of orange light framing a boarded-up window and moved towards it.

After a few minutes, the sounds of the voices of Drake's gang began to be audible outside. "Look how bright it gets when you blow," commented a voice David didn't recognize.

Peering out into the growing gloom, the first thing David saw was the glowing tip of a cigarette. He gradually made out that five shadowy forms surrounded it. Drake's gang had reached the corner of Staithe Road and Raglan Road, and by now were only about fifty metres away.

"You're supposed to smoke it, Ren, not muck about with it. If you don't want it, give it back." This was Drake's voice, a drawl unmistakeably hoarse already through overuse of cigarettes.

"No, no, I want it," Ren replied.

"Told you," said another voice in a disappointed tone. David recognized this one, too. Moxy, one of Drake's chief lieutenants. "There's nothing old enough to nick."

David, peering through a crack at an awkward angle, saw that the five boys were looking at three cars that had been recklessly left by their owners near the deserted end of Staithe Road.

"My brother could get one for us. I've seen him do it," said a fourth voice, another that David hadn't heard before.

"Yeah, well, he ain't here, is he?" sneered Drake. "Clegg, see if there's anything in them worth having." Clegg was much shorter than the rest of the gang, possibly a consequence of trying to keep up with Drake in the smoking stakes. He popped his cigarette in his mouth and jammed his hands in his pockets, adopting what he hoped was a gangsterish gait as he wandered over to the three cars and peered inside them one by one. "Nothing," he said, returning a minute later, speaking around his cigarette.

"Listen," Drake said, ignoring the report. "I've got something to tell you. I might be getting out."

The other four waited for clarification: none came. Finally, Moxy said nervously: "Getting out where?"

"I could be in trouble. I may need to disappear – and I'll be counting on you guys to help me. If it wasn't for Becks I would've gone already."

The guys looked at each other – movements visible even to David some distance away in the dark.

"Is it the cops?" asked Ren, the boy who was trying not to smoke his cigarette.

"Do you think I'd be running if it was the cops?" sneered Drake.

"Your dad then…" Moxy suggested. The way his voice trailed off into silence suggested that he was having second thoughts about mentioning Drake's father.

"No, it's not Da'. I can handle him. It's who he works for. You know he gets steaming sometimes."

"He batters you…"

"Cos I let him."

"Why?"

"Think about it and send me a postcard when you work it out, Moxy." Drake paused to take a dramatic drag on his cigarette. "When he gets drunk, he tells me things he shouldn't. If you guys breathe a word of this you'll be in it up to your necks."

"We won't," was the dutiful chorus.

"Come on, let's try somewhere else. I'll tell you as we go." At Drake's command the five boys started drifting casually back up Staithe Road. Soon they were out of David's view; shortly after, Nathan gave him the all clear to emerge from his hiding place.

"What was all that about?" asked David. "Maybe you should follow him. Find out what's up."

"Hot air," Nathan guessed. "Never mind that now. You were right about the other factory – there is a link to the Solvent Man."

"There is?"

"I don't know exactly what it is – there is a presence there, more of an atmosphere than a discrete entity. But there is definitely some part of the Solvent Man there – like an echo or a memory that he left behind – it filled my mind when I was there. He's been there – but whether he has been there recently, I couldn't say."

An hour later, Robbie Drake returned home. He lived half-way up Miles Hill, in a softening row of Victorian terraced houses. Most of the houses this far up the hill were empty, boarded-up shells, and Robbie's house was flanked by two others that had been deserted for as long as he remembered.

Da' was home. Robbie could see his father's car parked outside their house from far away, when he was still near the bottom of the hill. It sat incongruously among the few other cars, large, black, with tinted windows. Da's car was a limo, but it wasn't really his. He only drove it. Robbie and Becks never got near it. The limo was in very good condition and its chrome finish gleamed in the golden wash of the sodium streetlights. Further up, a little way above their house, they didn't bother to turn the streetlights on any more, because *all* the houses were empty. Nobody wanted to live near the house at the top of Miles Hill, because everyone knew that it was haunted.

Robbie decided to let himself in and go quietly up the stairs to see how Becks was getting on with her homework. Da' would be in the back, with a bottle. The TV would be on, so if he was quiet enough...

"Robbie!"

"Hello, Da'." Robbie froze on the doorstep. For a split second he considered backing out of the house and heading back the way he had come, but then he remembered his little sister. He checked a mental list of mischief he had got up to recently that his father might have got wind of. There was, as far as he could recall, nothing serious that word of could have found its way home. Nevertheless, it was with a pounding heart that he went down the hall and into the back room.

Da' was drunk. Half-past drunk. Quarter to floor. There was a bottle on its side on the carpet, and another half-empty on the table.

"You're late," Robbie's father said, without taking his shiny, bloodshot eyes from the TV.

"Am I?" It seemed safer to act innocent than to try to make up some excuse. Best not to mention that he had been out looking for an old car to take a joyride in.

Now Da' looked away from the TV, sizing up his son's expression. Whatever he saw there seemed to satisfy him, because he said: "Get down to the corner and get me another bottle of Harry. This one's not got long left."

"Okay, Da'."

"What did you want me to do? Send your sister? You come home on time in future."

"Okay, Da'," Robbie said, but what he thought was *you could try getting it yourself*. He waited for his father to give him some money. He waited for about a minute, shifting from foot to foot. His father had forgotten about him, his attention drawn back to a mindless quiz show on the TV.

"What are you waiting for, money? I had a *job* when I was your age." Da' tore himself away from the TV long enough to toss his son a much-folded fiver.

Robbie backed out of the room.

"And be quick about it!"

"Yes, Da'!" Robbie said, but his jaw was clenched and his fists were knotted, and he felt a sudden urge to punch someone. Anyone.

By the time Robbie returned, the half-empty bottle was an empty bottle and the mindless TV quiz show had become a different mindless TV quiz show. Da' took the new bottle with an eager, clumsy hand. "Any trouble?"

"No…" purchasing the Harry had been easy enough.

"It's for your dad, right?" the man in the off-licence had asked when Robbie Drake presented him with a bottle of Good King Henry. Good King Henry was a cheap fortified wine flavoured with a bitter herb. To Robbie the taste was disgusting, but Da' loved it. Da' also thought he was being clever by calling it Harry.

"Yeah."

"He's already been in and bought two today," the shop assistant added.

"Yeah, he's got a mate over," Robbie lied.

"Oh, that's good. Because anyone who can put away three of these in a night is asking for trouble."

Robbie would have gone to a different off-licence to avoid dumb conversations about his Da's drinking, but for the fact that they knew him at Lamb's and would sell him stuff he wasn't old enough to buy.

"Any change?" Robbie's dad asked.

Robbie reluctantly placed a pound coin and a fifty pence piece on the table.

"You're a good kid, Robbie."

"I better check on Becks."

"Stay! Siddown. Have a drink."

Robbie got himself an orangeade from the fridge, which was otherwise empty apart from a half-full bottle of milk. He sat on the low sofa, Da' in his armchair looking down on him like an enthroned king.

"Come closer! I'm not gonna bite you."

Robbie shuffled along the sofa a little way.

"That's better."

There was silence between them for a few seconds, an awkwardness filled by the wittering of the TV.

"How was school?" Da' managed at last.

How was school? Robbie thought. *Hell on Earth*. But it beat being here by a long, long way. "Great," he said.

"It's no world for kids, this," Da' said. "Not with what's happening. You hear things in my line of work. The Fathers. I had the Master in the back once. It's easy to believe what they say about him…"

"What's that?" Robbie asked, as his father trailed into silence.

"Shut your mouth! Don't ever mention him to anyone, right?"

"Okay, Da'."

"If they ever found out, my life wouldn't be worth a cup o' Harry, nor yours, nor your precious sister's! So you mind me."

"Okay, Da'."

"God knows we can't get by on what they pay me, but…" Once more Da' stopped speaking in the middle of a sentence.

Robbie realized that his hands were balled into fists. But he would never hurt his father. Or fight back. Even though Robbie was as big as his father now, and certainly stronger. Even if his father said things like "precious sister."

"I'd better see what Becks wants," Robbie said, after a suitable pause had elapsed, which Da' had filled with Harry.

"I didn't hear anything."

"Yeah, she called." She hadn't done so, of course, but it was all that Robbie could think of to get himself out of this hot little room, away from the court of the King of Harry.

"Go on then, see what she wants. Then you'd better make her tea."

Robbie thought of the empty fridge. "Okay Da'," he said.

Becks was sitting on her bed, not doing anything. "I wish Mum was here," she said in lieu of hello, as her brother knocked and entered.

Mum had been gone a long, long time.

"Me too."

Becks rubbed at the scar on her cheek – it was a little comma-shaped mark that everyone thought had happened when she fell off a climbing frame. "Is he all right?" she asked.

"The usual."

"We can't stay here. There isn't much time," Becks said.

"I'll protect you from him."

"It's not just Da'." Becks lowered her voice. "Something bad is going to happen, and I can't see how it's going to turn out."

"Like what?"

"Robbie: promise me you won't hurt anybody."

Robbie shrugged and allowed himself a little smile. Sometimes he worried about his sister, and more than just about her physical safety. "You know me Becks. I always do what you want."

Chapter 6: Elder Lore

Straight after school, David walked to the library. It had taken some persuasion from Nathan to get David to skip football practice in favour of finding out how to shake their neighbour, Michael Andersen, free of his possession.

"Football, or someone's life. I mean, it's not as if —"

Nathan did not finish his sentence. He didn't have to: David knew what he meant. *Not as if you're ever going to make the team.* In truth he did not go to football practice with any hope of making the team: he went because he enjoyed it, because his friends went. Nevertheless, he had agreed to go to the library instead. There might be an answer on the dusty shelves of the library that he had been unable to find in the bottomless recesses of the Internet.

The library was a huge, modern, glass-fronted building; in the windows, Christmas lights flickered, although it was still only November. The research area of the library was right at the back, and incorporated the remains of an older building, which now partly sheltered under the huge glass panels of the roof of the newer one. David and Nathan passed through well-populated forests of internet terminals, through the bright and airy expanse of the children's section, and through the popular fiction section on their way to the old building. To David, the ornate, red-brick building at the end of the hanger-like modern structure seemed like a Santa's grotto in a department store. Christmas had even penetrated to the research library, which was draped in tinsel, its doorway framed by an arch of fairy lights. Once beyond the threshold, though, all evidence of Christmas, in fact anything remotely non-academic, disappeared; the only decorations were the omnipresent handful of dried-up old men who sat about the ample desks, books and papers scattered around them.

Shelves ten feet tall surrounded the reading area, the shady gaps between them barely wide enough to walk down. The research department probably took up a quarter of the area of the library as a whole, yet must have contained three-quarters of all the books.

David began to wander through the deepest shadows of the tall bookshelves where, it seemed, no-one had passed for days, perhaps months, and as he found them ticked books off the list Nathan had recited to him. He ignored some for now, concentrating on the ones he thought might be of most relevance. A few of the books were very old and crumbling, while others were twentieth-century copies of ancient works. The ripe, musty smell of the old books intoxicated him as it always did when he came here: it was like the distilled breath of knowledge, wisdom that over decades had seeped from the laden shelves into the very air of the place. It was as if all he had to do was to stand there, breathe that heavy atmosphere, and knowledge would impart itself to him; he would absorb it just as he might absorb radiation near a nuclear power station. Finally, after a hundred years or more, all a book's knowledge would have leaked out, and spent, it would crumble to dust.

As he wandered, David occasionally removed old, never-read, never-consulted tomes from the shelves at random, blew the dust from them and briefly flicked through their brittle yellowed pages, just to cheer them up a bit.

"Come on," muttered Nathan. "What's *'The Articles of Fascination'* have to do with exorcism?"

David laughed at that, mainly because he hadn't yet worked out what *'The Articles of Fascination'* was actually about. He replaced the book and moved on, choosing another, this one actually on the list, with Nathan peering over his shoulder. It was called *'The Dead and the Undead'*.

David added *'The Dead and the Undead'* to the pile of books he was carrying, and looked again at his list for the class mark of the next book: *'Old Ghosts'*. A large, bottle-blue fly landed on the paper, scuttling across the list of books; he blew it lightly, and after a moment's thought, the fly flew off.

As the insect vanished in the gloom of the stacks, David caught the merest hint of a smell, as if the air stirred by the fly carried the memory of a monster. It was a smell that instantly dispelled his calm.

He glanced around and listened; it was so quiet now that it seemed as if he and Nathan were the only ones left in the research library. The shelves stretched away from him in all directions, seemingly without end. The only things he could see were books and shelves, books and shelves, books and shelves, shadowed or bright, the strip-lights in the suspended ceiling on, off, or occasionally in a state of flux, flicking on to off and back again.

The fly came back and landed on David's hand. He watched as it rubbed its forelegs together merrily. The boy tested the air, but there was no trace of the chemical scent. His heart slowed a little. Just his imagination.

The glittering insect, wandering across his hand, reminded David of something Uncle Charlie had told him once: that flies could sniff out the dying, and would land on them to lay their eggs before the person was even dead, to be the first in line for the grand feast that awaited... that thought was bad enough, but the next thing Charlie had said was worse: that it had once been thought that the flies emerging from corpses came from within, had been waiting within people for them to die...

"Dave?" asked Nathan. "Are you okay?"

Nathan's words broke the spell of the fly, and David blew it away again.

"I thought I smelled something..."

"What?"

"I'm just on edge, that's all. It's nothing."

They made their way back to the tables. Only one reader remained: an old man with snow-white hair that stuck up like a brush, who was engrossed in an ancient, cracked tome as thick as a brick. For an hour or more David and Nathan read, David sometimes ducking back into the stacks for more books. After one such excursion, Nathan said: "That old man. He came over to sneak a look at our books while you were gone."

"H'mm," said David, unwilling to say more in the quiet of the library in case the old man overheard him.

A few minutes later, as David flicked through a nineteenth-century book called *Elder Lore – Dialogues with the Spirit World*, he found a passage on the use of what were described as efreeti jars. As he and Nathan were reading this, the old man began tidying his books away. David looked at his watch; it was nearly closing time. He tapped the watch to alert Nathan.

"I wish I could turn pages myself. I could stay here all night," Nathan moaned.

"They probably turn the lights out when they leave," retorted David automatically. Then he remembered the old man, and looked up, feeling sheepish. But the old man had gone.

"An interesting choice of book for one so young," said a gravelly voice. The old man was standing immediately behind him. "Efreeti jars. Fascinating. Might I ask what your concern is with matters of the occult?"

"Oh," said David, hoping that Nathan would supply him with an answer.

At length, he did. "School project."

"School project," echoed David gratefully. He could feel the old man staring at the back of his head, but didn't look around, pretending to be engrossed in the book instead.

"School project. I see. Then perhaps I can recommend something else that you might find useful," said the old man.

A scrap of paper fluttered down on the table in front of David. On it was written:

Museum Cottage, Marsh Lane

Tomorrow, 3.30 p.m.

Tell no-one

"What's this about?" asked David, turning around to look at the old man. But he had already walked away, and was by now almost at the door to the research library.

"I'll follow him," announced Nathan, and whisked off to the door in pursuit before David could argue.

"Tell no-one," David said to himself. "How stupid does he think I am?" After aimlessly flicking through the pile of books in front of him for a while, David picked out one or two to borrow, and headed for the door.

Chapter 7: The Professor

Museum Cottage was set back from the road, behind a screen of ancient cypress trees. To the left, a short gravel driveway led to the side door of the old house. Although it was only half-past three, it was already almost dark, and from where he stood on the pavement David could see the light of an imitation brass gas lamp over the door. He hesitated. Where he stood, he was safe; but one step onto the property of Museum Cottage would be one step into the unknown.

"Come on!" hissed Nathan. "What are you waiting for?" The ghostly form of David's brother had drifted on ahead, and was half way to the door.

"I'm waiting for someone to come and examine my head," muttered David.

"I've already told you. It's safe. He's not going to hurt you."

Nathan had tracked the old man to Museum Cottage the previous night. He had returned to David's bedroom some time after tea, enthusing about all the 'fantastic stuff' that the old man had lying around his house, including shelf-loads of books about ghosts, hauntings, devil-worship and other 'cool' subjects. Nathan was convinced that the old man was genuine, and wanted only to help David in his research. David, having yet to see what lurked behind the walls of Museum Cottage, could only doubt that anyone with a genuine motive would approach him in such a suspicious way. "He might be a little cracked, but he wouldn't harm a fly," was Nathan's opinion of the old man.

The wind stirred dead leaves among the roots of the cypress trees, and rattled a few pieces of gravel down the driveway. Nathan was standing by the door, glaring back at David with spectral hands on phantom hips.

"Okay," announced David at last. "But if he kills me, I'm going to come back and haunt you. Just so as you know." He walked down the gentle slope to join Nathan at the door.

There was a small square window in the middle of the door, illuminated faintly by light shining through a curtain. Below the tiny window, there was a brass doorknocker in the shape of an elf, or maybe an imp. David knocked twice, putting more confidence into his knocks than he felt inside.

Nothing happened. There was no sound of movement from within the house. After about five seconds, David said: "Oh well, he must be out. Let's go."

"Give him a chance," ordered Nathan. "This is an old man we're talking about."

Before David could respond, the curtain was suddenly drawn back and the door opened. "You came. Good. Come in," said the old man, rheumy eyes twinkling, and stood aside for David to step past him.

David went inside, finding himself in a small kitchen. He noticed how immaculately tidy it was – no washing up on the draining board, no empty tea cups waiting to be washed up, nothing out of place at all. The old man's kitchen was even tidier than Mrs Read's, which was saying something, because so much as an empty cup deposited next to the sink there normally resulted in a telling off ('that cup won't wash itself up, you know').

"Keep going," he heard Nathan advising him. "The study's straight ahead."

If the kitchen had been unnaturally tidy, then the study was chaotically messy. It was not unlike an upmarket version of Uncle Charlie's living room; the level of mess was the same, but instead of engine parts, newspapers, unwashed mugs and old photographs tacked to the walls, the clutter in the old man's study consisted of leather-bound books, pages of manuscript, and figurines of jade and obsidian. On the walls, David was first struck by a pair of samurai swords hanging over the fireplace, and then noticed a hideous metal demon-face with backlit eyes on the other side of the room. In the fireplace itself, burning logs sparked and snapped.

Nathan was speaking, something about all the cool stuff and didn't David see what he meant, but David was only half-listening. He wandered over to the evil metal face, all nervousness forgotten. It was made of burnished steel, and was big enough to cover a man's face. Behind it, a hidden light bulb produced the sinister glowing-eyes effect.

"You like my *mempo?*" asked the old man.

"What is it?" asked David.

"A samurai battle mask, representing what the Japanese call a *tori-tengu*. A devil of the woods. Please. Sit down. I'm going to."

David heard a chair creaking. He turned away from the *mempo* to face the old man. In the warm light of the study, he looked younger than he had in the library. He was old though – there was no doubt about that. His pale face was heavily lined, his eyes sunken and rimmed with black. His hands were specked with liver spots. His hair – though pure white – lent him a token of youth, because there was still lots of it, and it stuck straight up as if he was standing next to a Van de Graaff generator.

"I'm Professor Robert Fuller," said the old man.

"Oh," said David, suddenly realising that he should respond, "David. David Carraway."

A frown immediately creased Professor Fuller's face. "Carraway... Carraway... now where have I heard that name before?" he launched himself out of his chair with the vigour of a much younger man, tore open a filing cabinet, and began to rifle through the documents inside. He searched for a few seconds before abruptly stopping. "Did you tell anyone you were coming here?" he demanded, still staring into the filing cabinet.

"Yes," said David, although in truth, the only person who knew his current whereabouts was Nathan.

"No," hissed Nathan.

"No," repeated David.

Fuller fell back into his chair and swung around to look at David. The burst of energy he had shown in jumping to his feet a moment earlier had gone –

now he looked tired, forlorn perhaps, and even a little less alive. There was no light in the eyes that he fixed on David – just the mist of age. After a moment, he looked away and chuckled to himself. "It's all right," he said to the floor. "You don't have to fear me. I'm not interested in boys. Not in the way you're thinking."

"I never thought that," David told him. There was a crack, and a spark leapt out of the fireplace, onto one of the many pieces of paper scattered on the carpet. David stamped on it instinctively.

"Your caution does you credit. I could be anybody. So, indeed, could you. Please – sit down." The professor indicated a small couch set against the wall. He swung a gnarled hand onto the door as David sank into it, pushing it shut so that they could see one another.

"The reason I asked you not to tell anyone is simple. There are… people… to whom my existence is unknown. Should I become known – and my location revealed – I would not be around for very long."

David resisted the urge to roll his eyes.

"Believe I'm paranoid if you like, but the fact remains they *are* out to get me," the professor went on, apparently sensing David's disbelief. "I can help you. Whether you choose to take that help or not – that's up to you. And this isn't a school project we're talking about, is it?"

David shook his head slowly.

"Then where do you want to begin?"

"Ask him about exorcism," advised Nathan. He sat down beside David.

"Do you know anything about exorcism?" asked David.

Fuller sighed – a deep breath drawn in and expelled harshly, as if he couldn't make up his mind whether to share whatever pearls of wisdom he might know with this young schoolboy. "How old are you, David?"

"Fifteen," answered David automatically.

"I performed my first exorcism when I was thirty-three, and I was…" here the professor paused to remember, "...lucky." He rolled up his left shirt sleeve to reveal a shocking network of white scars. "Are you sure you want to be getting into this sort of thing at your age?"

There was a question to be answered, but David's mind was distracted, fixated on the words 'my first exorcism'. Here was a man who not only had a hundred books about ghosts, he also believed in them. And had *exorcised* them. At the cost of a few scars, admittedly.

"Didn't I tell you?" Nathan asked.

David nodded curtly, a movement he hoped that the professor would not notice. "No," he said, "I don't want to get involved in exorcism. But no-one else is going to do it – and someone stands to gain a lot from it, I hope."

"Just so long as you know, this is not a game. It can have deadly consequences if mishandled. Now," Fuller tapped a sheet of paper on the desk beside him. "I've scratched out some notes about exorcism using an efreeti jar. If you follow the instructions here, you shouldn't come to any harm. However, I don't rate your chances of completing an exorcism."

"Why not?"

"The mouth of the jar has to be in close proximity to the ghost at the appropriate time. It's like trying to grab a ferret in the dark. And you only get one shot at it."

"He means we have to know exactly where the ghost is, Dave," said Nathan. "Tell him!"

But David still couldn't quite grasp the fact that Fuller believed in ghosts. He couldn't work out how to explain how he knew exactly where the ghost he wanted to exorcise was going to be without mentioning Nathan. And, for some reason, he didn't want to talk about his brother. If it was possible to limit the conversation to the exorcism of a hypothetical ghost, so much the better. "You believe in ghosts," David said quietly.

"Do you believe in air?" asked Fuller.

"Of course, but…"

"Yet you cannot see it."

"It's just that … well, you're the first person I've spoken to who does."

"Why do you think that is?"

"Because they haven't seen one," Nathan suggested.

"Yeah," said David. "Because they haven't seen one." Suddenly he realized he had all but acknowledged the presence of Nathan.

Fuller did not seem to have noticed. "There are thousands of churchgoers in Fairfield who believe in God without ever having seen Him," he said, and fixed David with his milky eyes.

"But that's different," said Nathan. "They've been brought up in the Church."

Nathan was right, David realized. "People have been telling them there's a God all their lives. But if I suddenly try to persuade them there's a ghost…" he stopped speaking. He had been about to add the words 'sitting beside me'.

"Tell me about *your* ghost," asked Fuller. He fixed David with that intense stare once again.

David felt instantly under pressure – as if he was being examined like a beetle under a microscope. He had no idea what to say about the monkey-ghost without revealing more than he wanted to about Nathan.

Sensing his reluctance, Nathan said: "Tell him everything."

David took a deep breath. For a few seconds he held it. In that pause he noticed the ticking of an antique clock that sat amid the clutter on the mantelpiece. Next to the clock, a glass sphere sat on a tripod, strange mist swirling within it. Logs spat and sparked in the fireplace; the heat from the fire was intense, scorching his cheeks, and was making him begin to sweat in his winter coat. Fuller just stared at him, saying nothing.

"Okay," said David at last. "There's a ghost, living in the house across the road."

"You're sure?" asked Fuller. "How?"

"Why don't you just tell him?" asked Nathan impatiently.

"All right," David replied exasperatedly. To Fuller, he said: "My brother can see it."

"And where is your brother now?"

David pointed to what to Fuller's eyes was only an empty space on the sofa beside him.

"Your brother is a ghost? Can you see him?" asked Fuller. David nodded. "Can you see other ghosts? No? Only your brother. Did he... die recently?" Again David nodded. "Amazing. I myself have never seen a ghost, although I have spent years searching for them."

"But you believe in them," objected David.

"Temperature gauges, microsound detectors, infra-red cameras, fluoroscopes, gaussmeters. Those are my eyes. Not these," Fuller indicated his real eyes. The old man held out a piece of paper, smiling. "Read it before you try anything. You know where I am if you need help."

It was still only half-past four when David and Nathan arrived at Uncle Charlie's shop. David had wanted to go home, but Nathan dragged him along, muttering about 'striking while the iron was hot.'

As usual, the only person in the shop was Uncle Charlie himself. At the moment he was working on what looked like an utterly obsolete ribbon printer, his club-like hands appearing totally unsuited for such delicate work. "Don't make 'em like this any more," he said.

"No," agreed David uncertainly. There was probably a very good reason why not.

"How are you, anyway?" asked Charlie. "I'll shut up shop and make a cup of tea. Not very busy today anyway."

"Oh, fine," said David automatically. "Actually, I was wondering if I could borrow something for a school project."

"Oh yes," answered Charlie. "What sort of thing?"

"We're doing a project on Arabian folklore, and I remembered seeing some interesting jars upstairs that looked a bit Arabian," David told him.

"Ah – those old things. Fantastic buy, they were. Job lot of fifteen for a ton. Bought them off a mate who I met in the war – he still goes back to the Gulf now and then and fills up a container with local artefacts, ships them back here, and sells them on for a huge profit. This lot were rain-damaged, that's why they were so cheap. Leaky container. They're still in pretty good nick. Here, I'll get you one. Think I've sold one of them. Ought to get them on display, there just isn't any room. Hang on. See if you can fix this," he said, referring to the printer. Still muttering, as much to himself as to David, Uncle Charlie limped off up the stairs.

There was a series of thumps and rumbles from above. About five minutes later Uncle Charlie could be heard thudding back down the stairs. David had given up trying to fix the printer – he couldn't see what was wrong with it, for a start. "Right, here we are," said Charlie. "Two for the shop, one for you."

The jars were about twenty centimetres tall, and almost as wide, the widest point being quite close to the neck. All three were covered in black lacquer and had a cork lid with a string handle. They were decorated with intricately marked golden bands, although the number and position of the bands and the characters drawn on them varied between the jars.

"Pick one, and I'll try to sell the others," said Uncle Charlie. "What do you reckon? A tenner?"

"They look as if they're worth more than that," said David.

"For keeping genies in," said Uncle Charlie solemnly. He pulled at the string handle of the nearest jar. The lid came out with a pop. "Your wish is my command," he said with a chuckle.

"Charlie," asked David, thinking of the crystal. "Were my parents into that sort of thing?"

"What? Aladdin?"

"No – you know, supernatural things. Magic."

"Mumbo jumbo?" For a moment, Uncle Charlie's face seemed to darken, as if an unwelcome memory stirred in his mind. He dropped his gaze. "No. Not really. Not that I know of. Cannabis. That was about the extent of their dabbling in the Dark Arts. You don't smoke cannabis do you?"

"No."

"Good. Don't."

"Why not?"

Uncle Charlie scratched his stubble for a moment, stuck for an answer. "Don't know," he said at last. "But it's the sort of thing parents are supposed to say – and as I'm your nearest living relative, there you are, I've said it."

"Charlie?"

"H'mm?"

"What do you remember about that night? You know, the night Mum and Dad disappeared..."

"They brought you here with your brother. Said they had to leave town for a little while, but that it was too dangerous to take you two. That," Charlie swallowed deeply and clenched his fist, "was the last time we saw them alive. One day you'll find out what happened to them, and that's a promise," Charlie said. He would not amplify what he meant by this somewhat cryptic statement, despite David's persistence. Talk of his parents' demise was something of a conversation-killer. Shortly thereafter, David chose one of the efreeti jars, and Uncle Charlie wrapped it in tissue paper. "Good luck with your project," he said, as David went out of the door.

"I'll need it," muttered David, more to himself than to his uncle. "Charlie?"

he called, suddenly remembering. "What does the painting look like to you?"

It was a while before Charlie answered. "A face. I see a face. I see the face of someone... dead," he finished lamely.

"My mother?"

Charlie nodded dumbly. David doubled back from the door and gave him a hug, which inexplicably started his uncle crying.

Chapter 8: Binary Solution

Almost a week had passed since David's visit to Professor Fuller's house. In that time the efreeti jar he had borrowed from Uncle Charlie had been nestling in the back of his wardrobe. He and Nathan had as yet made no attempt to exorcise Michael's ghost. Now that they actually had the opportunity to do something about the haunted boy, all sorts of practical problems kept getting in the way. Fuller's instructions on the use of an efreeti jar insisted on meticulous preparations; they also required David to get the person he wanted to free of their ghost on their own, out of earshot of anyone else, if the exorcism was to be successful. So both David and Nathan kept watch on Michael whenever they could, trying to work out a way to catch him on his own. David had tried using the shadow lens to look at Michael to see whether he could see the ghost around his neck, with limited results. A kind of haze was visible around Michael's head, but it was so faint that it could almost have been a smear on the bedroom windowpane. Nevertheless, the lens definitely worked on Nathan – and whenever he was particularly transparent, David only had to look through it to see his brother as solid and real as he had been when he was alive. Their watch had similarly limited results. Michael, when he was at home, was always in the company of Dr Andersen. David, with a mounting sense of relief, was beginning to think the whole thing would never happen.

At least there was football practice that afternoon. His friend Kelly had noticed his absence the previous week, and had begged him to come back.

"Come on, Dave – you'll never get picked if you don't turn up," Kelly said.

"Hughes is never going to pick me – unless it's out of sympathy," countered David. And yet he had agreed to go, mainly because he enjoyed the ten-minute five-a-side matches at the end of the practice sessions. As it turned out, football practice went badly. David missed an open goal; after that, it seemed that no-one would pass to him any more.

When he and Nathan arrived home, they bumped into Dr Andersen and Michael coming out of their house. Nathan, as usual, fled immediately when Michael came into view.

"David, could I have a word?" called Doctor Andersen.

"Of course," he answered nervously, wondering if she had noticed him spying from his bedroom.

"Just a minute," she told him, and led the mute, unresisting Michael to the Hummer. She buckled him in on the passenger side, then closed the door and came back around to David. "Would you mind coming over and playing with Michael some time? I think it would do him good to play with someone like you. He… doesn't have many friends."

"Of course," answered David, quite unable to believe his luck, but wondering with a sinking feeling whether it was good luck or bad. "Whenever you like."

"Would Saturday morning be all right?" asked Doctor Andersen, with a quick glance behind her at Michael.

David forced himself to smile at her. "That would be just fine," he said.

Tea that Friday was fish and chips. Mr and Mrs Read and David sat in the kitchen eating their chips out of the paper. Chips out of the paper was one of the few nice things about living at the Reads' house.

"Are you up to anything interesting tomorrow?" Mrs Read asked David.

"I'm going over the road to play with Michael," David replied.

Mr Read snorted. "Play with him? The child's a robot."

"I think there's a little more to it than that," muttered David.

"Ignore your father David," said Mrs Read. "He doesn't mean it. Good for you."

Mr Read snorted again.

"Are you doing anything interesting, Guy?" Mrs Read asked him.

"No. Visiting that old factory we're trying to turn into executive flats."

"That sounds nice. Well, I might as well go into town to do some shopping, if I'm going to be the only one here."

Again David couldn't believe his luck – although he was beginning to think that the fates were conspiring to give him a chance to make a fool of himself. The absence of Guy and Rebecca tomorrow would leave him free to make all the necessary preparations for the exorcism without risk of being disturbed. The opportunity was coming. His career as a ghost hunter would begin in the morning.

In the middle of the night, David awoke from a nightmare about a wizened, monstrous monkey that was riding on Michael Andersen's neck. He succeeded in pulling the screaming monkey free – but then it clung to *his* throat, and he couldn't budge it. The monkey didn't mean to possess him as it had Michael – it was going to throttle him to death, before returning, satisfied, to its former host.

When he awoke, heart racing, David saw Nathan sitting beside the bed, obliviously absorbed in an open book. He was trying to turn the page. He watched the intense concentration on his brother's face. Slowly the page began to flutter. Nathan's hands were shaking more than the paper. The page lifted into the air a centimetre, but then it began to fall back. Nathan let out a gasp of annoyance.

David reached out of the bed and turned the page for him. He sat up for a while, staring at his mother's painting. Now he too was convinced that there was a face represented in those blurred smudges: but it was not his mother's face that he could see, it was the face of a monkey, screaming at him with diabolic fury. He did not mention this to Nathan, who would only have interpreted it as David's fear of the morrow.

On Saturday morning, David woke up with a sick feeling in his stomach, as if he was taking an exam that day. It was raining, a hard, steady rain that drummed on the window and boiled down the guttering. Mr Read was the first to leave the house, soon after breakfast, on his way to inspect the Tipler factory; David wondered whether he too, would sense a presence within. Something told him that Guy Read was so down-to-earth that he would not sense anything unusual about the place, which would make him even more cross with the surveyors who refused to work there. Mrs Read left too, about an hour later, taking the other car, and David, already sick with anxiety, was free to begin preparations for the exorcism.

The brothers sat in David's bedroom with the efreeti jar between them. Nathan was amazed by the jar – he could neither pass through it as he could normal objects, nor could he pick it up. He could touch the jar, but it was far too heavy for him to budge. There was something about the black lacquer coating the surface of the jar that his essence could not permeate. David could pick the jar up and use it to sweep Nathan away, as if he was no more than a cobweb. David suggested he might first practice by exorcising Nathan, but Nathan would have none of it. "You're not squashing me into there," he said flatly.

David placed a standard white candle in the open jar and lit it with a match – a difficult job, because the candle was slightly shorter than the jar, and the lit match had to be lowered down to light the candle. They watched as it slowly burned down, Nathan with half an eye on David's watch.

The flame began to gutter and smoke. Not enough fresh air could get into the jar. Just as it seemed that the candle would go out, Nathan said: "Time's up."

Immediately David picked up the lid and fitted it into place on the jar.

"Now for the list of five-figure binary primes," said Nathan. David got a piece of paper. He began writing out a list of ones and zeroes. Then he wrote normal numbers beside these. The binary numbers started out with two digits, then three, then four, then five. When he had reached 11111, David stopped adding to the list. Next, with Nathan supervising, he placed ticks and crosses against some of the five digit binary numbers. Eight of these he copied out onto a new piece of paper.

"That's it," said Nathan. "Now we just have to sort out the stuff in the kitchen, and we're ready."

"I don't feel ready," complained David. "I feel sick."

"Just think how Michael feels," Nathan told him.

Nathan was looking particularly faint this morning. David took the shadow lens out of its box and peered through it at his brother. That was better. Nathan was grim-faced, determined. He grinned, posing as if David was taking a photo.

From somewhere the nightmarish sensation of scrawny limbs around his neck came to David. He zipped his top up as far as it would go, turned up the collar, and carefully put the crystal in his rucksack.

"You fit?" asked Nathan.

"No," answered David, standing up.

Outside, the rain still poured and laughed along the gutter and down the drainpipes.

Nathan stood in the middle of the road and watched as David approached the Andersens' house. He could go no further yet — for one thing, he didn't want the monkey ghost to see him, and for another, he didn't want David to trap *him* in the efreeti jar by mistake. He would stay within earshot, and in case of emergency would come as fast as he could — although what use he could be neither of them knew.

Doctor Andersen opened the door when David knocked. "Are you all right?" she asked. "You look a bit green."

"No, I'm okay," he said. David was not surprised to see that she was still wearing black. Perhaps she only had black clothes.

She invited him in; he followed her down the short hallway to the foot of the stairs. David refused the offer of a drink with a dry croak.

"Michael's up in his room," explained Doctor Andersen. "He likes lining things up, arranging things. Sometimes he likes to draw pictures. If you need me, I'll be just down here, getting on with some paperwork."

"Right," said David, hardly able to speak.

"Michael!" called Doctor Andersen. "David's here to see you."

There was no response from upstairs.

"Good luck," the doctor wished David.

"Thanks," he muttered, and started up the stairs. Once at the top, he quickly located Michael's room, knocked, and without waiting for an answer, walked through the half-open door. Inside, Michael was sitting on the floor, lining up his toy cars. David noticed a gold identity bracelet around his wrist. *In case he gets lost*, he realized. Michael looked up momentarily as David walked in, and then returned his attention to arranging the car he was holding precisely at the end of the line of fifty that already stretched most of the way across the room.

It seemed dark in the room, although the overhead light was on. Rain squalled against the window. "Hello Michael," David said. There was no response from the haunted boy. David sat on the bed and opened his rucksack. The first thing he took out was his shadow lens. This he gently placed against his eye and peered at Michael. This close there was definitely a suggestion of a few cobwebby strands of mist in the air around Michael's head, but they were faint, formless, not the monkey Nathan spoke about. David stowed the lens in a side pocket of the rucksack, leaving the main compartment open, but not yet bringing out the efreeti jar inside. Instead he took out a piece of paper from his back pocket, swallowed deeply, and spoke.

"Greetings, noble spirit," said David. At once Michael froze, the next car to be placed in line still in mid air. "One one one, zero one," continued David. At this, Michael slowly began to turn around to look at him, his face blank. "One zero one zero one," said David. The light bulb dimmed, its luminance returning a few moments later.

Michael's brow furrowed in confusion.

"One zero one one one," David told him, took a deep breath and added: "one zero zero one one."

The car that Michael was holding fell to the floor with a clatter.

"One zero zero zero one," said David.

Michael lurched unsteadily to his feet. Although slightly younger than David, he was big for his age. The confusion on his face was replaced by anger. His eyes seemed to be clouding over like a snake's lidless eyes when it sheds its skin.

David saw this with a glance, and said quickly: "One one zero zero one."

Tension knotted the muscles in Michael's arms, and he leapt on David, just as he was half way through another string of numbers.

"One one zero —" David began, but at this point Michael's hands closed around his neck. "…one…one…" David got one leg on the ground, and tried to push Michael off him by bracing his other leg against the bed, while simultaneously blindly groping with both hands for the mouth of his rucksack. Together they staggered back a couple of steps, scattering the lovingly arranged toy cars all over the place. There was a growing thready film on Michael's body, condensing out of nothing like grey candyfloss.

"One…one…" choked David. White spots were flashing in his eyes. He could dimly hear Doctor Andersen calling up the stairs, asking whether everything was all right. He couldn't get hold of the jar. "Nathan…" he called, but his voice was no more than a whisper. Suddenly Michael lost his footing on the scattered toy cars, and together they slammed into the wall. The grip on David's throat slackened for a moment, and he glanced down to get a bearing on the efreeti jar. Then the death-grip resumed, but by now he had the efreeti jar in his hands, the rucksack falling free. He felt for the string handle and pulled it. Michael seemed to be screaming and roaring at once. There was a rush of cold wind, a blast of a sewer-stink stench, and suddenly Michael's hands released their hold on David's neck.

"Be gone, noble spirit," David said hoarsely, and, turning to face Michael, held up the jar. It was as if Michael had been punched by a heavyweight boxer: his contorted face relaxed, his eyes rolled to the whites. He seemed to be held up, puppet-like, for a few moments, even though he was already unconscious. Then he sagged, slumped to the ground, and lay there lifelessly. Instantly David re-capped the jar.

At that moment Doctor Andersen appeared in the doorway. David watched helplessly as she saw Michael lying unconscious on the floor. Her worried expression turned to one of anger. "What have you done to him?" she hissed.

"Nothing," David said, and turned to put the jar in his rucksack.

"What's that in your hand?"

"Nothing."

"Did you hit him with it? Give it to me!"

"No!"

Doctor Andersen grabbed David and snatched at the efreeti jar. He tried to duck out of her grasp and dive for the door. He managed to free himself from her grip, but the jar fell out of his hand and began to roll along the landing. It was trundling for the stairs.

"Nathan!" screamed David, and dived for the jar. He didn't get there; Doctor Andersen had a hold on him again. He lay on the landing, pinned by her weight, as with tantalising calm the efreeti jar inched towards the top stair, slowing all the time. Just as the jar began to teeter on the brink, Nathan surged up the stairs and hurled himself against the jar like a wave crashing into a sea wall. The jar carried on rolling, pushing him back. It was going to fall. And then, miraculously, it stopped; beneath it, Nathan groaned like Atlas holding up the Earth.

David felt the weight lift from him as Doctor Andersen got up. "Michael — are you all right?" she asked. "What has he done to you?"

"Come on," grunted Nathan. "I can't hold it much longer."

David scrambled to his feet, grabbed the efreeti jar, stuffed it back in his rucksack, and hurtled down the stairs, leaving Doctor Andersen kneeling by her prone son. He heard her shouting down the stairs behind him as he ran, but he ignored her, and fled out of the front door of the house, not bothering to close it behind him.

"Now we're for it," David gasped, as he crashed through the kitchen door. "Did you see the state of him? He could be dead for all we know."

"There's nothing we can do about that now — just get the jar sealed," Nathan told him, sounding equally panicked.

On the cooker top, David had left a pan of melted wax. Now he peered into it, and was dismayed to see that it had already almost completely solidified. He put the efreeti jar down and lit the gas under the pan.

"Hang on a minute," said Nathan. "What about the blood? It's supposed to be one percent blood, isn't it?"

"Well, how much is that?" asked David. "And where am I going to get it from?"

"I don't know, and take a wild guess," said Nathan, staring at him evenly.

"Brilliant," muttered David, and pulled a large knife out of the knife block.

"Hurry up," said Nathan. "Our six minutes are almost up – the lid's moving, I can see it." With that, he leapt onto the worktop and stood on the efreeti jar, trying to keep the lid on.

David, his teeth gritted, sliced through the little finger of his left hand. The knife was sharp, and the cut was bigger than he had intended. Blood started to drip on to the floor. Quickly he held his hand over the melting wax. Red drops fell into the pan. "How much?" he gasped.

"That'll do," Nathan told him. "Just hurry up, Dave, because this blasted thing's coming out."

They heard the front door open. It was Mrs Read; they could hear her humming contentedly to herself.

"Do it now!" Nathan shouted.

David grabbed the efreeti jar and inverted it into the pan of wax and blood. Half of the pan's contents gushed out over the cooker top, splattering the walls and floor.

"Guy? Is that you?" called Mrs Read from the hall.

"Get out of here," ordered Nathan. "If she catches you in here with her precious kitchen in this state, she'll open the jar for sure."

David agreed. He grabbed the jar – the wax all over it still painfully hot – then swept up his rucksack and awkwardly tried to shrug it onto one shoulder as he fled. He threw open the back door and ran out into the rain. Behind him, he heard Mrs Read screaming. She had seen the state of her kitchen.

"Run!" Nathan told David. He needed no second bidding, but sprinted down the garden, the efreeti jar in both hands, solidifying wax congealing around his fingers.

"David! Come back here this instant!" shouted Mrs Read.

But David had no intention of going back. He scrambled over the back fence, using one hand to climb, the other keeping a tight grip on the jar, which had almost welded itself to him anyway. He fell into a flowerbed on the other side, protecting the jar at the expense of a few bruises. A dog was barking – a big dog – and the sound was getting louder. David was only half way to his feet when the dog – a huge, black and brown beast dribbling gluey saliva – appeared around the corner of the house. The dog stopped for a moment, barking even more ferociously, and then it came on at a run. David turned back to the fence, over which he could still hear Rebecca Read demanding his instant return. There was no way to run.

At that moment, Nathan floated through the fence. He quickly grasped the situation and roared at the dog at the top of his voice, which stopped in its tracks before fleeing, whimpering, back around the corner of the house and out of sight. "Right," said Nathan, unperturbed. "Let's go."

"When did you discover that dogs could see you?" demanded David.

"I'm not sure they can actually see me – they're certainly aware of me, but to what extent I don't know. Come on, get moving. We've got to get out of here."

David could not deny that. But where were they to go? Where could they hide the efreeti jar where it would never be found, and never be opened?

Chapter 9: Broken Pottery

For a while following the exorcism David walked aimlessly, Nathan floating along beside him, neither speaking. It was still raining hard, and the streets were quite empty apart from the occasional passing car kicking up sheets of water onto the pavement. At last the apparently random sequence of turns led them to the city cemetery.

"What are we doing here?" demanded Nathan. "We can't hide it here."

"No," agreed David, but he said nothing more. He led his brother up an avenue under the oppressively thick crowns of gnarled cypress trees, and then to the right towards a small round chapel, which was surrounded by a ring of benches protected from the elements by a portico. It was to one of these benches that David was heading; once under the roof of the portico, he dropped his rucksack on the nearest bench and slumped down beside it, exhausted and soaked to the skin. After a moment's stillness, David examined his cut hand, which was wet with a mixture of rain and blood. As he watched, a red drop gathered together, trundled down his finger, and splashed onto the dry concrete. "Sharp knife," he muttered. "This thing won't stop bleeding."

"Don't worry. You won't bleed to death," said Nathan, hovering over him nervously.

David did not reply; he just stared at his cut, as if transfixed.

"You've got to go back to the Reads'," Nathan said.

David looked up. Nathan was misty, faint. Had he not been able to hear him, he might almost have missed his brother altogether. Beyond him, the cemetery hissed with rain. The grey skeletons of great specimen trees, shorn of their summer glories, were all around them, looming unbowed among the rows of ancient cracked tombs. Piles of golden brown leaves were heaped up everywhere in wet drifts. Here and there, a yew or holly tree remained stolidly green in defiance of the coming winter. Beyond them, the avenue of cypresses led away down the slope into deepening gloom.

Slowly David shook his head, and looked down at his hand again.

"What about the library?" asked Nathan. There was urgency in his voice. "You can't stay here – you're soaked through. You've got to get in the warm. At least the library's warm."

David said nothing, gave no indication that he had heard his brother's entreaty.

"Dave?" Now Nathan seemed close to panic.

David smiled faintly. "What have we done?" he asked. "What did we think we were doing? We went charging in like fools and now look what's happened."

"We meant well, and no-one can say otherwise. Maybe Michael's okay now. I could go and have a look."

"Okay," David agreed, without looking up.

"I'm not going anywhere – not with you in this mood."

"What mood?"

"Look – we have to do things in the right order. You have to get warm and dry. We have to hide the efreeti jar. Then we can worry about Michael."

David shivered. His feet were going numb. "I can't go back to the Reads' house until I've found a safe place for this. Or maybe I should just smash it. At least then we'd be back where we started."

This suggestion hung unpleasantly in the air for a time, until Nathan countered: "I can think of one place it might be safe."

"Okay," David said in a resigned tone.

"Okay?" asked Nathan, surprised by his brother's sudden acquiescence.

"Too cold to argue," explained David. With that, he stood up stiffly, hoisted the rucksack onto his shoulder, and walked out into the rain.

What on a sunny day would have been a ten minute stroll to Professor Fuller's house turned into a half-hour-long trek dragging through puddles, weighed down as David was by soaking clothes. And worse was to come. For knock as he might at the door of Museum Cottage, no reply came. Fuller wasn't in.

"Maybe those people he reckoned were out to get him… er, got him," wondered Nathan.

"You really know how to cheer me up," retorted David. "Brilliant. Just brilliant. Here I am, soaked to the skin, bleeding profusely –"

"I wouldn't exactly call it profusely," interrupted Nathan.

"Here I am, soaked to the skin, bleeding profusely," went on David, ignoring him, "when I go to what I loosely call home there'll be hell to pay, God only knows what happened to Michael… Mrs Read's kitchen looks like it's been hit by a missile… and still I can't get rid of this damned jar. I'm going to drop it soon, I know I am. My hands are going numb." With that, David swung the rucksack off his back, catching it clumsily with his cold hands, and lowered it with exaggerated caution onto the driveway. "Now I'll probably fall on it, or kick it over. And did I mention? It's raining."

"It isn't all bad," Nathan commented, hovering nearby.

"It isn't?"

"You did it, Dave. You got the ghost."

"The ghost nearly got me," objected David, rubbing his neck.

"Do you want me to check on Michael now?"

David laughed briefly. With his earlier outburst, some of his good humour seemed to have returned. "No," he said. "If I'm going to be miserable, I might as well do it with you to moan at. Besides. I can delude myself with the hope that he's made a miraculous recovery, so long as you haven't been to check."

"Okay. In that case, I'll have a quick check around inside, just in case Fuller's having a nap." So saying, Nathan floated through the kitchen wall and disappeared.

David sank down on the wet step and turned his collar up. It was an ineffectual gesture of defiance of the rain, which still drummed down relentlessly. He sat for a while, thinking of nothing, but images, real and imagined, kept popping up in his mind: Michael's eyes rolling back as he fell to the floor; Doctor Anderson's expression as she took in the scene; an ambulance rushing Michael to hospital; medical staff gathering round… a medic shaking his head…

The sound of a car turning into the driveway snapped David to his senses. It was a small, racing green sports car with a black soft top, and it came in at quite a speed before skidding to a halt. As it did so David lunged to snatch the rucksack out of the way. Then he saw that behind the wheel of the car was Professor Fuller, who was gesturing at him, pointing at the garage door, raising his hand. David walked over to the garage door and pulled at the handle; it rose smoothly into the air. He stepped aside, muttering: "Unbelievable!" He could have spent the last ten minutes in the dry.

Fuller eased the car into the garage and emerged slowly, leaning on his cane. Concern registered on his face. "David? Is everything all right?"

David merely showed Fuller the rucksack.

"You have it? Well done. Very well done. Come on. Let's dispose of it." The professor led the way to the door.

Once they were inside the kitchen, Fuller took the rucksack and with gnarled fingers pulled out the efreeti jar. "Where is your brother?" he asked.

"He'd better not follow us."

Nathan, having just appeared from the direction of the study, had heard the professor's words. "Okay," he agreed, and hung back as Fuller led David down the hall to the front room. A battery of equipment was set up within. It reminded David of a photographic studio – what seemed to be lights on stands were arranged in a circle, all pointing at an old tea chest. To one side, a metal trolley was stacked with equipment sprinkled liberally with dials, switches, and lights, looking not unlike an obsolete stereo system. There was even a hum in the air, as if a huge amplifier was waiting for a signal. Strangely, for a living room, the everyday trappings of life were absent. There were no armchairs, no sofa, no TV, no coffee table, not even a carpet – just bare floorboards, bedecked with trailing wires and boxes full of discarded circuit boards and other electrical equipment. To one side, a crude wallpapering bench overflowed with more equipment, including an oscilloscope, a soldering gun, and a tray of assorted resistors.

Fuller moved into the middle of the room and gently placed the efreeti jar on the tea chest. Then he moved over to the bank of equipment on the trolley, twisted a dial, and flicked a few switches. The background hum in the room rose noticeably in pitch. "Now we'd better retreat to the study," Fuller said, and walked out of the door.

Once again David followed him. Strange: the professor was moving much more freely than he had seen before… he had left his cane at the outside door, and no longer seemed to need it. Was this the same shuffling old man he had seen in the library?

Nathan was fluttering nervously in the kitchen. "What's going on?" he asked.

"Don't know," replied David.

"I hope he knows what he's –"

"I must apologize to you," Fuller said, obliviously talking over Nathan and almost walking into him on his way to the study. Once there, he took some matches from the mantle and knelt down slowly to light the fire.

"What for?" asked David.

Fuller did not reply at once. He struck a match. Before he could get it to the grate, a draught blew it out. He lit another match, which this time faded as it reached the balled-up paper that Fuller was aiming for. Finally, using two matches together, Fuller managed to start the fire.

"Apologize. Oh yes. I must apologize because –" Fuller was interrupted by a sound like a gunshot. David's heart nearly stopped. "I didn't tell you a loud bang was coming."

David looked at the old man quizzically.

Fuller grinned and levered himself upright on fists as knobbly as rootstocks. "Sorry. Joke. Now I can show you. Come this way."

In the front room, there was a pile of ash and broken pottery on the tea chest. The humming had become a high-pitched whine. Fuller turned a dial, flipped some switches, and the noise abated. He pointed to the remains of the efreeti jar. "The exorcism is complete. Your ghost no longer exists in this world – we have squeezed it into another."

"But the pot! The ghost didn't escape, did it?"

"No, no," Fuller told him with a smile. "The pot merely imploded when the spirit within had gone. Come – back to the study. You look as if you need to warm up."

But even huddled in front of the fire, which by now was roaring merrily, and clutching a mug of hot chocolate, David was anything but warm. He was soaked to the skin, and chilled to the bone. "What are those things in the front room?" he asked, teeth chattering.

"Emitters. But now is not the time for questions – despite the number you must have. You had better get home, and get dry and warm. We'll talk more another day. If you're interested, that is."

"I can't. I'm in so much trouble…"

"Ask him about Michael," suggested Nathan.

"One question," said David. "The boy we exorcised – he collapsed. Does that normally happen?"

"The emergence of the real self may take time when a possession is removed."

"Time?"

"Hours… days…" Fuller swung around in his chair, pulling an old volume off a bookcase beside the desk. He flipped through it, wiry brows furrowed. "Here we are. A case of exorcism reported by Viktor Berezhov. The victim was a patient in a sanatorium… the exorcism was done by a Doctor Emil Majry. Oh."

"Oh?"

"After the exorcism, the patient slipped into a coma. When he awoke, he was mute and unresponsive, and remained so for nearly eight and a half years. After that, he awoke one morning as well as he had been before the possession, and with no memory of the intervening time."

"Eight and a half *years?*" repeated David incredulously.

"The real self may never emerge," Fuller said, snapping the book shut. "It has been protected, curled up inside. A man who has spent his whole life locked in a small room will eventually find the thought of freedom terrifying."

"What have we done?" asked David in disbelief, shaking his head.

"Tush!" snorted Fuller dismissively. "You must be positive. It depends on the character of the victim, how long the possession has gone on. There are ways… perhaps hypnotism may be of use."

"I am in so much trouble…" David said slowly. "Why didn't you tell me this before? I would never have done it."

"Firstly, you didn't ask. Secondly, you have nothing to regret. One who seeks reward will never find truth. One who seeks truth will never find reward. Now let's go – I'll drive you home."

Robbie Drake approached his house with feelings of trepidation that David Carraway would have recognized well. His mood lightened greatly when, still near the bottom of Miles Hill, he saw that his father's car was absent.

Robbie let himself into the silent, unlit house and called upstairs: "Becks!"

His sister's voice came from surprisingly close: the darkness at the top of the stairs. "I'm here," she said.

Robbie jumped in shock. His fingers quickly located the light switch and flicked it on. Becks was sitting on the top step.

"He's gone," she said.

"Gone? Gone where? What's happened… did he…?"

"I'm all right."

Robbie was already half way up the stairs. With the landing light falling on Becks's face, he calmed down a little. She was unhurt, outwardly at least.

"He didn't come back last night. It's been thirty-six hours."

"He's just out on the lash somewhere… you know what he's like…"

"No."

"No? How do you know?"

"It's just us now, Robbie."

Robbie sat down on the step below his sister. Becky was pale, thin, malnourished almost, with large, sad brown eyes. He took her little hand in his club-like fist.

"What are we going to do?" she asked.

"Is he dead?"

She nodded slowly.

"How do you know?"

Becks shrugged. "Everything is being stretched out thin. Today, tomorrow, yesterday… I have to try to think… but it's hard to make sense of everything…" Becky rubbed her eyes.

"I think you need to rest," Robbie said. "I'll see if there's any food…"

"There isn't."

"We need to find some cash. Then we'll just get on a train…"

"We can't just leave. And we can't tell anyone. I can't see a way out this time…"

"The social…? The cops?"

Becks shook her head. "Everything is black that way. But there is something… a little light… a chance…"

"Yeah?"

"You have to tell David."

"David? David who?"

"In your year. David Carraway."

"Carraway! No chance. ! I might tell him what a git he is, but I'm not telling him about this."

"He can help us. I think he's going to save my life."

"Carraway? Save your life? You have some weird ideas sometimes. He wouldn't cross the road –"

"You must get a detention on Monday. Then, tell him. Promise me."

"Look, Becks, this is crazy…"

"Promise!"

"Okay, whatever you say, I promise to get a detention and tell Carraway afterwards."

"And whatever happens…"

"Yeah?"

"You must *never, ever,* hurt anybody."

PART TWO

*

IN DIM RUINS IT LURKS

One of my wishes is that those dark trees,

So old and firm they scarcely show the breeze,

Were not, as 'twere, the merest mask of gloom,

But stretched away unto the edge of doom.

Robert Frost

TIPLER

Chapter 10: Blood on the Playground

David's punishment for making a mess of Mrs Read's kitchen was far more bearable than he could have hoped. The kitchen was still in exactly the same state as he had left it. As soon as David arrived home, Mr Read ordered him to make the kitchen spotless, which included cleaning up spatters of his own blood and the near-impossible task of getting all the wax out of the saucepan. He wasn't even allowed to melt the wax again. He offered to buy a new saucepan out of his pocket money, an offer that met with derision from Mrs Read ("Have you any idea what these *cost?*"). When he had spent half an hour cleaning, still in his soaking clothes, Mr Read inspected the saucepan, pronounced it useless, and tossed it into the bin. ("Any more of this behaviour, and it's the children's home for you my lad," he announced, predictably enough.) Strangely, though, neither of the Reads were interested in *why* he had done what he had done. They seemed to assume that he had done it for pleasure or during an attack of idiocy. The lack of an interrogation suited David, who scrubbed away in silence. Occasionally one of the Reads would appear in the kitchen doorway to assess his progress, before disappearing once more with a snort.

Finally the kitchen was acceptably clean, and David was sent to his room. ("And don't bother coming down for your tea.") David took all his wet clothes off, put several layers of dry ones on, and buried himself under his duvet.

Of Michael, meanwhile, there was no news. Nathan had gone straight over to check out the situation at the Andersens' house, but had found it empty. He kept flitting back and forth, but as afternoon became evening there was still no sign of Doctor Andersen or her son. Nathan promised to go over to the hospital to look there as soon as David had fallen asleep.

"Are you kidding?" replied David. "I can't sleep until I find out how he is."

But he was wrong. He was exhausted. For a time he sat up and stared at his mother's painting, letting his tired eyes defocus. There *was* a face, as he had thought yesterday – but it was not as he had thought the face of a screaming monkey. Rather, the portrait seemed to be of a beautiful girl. He mentioned this to Nathan, who could make out nothing beyond random splotches. "It's like a Rorschach inkblot," Nathan surmised. "Your mind forms it into a pattern that isn't there." David stared until all he could see was a dim tunnel with the painting at its centre, with at *its* centre the portrait of the girl, who now seemed to be smiling coyly at him. Finally, despite the incessant gnawing of his conscience and the hypnotic quality of the painting, by half-past seven he was sound asleep.

"Sleep well," Nathan said softly. He reached out an almost invisible hand to touch his brother's head. Then he turned, and walked through the wall, into the darkness outside.

Monday did not start well, and got progressively worse over the course of the morning. Firstly, there was still no sign of anyone at the Andersen house. Thoughts of where the Andersens might be and how Michael was preoccupied David to such an extent that he was late for school. On the way there he got caught in a sudden shower, which everyone else seemed to have missed by arriving on time. He had to sit through double maths in wet clothes, which made his second-worst subject even less bearable than usual.

Nathan had been gone all night, and only returned at morning break, having given up his search for the Andersens to return to the abandoned factory. He found David in the playground, and delivered an extended report on the deserted building, in between David's protestations that it was absurd to think about more exorcisms given the result of the first one. Nathan scoffed at his negativity and went on regardless. The whole structure of the factory, he said, looked as though it was about to collapse at any moment. There were no easy access points for 'corporeal organisms' – those without keys to the various padlocks, at any rate. There was definitely something supernatural about the place, and it was somehow related to the Solvent Man – but rather than a distinct entity, like the monkey demon had been, it seemed to be more of an atmosphere, a poisonous miasma that permeated the whole place, and instilled in all visitors a sense of foreboding, of being watched. Nathan had scoured the whole place, and there really was nothing there that could be collected in an efreeti jar. This began to cheer David up – it sounded like Nathan wasn't going to push for him to try another exorcism. He likened the situation to two states of water – ice and vapour. Whereas the monkey demon had been concentrated in one place – like an ice cube, easy to collect – whatever was causing the problems at the factory was more like a fog, impossible to gather. He was then moving on to say that, strictly, fog was more of a suspension of liquid than a gas – gaseous water is steam – when he interrupted himself.

"Look out – it's Drake," he hissed.

David immediately became intensely interested in the scuff marks on the ends of his shoes. "Where is he?" he asked, out of the corner of his mouth.

"Ssh, he's coming this way."

David kept his head down and listened to the babble of noise on the playground, trying to pick out Drake's rough drawl. At first there was no hint of Drake's voice: just the familiar racket of running, shouting – a football game in progress – and scores of chattering children. Then, from not so far away, came an unmistakable sneer.

"All right, Morley?" Drake asked. This question was followed by what sounded like a cuff around the head – a mock-friendly gesture that Drake frequently used in his playground tours to intimidate those children he wasn't going to single out for particular attention that day. This sort of thing kept them on their toes, and softened them up for when he decided to tap them for cash.

"Keep your head down," ordered Nathan.

What does he think I'm going to do, David wondered: jump up and do some Cossack dancing?

"Hey, Mox. Who's that sitting over there, pretending they haven't noticed me?"

David's heart tripped over itself. He looked up, ready to run; but when he got a bead on Drake, he saw that the bully and his cronies weren't even looking at him. They were gathering around a girl who was sitting on a bench between two yew bushes. The girl was in David's year, but he didn't know her well. She had a slightly odd way of looking at people, her head cocked and her eyes apparently defocused. David had himself been subject to such a gaze on a few occasions. He thought nothing of it. She was a little odd, that was all. What was an odd stare compared to talking to the ghost of your brother?

However, being odd was enough to single her out for cruel treatment at the hands of her peers. And at the hands of Robbie Drake.

"It's the mutant. *Woop!* Hey, mutant," Drake said, standing over the girl.

"I'm not a mutant," she said sullenly.

"*Woop*, it talks! The mutant talks!"

Drake's cronies Moxy and Clegg laughed dutifully.

"It must be a mutant, mustn't it boys. Look at its face. Hey, mongrel child. Does your face come off? *Woop!* What's underneath?"

"Help her Dave. She's going to cry," said Nathan.

"There are three of them," muttered David, looking on helplessly. "What am I supposed to do?"

"I'll be right there with you."

"Fat lot of use you'll be — and anyway, there are over a hundred kids on this playground —"

"So why should you be the one to stick your neck out?"

"Bingo."

"Just say what I tell you to say. Come on."

David stood up and watched as Nathan fluttered a little way towards the drama, dodging between clusters of students. He shook his head in disbelief, and instead of following his brother he walked away from the scene, heading towards the double doors that cut through a corridor and led to the playing fields beyond. After a moment or two Nathan noticed that he was trying to sneak off and caught up with him. "Where are you going?"

"I'm not sticking my neck out for a complete stranger. I'm not you, Nathan. You don't seem to be able to get that."

"All your friends were complete strangers when you met them."

"I don't care," said David flatly, and walked on.

"Fine. Do what you like."

"I've got science homework to hand in that I haven't done yet."

"Science is easy."

"No," said David bitterly. "Science is easy for you."

There was no reply from Nathan. Perhaps he was no longer following.

David carried on. He got to the double doors and hauled one open. Instead of stepping through, he stood there a moment, holding the door for four or five year nines. Then, without moving, he let it go, and watched as the door creaked shut.

He turned around. "I must be crazy," he said.

"According to most people, you are," Nathan told him. He *had* evidently been following, but silently.

"You're doing my science homework tonight."

"Fine." Nathan began to laugh.

"What's so funny?" demanded David angrily.

"You won't stand up to them because it's the right thing to do, but you will if there's a chance I'll do your science homework for you."

"It's not a chance. It's a definite." David briefly joined in the laughter. By the time he had walked the fifty metres to where Drake and his mates were picking on the girl, the laughter had been replaced by a cold feeling of dread.

"*Woop!* The little diddums is going to cry in a minute," Drake was saying. The girl was trapped between the three of them, Drake, Moxy, and Clegg. They had snatched her rucksack, and were passing it to and fro while she made half-hearted attempts to grab it back. David approached silently. As Clegg made to pass the bag to Drake, he stepped forward and snatched it out of the air.

"Leave her alone, Drake," said David, in as firm a voice as he could muster.

"*You?*" Drake asked, and a flicker of uncertainty at David's intervention crossed his features.

"Me," David said.

Drake looked down for a moment, as if he had to break contact with David's gaze to regain his composure. Then he looked up again, hunched his shoulders, set his jaw, and formed a deliberate humourless grin. "I've been looking for you, Carraway. So the little freak's got a boyfriend, has she? You're both freaks, after all, so you must be made for each other."

David gave the girl back her rucksack. As he let go of the bag, Moxy and Clegg grabbed his arms.

"Tell him he's really big with his two mates. How hard is he on his own?" Nathan ordered.

David relayed this, trying to sound convincing, but unable to keep a tiny quaver out of his voice.

"Harder than you, you freakface," Drake said flatly. "Your brother's not here to look after you. Because he's dead. Like you're going to be in a minute. Let him go, boys." Clegg and Moxy let go of David's arms. The next move was his. He saw that the girl had slipped away; that meant he could run, if he had the chance –

"Move into the middle of the playground," Nathan told him. "I want everyone to see this."

He's the crazy one, thought David, *not me*. Nevertheless, he obeyed his brother, shuffling sideways out into the open. Drake followed, staring at David with an expression of pure hate. Then, curiously, Drake's dark brows furrowed and his stare dropped once again. For a moment his tense muscles relaxed and it seemed, incredibly, that he might back down. But he breathed in deeply, straightened up, and fixed the slighter boy with what was if anything a more hate-filled stare than before.

There was a cold, heavy stone in the pit of David's stomach. Nathan was giving him advice, but he could hardly hear it. He heard something about going in hard, not holding back. He couldn't believe it. He had just volunteered to get the beating of his life.

A group of boys had noticed what was going on. "Fight! Fight! Fight!" they chanted. Others took up the call. Children were gathering around, encircling Drake and David, who were facing each other, three metres apart, as still as posts. David did nothing. A moment – it could only have been a moment – seemed to stretch out, thin, like melted toffee. He was aware of everything around him at that instant. He noticed a dozen tiny, tiny, irrelevant things in the wing beat of a fly: Drake's frayed coat, a red and white badge on the school sweater of one of the onlookers, a billow of grey clouds overhead, and a fragment of gravel grating under his shoe. Gone was his fear, the sweat dripping into his eyes, and the rubbery weakness in his legs. He seemed to be everywhere, and nowhere, all at once. For a moment, it seemed David knew everything about everything in the Universe. The most important thing he suddenly realized was that Drake was only a human – twice his size, perhaps – but a human, not a devil. David had beaten a ghost. How hard could it be to fight a boy? He realized that he was now smiling at Drake; the bystanders must think he really had lost his grip on sanity. Drake laughed back at him silently, his jaw hanging open as always, eyes now brightly empty.

Then the spell was broken.

"Come on then," Drake sneered. "If you think you're hard enough."

David took an unsteady step forward. Drake charged. In the instant of their closing, David threw a fist, felt it connect with Drake's cheek, felt, painlessly, his own head rocked back by a punch. Then they were too close for punching, grappling silently while the crowd surrounding them bayed for blood – whose, they probably didn't care. David's legs were weak with adrenaline – they could hardly hold their own weight, let alone keep him steady under Drake's onslaught. He managed to grab Drake's shoulders, tried to bring a knee into his adversary's solar plexus; Drake was trying something of the same. Unbalanced, they fell together, David underneath.

"Roll him! Roll him, Dave!" Nathan was screaming.

That was exactly what David was trying to do. But Drake was too heavy. He had David pinned down, had hold of his face, and was trying to smash his head against the tarmac. David scrabbled to prevent this, both hands grabbing Drake's wrist, fingernails digging in. Drake's spare left hand, bunched into a fist, caught David squarely in the side of the face. He saw only red for a moment, but wriggled, twisted desperately, and tried to grab Drake's left hand. Another blow came in, this one half-deflected, only glancing.

Then David somehow managed to get his knee in place under Drake, and drove it upwards. Drake fell sideways, his grip slackening for a second. They rolled. For a second David was on top; then Drake, his strength far greater than David's, was rolling *him*, and was suddenly on top again.

Then came a new, unexpected pain. His ear was being twisted. Drake was being hauled off him. The crowd had stopped chanting, and had started to disperse, pretending to a student that they hadn't really been interested at all, had only been passing by.

It was Mr Hobbs, the deputy head, who had an ear lock on both David and Drake. "Come on Drake – and you, whoever you are. You know where you're going." So saying, Hobbs half-led, half-dragged the two boys off the playground.

Chapter 11: Milla

David set down his bucket of soapy water and stared at the wall in front of him. The wall was more than two metres tall and screamed a cacophony of graffiti for most of that height. He solemnly regarded his scrubbing brush, and then looked back at the wall. The two were ill-matched. It would be simpler to overpaint the graffiti with a clean, slick coat of brilliant white. But then, he realized, he wasn't here to get rid of the graffiti. Not really. He was here to be punished.

Hobbs had hustled David and Drake to the head's office, and with a heavy hand pressed on top of their heads had sat them down outside to wait. They did not have to sit there long, which was a blessing, because David's face was throbbing, and Nathan was standing next to him rattling on about how proud he was. David had no pride in what he had done: he had never been sent to the headmistress before, and all he could think of was what the Reads would think when this incident got back to them, and how this might be the catalyst for them finally to shake this troublesome orphan out of their middle-class lives. The children's home waited. He could imagine it well enough: cold, dark, walls wet with tears, a babel of despairing children, each locked in a room no larger than a cupboard…

"You may go in." It was Hobbs' voice.

David stood up and followed Drake into the office, trying to keep behind the bigger boy; but once they were in, and Hobbs had shut the door on them, he made himself edge out from behind Drake to stand beside him. Drake himself had been silent for several minutes; with his head down and his eyes on the floor, he seemed cowed, beaten. David forced himself to look at the headmistress, Ms Alderney. Alderney looked like a businesswoman in her smart suit, hammering away at her computer keyboard, a dozen files open on the large desk in front of her. David watched her for a moment – her cold blue eyes were fixed on her computer's display – but dropped his eyes as she swung around to face the two boys. That brief glimpse was enough to convince him that she would stand no opposition, that whatever was placed in her way, she would cut through it. David determined not to get in her way.

"Don't worry, Dave. Her bark is worse than her bite," Nathan was saying from slightly behind David.

The office was cold. There were no plants; just box files and books. There were seats for visitors, but they were over by the wall, to be pulled forward when needed. Clearly, they were not needed now.

"Well, if it isn't Mr Drake," said Ms Alderney. "Fancy seeing you here." She spoke with her mouth twisted up in distaste, as though she had just been sucking a lemon. "And you are?"

David realized a second later that she was talking to him, and panicked. "Carraway, Sir – I mean Miss, Ms –"

"Ma'am will do. I don't recognize you, so I take it that you have only recently joined us. First name?" Alderney was out of her chair, heading for the box files.

"David. I've been here since Year 7." At least he managed to get that right.

"Whose class are you in? Mr Ahmadzi's?"

"Yes, Ma'am."

Alderney selected the relevant file and sat down again in her leather swivel chair. She leafed through card folders; she flicked through different-coloured pages in one of the folders. David and Drake watched as she did this, but then looked down as one when she closed the folder and the box file. "I expect this from you, Mr Drake, disappointing as it may be. You, though, Mr Carraway – there's no indication in your report that you're a troublemaker. It seems the reason I don't know you is because you've never been sent to me before. Rest assured, I will remember your name from this point forwards. Now, I want to know what happened. Who started the fight?"

Drake spoke up for the first time in the interview. "Not me. It was him. He attacked me for no reason… he's mental, everybody knows that."

Thanks Drake, thought David.

"You seem dogged by ill fortune, Mr Drake. Several times each term you are set upon by random passers-by – generally much smaller than you – for no discernible reason. And you, Mr Carraway? How do you explain this unpleasant incident?"

Before David could reply, he heard Nathan whispering in his ear. Whispering. As if anyone might have overheard him. "I've got an idea," he said.

Another one, thought David wearily.

"Tell her you started it. Trust me."

"Well?" demanded Alderney. "What have you got to say for yourself?"

David sighed. "Drake's right," he said. "I started it. It's my fault."

Alderney stared at him, the lemon in her mouth getting sourer, disbelief puckering the lower half of her face. Drake half turned towards him and gaped, his big jaw slack with surprise.

Eventually Alderney came to her senses and ordered Drake out of the room, evidently guessing that David was scared to put the blame on him in his presence. She told David that she could protect him from Drake – she was adamant about that – but David didn't change his story.

"It was my fault," he said.

"You're sure."

David nodded. He didn't know why Nathan had made him do this, but whatever the reason, it had benefited him. He seemed to have put Alderney on the back foot, and to have taken control of a situation he had no right to. He would never have dared respond with no more than a nod a minute ago.

"Well! I must say it's rather refreshing to hear a different tune once in a while. Your honesty does you credit, Mr Carraway. However. Detention. One night, instead of the two I was going to give you both. Report to Mr Turner's storeroom after school. I'll notify your parents that you'll be delayed arriving home."

"Foster parents," muttered David automatically.

Alderney stared at him again. This time though, her face was calm, a mask of authority. She ignored his interruption, and after the brief stare, returned her attention to the computer screen. "Send in Mr Drake on your way back to class."

At Nathan's bidding, David waited around in the corridor outside Alderney's office for Drake to come out. He walked away a few steps, but then wished he had sat in one of the chairs outside the office, because his legs were weak, wobbly with adrenaline. He decided to prop up a wall instead.

"Carraway?" came a voice. It was Mr Gough, his science teacher, a young, tall man with a plume of prematurely grey hair. "What are you doing hanging about? And what have you done to your face?"

David automatically put up a hand to his face. The flesh over his left cheekbone was swollen and tender.

"Don't forget your homework for tomorrow," added Gough, and before David could reply, he was hurrying on towards the science block. David levered himself off the wall and made a brief show of heading to his next class. When Gough had gone around the corner, David sank back against the wall once more.

Seconds later Drake came back out of the office. The ebullient, cocky Drake was gone; the version David was seeing now seemed to have shrunk. He was pale, drawn, and – David was grimly pleased to see – there were scars of battle on Drake's face too, a bruise on his right cheek. "What'd she give you?" asked Drake.

"Detention," replied David. "What about you?"

"Nothin'. She didn't give me nothin'. Why'd you do it? Why'd you take the blame? You could've stuck it on me and she'd've bought it all right with my history."

"Forget it," said David, taking this as thanks. He pushed himself away from the wall, and started to leave, trying not to stagger.

"Hey, Carraway!" called Drake.

David turned to look back, which set him off balance. He straightened up quickly.

"Would you do that for my sister? Stick up for her, like you did for…?"

"Your sister…?"

"Becks. Year 9."

"Say yes," Nathan said.

But David needed no advice at that moment. "I know her," he said, "Yeah, if she needed it. But why would she need my protection when she's got a brother like you?" He expected a burst of Drake derision. Instead, Drake seemed to wilt visibly.

Drake looked over his shoulder. They were still alone. "You're all right, you know that?" He paused, then spoke again, stumbling awkwardly over his words: "We're in trouble, god help us. Da's gone. Can we talk to you… me and Becks… tomorrow… break time…?"

David shrugged. What on earth was happening to Drake? He nodded.

"It's not for me. It's for Becks. You understand me. I'd do anything for Becks. Keep your head down, Carraway. That's what I'm planning on doing…" trailing off with a curious grimace, Drake strode off down the corridor, leaving David and Nathan standing there, bemused.

And so, after school, came the wall. David dipped his brush into the soapy water and applied it to a particularly offensive line of graffiti. Whoever Richard Roberts was, he was doing him a favour. He scrubbed for a time, but quickly gave up and moved on to try to clean something else, because the line about Richard Roberts wasn't shifting. "Sorry mate," he muttered.

Everyone else had gone home, and the area behind the bike shed was completely empty. Even Nathan had deserted him – just when having someone to talk to would have been a useful distraction. David's only companions were three broken bikes gleaming in the deep shadows of the bike shed.

Some of the graffiti came off in a second, whereas other patches would not shift no matter how hard he scrubbed. Some of it was actually quite good – for example, an unknown delinquent artist had created a metre-wide picture of Jupiter and its moons. Jupiter's great red spot had been made into a half-lidded eye. He didn't want to clean that off – it was a work of art. Others had taken marker pens and used Jupiter as a page to write their tags on. He tried scrubbing off these primitive defacements, but it was no good. Jupiter came off quicker than the writing.

He kept thinking back to the way Drake had looked when he came out of Alderney's office. The hyena seemed to have been savaged by a lion. Was it something she had said to him to make him look so... frightened? If only Nathan had hung around in the office to eavesdrop. She must have threatened him with something, even if she hadn't punished him. And asking to meet up the next day... what was that all about? *Da's gone...*

"Need a hand?" said a voice. David almost dropped his brush in surprise. It was the girl. He looked at her as if he was seeing her for the first time – her clothes ill-fitting her slight frame, her long, dark hair, her brown eyes. She was, he only now realized, quite pretty. Easy on the eyes, as Nathan would say. Her skin was a beautiful colour like milky coffee. He remembered a racist boy in his previous year warning him that if something wasn't done then there would be no white people any more, that everyone in the world would have coffee-coloured skin. He remembered clearly what the kid had said, but not his own response, which had probably been inadequate. He now realized what his response should have been: *"Well, then there won't be any racists, will there?"*

The girl was looking at him curiously, waiting for him to answer.

"Only one brush," David heard himself saying.

The girl raised her right hand into his line of sight. She already had a brush. "From the cleaner's cupboard," she explained.

"It's all right. You don't have to," David told her.

"I know," the girl said, and moved to stand beside him. She dipped her brush in the bucket and started scrubbing. After a few seconds, she paused, and said: "I'm Milla."

"David."

"I know."

"You do?"

"Everyone knows about the boy who goes around talking to himself."

"I think I proved how mad I am by standing up to Drake earlier," admitted David. "At least –" he stopped himself. He had been going to say, 'at least Nathan is going to do my science homework.'

"Everyone thinks you're pretty cool now. You might set a fashion for soliloquy."

"Oh no," groaned David.

"Why did you help me? You don't know me."

For a moment David scrubbed away furiously, unable to think of anything to say. "All my friends were strangers when I met them," he managed lamely. And then, with those words hanging in the air, it all began to make sense. Nathan had made him do all these things – stand up to Drake, take the blame for the fight – not out of some sadistic maliciousness, but for a definite reason. Was he trying to manoeuvre David into a position where he was more popular in the school? To a situation where he could finally shed the dreaded playground encounters with Drake? Or simply – as his words had hinted – make friends with this girl, Milla?

It was just getting dark when Robbie Drake arrived home. It was earlier than it should have been because he had failed to get detention as Becks had instructed him. But he had at least told Carraway. Or told him that he wanted to tell him something. It was a start.

Drake stopped sharply when he saw what was ahead of him on the road.

The limo was back.

Da' was back.

So Becks had been wrong after all. Robbie found himself having mixed feelings about his father's return. On the one hand, everything was back to normal and he wouldn't have to shoplift their tea. On the other hand, Da' was back.

Drake moved on, more slowly than before. He was still fifty metres from home when his front door opened.

There was a scent in the air, faint, but sharp. Like glue, or petrol, or something in between. Chemistry had never been Robbie's forte.

Robbie Drake's father came out of the house carrying a bundle over his shoulder. No, not a bundle. Becks. He was…

Carrying Becks over his shoulder. Becks – he'd killed Becks…

Robbie started to run towards them.

Then he saw that the man was not, after all, his father. It was someone else, another man, one with a shabby black overcoat, lank black hair and a curiously flat fat face.

Another man (still not Da') emerged from the limo. This one was thin, with an ill-fitting suit.

Both men saw Robbie running towards them at the same moment. They said nothing to one another. The limo's boot popped open.

It was Becks. They were taking Becks. She was unconscious, or dead.

The thin man advanced towards Robbie Drake a few steps while the other man put his sister in the limo's boot with the carelessness of someone throwing down a bag of rubbish. Then the boot was closed, and the man with the strange flat face began to head towards him. The thin man got back into the limo and started the engine.

The smell of solvents grew as the lank-haired weird-looking man approached him. Robbie waited as long as he dared, wanting to engrave the flat-faced man's features indelibly upon his memory. Then he turned and ran.

Chapter 12: A New Michael

t was already dark, cold, and steadily getting colder by the time David got back to Chapman Close. The sky was clear, and hundreds of stars were shining in the black night. The ancients thought they were pinholes in the fabric of the sky, Nathan had once told David. Despite his brother's best efforts to teach him, the only constellation that David could recognize was Ursa Major, the great bear. The great bear was more like a saucepan, and tonight whatever it contained would be tipping out of the sky to land half-cooked on Fairfield's rooftops. Nathan not only knew most of the constellations, he could also name a lot of the major stars, pick out planets as easily as if they were all labelled up there in the sky, and would rattle on at length about how this star or that one wasn't a star at all but a galaxy two billion light years away. Information like that fascinated David but never stuck.

Thinking about Nathan made David realize that he hadn't seen his brother since just after his interrogation by Ms Alderney. David quickened his stride and broke into a trot over the last hundred metres of the way. Perhaps Nathan was waiting for him up in his bedroom; unfortunately the Reads intercepted him in the hallway and they weren't looking too happy.

"Oh my God," gasped Mrs Read. "Look at the state of him."

Both the Reads had the habit of talking about David rather than to him.

"What on earth is going on in that head of yours?" demanded Mr Read. As he said this, he stepped forward and knocked, tap-tap, on the top of David's head.

"Guy," said Mrs Read reproachfully. She ushered her husband to one side and pulled David forwards a little, until he was right underneath the hall light, so she could assess the state of his face.

"No tea for you my lad," muttered Mr Read, and walked off. He could still be heard talking as he disappeared into the living room – something about how Nathan had never been any trouble, how he couldn't understand where David got his attitude.

"Your face looks like a side of beef," Mrs Read told David. "Ms Alderney said you'd been in a fight, but this! You should have been sent home."

"I stepped in to protect someone," David murmured.

"You look after number one in this world, remember that," snapped Mr Read, reappearing in the doorway.

David started to snap back at Mr Read, but choked his words just in time. Leave it, Nathan would say. Where *was* he? "I think I'll just go and rest," he said, making for the stairs.

"I'll help you to your room," Mrs Read offered, and took hold of David's elbow.

"If he can fight, he can walk," muttered Mr Read.

"Guy – make a cup of tea. And bring some biscuits with you." Mrs Read led David to the foot of the stairs, and together they started up. "Ignore him. He's just worried about that silly old factory." She left him at the door of his bedroom, promising to return with the tea and biscuits.

David sank down on his bed and kicked off his shoes. "Nathan?" he whispered. There was no reply. He closed his eyes and immediately felt weariness flowing over him. He was already drifting towards sleep when Mrs Read tapped lightly on the open door and came in with tea and biscuits on a tray. It was an effort to sit up and dip a couple of biscuits in his tea. He felt strange, light-headed; he could hardly feel Mrs Read sticking a new plaster on his cut left hand while he dunked biscuits with his right. As she left the room again, Mrs Read closed the door behind her. And there, crouched in the corner, was Nathan.

"Nathan – you're here – I was beginning to wonder… Nathan! Are you all right?"

Nathan's eyes flickered towards his brother, but he said nothing. He was ashen, faint, the ghost of a ghost. He was shivering. David levered himself up, tiptoed across the bedroom, and sat down next to him, reaching out. The touch was like being enveloped in freezing fog. Within seconds David's cut hand was throbbing again with the cold; in half a minute, his whole arm was as achingly useless as if it had been held in icy water. Nathan was draining what little energy was left in David's already exhausted body.

Nathan, though, had brightened, become more opaque. He quickly stopped shivering. Then he leapt to his feet and went to the opposite side of the room, staring at their mother's painting on the wall.

"Better?" asked David, slowly moving back to his bed. The effort of walking those few steps was like pushing Sisyphus' rock. He felt light-headed and his legs were like wooden posts. He slumped down on the bed, hoping fervently that he wouldn't have to move again soon.

"I haven't got much time left," Nathan said, still staring at the painting, apparently oblivious to David's state.

"Rubbish," snapped David, his tiredness making him impatient.

"I'm fading away like mist in the sun. I'm taking too much from you now. This wasn't meant to be. Or meant to last."

"I'm feeling better already," David lied. He still couldn't move his left arm.

"I haven't got long left," insisted Nathan. "I'm losing it – I'm becoming like that thing that hung around Michael's neck. It's getting painful to be away from you. Soon I won't be able to leave you alone. Next thing you know –"

"What's the solution?"

"I'm going to have to leave – lose myself, hope that I forget about you, forget who I am, before the urge to come back gets too strong to fight..."

"You're not leaving. There has to be something else."

"I can keep going for a while, a couple of weeks perhaps. We either have to figure something out by then – or else you might be using an efreeti jar on me."

"We'll think of something," David told him, trying to sound convincing.

"How was detention?" asked Nathan, changing the subject.

So Nathan *had* engineered his meeting with Milla. But how had he known that she would seek David out? "I know what you're doing," David told him. "I'm not lonely, and anyway, you're not going anywhere."

"Was it that obvious?"

"No – not at first. But I'm not stupid, Nath. Just a bit slow. I figured it out."

"She's nice though, isn't she?" persisted Nathan.

David shrugged – but lying down, and with a half-numb shoulder, the gesture didn't quite come out right, so he said, by way of clarification: "She's okay."

"You're going to see her again?"

"If I bump into her in the playground."

Nathan chuckled, but said nothing. Embarrassed, David said: "I believe you owe me some homework."

It was about half an hour later, and a mostly-recovered David was sitting up on his bed, still dressed, writing furiously as Nathan dictated the answers to his science homework. Nathan was saying something about pH, which David was trying to get down on paper and understand at the same time (he was already imagining that Gough, the science teacher, would guess that he had copied his homework from someone else and would get him to prove that he actually understood what he had written; he was wondering if it would be better to get an honest C rather than a cheating A).

At this point the doorbell rang. Nathan immediately sank out of sight through the floorboards like a ship foundering at sea. David read back what he had just written, and didn't understand it. He would have to get Nathan to explain it to him, preferably in words of one syllable.

"Dave!" shouted Nathan from somewhere under the floorboards. "It's the Andersens!"

"Oh no," said David quietly, "now I'm for it." He dropped his pen, jumped out of bed, strode to the door, then changed his mind and walked away from it again, went to the window, parted the curtains and peered out. Across the road, at the Andersens' house, the Hummer was back, hulking like a tank on the driveway. Below, he could hear someone (Mrs Read, at a guess) opening the door. A moment later, Mrs Read called to him up the stairs.

"David! It's for you."

"Okay," he called back. He twitched the curtains closed once more, and stood silently for a moment. Then, resigned to his fate, he left his bedroom and walked down the stairs to the hall. Doctor Andersen was there, just inside the door, making small talk about the weather with Mrs Read; she looked paler than usual, drawn, with exhaustion blackening small arcs beneath her eyes. David was unsurprised to see that she was dressed in black – black coat, black trousers, and black boots. Behind her stood her son Michael, hiding in her shadow. He was all right – at least, he was on his feet again. David almost sagged to the floor with relief.

"Hello David," said Doctor Andersen, her tone surprisingly light. "What happened to you? You look as if you've been in a war."

"I'm all right," David told her shortly. They had an audience. Mrs Read still stood at the foot of the stairs, Mr Read had arrived at the end of the hall to see what was going on, and Nathan had appeared too, standing next to Michael, smiling at David. David tried to keep his eyes off his brother, on Doctor Andersen. "How's –" he began.

"Michael?" she interrupted. "He's fine. He's why I'm calling, actually. He seems to be a lot better since you came to play with him at the weekend. I wonder if you might like to come over and play with him again? I know

Michael would appreciate it."

"Of course. Not a problem."

"How about next Saturday?"

"Yes, fine."

"Okay, well, we'll let you get back to your evening. Oh, by the way, you left this." Doctor Andersen held out her hand. Only now did David see that she was holding his shadow lens. It must have fallen from his rucksack in the struggle. He took the lens, and the Andersens left, with Michael, following his mother, actually saying goodbye – the first time David had heard him speak.

"Strange woman," muttered Mr Read, when the door had closed behind them.

David went back up to his room and found that Nathan had got there ahead of him. "He's all right," marvelled David, a smile breaking out on his face.

"He no longer has a monkey around his neck, and even better, I can stand near him without feeling sick," Nathan said.

David flopped down on the bed, still unable to keep a straight face. "I hardly dare believe it," he said.

"I'm going to go over there. See just how improved he is. But there's definitely no sign of the monkey-demon." With that, he was gone, flitting through the wall, into the night.

David was one of the last to arrive for registration the following morning. His form tutor, Mr Ahmadzi, was already there, standing at the head of the class waiting for everyone to get in and sit down. Mr Ahmadzi was one of the few teachers that David liked – he was always smiling and making jokes, in contrast to the other teachers who were all dour and serious. He was a small man, dark-skinned, with black hair and a shiny face. He always seemed to be sweating, even in winter, but always wore a smart long-sleeved white shirt with buttoned cuffs, never a t-shirt.

David, still sore and stiff, slipped into his seat and dumped his rucksack on the desk in front of him, hoping that no-one would notice his black eye. One or two people were already staring at him, but he pretended not to notice. Nathan lurked at the back of the class.

Mr Ahmadzi cleared his throat and started talking. "Before I take registration today, I have some serious news to tell you. This has to do with our own Mr Carraway."

David shrank down behind his bag, out of sight.

"Mr Carraway was involved in a fight yesterday," continued Ahmadzi. "David? Where are you?"

"Here, sir," muttered David, straightening up from behind his bag.

"Come out where we can all see you – come down to the front."

Everybody stared at him as he pushed his chair back and slowly made his way to the front. Some, including a boy called Rowse, were grinning at his discomfort. Others just gaped. David's friend Kelly stared at the desk in front of him.

"What have you to say for yourself?" asked Mr Ahmadzi sternly.

"Sorry, sir," said David quietly.

"Sorry?" suddenly Ahmadzi was grinning. "Don't be sorry. You don't know how many of the teachers here wish they could give that obnoxious little… bully… a good old-fashioned kicking… a round of applause for Mr Carraway."

At this, the class erupted, beating their hands together, kicking the tables, and cheering. Kelly put two fingers in his mouth and blew a shrill whistle. David just stood at the front, not knowing where to look.

"All right, Carraway," said Ahmadzi. "Don't milk it. Back to your seat. And don't take this as permission to do it again."

"But I didn't win," protested David as the applause died down.

"Tush, man! From what I hear, you had the best of it," Ahmadzi told him.

When, a few minutes later, Mr Ahmadzi was reading the names out of the register, there was a muted cheer as he reached David's name. Then, as the class was filing off to science, Rowse caught up with David, and slapped him on the back so hard that it nearly knocked his teeth out. "Good on you, Carraway," he said.

"Why does everyone keep saying that? It's nothing to be proud of."

"Yes it is," Kelly told him.

Rowse yanked David's arm. "I hear Farelly wants to take you on next," he said.

"But I don't want to take on anyone," objected David.

Rowse shrugged. "Tell it to Farelly," he said, and hurried ahead.

"Stay out of his way," suggested Kelly.

"I intend to."

"Missed you at footie yesterday."

"Detention," David said tersely.

"Bad luck."

"Could have been worse."

"Done your homework?"

"Yep."

"You never cease to amaze," said Kelly.

In science, Mr Gough collected in the exercise books to mark the homework. At the end of the lesson he returned them. David flipped through to see his mark: a large, red, 'A' was scrawled at the bottom of the page. He stared at it, not quite believing what he was seeing.

"What's the matter, Carraway," demanded Gough, looming over David. "Never seen an A before? Let's hope it's as good next week."

"Thank me," invited Nathan at break.

"H'mm." David was scanning the hundreds of students milling around, looking for a particular face. "Maybe I would have been better off with a B. Now Gough is going to expect an A again next week."

"You didn't ask for a B. You asked me to do your homework."

"H'mm."

"Looking for anyone in particular?"

"No, just looking," said David defensively.

"She's over there," said Nathan, pointing. "On the bench by the yew bushes."

Milla looked up as David approached. She smiled at him. "How's the eye?"

"All right," he said. He looked for Nathan, but his brother had hung back, out of sight – though probably not out of earshot. He sat down.

"What did your parents say?"

"Foster parents. They weren't too bad about it."

"I told my grandmother about you. I told her you were like an old-fashioned knight. Saving helpless people from the forces of evil."

"Not me. I'm more of an old-fashioned coward."

"If you want to know someone, they say you should ignore what they say and concentrate on what they do."

"Yeah. Well, I get up to some pretty strange things."

"I wouldn't expect a gallant knight to take credit for good deeds. More likely to shrug them off or pretend that it wasn't him."

"I can't win this argument can I?"

"A knight never argues with a lady," Milla told him.

David turned to see that she was smiling at him. For some reason he could not help smiling back. Then he remembered Drake. "Drake wants a word with me for some reason. You haven't seen him, have you?"

"He wants to knock your block off, you mean. But no, I haven't seen him."

"I'll see if I can find him. It sounded like he was in some kind of trouble. I don't know what had got into him. He was like a different person after we'd seen the Head."

"And you're going to help him?" Milla was incredulous.

"I don't know. I'll see what he wants. He seemed to be worried about his sister for some reason."

Milla stood up. "I'll check the field. You try the bike sheds. See you back here in five minutes."

"You don't have to…"

"I know. Neither do you."

Five minutes later, David and Milla rendezvoused by the bench between the yews. Neither had seen Drake or his sister.

Chapter 13: The Indestructible Carraways

David spent the rest of the day grinning to himself and humming happily. As soon as the bell went for the end of school, he hurried outside to where his bike was chained up. He got on and started wobbling into the gathering gloom, pedalling hard; the faster he rode, the more fluent and graceful the bike became. Rain drove into his face as he shot out of the school gates, over the road, jumped the kerb on the other side and sped into an area of waste ground which served as a shortcut to one of the nearby estates. The rutted and potholed path along which he raced had been scored into the ground by the feet and wheels of decades of children. David could hardly make out where he was going in the dark with rain in his eyes, but he didn't slow down – seeing a pothole at the last moment and jumping the bike or swerving wildly was all part of the game. While David sloshed through muddy puddles and slid on the steep sides of the path, Nathan easily drifted along beside him.

The estate beyond the waste ground was virtually empty. Even the little promenade of shops – grocer, butcher, newsagent, hairdresser and chippy – seemed deserted. There was little traffic; as soon as he was off the rough ground and under the amber streetlights, David got off the saddle and risked taking one hand off the handlebars for long enough to punch the air. "Come on!" he shouted.

"Are you all right?" asked Nathan coldly.

There was a long drag uphill now, to where the estate opened onto the main road, and David concentrated on his cycling, determined not to lose any speed. He could already see cars streaming along in the distance as people headed home from the city centre.

"He slays the ghost. He slays the giant –"

"What, Drake?"

"He saves the fair damsel…"

"Oh come on," Nathan snorted disparagingly.

"He gets an A in science…"

"I did that, not you."

"That's not what it says on the top of the page…" laughed David. He cycled on, legs burning. Despite his best efforts, he was slowing up, but the top of the hill was nearing, and from there it was downhill all the way to Professor Fuller's house. Knowing that he could soon coast for a while spurred him on, and he redoubled his efforts, reaching the main road in a breathless sprint. He swerved left, onto the pavement, hunting for a gap between the queuing cars as they edged up and sat waiting by turns. Raindrops swarmed like flies in the gleam of the headlights; water gushed over the tarmac, a river of gold in the streetlights. There was a gap; he darted for it, just as it began to close, the driver behind intent on the two metres between himself and the next car and nothing else in the Universe. David just had time to check that there was nothing coming the other way before he plunged out into the road. He was aware of the shocked expression that flitted over the driver's face as he saw a crazy kid hurtling out in front of him. It didn't stop the driver from closing up the gap to nearly nothing, but by then David was well gone, looking back just to enjoy his expression once more.

"Dave!" shouted Nathan. "Take it easy! You're not indestructible!"

"Says who?" shouted back David, laughing. He hopped the bike back onto the footpath, skirting the roundabout that the traffic was queuing for, and swung right, downhill. Once more he had to dart through traffic, but this time, he waited until he had passed the tail of the queue for the roundabout before launching into the road again. Halfway down the hill he turned sharp left, onto a dirt track. At this end it was used as an access to a row of back gardens, so was quite wide and well maintained; further down, the track withered until it was only an overgrown footpath with waste ground on one side and scrub on the other. Once beyond the street light, David could barely see anything, only two humped shadows on either side of him that represented the line of bushes encroaching on the path, but he didn't slow down, letting gravity take him, whipping through the wet rank grass, his legs soaked, relying on feel and guesswork to keep him out of the morass of thorns on each side. Ahead, he could see a faint lightening in the gloom where the footpath met a narrow road, Marsh Lane, where Professor Fuller's cottage was. A passing car briefly silhouetted the gate at the end of the path. It was closed. To the left, David knew, was a style.

"Dave! Stop!" called Nathan, a note of panic in his voice.

But David didn't. He kept on at full speed, pedalling now to maintain his velocity. The gate loomed. He drifted out to the right, where the path widened somewhat, then slammed on both brakes and swerved hard left. He came at the style obliquely, the wheels sliding now, then hopped off the bike, onto the style, keeping a hold on the handlebars, letting the bike's momentum pull it up, into the air; he swung it up, to the right, and over the gate. For a moment – just a moment – the motion of boy and bicycle was pure poetry; then reality clicked back in, corrupting the majesty of the moment: trying to keep up with the movement of the spinning bike, David lost his balance and tumbled into space, hitting the ground hard.

"Dave!" shouted Nathan. "Are you all right?"

David could see his brother's face looking down at him, bright with anxiety. The rain was falling straight through Nathan, drumming on David's upturned face. David, though half-stunned, began to chuckle. The chuckle, magnified by Nathan's glowing seriousness looking down at him, became a laugh. Eventually even Nathan softened a little and, shaking his head, laughed along.

"Hey – did you see that move?" demanded David.

"I saw where it ended up."

"I was nearly there," David showed his brother a finger and thumb a little apart, "that far from a perfect jump."

"Yeah? Well I went straight through the gate as if it wasn't even there."

Chapter 14: Checkmate

The breath may have been knocked out of David, but his good mood was very much intact. He pushed his bike between the cypress trees and up the dark driveway of Museum Cottage. Before he could knock at the side door, he noticed a light shining from behind the house. There was a sudden swishing sound, and then another, coming from the same direction. Then there was what sounded like a couple of footfalls and another swish. Nathan hurried ahead to investigate; David leaned his bike against the wall, and quietly followed his brother, who was already standing and staring around the corner, transparent as gauze in the white glare.

The back garden of Museum cottage was bigger than David had expected. It started off as lawn, narrowed into a couple of unkempt flower beds, then widened out again to another large patch of lawn where the light glinted on what looked like a stagnant pond, before fading straight into a patch of woodland. He couldn't be sure from here in the deep gloom at the end of the lawn, but David thought that at least part of the wood must belong to the garden – he certainly couldn't see an end fence.

But what his attention quickly fixed on was at this end of the garden, under the glare of a pair of floodlights mounted halfway up the back wall. Professor Fuller was out in the rain and cold. He was blindfolded. He was holding a sword in each hand. The light gleamed on the two blades as he moved, slowly, deliberately, gracefully, cutting the air to left and right, behind, in front. In slow motion, but with great suppleness, Fuller moved up and down the first large patch of lawn. A washing line crossed the lawn; from its centre, near the middle of the lawn, an apple hung by a string, at about head height. The professor swept around the apple, to left, to right, turning, spinning, all with oil-like smoothness, smiting invisible opponents as he went. Then suddenly, momentarily, the tempo increased; the old man leapt, spun around and slashed the larger of his two weapons through the air. With a chop, most of the hanging apple fell to the ground, the remainder dancing lightly on the end of its string.

"Wow," whispered David.

The professor turned at the sound of his visitor's voice and peeled up his blindfold. "Evening, David."

"That was incredible! You remembered where the apple was after all that moving up and down."

"Not to mention being distracted by your arrival. But as you see," the professor showed David the small amount of apple left on the string, "I missed."

"Missed? Why?"

"I was aiming to cut it in half."

"But that's impossible," blurted Nathan. David relayed this.

"Your brother is a philosopher," Fuller smiled. Then concern etched his face. "Are you okay? You look as if you've been a few rounds in the wrong weight class."

David touched his black eye. It was still tender, but was much better than it had been. "You should have seen it yesterday," he said.

Professor Fuller smiled. Then he turned away and started wiping the apple from his sword.

"I didn't know you knew sword-fighting," David said, edging forward.

"Not sword-fighting. Kenjutsu," said Fuller shortly. "The technique of the sword."

"Can you teach me?"

The professor stopped wiping his sword. "Can *you* teach *me?*" he echoed.

"I don't understand."

"My sensei taught me a very important lesson. There are no kenjutsu masters. Only students of varying competence. All students have something to teach. All have much to learn. I will spar with you if you like." Fuller walked over to one of the flower beds, and using his shorter sword, chopped out a couple of long stems from a leafless shrub. "We'll use these," he said, "in case you do yourself another injury."

David walked forward nervously to take his stick.

"The stick is part of your hand. Your hand is part of your body. Your body and mind are one. There is only one weapon." Fuller tapped his head. "Your mind. Now you advise me."

"But I don't know anything," stumbled David. Then he suddenly thought of something that he did know. "Wait, I do know something. Go in hard. Don't hold back. That's it."

Fuller nodded gravely. "Then come on," he said.

David did so. He lunged, slashing with his stick from right to left. But he didn't follow his own advice. He held back on the blow.

Fuller blocked the attack easily. "Practice what you preach," he said.

"Go on Dave," David heard Nathan say. "Give him some."

And so he did. Or rather he tried to. He lunged, slashed, and jabbed with his stick, at first not wholeheartedly, but as Fuller turned each of his attacks aside, he swung it harder and harder until he was striking as fast and as hard as he could. Still not one of his attacks hit home, although at least now Fuller was moving a little faster as he blocked them. At last, after about five minutes, David lowered his stick, stood back, and puffed out his cheeks. "You're too good," he said.

"I started late. But I've been learning for more than thirty years," Fuller told him. He was out of breath, David noticed, and seemed to stagger slightly as he moved to sit down on a tree stump near the back of the house. Gathering his breath, he told David: "There are places you can learn. You can practice on your own. There are books. Usually in Japanese. But often with pictures." Fuller was holding his chest. His thin white hair was plastered to his head by the rain.

"Are you all right?" asked David nervously. "I'm sorry – I didn't mean to, you know…"

Fuller put a hand out, and patted one of David's. The hand was cold, large, its knuckles swollen with arthritis. "I'm okay," he said. After a few seconds the old man took his hand away and gestured over at the lawn with it. "I was doing a formalized samurai practice before. A *kata*. Samurai against three peasants, two with sickles, one with a rake."

"Could you really beat three peasants like that?"

"Depends on how well they had mastered their own arts. In ancient Japan, everyone learned how to fight."

"Not moving so slowly, surely?"

At this Fuller chuckled. "The student writes the exercise in the pages of his mind. Should the occasion arise, those pages would be turned as fast as necessary."

"Ask him about the apple," Nathan said. David did so.

"Of course there is no apple in the formalized practice. The apple cut at the end is a device of my own addition. But tell me the good news. The person you exorcised is okay."

David was dumbstruck. "How do you know about that?"

"I know you didn't come here for a martial arts lesson. From your cheery demeanour I deduce that the recipient of your first exorcism must be showing a marked improvement."

David briefly explained how Michael had recovered physically, and how he had actually heard him speak for the first time.

Fuller offered his congratulations, but quickly added a caveat. "Not all spirits will be vanquished so easily. I don't want to dampen your spirits. Really. But if you continue your career as an exorcist you will meet a spirit who will deflect your efforts to entrap it. And you will find yourself in grave danger."

"I just hope I don't have to exorcise Nathan," commented David, and then wished he had said nothing.

"What do you mean?" demanded the professor.

David hesitated.

"It's all right, Dave," said Nathan. "Tell him."

So David explained about Nathan's fear that he was fading, and that he might end up like the ghost they had exorcised.

"It is possible," commented the professor, "distinctly possible. Such a relationship as yours is, I fear, not supposed to last for long. How it ends will be the choice of your brother." He made David a cup of hot chocolate and listened intently as David told him about the ghostly presence at the old factory. He was especially intrigued by the mention of 'the Solvent Man.'

"That name I do not recognize, but I may know to whom you refer," the professor said coolly. "My advice would be to stay away from the place."

"You know him? You know who killed Nathan?"

"The miasma you speak of does not sound like the man you describe in the cemetery, would you agree?"

"Nathan can sense a connection…" David began, then realized that the professor had ducked the question.

The professor smiled. "I cannot order you to stay away, but I strongly advise it. If you do go, let me know in advance." He asked about the efreeti jar, and produced some money ("for a replacement, as I seem to have broken yours.") They took their drinks through to the study.

"I have a lot to tell you, including about your 'Solvent Man,'" said Fuller, as he placed a couple of logs on the fire. They both sat down, squelching, in the warm room. "You see, I have remembered where I heard your name before." He tapped the filing cabinet beside him. "First, your brother's disappearance. Second, but earlier, the death of your parents. But I can say no more. Not now. There is danger in this knowledge."

"If there is something in there about either of those things, I'm going to look for myself," said David, got up, and made a half-move towards the filing cabinet.

"Wait. Please," the old man told him.

"You don't trust me – is that it?"

"Trust?" the professor smiled sadly. "Of course I trust you. Your efforts to free a stranger from demonic possession establish that you can be relied upon."

"Then what? Tomorrow we're going to this factory whether you tell me what this thing is or not. You better tell me what you know."

"I do not think you will find your Solvent Man there. But if you do, you must run. Do not try the jar. The jar will be useless."

"But there's a link," Nathan protested, "I know there is."

"If you don't want me to go to the factory," David said, "you can tell me where the Solvent Man is."

"That I cannot do, since I do not know where he is. I would not tell you even if I could. To face him is death."

"We owe him!" snapped David.

"You think you are alone in that?" asked Fuller calmly. "The being you describe is a ghost. Perhaps there is some connection –"

"Then we have to go there!"

"Do you intend to simply ask it what its connection to the 'Solvent Man' is?" demanded Fuller. He winced, and clutched at his chest.

"Are you okay?" asked David, half-rising again.

Fuller laughed, once. "I am as well as can be expected."

Did this mean that the professor was dying? "Can I get you something? I mean, do you have some pills or something..."

"No." Fuller shook his head. "No medicine. I know what you're thinking," he added quickly. "What if I die before I tell you all you want to know? Don't worry. You know that trick with the apple? Every day, I cut it in two. So if the apple isn't fresh, you'll know that I'm gone. You have my permission to come in and read your file. I have filed it, for convenience, under Shadowland."

"Shadowland?"

"Where your brother lives. It is the realm of ghosts, a shadow of the real world. It is the tissue that divides this world from the next. The Shadowland."

"And you want me to break in?"

"If I'm dead, I really won't care, will I? On the other hand, you could use the key I've hidden. Between two bricks, around the back of the garage, by the Wisteria." David didn't know what a Wisteria was, but he wasn't saying so. Fuller continued. "Come in, take the file, go home, and read it. It would probably be wise then to burn it... don't hang around leafing through the other files. Get in, get out. Don't look back."

"And my parents. There's more to the death of my parents than I know, isn't there?" asked David.

"You'll find out, when the time is right," Fuller told him. The expression on the old man's face was inscrutable. "Finish your cocoa. You'd better get home, and into some dry clothes."

It was half past seven, and David had already gone to bed. At least, he had gone up to his room so that, away from the Reads, he could talk freely to Nathan. They were playing chess on the bed. Nathan, of course, couldn't touch his pieces, so he gave commands to David regarding what he wanted to move and where. David, who had never beaten Nathan, had already lost two games, and had just set up the pieces for a third. The game followed one of the most common lines – Nathan played his king pawn, and so did David. Queen's knight followed king's knight into the fray, and then Nathan brought out his king's bishop.

"What is it that you think Fuller knows that he won't tell me?" David asked, absently moving out his king's knight.

"Knight to g5," said Nathan. "More to the point, why won't he tell you? It's a bit suspicious if you ask me."

David was staring at the board in dismay. There were now two attacks on his king bishop pawn, and he couldn't see how to save it. He had only made three moves and he was in trouble already. "Suspicious? Why?" he asked, playing for time.

"Because it's dangerous? It's dangerous to be ignorant, especially as he knows we're going anyway. Are you moving or not?"

At last David spotted a way out of his predicament. He advanced his queen pawn, blocking the attack of Nathan's bishop. At this Nathan exchanged pawns and sacrificed his knight. David was in two minds about whether to take it – whenever he accepted a sacrifice he seemed to lose more quickly than usual. But he had no choice. His rook was gone otherwise. "Maybe we should leave it," he said.

"We could try automatic writing. Queen f3 check. Like before."

David shuddered. Their previous attempt at automatic writing had somehow summoned the Solvent Man and led to Nathan's death. He said as much. Meanwhile he could only see one way to save his knight. It meant moving his king into the middle of the board, at the mercy of Nathan's forces.

"It's worth a go. At least this miasma of doom or whatever it is can't strangle you. Pawn to d4."

From then on, David's moves were all forced and purely defensive. At last he found an outlet for his queen – his only active piece. "Do you think it will be safe for *you?*"

The question seemed to throw Nathan, and he made an uncharacteristically rash move. David saw the chance to take Nathan's queen pawn, swap queens, and liquidate the position. After the dust had settled, he found himself with an extra bishop and a seventh rank pawn – surely he couldn't lose from here?

"It could be dangerous," Nathan muttered. "But for you, not me. I'm already dead, remember? What have I done to this position?"

Nathan harried David for a while – his pieces were still more active – but there weren't enough of them now to be a danger – were there? Then David retreated an attacked bishop with check and skewered Nathan's rooks with his other bishop. He was hot now – he had won at least the exchange of rook for bishop...

Somehow Nathan spotted a way to save his rook with a check. David was still okay though. Now he was able to activate his own rooks... his superior forces were beginning to tell.

"If you don't want to do it, we won't," said David, feeling uncharacteristically brave.

"All right. We'll do it." Nathan was sparkling with anger. His mind was working like a vast calculator, desperately seeking a way to salvage the wreckage of his position.

A few moves later, Nathan had somehow worked himself a seventh rank pawn too, but David ignored it. It was like a fly... a distraction from where the battle was about to be won... in times gone by David would have switched his attention to deflecting this new threat. Not today. Was he finally going to beat his brother? Nathan clearly thought so. Nerves that he had never felt before playing chess came from nowhere. His heart was pounding, his palms, he noticed as he moved a rook to attack Nathan's back rank, were wet with cold sweat. There was an exchange of rooks, and now Nathan had to provide his king with an escape route through his wall of pawns to avoid imminent checkmate. Bishop checks... pawn blocks... rook checks again (which famous master was it who said 'when I give check, I fear no-one'? Nathan would know, but David wasn't about to ask). But how to finish the game? Where was the *coup de grâce?* Then he saw the answer. Bishop takes rook. There was no defence… it was checkmate in one move… bishop takes pawn – so there was a defence – but it was a desperate, rook sacrificing, temporary defence.

Bishop checks… king moves… where? Not to h1, surely… no, immediate mate there, f1 then, attacking the rook. Bishop takes pawn with a discovered check to follow…

"King move," said Nathan.

David picked up his brother's king. "But you can't move it," he said after a moment.

"Oh yes I can," said Nathan, and David had a sudden panic that despite his overwhelming forces, he was still going to lose. "Take my king, and lay him down. The game is yours."

"I've won?" asked David, incredulous. "I can't believe it. You give in? Really?"

Nathan chuckled. "Congratulations. I keep telling you that you're getting better…"

"But you were all over me," objected David. "All over me as usual. Only this time… somehow… I don't know how…"

"I do," snapped Nathan. He jabbed a finger through the board at f4. "Biggest blunder I've made in years. And there were others. I told you… I'm losing it. Fading away. My mind is going now."

"So it wasn't anything to do with me? Cheers mate," David muttered bitterly.

Nathan laughed. "You played well. Really."

"How about we test your theory with another game?" Nathan would wipe the floor with him as usual. Still, maybe it would cheer him up a bit.

Nathan did not respond for a moment. David was already setting up the pieces again when he finally replied. "No – I don't think so. Something tells me that we won't be playing again. I'll see you." Nathan began to drift over to the wall.

"Where are you going?" asked David, concerned at his brother's dark tone of voice.

Nathan floated back a little way. "I'm going to check out the factory one more time," he said. Then he left the bedroom.

David watched him go and then turned his full attention to his mother's painting. It was not lost on him that the day before he had met Milla it had appeared to be the portrait of a girl. If he had any doubt that the painting was magical, that doubt disappeared now – for stare as he might his mind could not, tonight, conjure any image from that dark canvas. In fact, the smudges of paint themselves seemed to have spread and faded, so that all that remained to be seen was blackness. The painting seemed to be suggesting that it was going to be dark in the abandoned factory.

Chapter 15: The Thing in the Factory

"Getting in is going to be a problem," David pointed out. He thought for a moment. "And so is getting out." But Nathan did not reply; he had already gone on ahead, straight through the three-metre-high brick wall that surrounded the front yard of the deserted factory. Now he popped his head back through, making David jump. "Hurry up," he said. "Don't forget, you're supposed to be going to the Andersens'." With that, he disappeared again.

It was Saturday morning, and it was raining again. It seemed to have been raining for ever. As Nathan drily noted, "If you see a man with a long beard building a huge boat, don't laugh at him, because he might be doing you a favour in a few days' time."

The alley beside the factory was choked with brick rubble, aerosol cans, rotting wood, old nappies and broken bottles. There was even the carcass of an ancient, rusting motorbike, its wheels long gone, its dials smashed, its cables hanging out like severed veins. In the cold rain, a stinking mist rose from the ground. David, with Nathan acting as his tour guide, had already made a circuit of the site: the only obvious access point was the pair of gates in the yard wall, their rotting wood flecked with colour where paint had fallen away, revealing older layers beneath. Although rotting, the gates were held together by a large, shiny new padlock, and were still sturdy enough to block the passage of an average-sized boy. Two sides of the factory were sheer, featureless walls: no problem for Nathan, but no use to David. On the fourth side of the factory, where its grounds met the River Fair, a chain-link fence decked with rusted barbed wire protected the ancient building. Climbing it would not be easy for David, and an attempt at it was pointless anyway, because even if he could get over, Nathan could find him no way in to the factory itself on that side. So David was left, by a process of deduction, with the task of having to climb the wall into the yard, and trying to find an entrance to the factory from there.

David parked his bike, locked it, and began to cast about for a place where he could climb high enough to reach the top of the wall. Nowhere were the unsteady piles of rubbish high enough. He felt trapped, suffocated, under his hood, and could neither see nor hear well with it on, so he pulled it back. Refreshing rain fell on his exposed head, collected in little streamlets, and dripped from his chin. The water was already soaking through his raincoat. He began to think about coming back another day. "There can't be much water left up there, surely," he moaned.

"Tons," responded Nathan from somewhere out of sight. "Come on, what are you waiting for?"

At last David spotted a plank of wood that he could use. Orange fungus bloomed on it in places, and it was filmed with viscid green algae, but when he propped it against the wall and gingerly walked up, it took his weight okay, bowing only a little. From the top of the plank he could easily reach the top of the wall, and was able to hoist himself up. From his vantage point he could look down on the forecourt, and see beyond it the tumbledown factory itself.

The yard was strewn with debris. The piles seemed to have begun in the corners, but over time they seemed to have spread, scattering their contents far and wide. David had emerged above one such pile, which would greatly ease his descent from the wall and, later, his climb back up. Forlorn weeds strained from every crack in the concrete, mere dead sticks now, but with splashes of green at their bases promising a return to life in the spring. Right in the middle of the yard was a car, or rather its stripped, partly burnt remains.

The factory itself had three floors. An ostentatious doorway was flanked by false columns and topped by a square lintel, on which the graven image of a huge round face was set. It took David a while to recognize it as a stylized representation of the sun, once a sign of welcome. Now, covered with moss and lichen, the giant face had taken on a hideous, demonic appearance, and had become a sign of warding. Below this gargoyle, the legend 'TIPLER' could still be seen. The rib-like stems of butterfly trees erupted out of a dozen places in the front of the factory, their roots growing in, spreading, and lacing the masonry with deepening cracks. On the ground floor, both the doors and the windows had all been recently boarded up. The windows of the two higher floors had long since been smashed by an earlier generation of stone-throwing kids, and the tooth-edged wooden squares allowed glimpses of what seemed only a void beyond.

"Good-looking place, isn't it?" commented Nathan.

"No," said David, awestruck. "This is how the world will look when there are no people left."

"No bad thing for the planet."

"No good thing for the people," muttered David. "I thought you said there was a way in."

"Come on — let's get the stove set up first. This way," Nathan said, and his glowing form started moving ahead. David dropped down from the wall and followed as his brother led the way to the shell of the abandoned car. The front seats were gone, but the back seat was still there, partly blackened and crisped by an old fire, and with odd springs sprouting out like metal seedlings. Inside, with the rain roaring in frustration on the roof, David took a camping stove out of his backpack and set it up on the floor in front of him. As he melted some wax, he said: "Uncle Charlie knows something fishy is going on."

"He sold some jars. And a camp stove. He's happy."

David was not so sure. Uncle Charlie had sold David the efreeti jars, it was true, but to David he seemed to do it reluctantly, as if he had an inkling of what the jars were really needed for. The camping stove, which Nathan had found on a hidden shelf, made him even more suspicious.

With a penknife, David nicked the third finger of his left hand to add a few drops of blood to the pan. Its neighbour – his little finger – could do with some rest and recuperation. They left the wax on a very low heat and moved over to the factory, Nathan leading the way, David dragging his heels. He still couldn't see a way in. The main door had been reinforced, and was secured with a heavy padlock. The boards over the windows looked solid. Nathan directed him to a heap of rubble that was piled up against the inside of the courtyard wall. There were some lengths of wood amongst the brick and concrete which might be enough to tear off one of the boards. But the wood was old, rotten; the boards were newer, harder. Too hard.

When he had broken three pieces of wood without making any impression at all on any of the boards he had tried, David said: "We need a crowbar."

"There's another way," offered Nathan. He pointed up. High above, one of the third floor windows was hanging open, swinging gently in the breeze.

David snorted with derision. He stood back to trace the route he would have to take. He would have to climb some six metres up a water pipe and then swing out over a sheer drop to reach the window. He snorted more loudly. "Who do you think I am, Spider-man?"

Nathan faced him squarely. "You're indestructible, remember? It's an easy climb. I'll see you inside." With that, Nathan walked through the wall, and was gone.

"Hey!" shouted David. Nathan did not reappear. Shaking his head, David went over to the pipe and gripped it with both hands. The pipe was cast iron, and although warty with exploding blisters of rust, it still seemed to be in reasonable condition. Water gushed out of the bottom and over his feet; the drain the water had once disappeared down was choked with gravel and weeds. "I don't care enough about Guy Read to do this," he called. "The Solvent Man obviously doesn't come here either unless he can walk through walls..." There was no answer. He pulled the pipe, to see how much weight it would take. It didn't budge, which was promising. Finally, with a heavy sigh, he began to climb. At first the going was actually surprisingly easy. Within a minute David was at the level of the first floor windows. Then climbing got considerably harder: the pipe's stays started coming out of the wall, and it began shifting alarmingly, to such an extent that he seriously considered giving up. Looking up, he saw that the next bracket seemed to be more secure, so, rain pelting his face, he carried on. "This place is falling down – you don't need a surveyor to see that." There was, once more, no reply from his brother.

David imagined the pipe peeling away from the wall in slow motion with him dangling off it like in a scene from a slapstick movie. His hands were going numb from keeping a death grip on the cold iron, and he was by now completely soaked, mainly by water that had slopped out of the gutter high above or found its way out of joints in the pipe. He had at least reached a height where he was only a little below the open window. The window was larger than it had looked from ground level, and was no more than an arm's reach away. It was divided into four panes; in each of them, only a toothy rim of glass remained. He grabbed for the window as it swung towards him, but a taunting blast of wind tore it from his clutching fingers and slammed it shut. He was momentarily unbalanced; his foot slipped, and he had to hang on to the pipe for dear life.

The window swung open again, and he made another grab for it; this time he reached it. But now he was swinging away from the pipe, and the rotting window didn't look like it had the strength to hold him. For a moment he was in limbo, his right hand on the window, right foot scrabbling for purchase, his left hand and foot still anchored to the pipe; then with relief he found firm ground on the lip of the tablet bearing the graven image of the sun. Relying on this surer footing he was able to swing himself across and dive headfirst into the factory.

David got to his feet and pulled a torch out of his bag. It was noticeably colder inside the factory than in the courtyard. There was little enough light outside under the suffocating blanket of grey clouds, but the factory's second floor was already night-dark. The raggy, mould-blackened remains of net curtains at the windows danced like wraiths in the breeze, the sky a heavy gunmetal grey behind them. Columns of ashen light and rainwater sifted down through holes in the high roof, a fall of glittering gemstones in the dark. "You're trying to get me killed," David said loudly, aiming his comment at Nathan. But there was no sign of his brother. He clicked on his torch. The light picked out the few features of the vast, open interior: the cast iron columns supporting the roof, a stairwell and the windows of former offices in the distance, and close by, tattered wisps of ancient cobwebs hanging from beams high above, ghoulish party decorations. The place was nearly empty – everything of worth had long since been stripped out, and all that remained were the brackets and fixtures that had once held them in place.

Something evil lurked in this emptiness, invisible even to Nathan's secret vision. Left behind when the factory had closed, here it had festered, alone, as the roof and walls around it crumbled. And now here came men who wanted to turn back the hands of time, to bring light to the gloomy places it liked to hide. David could already sense a presence, just as the surveyors had before him. He was observed, his presence here was known, and – without question, he could feel that – he was not welcome. He swept his torch around again, this time taking in the roof, pocked with glimpses of the clouds above, and the floor, dotted with puddles. He took out his shadow lens and peered through that for the ghost, but there was nothing to be seen. As he moved gingerly forwards, the floor creaked alarmingly underfoot, the sound clear even over the spattering of falling water. Then, far to the left, something moved – he swung his torch, and its beam picked out a huge, hurrying spider, white as cleaned bones. He shivered. Evidently the cobwebs were not so ancient.

"You made it," said Nathan, abruptly appearing through the floor.

"Just," David said.

"Do you sense it? The presence?"

"Of course I do. And I don't like it," David muttered. He sniffed. He could smell the faintest of scents. Somewhere, far away, or a long time ago…

"Light the candles. The sooner we find out what's what, the sooner we can get you out of here. You've still got your triumphal return to the Andersens', remember?"

David obeyed silently, deploying two candles in glass jars just as they had that night in the cemetery two years before. Nathan was already muttering the same incantation that he had read that night and had now memorized. David had the feeling that a baleful attention had been turned on them, and that it was waiting to see what they were going to do next.

"Paper," Nathan reminded David. "And think of the Solvent Man."

David didn't have time to think of the Solvent Man, for at the mention of his name there was a sudden gust of wind that blew out the candles and snatched the notebook from his cold fingers. It landed, pages fluttering, some metres away near the middle of the huge room. Behind him, the window he had climbed through slammed shut and some of its broken glass tinkled to the floor. The entire atmosphere within the factory seemed to heave, twice, almost as if the vast structure was alive and breathing. Then once more all was still apart from the water cascading from above.

"That was not a coincidence," hissed David, panicked.

"Agreed," Nathan said. "I think maybe you should get out of here."

David looked at his brother, surprised.

"It can move stuff," explained Nathan. "That could be dangerous. Come on.

Let's go."

They moved swiftly to the window, David feeling a growing sense of relief as they approached it. But try as he might, he could not make the window open. The ghostly presence in the factory was holding it shut. The brothers exchanged looks. From somewhere far below in the depths of the factory came a huge booming sound. David peered around through his crystal. He could see nothing. "If you don't want us here, let us go!" he shouted, his voice echoing in the darkness.

"The jar," Nathan said. "Try the jar."

"What's the point? I don't know where it is."

"It's everywhere."

"Is it *him?*" asked David. "Is it the –?" he did not complete the sentence, for he suddenly remembered what had happened the last time that name had been mentioned.

"What's the difference? It's not letting you out of here. Use the jar."

"I'm not sure that's a good idea."

"Have you got a better one?"

"Maybe we could wait… wait until it gets bored…"

"Do you think it's got anything better to do?"

David shook his head numbly.

Nathan laughed and backed away a little. As if recharged, he gleamed more brightly in the darkness. "That's the spirit," he said.

David moved further into the middle of the room. He swung his bag off his back and laid it on the floor at his feet, loosening the drawstring, but keeping the efreeti jar well hidden.

"I'll be within earshot if you need me," Nathan said, and fell through the floor.

David was alone in the darkness. Water fell all around him like the pattering of tiny feet. He took one last look around with the torch and the shadow lens, picking out the large white spider again, and then he pocketed his lens and pulled out his sheet of prime numbers. This was easy, he reminded himself.

"Greetings, noble spirit," he said, as loudly as his nerves would let him. "One one one, zero one." As soon as the first five digits were out of his mouth, there came a change. It was suddenly very cold – he could see the mist of his breath drifting through the torchlight. "One zero one, one one," he continued.

Something strange was happening. Deeper shadows were falling like velvet drapes in the corner of the room; blackness was beginning to gather in the factory. It was as if a theatre's house lights were dimming ready for the performance to begin. The more distant walls of the place disappeared almost immediately. David kept talking, trying not to blurt the numbers out, but to say them in a calm, firm voice.

It was not so much a lack of light, he thought, more as if something was drawing in the darkness about it like a cloak. Impossibly, the tone of this darkness seemed to be darker than black, as if the black he had always known was no more than the ghost of its true self. The walls had completely gone now. One of the shafts of daylight was swallowed up as if it had sunk beneath the surface of a night-black sea. He was hemmed in by an advancing wall of night. The torch revealed nothing; its beam vanished where the unreal darkness began, which was now no more than a few metres away. He stood in a pocket of grey light in an endless void, an actor in a spotlight.

He called out the last number and bent down to his bag. The darkness was closing in. His fingers, numb with cold, dropped the torch; it rolled away and disappeared from view as absolutely as if it had been kicked under a curtain. He groped blindly for the jar. He couldn't get hold of it. Rough hands were trying to pull the bag from him. He couldn't breathe; there was no air in this darkness.

The jar! He had the jar at last. He gripped the string handle, uncapped it, and ordered hoarsely: "Begone, noble spirit!" The instant he uttered these words, the blackness seemed to relax its hold on him a little. Then he could faintly see, or imagined that he could see, an oily river of night begin to flow into the jar… the blackness poured and poured into the jar… he couldn't believe how much there was, nor did he know how long to wait before recapping it. At his feet the torch beam reappeared. Around him, grey light was inching back into the factory. The river of oil seemed to be thinning, slowing… now was the time to cap the jar… as he did so, the remaining darkness dispersed around him and faded away. The factory was dark still, but no more than it ought to have been, no more than it was when he had first climbed in the window.

"Nathan!" he called unsteadily.

In seconds, Nathan rushed through one of the walls. "Have you got it?" he asked.

David nodded. "Let's get out of here," he said. He noticed that his hands were cold, and looked down at the jar. Except that the jar was gone. In its place there was only a clot of darkness, a hole of nothingness into which his hands disappeared. Instinctively, his hold relaxed. He dropped the jar.

"Dave – no!" shouted Nathan.

Reflexively David stuck out a foot to try and cushion the fall of the jar – but the jar only glanced against his trainer, hit the floor, and smashed into a hundred pieces.

"Run," hissed Nathan.

But David could only stare in disbelief at what was happening. The strange, infernal oil, freed from the jar, was oozing out all over the floor. In seconds the darkness had spread across the whole of the top floor of the factory like a tide of pitch. David's feet were immersed in what felt like icy water. He could vaguely hear Nathan imploring him to move but all he could do was watch helplessly as tentacles of darkness began to creep up the walls and windows, gradually blotting them out. Hideous, unreal night was falling again. Then he noticed that the blackness was also creeping up his legs, as if he was standing in rising waters. He couldn't move his legs at all, and trying to get them to go was threatening to unbalance him and pitch him over into that foul lake of black ichor.

"I can't move," he managed to say at last. He was aware of Nathan under him, touching the blackness that was crawling up his legs, trying to *peel* it away. It came free, but quickly – more quickly than Nathan could cope with – closed in again, bringing with it a terrible, penetrating coldness. Around the edge of the huge room, the darkness was nearly at the ceiling, and the light from the windows was gone again. There were only the grey shafts of light filtering down from above to reveal that Nathan was losing the battle against the rising tide, and that David was being swallowed up by greedy, slurping sentient oil. For a few seconds the evil liquid slowed down and set like tar; then, as smoothly as it had risen, the tide of night began to ebb. As if a plug had been pulled out, the level of the strange ooze started to fall, and light peeped again through the tops of the windows. Soon only a skin of blackness was left covering the floor, and then even that trickled through gaps between the floorboards and disappeared. The window, released from its unnatural grip, swung open once more and began tap-tapping against its frame as if beckoning David towards sanctuary.

The presence had gone. David tried to move his legs, but they were both numbed and weakened, and all he managed to do was overbalance and fall over. At least it didn't matter now. He grabbed his torch. Around him, shards of broken pottery littered the floor. "What was that?" asked David.

"Our ghost, at a guess," replied Nathan.

"Well, whatever it was, it's gone."

But Nathan suddenly darted away a few metres, heading over towards the stairs. He turned to face his brother. "No it hasn't," he said urgently, "get up.

We've got to go, now."

"What is it?" asked David. His legs wouldn't get under him. He decided to crawl to the wall, so that he could lever himself up there. But even at crawling his legs were all but useless; progress was both painful and slow.

There was a heavy crash somewhere below, down in the unknown depths of the factory. David looked behind him as he crawled; he could see Nathan at the top of the stairs, peering down anxiously, no more than a faint glow in the shadows. His legs still wouldn't work. The wall, three seconds away at a run, was still a lifetime away at this pace.

"Hurry Dave," Nathan called, a quavering note of panic stealing into his voice. "It's coming."

Somehow the phrase *it's coming* was the most terrifying thing that David had ever heard. He redoubled his efforts to get to the wall. He was now flopping along like a seal, gasping for breath, using every joule of energy his arms could generate. His legs, dragging behind, still wouldn't even bend in the middle: they were cold and clammy, like dead flesh.

Then he realized that Nathan was standing over him. "Hurry," he hissed.

"I am," retorted David. "I can't move my legs."

"Oh no," breathed Nathan. "Can you hear that?"

David felt his brother move into the same space as his legs – a joining marked by a rush of painful pins and needles. A little warmth returned – but not enough. Nowhere near enough.

There were footsteps coming up the stairs. Heavy, quick, stamping footsteps. David tried to flex his legs. Movement was returning, but painfully, and gradually, too gradually. He managed to lurch to his feet, but as he did so he couldn't resist taking a look over his shoulder. A shadow was growing at the top of the stairs, swelling and taking form. At first David could see nothing more than a column of darkness, then, underneath the wreathing, curling tongues of smoke-like stuff, he could make out legs, arms, and a pale head

153

thinly streaked with black hair. A pair of curiously flattened, gleaming eyes swam in the round white face. Blackness dripped from the creature like oil; it wrapped itself in the darkness as a cloak. But it wasn't at the top of the stairs any more. It was half way across the room, coming fast, smiling insanely. It bore with it the solvent stench that David and Nathan knew too well.

"Come on, Dave," implored Nathan, who had moved ahead, over to the open window.

The window might as well have been a light year away. David shuffled towards his brother, towards salvation. Behind him, he could hear charging footsteps. In front of him, he could see Nathan's eyes widen in terror. Then the thing smashed into his back, and he fell forwards, onto the floor. *It really was the Solvent Man*. Even as he tried to squirm onto his back, he couldn't quite believe that it had touched him; where before had only been some poisonous vapour there was now the physical embodiment of his worst terror. Water was pouring down on him from a hole in the roof, a hole that was also letting in a whisper of daylight. Then darkness loomed over him, and the light was blotted out. The ghost reached down for him. It was smiling at him as its arms plunged straight into his chest. The shock was like falling through a crust of ice into a frozen river. *It's doing what Nathan does*, he thought, fading fast. That was when his brother arrived.

Nathan surged into the fray like a fiery comet, sparkling with anger, and slammed into the much larger creature, his fury pushing it back. "Run! Run!" he was shouting. The two ghosts grappled, staggered, and rolled together, locked in battle. David tried to do as his brother was urging, but was as shocked and stunned as if he had been hit by a car, and the last thing his body wanted to do was get up and run. Instead he could only watch as the incandescent heat of his brother wrestled with the cold black creature, which seemed to be able to change shape, to flow out of the way of attacks, and extrude rope-like, snaring tentacles of night at will.

At last David got to his feet, despite the screaming protests of pain and the inexorable downward pull of tiredness that tried to stop him. The floor here was spongy, wet with rot where water had poured onto it for untold years. He took one step, and then another, with Nathan screaming behind him; then his balance went, and he was falling again. As he crashed onto the rotten floor, it splintered to pieces and he was suddenly in a rushing void, falling, falling, falling into space. Below him there was only darkness – he saw a brief flash of light from the windows, but the first he knew of the floor below was when he smashed into it. Pain lanced into his left wrist. Lights popped and wheeled before his eyes, and were followed by waves of darkness that tried to pull him under. He needed to move, but his body would not respond. Eventually, with a colossal effort, he managed to roll onto his back, but that was as far as he was going to go. Above him, through the hole he had made in the floor above, he could see the dancing lights of Nathan's struggle with the ghostly creature.

"Run! Run!" He could still hear his brother calling, but his voice was far away, as if muffled by layers of cloth. The light of Nathan's fury was dimming. The shadows were swallowing up the light. David watched helplessly as the struggle above him gradually subsided into an eerie peace; Nathan was not shouting any more, nor could he be seen. For a little time there was complete darkness, and a quiet interrupted only by the sound of rain running through the innards of the factory. The fight was over. David did not doubt who had won. The silence and the darkness were evidence enough. Then, over to his right, a pool of deeper shadow started to clot around the foot of the spiral stairs. The winner was coming to claim its prize.

David lay still, an immovable weight on his chest, and watched the ghost as it gracefully descended the stairwell. He was too tired to worry about what was about to happen to him. Then something unexpected happened to the shadowy spirit. Its flowing approach to him stuttered, faltered. A distant gleam of light appeared amongst the cloaking darkness, which grew brighter by degrees… David watched, fascinated despite his terror. A glowing arm erupted from the heart of the ghost, then a head. Nathan's head. Tentacles tried to snare him once more, but with a desperate effort he pushed them away and struggled free. It was a pale, grey, dim Nathan who emerged.

The two brothers locked eyes. David could see the ghost bearing down on his brother from behind; he tried to warn him, but couldn't find his voice. Nathan staggered towards David for a few metres, despair etched into his features.

"Dave, please, run," muttered Nathan. "Run, I beg you…"

Even as he said these words, the darkness quietly caught up with him, folding around him like a gentle caress. In a second, Nathan had been completely consumed by the darkness. For a moment, a flailing hand emerged. But the darkness quickly drew it in again, and the light was gone forever.

There was something tugging at David's left wrist. Every touch brought with it a lance of pain which slowly began to rouse him from his unconscious state. A voice was speaking to him – the voice of a boy.

"Come on," said the voice. "Before my uncle gets here…"

Uncle? What did he mean? David managed to open his eyes. The boy was younger than he was, and was dressed in a smart grey jacket and long shorts.

"Come on," the boy insisted. "I know a trick. This way." He gestured towards deep, impenetrable darkness. David managed to stand and allowed himself to be led, the boy taking most of his weight by putting his head under David's right arm. "You have to get out of here," the boy said. "It isn't much, but at least it's a little sheltered…" the boy's voice faded away, and David was lost to the world again.

The next thing that David became aware of was the roaring of rain above him. There was water splashing on his face. It felt like he was waking up. There was another sound nearby, coming to him over the sounds of the storm: a voice raised in anger.

"How could you even consider giving him up to them! John! Wait!" the voice was a woman's.

"I don't have any choice," replied a man's voice. "This is the only way they'll let us in. If you want this place to survive you'd better start..."

"He can hear you!" The voices were getting closer.

"Don't be absurd! And anyway, it's not as if he can understand a word we're saying. This isn't a normal boy we're talking about – it would almost be a kindness..."

"Hello, William dear," came the woman's voice, and David realized that she was talking to him. *My name's not William*, he thought dully. There was the sound of a car door opening. "I hope we haven't kept you waiting too long..." The voice seemed to fade away, and David opened his eyes to see what had become of its owner. He must have been dreaming, for there was no-one there. Above him, he saw blackened, torn vinyl. He didn't understand what he was staring at for a time. Then he looked about. There were empty windows. In front of him, there was a steering wheel; below, to the left, there was a small stove with a pan of molten wax on it. As he shifted position, a blinding pain burst out of his left wrist and squeezed sight and sound from his consciousness. After a few seconds, when the vice-tight grip of agony had relaxed a little, he began to see other things around him: rusting seat-springs, broken glass, and, outside the car, large puddles of water, almost forming a continuous lake after all this rain. In the distance, through a blurring veil of falling water, was the factory.

"Nathan?" he said. How had he got here? He remembered lying on his back, staring up; remembered a shadow coming down the stairs… then the boy… the voices… now this. He was slumped in the back seat of the burnt-out car on the factory's forecourt. He looked at his injured wrist. Then he wished that he hadn't. Nausea welled up within him. Then he remembered what had happened to Nathan, remembered that his brother was gone, engulfed by the silent demon in the factory.

"Nathan!" called David, as loudly as he could.

There was no reply from his brother; the only sound was the continuous, merciless rain. Nathan was still in the factory. He had been swallowed up by the darkness.

David crawled out of the car. He was cold, dizzy, and felt sick. In front of him the factory reared into the heavy sky, the carven sun staring down blankly at him. There was no sign of any forced exit in either the first or ground floors. How had he got out of there? There should be an open window, a ripped-out board, something to show where he had emerged. Only a ghost could have got out of there without leaving a trace.

"Nathan!" he called again. There was, as he knew there would be, no reply. He was now no more than a few metres from where he had begun his climb up the drainpipe an unknown time before. Above him, the high window slammed open in a gust of wind. An invitation. For a moment he even reached out with his good hand for the drainpipe… then drew it back, knowing it was hopeless.

"Nathan," he moaned. "Please. Please, Nathan. Don't be gone. Not again." He walked away from the factory a little way to get a broader view. "Nathan!" This time he shouted his brother's name. Again, high above, the little window slammed, mocking him.

He stared at the factory and waited for his brother to come out. Nathan did not come. David waited. An image came to his mind's eye: he was running across the road, away from the cemetery, screaming. Ahead of him, the lighted windows of a house promised salvation, but pound as he might on the door, no answer came. Behind him, he could no longer hear his brother. The memory of running away stood at his back like a wall. He could not abandon his brother this time. He willed Nathan to emerge, staring at the factory as rain lanced down on him like the derisive spit of the gods.

After a time, he didn't feel cold any more. Some time later, it began to get properly dark. And yet he stood, resolute, still as a tree, and waited for his brother. "I'm not leaving you," he muttered. He realized that tears had joined the raindrops running down his face. The darkness was folding around him, enveloping him just as it had Nathan; but this darkness was different – it was beautiful, friendly, a warm, comforting embrace. He hardly even noticed that he was falling. Consciousness returned briefly when he hit the cold, hard concrete. Then that insistent blanket crept back, covering him once again, and he was dead to all the world.

PART THREE

*

THE EXORCIST

All is not lost; the unconquerable Will,
And study of revenge, immortal hate,
And courage never to submit or yield:
And what is else not to be overcome?
That Glory never shall his wrath or might
Extort from me.

Milton

Chapter 16: Isolation Ward

There was an unknown length of time when David was aware that he was awake, but chose neither to move nor to open his eyes. After some time, he began to hear voices. They started as faraway whispers, faint and indistinct, but gradually grew in volume until they seemed to come from people gathered over him. The first voice he recognized was Guy Read's. He was angry. "I tell you, I've had enough of this!"

"Quiet, Guy! It's not you who's injured. Stop thinking about yourself for one second." The scolding reply came from his foster mother, Rebecca Read.

He couldn't believe it. Where was he? At home? He kept his eyes fast closed, and pretended to be asleep. Facing the Reads' questions was more than he could bear at this moment. There were other noises behind the Reads' voices, including lots of talking, a generalized surrounding murmur of deliberately lowered voices. There were irregular footsteps on a hard floor, getting louder. Somebody with a limp was approaching. Abruptly the footsteps ceased.

"How is he?" came a voice. He recognized this one, too. It was Uncle Charlie.

Mrs Read replied. "Oh, hello, Charles. They said he's going to be okay. They've set his arm, given him a sedative. Mild hypothermia, a few bruises – otherwise he's okay."

As Mrs Read's words drew his attention to his wrist, David realized that it was being squeezed by a throbbing bracelet of pain. He kept his eyes closed, but not too tightly, in case someone noticed that his eyelids were no longer in the relaxed pose of unconsciousness.

"How did it happen?" asked Uncle Charlie softly.

"We'll have to hear that from the horse's mouth," muttered Guy. "All we know is, a passer-by called an ambulance. Found him unconscious in some waste ground on the corner of Raglan Road and Staithe Road."

"Not many passers-by down that way any more," Charlie observed.

"He got lucky."

The corner of Raglan Road and Staithe Road? But that was a hundred metres from the Tipler factory. Had he managed to drag himself there? It seemed that no-one had an inkling about what had actually happened… but what *had* actually happened? David had flashes of memory, little more than dream images: creeping, suffocating darkness; the smiling ghost bending over him; Nathan's hot light battling the monster's cold darkness; falling… he remembered a moment in the ambulance, a plastic mask clamped to his face, the sick-sweet air too rich, making him vomit. He realized that he still had a sour, acid taste in his mouth. And Nathan… he almost cried out in sudden despair, but managed to check his voice in time. Nathan was gone.

Uncle Charlie was thanking the Reads for calling him. His great paw settled gently on David's unhurt right hand. Uncle Charlie was asking him a question, but he was speaking from a long way away, and his voice was receding into the distance. The other sounds were fading away too.

Time seemed to have passed. It was all quiet again now; there was only a faint hum as of distant machines and a little metallic *pink-pink* sound coming from closer by, over to his left.

David opened his eyes. It wasn't hard to guess where he was. He was in a hospital ward. Beds were lined up on either side of the room, some with sleepers in them. Erratic light spilled in from the corridor outside through a large open doorway, where one of the overhead lights was flickering. *Pink-pink*. The light was fighting against its inevitable end. There were no visitors or nurses in the ward any more, only still, slumbering patients.

David noticed that his left arm was in a cast that reached from below his elbow, took in half his thumb, and ended at his knuckles. A tube ran out of his right arm to a bag hanging on a stand beside the bed. He seemed to hurt all over: his left arm pounded with pain, a good deal more severe than it had been when he had been briefly awake before; his right arm stung where a piece of tape hid the join between the tube and his body; but the worst sensation was in his chest, which felt raw, as if his lungs had been sandpapered, and each breath brought with it a saw stroke of pain. Where the ghost touched me, he realized. Where it would have killed me if Nathan hadn't –

"Nathan?" David whispered his brother's name into the quiet darkness, without any real hope of reply. Nathan wasn't there – he was sure of that much. He remembered Nathan struggling, disappearing like a drowning boy pulled under black waters by entangling weeds. He remembered Nathan's look of despair as the darkness enveloped him: not despair at his own fate, but at his inability to save his brother. Even at the end, all he could think of was David. He wanted to save his brother, at any cost. Just like before, at the cemetery. And as before, David was safe, Nathan gone. Well, this time it was going to be different. This time he was going to go back for Nathan.

David ordered his tired body to get up. His muscles were stiff, weak; he barely had the strength to fight his way out of the tightly binding bedcovers. The floor was polished, cold underfoot. His shoes: he needed his shoes, and his clothes. He couldn't wander out into the night air in hospital pyjamas. As he tried to move around the bed, his drip tube pulled tight and a needle of pain dug into his arm. He could see that the drip was on a wheel stand... it was somehow fixed to the wall, but in the half-light, and with his brain not at its best, he couldn't see how to unclip it.

In the end it didn't matter that he couldn't free himself. His legs were too weak to hold him anyway, and after a few seconds staring helplessly at his drip, he simply folded up onto the cold floor. He thought he should call out: there would be a night-nurse on duty somewhere who would hear his cries and help him back into bed. But he kept silent. He just lay on the floor and gritted his teeth. His thoughts spiralled around his record of failure. Nathan was like a guardian angel who never failed in David's hour of need. But whenever Nathan needed help, David could never provide it, no matter how hard he tried. He would give a break in each of his three good limbs to see Nathan's disapproving face glowing down on him. But such a trade was impossible. The deal was done. Nathan was gone, and he was never coming back. David began to cry: it hurt murderously that Nathan was gone, but in truth, the tears were for himself. What a little thing he was, alone in the universe, nothing more than a speck of warmth in infinite coldness. A fly caught in a cosmic spider web, humming and buzzing in oblivious futility, becoming ever more tangled in its own inevitable failure.

Somebody was shouting. It was a man's voice, bellowing from some way down the ward. "Nurse! That patient needs some pain relief!"

In seconds strong hands were lifting him back into bed. The nurse was a man, who spoke with a warm, northern accent. "I know it hurts," he said, completely misunderstanding. "I'll send the sweet trolley down as soon as it gets here. You just lie back and rest a minute..."

The first thing that David noticed in the harsh light of morning was an envelope and a small parcel lying on his bedside table. He recognized the writing as Uncle Charlie's. Inside was a card, which wished him better soon and invited him to guess what the present was for. The present was a brass ring about the size of a finger and thumb made into a circle. One side of the ring was thick, the other thin and interrupted, so that the whole had the look of a fine crescent moon. There were six small screws set in the ring, which could be driven in towards the centre, but had nothing to join to there. A tiny ring had been braised onto the outside of the larger one, probably by Charlie himself. The function of this puzzled David for a while. Whatever it was for, he liked it; it grew hot in his right hand, and he could fidget the screws in and out with finger and thumb. Charlie had used an engraving tool to carve – somewhat crudely – the following legend onto the outside of the ring: TO DAVID CARRAWAY FROM HIS UNCLE CHARLIE.

Just after breakfast, his first visitors arrived: the Reads. Much as he would have liked to, David could not feign sleep this time. Mrs Read gave him a gentle hug; even Mr Read briefly rested his hand on David's shoulder. They had brought him grapes and a carton of chocolate milk. David, of course, lied about what had happened to him.

He had no memory of what had happened, he told Guy Read. A passing boy wearing a hood had asked him the time; the next thing he knew, he was in the hospital. It was dark, raining, he didn't recognize the boy, wouldn't know him again if he saw him. He admitted that he had been foolish to go wandering around the old manufacturing district.

"Bloody kids!" muttered Mr Read. "They want shooting, the lot of them. Or for something worse to happen to them, like the end of the world."

"Guy!" said Mrs Read.

"You know what I mean. They think they can get away with anything." After this, both the Reads moaned about the lack of space at the hospital, which had led to David being placed in a male surgical ward, because the children's ward was full. David himself hadn't really noticed. The men in the ward kept themselves to themselves. The thought of a children's ward hadn't even entered his head until Guy Read started muttering about where his taxes were all going, because they clearly weren't being spent on health.

Later on, David was able to call Professor Fuller on his phone. His clothes had gone, he knew not where, but Mrs Read had brought him fresh ones and his own pyjamas. His personal objects, however, had been rescued from his clothes and placed in the top drawer of his bedside cabinet, and amongst these was his mobile. He went out into a busy corridor to make the call for reasons of privacy.

The phone rang for an interminable length of time before the professor picked it up. "Professor, it's me, David."

"You're all right. Thank the stars."

"Was it you who called the ambulance?"

"No. I was too late. When you didn't come to see me, I worried that something was amiss. By the time I arrived an ambulance was already there. I thought it wisest to turn around. But what on earth happened – it must have gone badly wrong?"

David gave the professor a shortened version of events. He told him how Nathan had been taken, and as he did so, bitter tears started to flow again.

"Calm, David. It may not be impossible to get him back," muttered the professor. "I'll do some reading… but let's not forget, he seemed to be on borrowed time in any case…"

"But where is he, Professor? Is he dead, or trapped helpless in that darkness? I couldn't go on if I thought that…"

"I don't know. But I promise you this. If it is humanly possible to get him back, get him back we shall. Agreed?"

"Yes."

"But how are you? That's the most important question."

"A broken wrist, not too bad – I'm almost out of credit. I'll call you when I can."

"Stay safe."

"I will," David said, and ended the call.

The rest of the day was quiet and dull. There was a day room attached to the ward, but it was full of magazines of little interest to David. His fellow patients, mainly older men, had nothing to say to him – they had little enough to say to one another, it seemed, shuffling around in a cloud of their own personal despondency. David wondered how long he was going to be stuck in the hospital. He needed to get out, to get to the professor, so that together they could find a way to get Nathan back. But suppose there was no way to bring him back? If the professor exorcised the ghost, wouldn't he simply exorcise Nathan along with it? Who was the boy who had dragged him out and left him in the car? Were the boy who had helped him and the William that he had heard the couple discuss one and the same? Why had the Solvent Man spared him? Was there perhaps a grain of goodness about him? No, he sensed that the ghost was unalloyed evil, a loathsome, foul entity that delighted only in the suffering of others. Somehow that boy had intervened on his behalf – but how, and why? He wanted to get back to the factory – needed to – but he knew that when he got there, the darkness would be waiting for him. He sat and stared into space and worried himself down a spiral of despair until he reached the bottom – the very bottom. He was going to have to face life without Nathan: but to lose Nathan would be to lose the best part of himself, the sun in the daytime. He would always walk in the night, always alone, wherever and whenever he went. School without Nathan would be hell on earth. He imagined himself standing helplessly in the centre of the playground, doing little more than counting time, whilst all around him hundreds of children hurried purposefully towards their hopeful futures.

At some point the ward lights were switched off. A few of the men read by the warm light of their bedside lamps; most just lay back and invited a small sliver of death to bring them oblivion for a few hours. David stared at the ceiling, tracing with his gaze electrical conduits, the joints between the ceiling panels, and the housings of strip lights. Gradually, the readers closed their books and switched off their own bedside lights. Now the only sounds were a few gentle snores and, out in the corridor, the *pink-pink* of the light that still hadn't been mended but still hadn't been overcome by darkness.

Sleep, he told himself, but every time he closed his eyes, an image of

Nathan being dragged backwards to his doom swam to the surface of his mind. The expression on Nathan's face as he was swallowed up would never leave him. But each time he remembered that moment, a match of anger was struck, until at last he was burning with fury, ready there and then to confront the ghost, and to crush it with the sheer force of his hatred of it. He stared at the flickering light and plotted his enemy's downfall.

Pink – pink. Pink. There was no pattern to the flickering of the light, which was perhaps why it was so hypnotic. He watched the light and counted seconds: sometimes there would be a half-light, accompanied by a low buzzing noise, and then with a *pink* the light would come on for a second or two. Sometimes there would be darkness for five or ten seconds. As David stared, in his mind's eye he poured petrol all around the factory, a lighter clenched in his hand, ready to set a gleeful ally leaping through the ghost's home.

Burn it. Burn it all.

Pink.

The light went off. David counted seconds. By the time he got to twenty, he realized that the light had given up its half-life, and had finally died.

Then he noticed that as he breathed, a plume of mist appeared in the air above him. His arms, out of bed, were suddenly cold, and rippled with a rash of goose bumps.

The lights in the corridor dimmed until what had been a garishly bright opening on a never-sleeping world had become the mouth of a tunnel that led only to the deep darkness of nightmares. Now the only lights were the faint orange dots that marked the panic buttons over each bed.

Fear leaned over David and with a smile blew out the guttering candle of his anger. He knew that he should get out of bed and flee... but his instinct was to lie still, hardly breathing, and try to convince himself that he was mistaken, that the ghost was not here in the hospital, that it was not coming for him. At last, as the darkness felt its way up the ward towards him like a vast black amoeba, he managed to force himself to move. He got as far as the middle of the ward before he realized that there was no way out, that the only escape route was the very corridor from which the darkness was seeping. In front of him, even the lights of the panic buttons were being swallowed up, the sleeping men beneath them all oblivious to what was happening.

David backed away as the darkness crept towards him. He knew that he was on the first floor, so he could try for a window – even if he couldn't climb down he should survive the jump... but as, with a clatter against the Venetian blind, his back reached the end of the ward, he did not turn to the window. He was tired, and had been chased far enough. He wasn't going to play the game to the end.

"Come on then," he said angrily, and took a step towards the encroaching darkness. As he did so, he felt a weight of responsibility fall from his shoulders. His fear was still there, but it was his friend now, the last stagecoach out of a place he couldn't bear to be in any longer. "I'm not playing any more," he snarled at the ghost, "I'm here if you want me. Either give me Nathan back or take me too. Either way we'll be together."

The darkness, by now lapping at his toes, seemed to hesitate, and perhaps even fell back a little. Then for a time neither the panting boy nor the darkness looming over him moved an inch. The moment seemed to stretch for eternity. David wondered if the ghost, a cruel executioner, was waiting for his resolve to crack, for him to try and escape again before it finally engulfed him. The delay in his sentence seemed to feed his hope, and as his hope grew, the more he thought he should take his chance and run before the ghost lost patience and swallowed him up. Soon the only reason that he didn't move was the sure knowledge that the merest twitch on his part would see his doom. Then, abruptly, like a crab spider seizing a fly, the darkness fell on him.

But he did not die. The ghost was trying to open his mind instead... David fought against the invasion for all he was worth, but as a creeping starfish triumphs over a sturdy mussel, the ghost inexorably exhausted his defences. It had visions to torture him with… There was an old house on a hill… David found himself transported to a large, windowless room within. A dim light shone from high above through a tiny grille; he could vaguely make out a wooden staircase rising to a door above. Was this where Nathan was?

"Nathan?" David asked, but his voice was faint and whispery, like the sounds of a worn out old record. Then he noticed the coffin. It was large, shining black and gold, and sat in the middle of the room on a raised stone platform. For some reason, the coffin held a deep terror for him. He knew that he had to get out of the house before nightfall. He charged up the stairs and pulled on the door, but it would not open. Behind him, he could see that the light from the grille was fading, as though outside the sun was setting. He realized with mounting dread that this dying light was inextricably linked to his fear of the coffin. He ran back down the stairs, flying around the walls, searching for a way out or somewhere to hide. But there were neither.

Soon the light was almost gone. He found himself shouting: "Help me!" But he knew that his calls were in vain. He knew that of the two people who could hear him, one sat smiling in a room above, a click-shut silver case containing a solvent-soaked pad in his pocket, while the other lay in the coffin, waiting for nightfall. When the ebon sarcophagus finally opened, it did so with such ease and well-oiled grace that he did not hear it. He heard the thing coming out of it though. The creature clambering towards him over the rim of the coffin was grey-skinned, bald, and was wrapped in crude rags that spoke of the most abject poverty. The parts of it that he could see were both heavily scarred and tattooed all over with strange writing and symbols. It smiled at him, and its teeth were hideously malformed… all except the two upper canines, which were monstrously produced. Although it smiled, its eyes did not join the expression; they were dead, glittering, black shells. It came for him in a series of jerky, lurching movements, crooning faint words... "My dear... William, my dear..."

The sound of footsteps coming broke the spell. In a blink the dark cellar and its monstrous denizen were gone, as was the enveloping phantom itself; the lights in the corridor were back on, and even the broken light had resumed its jerky existence. A white-uniformed nurse swung into the ward and stopped short when he saw David standing by the window.

"Out of bed again, are you?" asked the nurse. It was the same nurse who had lifted him back into bed the previous evening. "Admiring the view? Not much to see out there – just the old riverside factories... come on, back to bed, lad."

David let the nurse lead him back to his bed. He could not help but look about him for the grey creature – but he knew that it was not here, that it was part of a memory he had been shown, the ghost's last memory as a living person...

"Are you all right?" asked the nurse, feeling his patient's forehead.

"Just scared," David told him.

"The men's ward is no place for kids. Still, you should be out of here tomorrow. Can't see why they'd keep you in. Tell you what – I've got some paperwork to do, so why don't I bring it in here and do it?"

David nodded mutely. The nurse went out and returned shortly afterwards with his paperwork. Then he drew up a chair at a vacant bed, switched on the reading light, and got to work. "Now get some sleep," he told David. "I'm only over here if you need me."

David felt sure that he would never be able to sleep again – but in spite of himself, within minutes he was slumbering soundly.

Chapter 17: Recuperation

David awoke to find the sun streaming in through the windows of the men's ward. He did not have much time to dwell on the events of the previous evening, because immediately after breakfast, a series of visitors arrived. The first visitor was his social worker, Teresa. Today, Teresa's hair had been tied back in a tight ponytail and she was wearing an ill-fitting roll-neck jumper. Her questions were of the usual kind, easily fielded, like the ubiquitous "Are you happy at home?"

"It's okay," said David, adopting his usual neutral tone to anyone in authority. To offer minimum voluntary information, that was the key. Respond to questions as briefly as possible, and give them nothing that they had not first had painstakingly dug up – that was David's strategy.

Later that morning, he was discharged. The Reads turned up unannounced and he was told to get dressed. He was helpless again, this time a prisoner of adults organising things over his head and behind his back. At least Uncle Charlie was in the loop; he was waiting on the drive of seventeen Chapman Close, eager to see how his nephew was doing. Charlie gave him a huge hug and helped him up to his room.

"Thanks for the present," David told him.

"Have you worked out what it's for yet? I hope it fits."

David hadn't yet worked out the purpose of the moon-shaped brass ring he had been given, but with the clue in these words, he guessed in a flash. He took out the ring and his shadow lens. They were clearly made for one another. "I couldn't do it one-handed," David lied. "How did you know how big to make it?"

Uncle Charlie placed David's crystal in the steel ring and tightened the screws one by one until it was held securely. "I'm not completely useless, you know. I am a man of hidden talents. Speaking of which, listen, David. I don't want anything else to happen to you. You're my only living relative, you know. So if you want me to sort out those kids, just let me know. I'm guessing you know who they are. I may have a dodgy leg but I'm more than a match for a few kids." Charlie flexed his vast biceps. Then he winked. "And I've got friends in high places."

David could think of nothing to say. All he knew was that he couldn't drag his uncle into this business with the ghost.

"You think I'm joking, don't you?" demanded Charlie. He showed David a giant clenched fist. "If you want it done, it's done. Just give me the word."

That afternoon, David was sitting in bed, staring at the lengthening shadows on his bedroom wall, when there was a knock at the front door. He heard voices, footsteps on the stairs, and then a tap on his door. Mrs Read showed the Andersens in, and then retreated again to make a pot of tea.

"If you didn't want to come over, you could have just said. You didn't have to go to these lengths," Dr Andersen told him, her voice deadpan. She was still dressed all in black, her blond hair pushed casually back behind her ears.

David smiled. He watched as Michael looked around the bedroom, finally approaching a poster of the solar system. "Nice," he said, staring at it intently. "Mercury, Venus, Earth, Mars, Jupiter, Saturn, Uranus, Neptune, Pluto… now considered a dwarf planet, of course… although that is a mistake in my view…"

"It was my brother's," David said.

"Jupiter is best," said Michael. "His great red spot could easily swallow up the Earth…"

"How are you?" asked Anna, the doctor in her coming to the fore. "Are you in pain? Are they prescribing you medication?"

David answered her questions as best he could. He wasn't quite sure what the tablets were that he was being given: he just swallowed them unthinkingly. Finally, having satisfied herself that David was being treated okay, Anna could skirt around the question she wanted to ask no longer.

"What did you do? I know you treated Michael. But I don't understand how."

The time for evasion was gone. David answered her question truthfully, without much hope of her believing him. "Michael was haunted. Possessed, if you prefer. I exorcised the ghost."

"That was what was in the jar," realized Anna.

Over at the poster of the solar system, Michael turned his attention to their conversation.

David nodded in reply. He still couldn't quite believe that Anna was going to accept a supernatural explanation so easily.

"Why didn't you just tell me?"

"With your son unconscious, I didn't think you'd listen," David told her, and smiled wanly.

"Yes, I'm sorry about that," muttered Anna, and turned to see what Michael was up to. He had lost interest in their conversation and was leafing through a battered paperback book that he had found. "I found him reading one of my medical textbooks – I'm sure he didn't know what it meant, but it's quite incredible how he is now…"

"I did know," said Michael, without looking up.

"I've taken him out of the special needs school. He's going to be going to Meadows with you after Christmas. I just can't believe how he's changed –"

At this point Rebecca Read entered the bedroom and placed a tray of tea and biscuits on the bed. When she had gone, Anna recounted what had happened when David had left their house after the exorcism. Michael had quickly recovered consciousness, and had shown such a marked improvement that she had taken him to see a friend and former consultant. "The first thing Michael did when he opened his eyes was to say that he loved me. He's never done that before."

David said: "I've got to say sorry. I didn't know the exorcism would work. I had no idea Michael would wind up unconscious like that – I should never have taken such a risk."

"We're grateful to you that you did," said Anna, and laid a cold hand on his. "You know, I don't believe in any of this alternative wisdom stuff. I didn't, I mean. I know a lot of other children with autism –"

"I can't cure autism," interrupted David. "I don't even know what it is. Michael was possessed."

"But what if the other children –"

"There's nothing I can do for them," he said flatly. "I wish I could."

"How did you know what was wrong with Michael?"

"My brother. He was a ghost. He could see other ghosts. He's –" David paused, searching for the right word. "He's gone now."

His words seemed to be a conversation killer. The Andersens left shortly after. As they did, Anna said: "If there's ever anything we can do – you know where we are." Michael had been patiently twisting a piece of scrap paper into the intricate shape of a swan; as he walked past the bed, he laid it on the tea tray, a silent thank you.

As David and the Andersens had been talking, the last of the sunshine had drained from the room. It was almost dusk. David switched all his lights on but left the curtains open. After tea, he stayed downstairs with the Reads for as long as he could, until he was sent to bed. He tried to read until Guy told him to switch the lights out. Then he lay in bed awake, the curtains still wide open, the coppery light of the streetlamps washing into the room through the skeletal weeping willow on the lawn. As soon as the Reads had gone to bed themselves, he got up again and sat on the cold windowsill, away from the gloomy interior of the bedroom, and waited, staring out. All was quiet on Chapman Close. He watched the willow tree dance in the wind. The orange streetlamps cast multiple ghastly, twitching shadows on the bedroom walls. Occasionally, wet leaves would fly out of the night and briefly pick at the window, making him jump. But of the creeping darkness, there was no sign.

In the depths of the bedroom, he could blearily make out the time by his radio alarm clock: a quarter to two. Sleep tugged at his body, pulling him down, but he resisted. He did not know what he would do when the ghost came, but he must be ready. He imagined it flowing over him like the tide washing into an estuary. Awake, he had some chance.

He tried to read, but it was too dark without the light, and he did not dare wake up the Reads. Instead he watched the fingers of shadow writhing on the bedroom wall, convinced all the time that they were coalescing into deeper darkness. Each instant, the shadows darkened, but always they stayed the same, waving, nodding, and beckoning to him. He watched them through his shadow lens, now hanging from a chain around his neck; he saw nothing. He looked at his mother's painting – but there was too little light to make out what, if anything, it was trying to tell him. He brought it close to the window and let the coppery street light bathe it. *Now* he could see... there seemed to be some sort of doorway framed by the grey smudges; in the middle, as if passing through, was a small figure. He knew with cold dread that he was looking at himself, although what this doorway represented, he could not tell: was it real? Or was it a metaphor, the doorway to death? Cold and stiff, he sat on the floor under the window and watched the shadows of the trees dancing over the painting. His eyelids drooped. The ghost! He snapped awake. The shadows were as before. He strained to keep his eyes open; for a few seconds he succeeded, but soon they began to close again.

The scolding note of a panicked blackbird outside the window brought him to his senses. He found himself on the floor, looking up at the grey rectangle of his bedroom window. It was dawn.

David spent most of Tuesday feeling like a prisoner. He was unable to call

Professor Fuller because Rebecca Read stayed in all day to look after him. Even school would have been preferable to sitting in bed, aimlessly reading books he already knew virtually by heart, or staring blankly at his mother's painting (still showing him that ominous doorway), or turning his lens over and over in his hands in its new mount. Even his wrist had stopped hurting most of the time. The worst thing was that he couldn't concentrate on anything because he alternated between wondering why the ghost hadn't come to finish him off last night and rehearsing all that had happened at Tipler's over and over again to try to decide what he should have done differently. The same thought kept occurring to him: that he shouldn't have dropped the efreeti jar. If only he had held on. Or stuck out a foot quicker and cushioned its fall. Or not looked down at it. But why had it been black? Had the ghost been halfway out of the jar even when he had dropped it?

Late that afternoon, he was watching television when he had another visitor. He distantly heard a knock at the front door and a surprised-sounding Rebecca Read saying "Yes?" He did not hear the visitor reply, but found out soon enough who it was, when his foster mother showed her in.

It was Milla. She hovered in the doorway, as though unwilling to come any further.

"Hello," said David, and tried to fashion a smile.

"Have you been saving damsels in distress again?" asked Milla, smiling back. "Do I have a rival?"

David chuckled politely. "No," he said. "I've been being a fool again."

"They said at school that some kids attacked you – was it Drake and his gang?" Milla was still standing in the doorway, looking ill at ease in her large coat and big scuffed boots, with her skinny legs in between.

"Come in," David said, and used the remote to switch off the babble of the television. Should he tell her, confess? He felt that he must tell someone soon, because quietly swallowing all his pain was slowly poisoning him. But he couldn't tell Milla and seem like a fool to one of the few people he knew who respected him. No: he would have to wait until he spoke to the professor. "No," he said. "I don't know who it was."

"You're going to be all right though," said Milla, perching on the sofa, still in her coat. There was a hole in the knee of her black tights.

"Back to school tomorrow," agreed David.

"Your arm – is it broken?"

"Do you want to sign it?"

"If you want my name on it."

"Why wouldn't I?" demanded David.

Milla shook her head, sighing as if she was talking to an idiot, and signed his cast, adorning her name with a bunch of flowers. "People will talk," she said faintly.

"About what?" asked David.

After that, they chatted for quite a time, during which Rebecca Read kept obtrusively out of the way. The talk turned to Meadows High and what a pit of hell it was. Talking of the school made David realize how much he would miss Nathan there, but at least he knew that he had found in Milla a kindred spirit with whom he could spend some of the time he would otherwise have been with Nathan. And that, of course, was what Nathan had intended: for Milla to replace him once his slow evanescence had reached its inevitable conclusion.

Chapter 18: The Witch

David was struggling to stay awake during double art. He had spent most of the night sitting up as before, waiting for the ghost to come, but again it had not made an appearance. Perhaps it was satisfied that he was no longer a threat to it, and had decided to leave him alone. Guy was not happy though. At breakfast, he told Rebecca and David how the new surveyors had taken one look inside the factory and had refused to go any further. He was also greatly upset that what he called 'vandals' had broken in to the place again. David felt a surge of guilt. He had completely forgotten about the surveyors. Luckily they hadn't come to any harm. He asked Guy what he was going to do with the factory.

"I'm going to try one more lot of surveyors. This time I'm going to call someone in from out of town, who hasn't heard that the place is supposed to be haunted. If they won't do it either, then there's only one thing I can do."

"What's that?" asked David.

Guy Read glared over his morning newspaper at his foster son. "Tear it down, of course," he snapped, and by raising the paper into David's eye line, made it clear that the conversation was over.

Now David was nodding off over his drawing of an old bottle when Miss Beauchamp wandered over to take a look at his progress. Miss Beauchamp was a thin, spectacled, frizzy-haired woman with an extremely relaxed attitude to teaching. She generally let the untalented children amuse themselves at the back of the class, also-rans cantering at the back of the field, while she devoted the bulk of her time to urging on those with more potential. She had evidently spotted that David (placed firmly within the also-rans) was more inactive than usual this morning.

"There are no angles in this bottle, David," she said, gently reproachful, and, sitting beside him, rounded out some of his angles into curves. She quickly got carried away with the drawing, and David, already nodding again, was only too happy to let her. At last she passed the pencil back to him. "Finish this up, and start on something else," she said, and drifted off to another set of tables. But that was one of his big problems with art. He never knew when a picture was finished.

At break time, the rain had temporarily cleared up, and the sun was shining brilliantly on the wet playground. David meandered towards the middle of the open space, while all around him children laughed and chatted, chased footballs and shouted to one another. He looked at his feet as he walked. From somewhere not too far away, he heard Rowse call out: "What's up, Carraway, lost your contact lenses?" David said nothing, didn't even lift his head; his bait not having been taken, Rowse soon wandered off.

David felt like crying, but knew that with the world and his dog watching, it would be a mortally embarrassing mistake, and so concentrated on staring at his shoes instead.

"Are you all right?" It was Milla's voice.

David nodded gently. He thought his voice would crack if he tried to speak.

"You still don't seem quite yourself."

David swallowed deeply and without looking at Milla said: "Sorry – I just – I guess I'm still not one hundred percent."

"Your brother not with you today?" asked Milla quietly.

"No, he –" began David, and then he realized what Milla had said. "*What did you say?*" he demanded, looking up at Milla's face for any sign of mockery, of which there was none, and immediately regretting the harshness of his tone.

"Do you think that you're the only one who can see him?" replied Milla.

David almost cried out with relief. But as this moment of near-joy (*she can see him, I'm not on my own any more*) swept over him, the strength seemed to weep out of his legs and he found himself sitting in a puddle. Milla's arm was quickly around him, helping him to his feet. She led him to a bench, and he sat down gratefully.

"Why didn't you tell me you could see him?" asked David.

"You only talk about such things with people you can trust," replied Milla.

"Didn't you trust me, then?"

"I don't trust anybody," Milla told him. "Except my grandma. She's a witch, you know. She says I've inherited the craft. My mum's livid. I'm not allowed to visit Grandma any more, but I do anyway of course. Mum says she mustn't fill my head with nonsense. Except it isn't nonsense, is it? It's true."

David said nothing, merely stared at her wild-eyed.

"You're not laughing," said Milla.

"Of course I'm not laughing," said David. Then he realized that Milla always seemed to be looking through people, or at something beside them, never at them. Was she seeing things that no-one else could? "Can you see lots of ghosts?" he asked.

"Sometimes it's just a feeling. With your brother I can see a shadow, usually right beside you. Sometimes your aura merges with his... it's quite beautiful," Milla said, slightly dreamily.

"My what?"

"Your aura. Today..." Milla's voice trailed off as she stared into space, just above David's head, letting her eyes defocus. After a few seconds, she nodded. "Yes, it's still grey. Sometimes when I've seen you it has been orange, sometimes yellow. When an aura is grey like yours it means you are ill or unhappy."

"You're incredible," David told her, and managed half a smile.

"Is that a compliment?" Milla asked, smiling in turn.

David opened his mouth to speak, but before he could say anything else, the bell rang for the end of break.

"Do you know the groundsman's hut? Down by the long jump pit?" Milla asked. David nodded. "Meet me there at lunch." She reached out, squeezed his good hand, and walked off without looking back. Everyone else was filing back into class again; soon David was the only one left on the playground. At last he pushed himself to his feet and headed off to the science block.

The hour-long science class seemed to last for a year; David had caught himself nodding off again on several occasions, and once Mr Gough swatted him around the head with his homework just as he was drifting into sleep. "Back to a D again, Carraway," Gough snapped. "That A was just an aberration after all."

"Sorry sir," David said. "I haven't been sleeping well."

When at last the class was over, David hastened straight down to the playing field. The vast field was empty at the moment; the kids who would later spill out and play football there were still eating their lunches in the dinner hall. The rain had returned, this time in the form of light drizzle, which was hanging and drifting in the air. Milla was already at the groundsman's hut, her head completely concealed by her large hood.

"You don't know what it means to have someone I can really talk to," David told her.

Milla grabbed him and put her arms around him, hugging him close, but said nothing.

David was slightly shocked at this. His first thought was that he didn't deserve someone being so nice to him. But he hugged Milla back anyway. "There's something I have to say," said David, over her shoulder. "If it hadn't been for Nathan, I wouldn't have helped you that day."

"Yes you would," said Milla in a voice that warned off any argument.

As they talked, children drifted out from lunch in twos and threes and set up several games of football. One of them was Peter Kelson. He spotted David lurking over at the groundsman's hut and called him over for a game.

"No thanks Kelly," shouted back David. "Stuff to talk about."

Kelly shrugged and got on with the game.

"Go if you want to," Milla told him, and gave him a little push.

"I don't want to," David said. "And anyway, there's something I want to tell you."

They leaned against the side of the hut, in the partial protection of the overhanging roof, and David explained all that had happened, from Nathan's reappearance at the cemetery to when he had been swallowed up by the ghost at the factory. He related how the ghost had found him at the hospital, and how rather than finish him off it had shown him a memory of a monster emerging from a coffin. He spoke about the professor, whom Milla thought sounded very strange and mysterious.

"I have to go and visit him after school – he'll know what to do if there's any chance at all that we can get Nathan back."

"Can I come too?"

"I'm not supposed to tell anyone about him – he's paranoid that some people – he won't say who – are after him. I'll ask him if he'll let me bring you along another time."

"You could always try the *chenda* first – see what *it* has to say," Milla suggested, looking out over the drizzle-soaked field, avoiding David's gaze.

"What's the *chenda*?" asked David.

"Your future. It's too wet out here – we'll have to do it in the groundsman's hut. If anyone finds us in there we'll just say we found it unlocked and wanted to get out of the rain."

"But it's locked."

Milla held the padlock in one hand and closed her eyes. *"lowev,"* she said softly. Three seconds later there was a quiet click and the hot padlock opened in her hand.

"Wow," David commented.

"That's pretty basic," Milla said, but she glowed a little with pride. "Come on into the dry and let's see what your future holds."

Chapter 19: The *Chenda*

The interior of the groundsman's hut was dusty, damp, and smelled of stale grass cuttings. There was lots of sporting equipment: piles of hula hoops, string sacks full of footballs or rugby balls, spring-loaded cricket stumps, hockey sticks, javelins and dismantled hurdles. In the darker corners there were hundreds of sheet cobwebs, their eight-legged denizens unseen in the shadows.

Milla sat down in the middle of the hut amidst the muddy detritus left by a hundred pairs of football boots and swept a small area of the wooden floor clear with the back of her hand. She gestured for David to sit down.

"Better pull the door to," he muttered, "or else everyone will be in here ransacking the footballs." With the door only open a crack, the grey drizzly daylight entering the hut was hardly enough to see by, so David was forced to push it back open a little: enough to let the light in, but not enough to advertise a sporting free-for-all to all the kids on the playing field.

He sat down and Milla took both his hands in hers. His left hand twinged a little as she rotated it palm up.

"You are right handed?" she asked him.

"Er – yes."

"Lucky for you, going by the state of your left hand," Milla said. She released his left hand and turned his right hand palm up, scrutinising it minutely. Her hands were warm. She peered intently at David's right palm for some time without saying anything. He watched as she traced over a pair of crossed lines on his left palm, close to his cut fingers.

"You see this?" she asked. "The cross of the Magus. Only those touched by the spirit world have this mark."

"Really?" asked David, suddenly interested despite an inbuilt scepticism. The cross of the Magus sounded like quite a cool thing to have.

Next Milla handed David a small leather pouch, which rattled lightly as he took it. "This is the *chenda*. Shake it, then empty it onto the floor," she ordered.

David upended the pouch. Out of it tumbled nine objects: three small mottled brown feathers, three flat, square stones, each of which had a different symbol etched into it, and what looked like three old dry chicken bones. The objects fell in three clusters: the feathers on top, the three stones next, and below them the three bones, which fell so that they were all connected.

Milla stared at the bones, stones, and feathers for a long time. She said nothing.

David waited for her interpretation. As he did so he pulled his water bottle out of his rucksack and swigged from it. "So what does it mean?" he asked finally, when he could bear the silence no longer. Still Milla did not speak. "Is it bad news? Am I going to die?" he asked, trying to make it clear from his tone of voice that he was joking.

"Well," said Milla, laying her hand on his, "that's just it."

"It is?"

"The thing is, according to your *chenda* you're *already* dead."

At this point a mouthful of David's water went down the wrong way and he spent the next three minutes doubled over coughing.

"I've come close to it a few times, including just now," David protested, "but that is frankly ridiculous." He looked from Milla to his fortune on the wooden floor and back.

"Not as ridiculous as it at first sounds," argued Milla. "The *chenda* thinks you are dead, even if you're clearly still in the land of the living. The feathers are the sky, spirit, the future; the bones are flesh, the present; and the stones are reality, the earth, and the past. The stones were placed exactly between your body and your spirit. The one under the ground, the other in the realm of spirits."

"But as you see, I'm still here," said David.

"Which a practitioner of the *chenda* would interpret as evidence that a powerful spirit, perhaps even a deity, had intervened to save you."

"Now I know that it's rubbish. It's hardly scientific, is it? The facts don't fit the theory, so the facts must be wrong." David immediately regretted his tone of voice.

"But what if it *were* true?" Milla asked, taking his disparaging attitude in her stride. "This isn't science we're talking about. Suppose something – it would have to be something with knowledge of the future – had altered your destiny? That would make you rather special, don't you think?"

David took a gulp of water. "I know I should be dead," he said quietly. "Because Nathan saved me. He should have lived, not me. No deity saved me – just a boy."

"Maybe that's it. He could see the future – as far as he needed to. He knew that it was a choice between him and you, and he picked you. His sacrifice has given you great power – the magical power to hide from fate, to tip the scales of chance in your favour –"

"No," interrupted David, "enough already."

"– and now that he's gone –"

"He's not gone until I say he's gone," David spat, glaring at Milla and daring her to argue.

"No," agreed Milla softly. She laid a hand on his arm and smiled.

David cycled to Professor Fuller's house feeling rather het up. When he arrived, the professor led David into the study, where he gave him a brief, firm hug.

"Everyone keeps hugging me," commented David.

"They're trying to tell you something," Professor Fuller said, but did not elaborate. "Now, tell me everything." He sat back in his leather armchair and listened while David reprised his encounters with the ghost of Tipler's. For the most part Fuller listened in silence, staring at the crackling fire, commenting only occasionally. This time David mentioned the vision of an arguing couple, at which Fuller muttered something under his breath. When David told him of his most recent encounter with the ghost in the hospital, the muttered words were "Interesting – very interesting – it wanted to show you how it died?" Finally, when he had finished speaking, David sat back and awaited a reaction: but a reaction was not immediately forthcoming. Fuller just sat there, staring into the fire, his angular features etched with flickering lines of deep shadow.

David remembered his tea, and phoned the Reads to let them know that he would be late. David spoke to Mrs Read, and explained that he was at Peter Kelson's house, and would be home shortly, surprised at how easily the lies tripped off his tongue.

"Actually, we're going out for dinner, so I've made you a sandwich," Rebecca Read told him. "Will you be all right on your own? You don't mind, do you? Only Guy sprang it on me, a bit of a surprise, you know what he's like..."

David was only too pleased to hear that he was not needed back. He returned to the study, and explained to the professor that, because the Reads were going out, he would not have to rush home.

"Going out?" repeated the professor, strangely interested. "Tonight? Really? Where?"

"Some restaurant."

"And they go out regularly?" he pressed.

David wondered where all this was leading. "Yes, I suppose so," he admitted.

"When do they come back – as a rule?" asked the professor, staring intently at David.

"Don't know. Elevenish. Not too late."

"I see. Would I be right in thinking that they were out on…" he turned away and leafed through a calendar, which was pinned up on the wall beside the desk, "October the twelfth?" so saying, he fixed David with a beady-eyed stare again.

"I'm not sure."

Professor Fuller nodded. "Make a note – discreetly – of the dates they go out, would you?"

"Why – what's this about?" asked David.

"Nothing, perhaps. Something, perhaps. Whatever, their absence will give us the chance to place a ward around your house to keep this ghost from coming to you there. You will at least be able to sleep peacefully tonight. Now," said Fuller, "about this ghost. Describe it to me again. The black, smoke-like form."

"It was as if the darkness was alive," David remembered, stumbling over his words. "He had a pale face, with streaks of black hair, thin on top. Eyes flat, watery… there was a smell – a smell of solvents – just like that night… the night Nathan was taken. But that was a man, at least I think it was. This – this was no man."

"It's all right," Fuller said kindly, patting David's arm. "And it manifested away from the factory… and was able to insert images into your conscious mind, images of a monster that came out of a coffin…"

David nodded.

"I would be lying if I told you these images did not mean anything to me. Exactly what I would rather not say immediately. But we have indeed got a powerful foe in this spirit," Fuller said. "It must be eliminated at the earliest opportunity; I do not believe it will remain contained in that factory for long, or that those who come to survey or tear it down will be safe. We need to find out who it was, if it is indeed a ghost and not something worse. Find that out, and we will find out what it wants, and knowing that might give us a way to bring it peace. Failing that, we'll just take the emitters down to the factory and fry it. But for now, it's nearly six, and we need to get you home and get your house protected. You could do with some sleep: there are rings under your eyes that you could balance a row of books on."

"Actually," David said apologetically, "it's ten past. I think your clock is running slow." Fuller's clock, which sat on the mantelpiece amid all the other clutter, was a beautiful object, but clearly wasn't very good at keeping time. A narrow waist connected the round clock face with a wide base, upon which grapes, butterflies and leaves in rich rosewood stood out against a mahogany background. As if on cue, the clock began to chime six o'clock.

"This clock has been ticking since Napoleon was rampaging across Europe," Fuller said, "so it can be excused for losing a few minutes, don't you think? We all slow down as we get older." With that, he tilted the clock forwards so that he could adjust the time and wind it up. "It's almost worth turning it back to hear it chime again, don't you think?" asked Fuller, somewhat wistfully.

"Er, it's nice," agreed David. But his worries could not be distracted by a Napoleonic clock. "Professor? It's my fault, isn't it? If I hadn't tried to exorcise the ghost, it wouldn't be as strong as it is."

Fuller shrugged, setting the clock back in pride of place in the centre of the mantelpiece. "It may be that you have stirred it up a little, as one might stir up a wasps' nest. But you did not invent this evil. For that we have to look elsewhere, into the past of that factory."

"What if it's more than a ghost? What if it eats ghosts, swallows them up and makes them part of itself – getting stronger each time..."

The professor sat heavily in his armchair and regarded David, a sudden spark in his milky eyes. "That might explain why it left you alone at the hospital – if there is a part of it that is Nathan, a part of it that loves you... but we won't know anything until we find out who or what it is, and for that, you need to get to the library."

"But what about you? Surely you're better at that sort of thing than I am?"

Fuller smiled. "Perhaps. But there are one or two other matters that I'm working on – I really can't spare the time. I'll help you when I can – but this is something that you must do. Get your new friend Milla to help you."

Ghost-proofing seventeen Chapman Close turned out to be a simple matter. Professor Fuller was only there for a moment, handing David a folded sheet on the doorstep and promising to return in the dead of night to lay a charmed salt-line around the house and its attached neighbour. The sheet – which David had been instructed to unfold and place under his mattress – bore a large double circle within which there was a five-pointed star; occult characters filled the space between the two concentric circles. It said a lot for David's confidence in the professor – and the level of his exhaustior – that almost as soon as the pentagram was arranged under his bed, he crawled into the covers and slept.

Chapter 20: The Monster in the Library

"You two want to *consult* the *microfilm?"* asked the librarian. A badge on her voluminous black cardigan gave her name: Pam. Pam was a large middle-aged woman whose fingers were dressed in chunky rings. A gold chain was hanging around her neck, and heavy earrings stretched her earlobes. Her half-moon spectacles hung from another chain.

"Is it a problem?" asked Milla, quietly determined.

"Heavens, no," said the librarian quickly. "It's just a little unusual for…"

"Young people?" Milla prompted. "So everything's on film, is it?"

Pam laughed. "Everything that we have, yes. What did you expect? That we kept the original newspapers?"

"I thought perhaps it would all be digitised, with a searchable index."

Pam began to turn purple.

David was standing next to Milla, enjoying the show. He was amazed at how confident Milla was with adults – instantly ready to engage them in conversation as an equal. They had come straight to the library from school, and were now at the help desk in the reference section – the old, original building behind the garish new extension. David would never have marched straight up to the desk and asked for help. Instead he would have spent an hour wandering around, probably find nothing, and resolve to come back another day. But Milla was far more organized. David knew that the Tipler factory had closed down in the 1950s – Guy had said as much – so Milla had decided that they should begin their search for information by looking at the Fairfield Daily from the relevant period.

Pam led them to the back of the reference library and through a fire door. They found themselves in a low, cinderblock corridor with bare concrete underfoot – another more recent addition to the old library. A fire extinguisher and a glass-fronted notice board were all that there was to break up the monotony of the corridor. The notice board's messages were cobwebbed, out of date; equally, David would not have put much faith in the condition of the dusty fire extinguisher. They passed several doors, marked ARCHIVE 3, ARCHIVE 2, and PRIVATE before they came to the microfilm room, marked ARCHIVE 1.

The room was narrow and cramped. A bench ran along one wall, almost lost under papers, box files and journals. On the other side of the room, what looked like a 1960s computer sat beside a row of filing cabinets.

"Here's the viewer," announced Pam, and flicked a switch on the side of what David had taken to be the ancient computer. The screen lit up, the machine humming. "The films are kept in here," she said, opening a fi ing cabinet. Within the large drawer was a jumble of small cardboard boxes.

"This needs tidying," observed Milla.

"Be my guest," agreed Pam, and swept out of the room, calling "the library shuts at half-past five," as a parting shot.

"Only one viewer," said Milla. "Do you fancy the microfilm or the local history section of the library?"

"Viewer," said David automatically. He didn't know what using the viewer entailed, but he knew that trawling through books was no fun, so decided to take his chance with the machine. It took them five minutes to load the first film, the first 1950s spool they found in the pile (May to August, 1956). After that, it was just a matter of winding the film on, scanning the headlines, focusing, zooming in and out, and reading. Milla went back into the reference library, warning David to keep a note of which spools he had checked through.

"What do you take me for?" asked David, slightly aggrieved at the veiled insult, but nevertheless grateful for the tip, which he hadn't thought of.

It took him perhaps fifteen minutes to get the hang of the viewer – two complete newspapers later – by which time the bright light had given him a headache and the job of turning the handle to move the film on had started to hurt his wrist (it was on the left-hand side of the machine). He sighed, sat back, and started doing some maths. There were… around one hundred and twenty papers on the spool. He had read two (one sixtieth) in fifteen minutes, which meant…at this rate it would take fifteen hours to do the first spool. At this point he nearly went to find Milla to suggest a change of tactics, but in the end he didn't. He would have to speed up, hope that something would leap out. He was supposed to be lucky, wasn't he?

He scanned the next ten papers in a little over five minutes, using his right hand to turn the handle, the awkwardness of which was making that hand hurt too. No mention of the Tipler factory or ghosts: lots about farming, sea defences, war, fishing, and local court cases.

He worked in near-silence: the only sounds when he wasn't winding the handle were the hum of the fan at the back of the viewer and the occasional drip from a squat dehumidifier just inside the door.

The only excitement for the next hour was the sudden appearance of a gigantic black fly an inch from David's nose. He jumped a foot in the air and his heart almost stopped at the appearance of this monster. A second after its appearance he worked out that the fly was no giant: it was a normal-sized insect that had somehow become trapped in the microfilm viewer. Next he had to work out how to free the fly, which was now getting increasingly agitated by the heat inside the machine. He had to remove a grill with his penknife and turn the machine off so that the fly, drawn by the light in the room, could find its way out. As it began to circle and bump into the bare lightbulb above him, he wondered why he had bothered to free it. He could just have waited until the heat in the machine cooked it: but if that seemed callous, dismantling the viewer to save it seemed beyond the call of duty.

Saving the fly reminded him that existence was binary: on or off, dead or alive. There was no grey area. Except for ghosts. He thought of Nathan then.

He thought of the on-off light in the hospital. He thought of Milla, and Drake, the ghost of the Tipler factory, and the white crow that had laughed at him at Nathan's mock funeral. But as he got back to scrolling through the micrcfilm it did not occur to him that he had encountered a fly in the library once already, when he had been researching exorcism with Nathan.

David had made his way through a month's worth of papers when Milla returned to see if he had made any discoveries. David admitted that he hadn't. He didn't mention the fly, but grinned to himself imagining how she would react if he did. Milla hadn't found anything either, but she presented him with a list of books that she had checked through, and suggested that they swapped over.

"This is going to take weeks," complained David.

"Unless we get lucky," agreed Milla.

Their fruitless search continued until closing time, carried on after school on Friday, and started again on Saturday morning. Then Milla had an idea. David was peering at a microfilm that was barely legible because it was so pockmarked with flowers of damp, when Milla came in, checked the list of papers they had looked through, then began to dig through the mess in the filing cabinet.

"Have you got a lead?" asked David.

"Maybe. Try this," said Milla, triumphantly holding up one of the spools.

David quickly wound back the spool he was looking at and inserted the new one in seconds (he was an old hand at this by now). "What am I looking for?" he asked.

"Third of June," Milla told him, leaning over his shoulder.

David reeled frantically through the spool, stopping every so often to check where he was. "What put you on to it?" he asked.

"Obvious really," she said. "Register of deaths. Thought I'd check for Tiplers and I found one. Might be nothing to do with the factory, of course..."

David had found the third of June. He scanned through. Nothing. Then he spooled through again, this time more slowly. There was no mention of a Tipler.

"Try tomorrow," suggested Milla. "I mean the next day."

David spooled on; and there it was, after hours of searching, the first piece of the puzzle of the ghost of Tiplers.

NEW TRAGEDY AT "CURSED" TIPLERS

Second Fatal Fall This Year

Yesterday William Tipler excused himself from a staff meeting, went up on the roof of his textile factory, and threw himself to his death.

William's brother-in-law, John Horton, who is also the manager of the factory, tried to prevent the suicide, but to no avail.

William Sr. had been "very unwell" since the death of his son earlier this year, which also resulted in a fall from the roof of the factory.

David read the tiny article through twice. Then he leapt to his feet, grabbed Milla's hands, and together they spun around the cramped room, scattering loose papers as they went.

"But what does it mean?" Milla asked, disengaging herself at last.

"Genius. It means you're a genius." David sat back down and spooled forward a day, looking for another item on the death of William Tipler, but there wasn't one. He spooled forward again.

"Who is the ghost? William or his son?" asked Milla. "That's the question."

"The son, of course," said David. "He chucked his own dad off the roof..."

"But why throw your dad off the roof? Don't you love your dad?"

"Don't complicate it. Please don't complicate it. Not when we're getting somewhere," moaned David.

"We need to find out more. See if there is anything more on William's death. I'll get going through the roll call of the dead to find out when William's son died."

After that, it was back to the drudgery of ploughing through the microfilm. Information trickled out, disjointed sentences scattered across what had until now been an absolutely blank page. William's son was also called William, and had died five months before his father. He had been "distraught at the death of his mother Amelia by drowning, to which event he was the only witness." Was Amelia Tipler's death significant? The report of her death was as dry as that of the others. What was certain was that Amelia Tipler's death had started a chain of events that had led to the death of her son and husband.

Just as David was contemplating yet another tiny nugget of data, he heard a door slam in the corridor outside. Heavy footsteps came down the corridor and halted suddenly – just outside the door to the microfilm room, it seemed. It was probably one of the librarians, wondering who was perusing the old papers. Then David noticed something else. There was a smell in the air that hadn't been there before, faint but clear. It was a high, nose-rankling solvent stink, a stink that David knew well.

David's hand froze in the act of winding the microfilm on. He turned – just his head, so as to make no noise – towards the door, which was open a crack. There was a moment – a long moment – when David could not decide whether to remain as still as he could, or to leap up and see if he could tip over the filing cabinet nearest the door, thus blocking it. But before his mounting terror could overcome his inertia, the footsteps started up again; the door into the reference library opened (he recognized the sound – it was a door he had heard open and close a hundred times while he had been sitting there), and the footsteps were gone.

David sagged in his chair. Could the smell be a coincidence, or was this the man who had killed Nathan? He could not be sure. And where had the footsteps come from? He had been sitting here for long enough to have heard the footsteps going the other way, coming out of the library – and there was nothing up the other end of the corridor, although perhaps it did connect in way unknown to him to the adjacent City Hall...

Two thoughts occurred to him almost simultaneously. The first thought was that here was a chance to identify the Solvent Man: the library was dotted with people, so he would surely be safe enough. The second thought was that he had to warn Milla to stay out of his way.

He was out of his chair, down the corridor, and slamming into the library ten seconds later. A dozen faces turned to see who had made the noise, and almost as one returned to what they were doing a second later. David hunted for someone walking away, someone with a heavy step... but the reference library was quite busy. There were at least thirty people in it. Many of them he had seen before. There was the librarian Pam, who was sitting behind her desk, reading; there was Edward, a considerably nicer librarian, replacing books on a shelf; there were the same old men who seemed to be there every day, reading the same books, David suspected more to keep warm than in order to learn... but where was Milla? He couldn't see her. He ran into the stacks, registering no more than a glimpse down each narrow aisle between; perhaps a third of the aisles had readers in them, but by the time he had got to the end, he still hadn't seen her. He doubled back, running faster... then he saw her, just beyond the central aisle that divided the long stacks. She was sitting on the floor, completely absorbed in a book that lay open on her lap.

There was a man walking away from David in the darkness between the bookshelves. He had a heavy, quick stride, which was eating up the distance between him and Milla.

David shouted automatically. "Milla!"

Milla looked around instantly. David imagined everyone else in the library looking over towards the shadowy stacks to see who was shouting. The man looked around too. Their eyes met. The faintest whiff of solvent lingered here, a token of the man's passing.

"Milla!" shouted David again. "Get out of there!"

Milla looked up at the man, who slowly turned again to meet her gaze. Then she was up and gone, running like a hare towards the far end of the stacks. David moved too, back along the stacks until he had reached the large open area in the middle of the reference library. As he arrived at a run, faces turned to look at him; then, at the far end of the library, Milla skidded into view by the doorway to the lending library, and everyone turned to look at *her*; then the man emerged from the central aisle and stood still, and everyone looked at *him*.

There was a moment's silence, before Edward, the nice librarian, let a book fall from his hand to the floor, where it landed with a heavy thud. He didn't pick it up.

The man was dressed in a long, expensive-looking woollen overcoat. His thin black hair hung in lank threads from his white, balding head. His face was pale, an almost deathly white blotched with purple – but the most striking thing about him were his eyes, which were flattened, fishlike discs, bloodshot and yellowed.

If David hadn't been certain before that this was the same man who had taken Nathan, he was now. "You killed my brother," he said quietly. Quiet as they were, the words would have been audible throughout the reference library. Nobody else was moving, or talking. Or, it seemed, breathing. Everyone was riveted on the ongoing drama.

The man said nothing, just stared at David and smiled, revealing two even rows of clean white teeth.

On impulse, David pulled his shadow lens out from where it hung on its chain under his shirt and put it to his eye, peering at the Solvent Man. As soon as he had brought the man into view, David took an involuntary step back and collided with a bookcase. The lens slipped from his wilting fingers and dropped to the end of its chain. His suspicion had been that he was looking at a monster. But he could not have conceived the true meaning of that word until that moment. *This* is who had me. *What* had me. *This* is what Nathan tried to fight… what chance did he have? David was afraid; he was terrified. But a slow-burning rage was building up in him, and as scared as he was, it would soon dwarf the fear that held him in check. *I will kill him*. Or he will kill me. David's hands knotted into fists.

The man was still smiling at him, but now the smile was even broader than before.

Everyone in the library looked from David to the man and back to David again to see who would make the next move, like spectators at a gunfight.

"Tristan!" said Milla sharply. Everyone glanced at her, but then returned their attention to David and the smiling man. Tristan? Who was Tristan? And then David realized that she was talking to *him*. But he did not have long to ponder why. The man, still grinning, put a forefinger to his face and pulled one of his lower eyelids down, exposing unpleasantly glistening flesh. *I'm watching you,* the gesture said. *Watching you with my fishlike eyes*. Then he turned on his heel and strode towards Milla and the exit. Milla danced out of the way, circling around one of the big tables; but he was not after her, he was leaving.

As the door swung closed behind him, there was a collective exhalation from everyone in the library.

"Who is he?" croaked David. Tension seemed to drain out of him; he felt unsteady on his legs. If Milla hadn't shouted, he might have snapped. What might have happened then he did not want to think about. He spoke again, his voice still dry. "Does anyone know who he is? He killed my brother."

There was no reply from any of the library users or either of the librarians. Milla was running over. "David, wait," she said.

David didn't wait. He swayed over to Pam at the counter. Milla arrived, grabbing him, but he twisted away. To Pam he asked: "Who was that? What was he doing down there?" he pointed towards the archive area. "I didn't hear him arrive."

"I'm sorry dear, but if you can't keep your voice down, I'll have to ask you to leave," Pam said, avoiding his gaze.

David leaned forward, dropping his voice to a whisper. "Who was it?" he asked.

Pam shifted uncomfortably in her seat. Her cheeks reddened. "I can't help you," she said quietly, and pretended to return her attention to her computer screen.

David turned to speak to Edward, the other librarian, but he had gone, the book he had dropped still lying on the floor. Everybody else was suddenly extremely interested in their books: no-one met his eye when David scanned the room for someone who was willing to speak to him.

Milla dragged a half-resisting David out of the reference library. When the door swung closed behind them, she said: "Come on. Let's get some hot chocolate."

As it turned out, they only had enough cash between them for one hot chocolate, and so sat together in a nearby café taking turns to sip from the same mug. The city centre was teeming with thousands of people, and there were dozens crammed into the tiny café. So many people gave them a sense of safety now, but they had felt anything but safe as they had crept out of the library, looking about for the Solvent Man, plunging into the thickest crowds of shoppers as quickly as they could.

"Tristan?" asked David.

"I didn't want to give him your name – like you gave him mine. He probably knows who you are now anyway, after that outburst."

"Sorry... I wasn't thinking. I shouldn't have used your name. There can't be many Millas in Fairfield."

"Maybe he thinks you were calling my surname: Miller. But next time call me Isolde if you want to get my attention."

"Who's Isolde?" asked David.

"Tristan's better half," said Milla quickly, taking a sip of hot chocolate. "Why did you tell him that you knew? Now he *knows* you know... I'm sure he was just going to walk past me, you know."

"Walk past you? No. Why would he detour that way if all he wanted to do was get out?"

"Maybe he didn't want to be seen. He could hardly have kidnapped me, could he? A cemetery at midnight is one thing, but a city library on Saturday afternoon..."

Milla's voice trailed off. David asked quietly: "Did you notice anything... odd... about him?"

"There *was* something strange about him, wasn't there? His aura was like a wriggling dark cloak... I've never seen one like it. Pam was lying to you by the way: she knows who he is, or something important about him anyway. But you saw something with your spook-detector, didn't you?"

David looked away, out of the window, where hundreds of flustered shoppers were scurrying past in the cold of December. Then he noticed an odd figure standing like a rock in the tumultuous, eddying surge of humanity: *himself*. He was looking at himself, but he was also looking at a ghost, a dead boy. His skin was as white as bone, his dark hair lank; he gripped a sword – like one of the professor's swords – tightly, and stared back at David, lost and desperate. The mass of pedestrians clutching their Christmas shopping walked by the dead boy without noticing him, as a mountain stream flows past a rock.

"Look! Do you see that?" He pulled out his shadow lens and looked again. Now the ghost-boy was alone: the shoppers were gone. The ghost stared into the café, as if he was looking for something within, as if he was straining to see where David and Milla were.

Milla looked. She saw nothing: he could tell by her expression. "See what?" she asked.

"Me… I'm standing out there…"

She looked again. "You're in shock, David."

"No, it's really –" he made to hand Milla the shadow lens, but then the figure was gone for him too: it staggered slightly, glanced over its shoulder, and hurried on, fading from view in a few moments like a dream upon waking. "He's gone. He just looked over his shoulder and hurried on, as if he was being followed."

Milla took the shadow lens and scanned the crowd of shoppers. She saw nothing out of the ordinary. "Weird. I'm supposed to be the one who can see the future."

"Do you think it's the future? I looked like I had been through the mill, and I was holding one of the professor's swords…"

"You generally *have* been through the mill. And if you're going to be swanning about the city with the professor's swords, you had better start learning how to use them."

"I wouldn't call what I was doing *swanning*… and you can't just go swanning about Fairfield carrying a sword…"

"Then let's hope you're seeing things."

"Yeah."

"Tell me about the Solvent Man," Milla said, poking him in the chest gently.

David sighed. He kept his gaze directed out of the window, still looking for his vanished doppelgänger. "He's not human," he said simply. He did not have time to say more, for suddenly a man sat down at their table. At first David didn't look over; when he did, he saw that they had been joined by Edward, the nice librarian.

Edward looked from David to Milla and back again, saying nothing for a moment.

"You know who he is," David said.

Edward looked over to the door. Then he scanned the room, looking carefully at every single customer one by one. Nobody seemed to be paying them the slightest attention. Finally he spoke, his voice a hoarse whisper. "Stop digging. For God's sake, stop digging, because you're digging your own graves."

"Just tell us what you know," David said. "That's all. That's why you followed us, isn't it?"

"NO!" Edward's voice was loud enough to attract a few glances. "No," he said, more quietly, "I came here to warn you. You don't know what you're getting into. Believe me, I wouldn't start down this path if I knew where it would lead. That man you saw..."

"That was no man," hissed David. He remembered that when he was small, when his parents were alive, the cat would sometimes kill a bird and leave it to fester and decay. He recalled finding dead birds whose body cavities were full of blowfly larvae. Sometimes the pressure of all those writhing insects would split the bird's skin open, and the maggots within would tumble out or burrow between one another, desperate to escape from the hateful light that had invaded their nest.

As those carcasses were, so was the Solvent Man. Under the gaze of the lens, he was a vast clew of worms, nothing more, giant glistening worms sliding and slipping over one another to form a heaving mass of living decay. David knew this now. The Solvent Man knew that he knew. And, quite clearly, the Solvent Man didn't care.

Edward covered his eyes and whimpered softly. "Forget what you know. If you pursue this, you'll end up dead. Don't come back to the library. It won't be safe." With that, he pushed back his chair and strode to the door, letting it slam behind him.

Chapter 21: The Corrupt

When David and Milla turned off Marsh Lane and into Professor Fuller's driveway, David stopped dead in his tracks and grabbed Milla by the arm to stop her too. "That's not the professor's car," he hissed. A large white estate car sat in the driveway. The professor's car was a small, racing green sports car.

"He's allowed to have visitors," said Milla.

"He doesn't have visitors," David assured her.

"What are we then?"

"Look – let's just check to make sure." David led Milla down the side of the house, creeping past the white car and into the back garden. Half an apple – clean and fresh – was hanging from the washing line as usual. They peered through the kitchen window, cupping their hands around their eyes. Almost the first thing they saw was Professor Fuller walking past. He noticed the two young faces pressed up against the glass out of the corner of his eye and turned to them, squinting quizzically.

The professor let them in the side door. "You must be Milla," he said, shaking Milla's small soft hand with his giant gnarled one. "I'm Robert. What are you two doing sneaking around?" he asked mildly.

"It was the car," explained David.

"Aha. Good thinking. It's mine. Had to sell the MG for a fraction of its worth – and that monstrosity is the best replacement I could find."

"You got rid of your sports car for this?" asked David incredulously.

"The MG stood out in a crowd – at least this heap is anonymous," said the professor. He led the way through to the study. The first topic of discussion was the history of the Tipler factory. David outlined what they had discovered while Milla examined the objects on the professor's mantelpiece. She was particularly interested in a glass sphere on a three-legged stand, which seemed to be full of thick, opaque mist, an object that David, too, had noticed on his first visit to the professor's house. "A crystal ball?" she asked.

"Not exactly," replied the professor, "more of a secret weapon. Best not to touch it."

Milla took her hand away sharply and moved along the mantelpiece a little way.

When David had summarized all that they knew, the professor leaned back in his easy chair and thought for a moment. "So," he said at last, "first Amelia Tipler drowns in Grey Lake, an apparent accident witnessed only by ten-year-old William. Then William is murdered and his body is thrown off the Tipler factory to make it look as if he fell, whereupon his father, seemingly distraught, leaps from the same roof – three deaths following one upon the other like dominoes, and within a year of the third of them, the factory is on the verge of closure – skittish workers mumbling about a malign presence and cheap foreign labour conspiring to bring about the end of one of Fairfield's oldest companies."

"That's just about it," agreed David.

"And the ghost, we presume, is William Junior, adopting a form that he himself feared, which means –"

"Professor," David interrupted. "At the library. The man who killed Nathan was there – if you can call him a man... through my crystal..." David pulled it out from under his shirt for emphasis, "through the crystal he looked..."

Professor Fuller turned several shades whiter. For a few seconds he stared rigidly at David. Then he said: "What do you mean by 'if you can call him a man'? What did you see?"

David stared at the gleefully crackling wood fire as he replied: "He is nothing but worms, huge red shiny worms turning and twisting and burrowing – under those posh clothes there is nothing but..." he groped for a word, aware of Milla staring at him in shock.

"Corruption?" asked the professor gently. He held his hand out for the crystal, which David passed to him. The professor peered through it, and then found a hand lens in a drawer and inspected the crystal through that.

"Corruption," David agreed. "In the cemetery, he was solid enough. He had me pinned down. He was real. Then at the factory… you're right. William Junior met the Solvent Man too, that's why he took on that guise. And now this – in the library, as solid and real as ever, with all those worms underneath…"

"I've only seen him once," Milla said, "but he's not a ghost, and David's right, he's not human, but I could only see a suggestion, a hint of what lies beneath his cloaking aura."

"You can see auras? Impressive," the professor said to Milla, then sighed and rubbed his forehead vigorously. "If you see him again, run, run for your life. If I had known there was a chance he would turn up in the library I would never have sent you there. For that matter I would never have set foot in there myself."

David and Milla waited for the professor to say more, and after a few seconds' thought, he did. "He was the one who took your brother, David. There is little doubt about it. As to whether he – it – killed him, that is another matter. The ghost of your brother was taken by a ghost, a separate matter entirely. It is the ghost of someone who has as deep a terror of that monster as you should have," the professor said. "One who, I think we agree, has taken the form of the creature it fears. Milla – would you rather I said no more? You must understand, knowledge is dangerous. Knowledge is something we strew unwittingly about us, a trail for others to follow… and follow they will…"

"I want to know everything," Milla said firmly.

"If he knows who you are, he will single you out," said the professor sadly. "There is nothing I, or anyone, could do to stop him."

"He already knows who I am," David said. "Why else would he have been hanging around the cemetery at midnight?"

"Don't assume your identity was known. It may have been predicted that two boys would be in the cemetery… less likely that it would have been known who they were."

"How could *anyone* have known we were going to be there?" demanded David.

"How could anyone have known you were going to be there, *even if* they knew your identity?"

Milla, apparently exasperated at the slow drip of this supposedly dangerous information, started to sketch out what facts she knew or could deduce. "He's not human. A monster made of worms. He kills children –"

"I didn't say *he* killed them," the professor said.

David had a sudden vision of that grey, fanged creature he had seen or imagined crawling towards him from the polished coffin… remembered the reeking pad clamped over his mouth and nose… "He gets them for someone else. *Something* else. Is that what happened to Nathan? That cellar… the coffin…?"

"You said your brother had no memory after being taken."

"He didn't – but William Tipler does. That's why he showed me that scene – that was what happened to him…" David trailed off.

"There are things…" the professor began slowly, "…things I have planned to tell you in time. You have just opened the book; you have read as far as page ten. Now suddenly you want to skip forward, to find out how the story ends; but the huge passage in between could be the difference between life and death, even if it does not hold the information you want. Do you see?" The professor sat back in his chair and helped himself to a splash of golden Hibiki. He drank a small quantity of the whisky, massaging his heart with his spare hand. "They call him the Alchemist. His age is unguessed at. He was probably resident in this fair city before gas lamps lit the streets. The

Ephemerae, a secret organisation dedicated to hunting down his master, called him simply The Corrupt. From what you have said, we now know why."

"So that vision I saw of the creature in the coffin…"

"I believe it was accurate. Listen – both of you. Why do you think I came back to Fairfield after so many years away? Not to die alone in this little cottage. I came back for them. The Alchemist and his master. Soon I'll tell you everything you want to know – but first we have a shot at getting Nathan back, and we need to concentrate on that. His presence could give us an edge without which our chances, already slim, would vanish entirely."

"This has something to do with my parents also," David surmised.

Professor Fuller stared out of the window. The sky was beginning to darken. He did not contradict David. "Meet me at the factory at eleven o'clock tomorrow morning. I have some modifications to make to that hideous contraption in the driveway."

"Are we going to…" began David.

"Fry it?" asked Fuller. "Yes we are. And bearing in mind certain complications that have just arisen, I think we should do so as soon as is humanly possible."

Chapter 22: Chasing Shadows

David met Milla at the bottom of her road at a little after ten o'clock the next morning. Milla looked the part of a teenage exorcist – her hair, normally arranged in demure fashion, was pinned up in an efficient-looking manner, and she was wearing a black PVC jacket and shades to match with round lenses little larger than two-pence pieces. These apparently made it easier for her to see auras, perhaps by partly dimming and tuning out everyday light. She could hardly look more different than the geeky girl he had met at school. As they walked, Milla pulled a string of charms from her pocket and fastened it around her neck.

"Didn't want Mum to see it," she explained, "in case she recognized it – it's Gran's. She'd know what it was for, too –"

"She knows you're going after a ghost?" asked David.

"No. I didn't tell her that. But she'd be okay with it. She would see it as part of my education," Milla said evenly. "She fell down the stairs a few months ago and has been in a nursing home ever since. She doesn't say much. But she hears everything."

"I'm sorry…"

"'s okay."

The morning was cold and crisp. Hollow, frozen puddles splintered under their feet they walked.

"You don't have to do this, you know," David said after a time. "It's my fight. Last time I barely got out of there…"

"I wouldn't miss it," Milla said dismissively. "Besides, the ghost got you out of there himself. He doesn't sound so bad. Just misunderstood."

"Whatever he is, he's got a fearful temper. How do you think he's going to feel when we start turning the professor's machine on him?"

They had reached the old industrial area at whose rotten heart was the crumbling Tipler factory. Boarded-up buildings skulked behind broken chain-link fences and weed-ridden redbrick walls. The factory yards, where they could be seen, were full of giant rusting pipes and obscure dead machines. It was as if the entire district had been abandoned in a hurry decades earlier – workers downing tools and departing with not a glance over their shoulders. Everything was quiet and still, but David could imagine a secret cacophony echoing in the empty rooms of these old factories. Ghosts watched them come.

"Charming," commented Milla.

"Ripe for redevelopment," David rejoined. "We're nearly there. That's it, up ahead." The Tipler factory was a hundred yards further along the road, its high brick wall standing out among the rusted chain-link fences of its immediate neighbours. There was no sign of the professor, and David found his footsteps slowing as memories of his last visit there fed his anxiety. The low sun gave the factory a metallic, emotionless light, as cold as the frozen puddles crackling beneath their feet. The factory's solidity, its permanence, began to sap what little confidence David had that this enterprise would have a successful outcome.

"How do we get in?" Milla asked brightly, apparently unaffected by the malaise that was growing in her companion.

"We walk the plank," David said tersely, and showed her the alleyway between the two factories. With a shock he recognized his forgotten bike, bright amidst the rusting, frost-filmed junk in the alleyway. Milla was all for going straight into the courtyard, but David was adamant that they must wait outside for the professor.

"Do you visit her much – your Gran?" asked David, unable to bear even a brief silence. From here in the alley the Tipler factory was out of sight. He didn't like the idea of it being so close and yet still hidden, and backed away until the roof of the factory rose into view over the high wall.

"Saw her last evening," Milla replied, following him. "The Acorns, the home's called. It's okay — the manager's always pleased to see me take Gran for a walk in her wheelchair. I did a little spell to protect her room against evil spirits. She did the same for my house back when I was born. Strange how we just carry on as if the world is completely normal — as if there are no monsters—"

Milla was interrupted by a loud crash. The sound had come from the factory next door to Tipler's, the smaller, more modern building. "I hid from Robbie Drake and his gang in there when I first came this way," David said.

"There's someone in there," Milla said, staring hard at the blank wall. "Was there anyone living there then…?"

"Dunno. Not sure. Didn't have a torch last time. Do now." David clicked his little LED torch on and off. "Whoever they are, we'd better warn them off trying to move in next door." He was already stepping over the collapsed chain-link fence to investigate. Rounding the corner, he recognized the loading bay and its triangular entry way formed by the bent-back corner of corrugated metal. "This is not the spot to set up home," he said, "and as for next door…"

"In half an hour it will be fine," Milla said.

David wondered where she got her confidence from. If his experience at Tipler's had taught him anything, it was that overconfidence was dangerous. "Hello!" he called. "Hey! It's not safe in here." His words brought an obvious response from within the factory: a scuffle of movement. "We just want to talk," David added. He banged on the corrugated iron sheeting forming the crude door, and recognized the sound: the sheeting slamming back into place had been the first noise they had heard. There was no reply. "You coming?" he asked Milla, and ducked through under the loose flap of metal into the gloomy interior. It took a few seconds for his eyes to adjust to the darkness within. The room they had entered was largely empty apart from some scattered debris. To their left was the stairwell that David had already once climbed; ahead, a broad opening led to the main space of the factory. What had looked like a miniature forest on his first visit turned out to be just that: the heart of the factory had been partly reclaimed by nature, and a thicket of butterfly bushes had grown up under what little remained of the glass roof high above.

"Wow," Milla said. "It's like the Eden Project."

"Yeah, except it's all weeds, the roof is broken and it's freezing cold." David led the way to the steps. In seconds what little light permeated from the doorway was gone, and they had to rely on the faint glow of David's torch to reveal their way. A few steps up there was a crunch as David stepped on something, and then another; he directed his torch down and saw that, as on his first visit, he had flattened two large snails.

"Sorry… forgot to mention the snails. Watch out for the snails."

"Urgh…"

"Couldn't see them last time… impressive beasts, aren't they?" David tried to sound cool, but he had never seen snails of such size outside of a pair of African land snails that had been kept as pets at his infant school. These molluscs, if similar in size, were different in shape – more apple-shaped than tapered like the African land snails had been.

"The idea of walking up here in the pitch darkness is making me feel sick," Milla said.

"Huh. You ought to try next door. Much more fun."

The two snails David had killed were only the vanguard of a legion: both under their feet and all over the walls, snails inched along in all directions, their silver trails catching the torchlight and reflecting it back. They seemed to be eating the peeling, mould-ridden wall covering, perhaps having strayed from their home in the indoor copse of butterfly bushes.

"Hello?" David called again. His voice echoed back to him in the silence. He was beginning to wonder whether they should just back out of the place and wait for the professor. Then he noticed something: on the step above him there was a freshly squashed snail, with a trail of juice running away from it and off the edge of the step. He put out an arm to stop Milla and showed her the dead snail. As they stood there, a faint susurration became audible, like static on an old record – it was, they slowly realized, the rustling of this nation of snails creeping over the walls.

A louder noise – the sound of movement – came from their right, along a balcony that led from the first floor landing. On his first visit, David had assumed that the stairs exited into a corridor – but in better light, with a torch, he saw that it was in fact a balcony that was completely open on one side. On their left, a rusted railing prevented the unwary from tumbling into the indoor woodland below; the tops of the bushes were a few feet below the first floor level, while far above them, grey daylight showed through the gaping roof. On their right, a succession of former offices opened up off the balcony. The staff in these offices had once had a good view of the workers below; now the offices were empty, and looked out only on a building slowly falling to ruin.

"Carraway?"

Both of them recognized the voice. Robbie Drake.

They exchanged a glance. David suddenly remembered Drake's request for a meeting he and his sister had not turned up for. It occurred to him that he had not seen either of them since.

"He's alone," Milla said quietly.

David led the way forwards, motioning Milla to stay clear of the rickety balcony rail. How close he might have come to disaster on his first visit, he didn't like to contemplate...

They passed two dark, doorless offices, empty apart from snails, brick rubble and aerosol cans; in the third room there was sudden movement as David played the torchlight around: his arch nemesis, Drake. His white face, caught in the light, was quickly hidden by an arm snatched up to protect its eyes against the glare.

"Drake?" David asked automatically.

"Get that bloody light off me," hissed Drake.

David directed the torch away from Drake. There was still enough light on him to make out that he was sitting propped against the wall, his lower half covered by a sleeping bag. He was surrounded by old newspapers and bin bags, some of which had split open, their vile-smelling contents sloughing out onto the floor.

"What are you doing here?" asked David. Drake must have run away from home. What had he done this time?

"Carraway. I might have known," muttered Drake. "If you tell anyone I'm here I'll kill you."

"We won't tell anyone if you don't want us to," David said calmly. A threat from Drake right now was as frightening as a butterfly. "But why are you here?"

Drake laughed bitterly by way of answer. "Who's that with you?"

Milla stepped forwards. "The freak, the mutant, the half-breed, the mongrel... what else have you called me this year...?" she said quietly.

Drake laughed. His mouth hung open, like it always did, and his eyes were as expressionless as usual. He still had the look of a hyena. But this hyena's confidence was gone: his laugh was empty, humourless, forced. "How's your arm?" he asked at last.

"My arm...?"

"It looks a lot better in the cast. God, I nearly hurled when I saw it the first time..."

And suddenly David and Milla simultaneously understood. Drake had been living here when David had tried to exorcise the ghost of the Tipler factory. It was Drake who had carried him to a place where the ambulance crew would find him.

"Nice to see you're still alive."

Before either David or Milla could gather their thoughts to reply, Drake spoke again.

"Thought you were dead. Seriously. What the hell were you doing there?"

Drake saved me. *Drake.* The kid I thought was a monster. The kid I hid from in this very ruin. David's thoughts spiralled; all he could muster to say was: "H-how did you find me?"

"How d'you think? Heard this voice. About two in the morning. Couldn't sleep – too cold. Had a look from the window – and there was this nutcase shouting something at the next factory along – then going down like a sack o' spuds, bam, spark out. I wasn't sure it was you 'til I got there. Had an inkling cos you were shouting 'Nathan…'"

"You saved my life. I can't believe it. I wouldn't have banked on you to save me."

Drake laughed again. "Is that what passes for thanks in Carraway land? You don't know me. Anyway, you owe me one now. Shame I can't cash in on that…"

"Where's Rebecca, Robbie?" David felt compelled to use his saviour's first name. He hadn't seen Robbie or Rebecca since the day of the fight.

"Don't talk about my sister!" Robbie Drake was instantly transformed into the Hyena that David knew so well: gleaming eyes, dropped jaw, knotted posture. He half-rose, a knife suddenly shining in his hand.

Milla raised her right hand, as if ready to send him back into the rubbish pile by a force of will. But the tempest blew itself out before it had really begun. The momentary rage in Robbie Drake's eyes faded and he slumped back.

"Don't say her name like that," he said quietly. "It's Becks."

"All right then: where's Becks?"

"We should have left. It's what I said we should do. But we didn't. I guess they thought he'd told us something. But he hadn't, not really."

"Who?"

"Da'! My old man. You know, I've been thinking about it, and she wanted to save me. The only way she could think of to do it was to keep me away when she knew they were coming for us. So they only took her. But I arrived too soon. I was supposed to get detention but didn't... thanks to Carraway playing the hero as usual... I was this close to getting it myself." Robbie indicated about an inch between a finger and thumb to show just how close.

"Who are they? Where's your dad?"

"Why? What do you care?"

"Like you said. I owe you one now."

"This ain't something you can help with. She wanted me to tell you, Becks did. But I thought it would be easier to smash your face in instead. Sorry 'bout that."

"And yet you pulled me out of the yard next door."

"Yeah, well, that was different. What do you think I am, a monster?"

I did until a few moments ago, David thought. Then he remembered why they had come into the factory in the first place: to warn its occupant about the Tipler place. "Robbie: don't go in the factory next door. The Tipler factory. There's a ghost. It's not nice."

"A ghost?" Drake said scornfully. "Ghosts don't scare me. Nor do giant snails or the dark. I'm scared of the guy who smells like the cleaner's cupboard, him and his scarecrow mate in their big black car –"

"The man who smells like the cleaner's cupboard?" David interrupted.

"Why? D'you know him? You don't know him. He took –"

"My brother."

"Becks."

"Tell me what you know about him."

Drake shrugged. "He works for the Master, or the Guild, or its Fathers. Same as Da' did. Except Da' was stealing from them. They did him in I reckon.

Don't suppose I'll see him again. Then they came for me an' Becks 'cos of what he might have told us."

"You have to go to the cops…"

Drake laughed at this idea. "There are four kinds of people in this city, Carraway. One: those who know nothing about the Guild and they mostly get ignored. Two: those who are *in* the Guild, and they are most of the important people and run the place. Three: those like Da' who work for the Guild. And four: those who aren't in the Guild, but know more about it than they should. The last lot don't stay around for long."

"How do you know all this?"

"I told you. Da' worked for them and told me stuff he shouldn't have."

"And Rebecca – Becks – could see the future. She knew the Alchemist –"

"Who?"

"The guy who smells like the cleaner's cupboard."

"Huh."

"She knew he was coming, so she told you to get detention so you'd get away."

"She used to claim she could see the future. Sometimes it seemed she really could. But that's impossible, huh?"

"No," Milla said.

David thought of his own vision of himself the day before, and agreed with her.

There was the sound of a car approaching and drawing up nearby. Professor Fuller.

"I'm going to come back – I want to know everything you know about the Alchemist. Is there anything I can bring…?" David asked Drake.

"Food would be useful," muttered Drake, as bitterly as if he was a soldier who had just surrendered to the enemy. "I can't remember when I last ate."

David went through his pockets. He knew that there was no food there, but he at least had a handful of change. Beside him, Milla produced some coins too. David handed over the key to his bike lock as well. "This is a loan. I want it back when I can cycle again."

"Yeah, sure. Thanks, whatever."

"Where're Moxy and Clegg when you need them?"

"To be honest, I'd rather trust my back to you two than them. Ain't that saying something? You're a peach, Carraway. Thanks for the tip. Now get out. Oh – and whatever your name is…" he gestured at Milla. "No hard feelings. Them things I said were nothing personal. I hate everyone the same."

"But I don't think you do," Milla said, and left the room.

David followed her, but hesitated in the doorway. "I'll be back," he called over his shoulder.

"Bring chips, and make sure they're hot, yeah?"

When David and Milla returned to the front of the Tipler factory, dazzled by the bright morning light, they saw the professor's battered white estate idling outside the gate, its diesel engine gushing black smoke. The old man emerged, looking unusually unkempt. His hair was untidy, smudges of grease decorated his face, and his eyes had black rims beneath them. "Everybody here?" he asked cheerfully. He looked at his watch. "Sorry I'm late. Damn thing needs work – and I'm no mechanic. I was up half the night modifying the emitters and when I got up this morning, the car wouldn't start. Now I don't dare switch her off. Idling unevenly. Dodgy valve maybe. Flaky starter motor as well. What a heap of junk. Sometimes you can keep them going by banging them with a hammer." He gestured behind him at the old car, which was idling unevenly: sometimes the engine sounded as if it was racing, while at other times it seemed close to cutting out. He produced a key from his pocket, marched up to the padlock that secured the gates, and unlocked it.

Milla and David stared in amazement. Neither of them spoke for a moment. Then Milla asked: "Where did you get the key for that?"

"From a hardware shop in town," muttered the professor, swinging the gates open.

"But how did you know how to cut the key?" persisted Milla.

"It came with the padlock. I snapped the other one off yesterday and replaced it with this one. Thought it would save time today. Any more questions?" Without waiting for an answer, the professor trotted back to the car and drove it through the gateway. "Close the lock behind you, could you?" he called as he inched past David and Milla. They each swung one gate closed and Milla clicked the padlock shut. Then they followed the car through the scattered rubble in the yard and past the burnt-out wreck until they reached the front door of the factory.

The professor got out of the car again, leaving the engine running. "With the gate locked behind us, we're not likely to be disturbed," he told them, and then turned to stare at the front of the old factory. "Charming place," he said.

David pulled his shadow lens from under his shirt and squinted at the factory through it. Everything he could see was grey and twisted, as if he was staring through a piece of broken, dirty bottle, but there was no sign of the ghost. "What about Nathan?" he asked. "If the ghost has swallowed him..."

"Won't the emitters fry him also?" finished the professor. "I don't think so. I've thought about it, and this is what I think we should do. If we hit the creature with the emitters on low, we should agitate it enough to split it into its constituent parts – if, as we think, it is a conglomerate of more than one spirit. Then we'll locate Tipler himself and give him the full dose. Okay?"

David nodded, still not entirely convinced. He looked at Milla, who was staring into space. "Milla? Are you all right?" he asked, grabbing her arm.

Milla's eyes refocused. "There's nothing here at the moment – not that I can see," she said.

The professor got back in the car, popped open the bonnet, then opened the glove box and plugged some black leads into a gadget within. Then he got out and fiddled with the car's battery with a pair of insulated grippers. Next he walked around to the back of the car. The seats were down and the back was full of equipment. David and Milla watched as the professor unpacked most of the gear until all that was left in the boot was a laptop computer.

"Right," said the professor. "Plan of action." He snapped open the computer and started it up. "Live video capture," he explained. "There are two emitters, so I think two of us – you and I, David – will go into the factory."

"Wait a minute," objected Milla. "Just because I'm a girl –"

The professor held up his hand. "You'll have a job to do, I promise. It's most important that the car doesn't stall. If it does – we'll be without power for the emitters. Should that happen at an inopportune moment –" he left the sentence hanging, and then switched to explaining how to start the car, despite her protestations that she knew what to do.

"Generally you more or less turn the key. However, this beast's a bit touchy. It doesn't like starting from cold and when it gets hot it flutters and eventually cuts out. If it really won't start, take this hammer," he picked up a machine hammer and waved it briefly before dropping it back into the back of the car, "and bang the starter three times. I'll show you which bit in a minute. Then try it again. Okay? You can also watch the live feed on the laptop. The cameras can see beyond the visible spectrum – so you might see something we don't." He showed her how to alter which of the two cameras and which of the five available channels were displayed on the live output. "Anyway, it can't be trusted to keep running on its own so we need someone to keep an eye on it."

"All right," Milla said, but she seemed reluctant to stay outside where it was safe.

Next the professor showed Milla how to pop the bonnet open and pointed out which bit of the engine she should bang as a last resort.

While this was going on, David wandered off a little way. He didn't think that hitting the car was a sensible way to get it working again, but he assumed that the old man knew what he was doing. Once more he peered at the factory through his shadow lens, and again it seemed to be nothing more than an old, abandoned building. "Nath," he breathed, "we're coming to get you." Then the professor was calling him over to demonstrate the operation of the emitters. They were the same ones that he had seen in the professor's front room, the ones that had disposed of the monkey ghost that had haunted Michael Andersen. They had each been modified by the addition of a protective frame and a tiny digital camera, gaffer-taped to the top; cables ran from the emitters to the laptop and the gadget in the glove box, which served some function known only to the professor. The controls themselves were simple enough. There was an on-off switch, a dial marked from one to ten (currently indicating three), and two LEDs – one marked 'power', the other 'charge', both of which were currently blank.

"How do those things work?" asked Milla.

"In a nutshell? They work on the principle of electromagnetic resonance. Universes are no more than vibrations in dimensions beyond our understanding – but after painstaking research I have found a frequency that harmonizes with both our universe and that of the Shadowland beneath it. Have either of you ever seen footage of the Tacoma Narrows suspension bridge?"

Milla shook her head. So did David.

"Look it up. You'll be amazed at what resonance can do. But not," added the professor quickly, "at the library. Why do you think prime numbers get the attention of ghosts? Because primes resonate in the Shadowland. They ring through to them like the chiming of a bell." He turned to David. "Are you ready?"

"No. But I'd go to the gates of Hell to get Nathan back if that's what it took. So let's go."

As he said the words *gates of Hell*, an image sprang into David's mind: he saw himself clinging to the top of a ladder… or a ladder with a section missing… and above him, on the bottom rung of the next piece of ladder, out of reach, sat a big black crow, fluttering its wings and laughing at him: *Krra!*

"Let's hope we don't have to go quite that far," commented Fuller. Then he saw the stunned expression on David's face. "David? Are you all right?"

"Fine," David muttered, and began to follow. The vision of the crow had vanished as quickly as it had appeared: but its laughing call lived on, an echo that only he could hear. Crows… first a white crow at the cemetery, now a black crow on a curious ladder… he looked up at the roofs of the buildings around them, suspecting that what he had just imagined had been triggered by a real crow: but there were no crows to be seen, no birds at all in fact.

"Good luck," said Milla.

"Good science," countered the professor, and walked on, leading David to the front door of the factory.

They carried one of the emitters each, their cables unspooling behind them as they walked away from the car. The professor had also brought a holdall overflowing with assorted equipment. When they arrived at the boarded-up door, he pulled a crowbar from the bag and started systematically ripping the boards off. David turned to look back at Milla, who waved with a smile. He gave her an abbreviated thumbs-up. Then the boards were gone, the way was clear, and he entered the Tipler factory for the second time.

Although occasional dusty shafts of sunlight punctuated the gloom of the factory, the sudden change in the level of illumination meant that David was unable to see enough to move any further for a few moments. The professor had already gone some way ahead of him, visible as a bobbing torchlight in the darkness. He stopped walking and muttered something, which David realized too late had been directed at him.

"Sorry?" he asked.

"I said we needn't go far. Don't move – I just want to scan you."

"What?"

The professor pulled something else out of his bag. David could vaguely see him waving whatever it was around. After a few moments there was a hum – like a wasp colliding with a light shade – then another, and another each time the professor swung the object through the air.

"Same as the emitters – but a passive, directional sensor. You'll be glad to know that you have a soul – or at least, some presence in the Shadowland." The professor pointed the sensor around and about, up and down; the only response was when it was pointing at David. "Here – leave the emitter there and take this torch, will you, while I make a few lines."

David took the proffered torch and pointed it at the floor while the professor cleared some pieces of rubble from a large area of floor, and then marked out a rough circle with chalk, string and a lump of putty. As he followed the professor with the torchlight, David kept his lens up to his eye, but all that he could see were faint beams of sunlight, twisted into brownish smears by the action of the crystal. The professor completed his circle – the two ends joined up quite well – then started forming another, slightly smaller circle inside the first.

"I don't see anything," said David.

"You will soon," replied the professor calmly.

"I know," David said, trying to keep the nervousness out of his voice.

When the professor had finished with the second circle, he began to fill the gap between them with symbols. "This is all gibberish – but don't tell anybody. Let's let William Tipler think we're here for a traditional exorcism – then we'll give him the *à la mode*. That ought to do it. Right. Let's get the emitters."

David and the professor placed the emitters within the inner circle, pointing outwards at the centre of the factory floor.

"Are you ready?" asked the professor. "Don't switch on until I say – and make sure it isn't pointing at either of us. Still set at 30%?"

David looked down. "Three," he said.

"That'll do. Now let's get his attention. This is how a priest might start… our friend should quite relish that… *Exerciso te William Tipler, spiritus tenebra, in nomini Patre…*"

David stood beside the professor, his emitter pointing into the darkness, squinting through his shadow lens for any sign of the ghost. He didn't have long to wait. The bottle-brown smudges of sunlight quickly disappeared as if the sun had gone behind a cloud. David lowered the lens from his eye; the beams of sunlight were still there, but they were weakening, fading into the darkness. "He's coming," hissed David, grabbing for the switch on top of the emitter while he could still see it.

"Don't switch on until I say," repeated the professor. He swept the sensor back and forth. There was definitely something there – a faint buzz, another wasp, this one hitting a light shade several rooms away.

Darkness was falling in the factory. David was taken back at once to the cursed day that he had lost Nathan. This time the darkness grew more slowly – the change was imperceptible moment by moment, but was definite over the course of a minute or so. He could see nothing with his shadow lens. Soon he could see nothing with his eyes – just the LED on top of the emitter, his torch, and the indefinite, fading outline of the professor. The noise made by the professor's sensor was growing louder. The wasp wasn't several rooms away any more: it was close, very close – with a swarm of a thousand of its kin. There was sudden silence. David guessed that the professor had switched his gadget off – at that moment it was as useful as a microscope is for observing an elephant.

David's torchlight, visible where it picked out the drifting streams of his cooling breath, disappeared into nothingness at the outer edge of the professor's concentric circles. They were completely walled in by the shadows. Only the little patch of ground within the circles was spared the absolute darkness, and even here the gloom was virtually impenetrable. The sound of the car's engine had faded away too, as if muffled under layers of cloth. It had grown cold, so cold that David was afraid that his rapidly numbing finger might not be able to activate the emitter; he wiggled it, trying to keep the feeling in it.

"Three, two, one, now," said the professor.

David pulled the switch.

The unreal darkness fled in all directions as if it had exploded. In the middle of his field of vision, David was left with a large, roughly T-shaped smudge of afterimage; as he blinked, the smudge turned purple, then green. It was as if a camera flash had gone off in his face.

"And off," the professor was saying.

David pushed the emitter's switch back into the 'off' position, still blinking hard to restore the affected part of his sight. Beside him, he could hear the professor's ghost-detector humming away faintly. "Did we get him?" David asked. "What happened? Where's Nathan? Is he here?"

"Several readings," replied the professor coolly, sweeping his detector around. "It seems we were right."

David was still finding it difficult to see anything. Wherever he looked, the smudge of afterimage followed. Then he had a thought, and raised the lens to his eye. *Now* he could see – the blinding smudge was gone, and there were several shapes drifting around in the distance. The shapes were grey, faint, ghostly...

"Nathan!" called David.

Immediately one of the phantoms ceased its wandering and turned towards him. He could see no details at this range – it was just an ashen blur with a suggestion of a gaping, black mouth and the clotted shadows of its eyes. "Nathan?" asked David, a hint of nervousness in his voice.

The ghost was coming. Its legs pumped as it sprinted towards him, claw-like hands reaching out. It was not Nathan, he was sure of that. Not the Nathan he had known, anyway. Its hair was long, black, and in disarray, streaming behind it as it came. As it neared, its claylike appearance was refined into a purple- and blue-tinged pallor. It was screaming at him, a silent scream of hatred and anger.

David screamed too, and instinctively switched on the emitter. For a moment, nothing happened; the ghost kept coming until it was almost upon him. Then its scream of anger turned to one of pain, and the ghost began to disintegrate, shrinking and folding in on itself, evaporating in the emitter's merciless glare like a cloud in the sun. In a second it was gone, leaving behind it no sign that it had ever been.

The professor was saying something. David had to focus to hear it.

"I said, watch what you're doing. You don't want to fry Nathan."

David switched off the emitter. He could see via the shadow lens that the newly-separated spectres all around him were scattering, disappearing through walls, floor or ceiling. "That wasn't Nathan," he said firmly. "Nathan!" he called. "Nathan! Are you here?"

There was no reply from Nathan, if he was there. All of the ghostly forms had now dispersed out of sight.

"It probably wouldn't have hurt you," the professor said, still swinging his ghost-detector around, looking for a strong signal amongst a dozen faint ones. "Would have breezed straight through you."

"No," spat David. "It wanted to latch on to me..." he realized that he was trembling.

"Are you sure it wasn't Nathan?"

"It wasn't Nathan," said David flatly. His vision, he was relieved to find, had returned to normal. He stood and watched as the professor waved his little gadget left, right, up and down... suddenly the swarm of wasps were back. Not as close as they had been before, but there nevertheless.

The professor's detector was pointing straight down.

"Come on," he said. "We need to find the cellar."

"What if we run out of cable?" asked David.

"Let's worry about that if the time comes," said the professor, and started towards the right-hand side of the factory, paying out his emitter's cable behind him as he walked. David followed a little way behind, still occasionally calling his brother's name, not optimistic that there would be a reply.

Chapter 23: The Tollund Boys

Milla was alone on the factory forecourt. She wrapped her coat tightly around her and stared intently at the computer display, trying not to cough. Standing behind the professor's old car made it hard to stay out of the plume of smoke it was emitting. The live feed from David's camera showed the back of the professor's overcoat and the walls and floor of a long corridor, lit intermittently by dancing torchlight. With her mouse she moved a slider above the window with the live feed in; the image stopped, blinked, and started to go jerkily backwards. She selected a time some three minutes earlier, back to around the time when the emitters had been switched on, but quickly found that she had gone back too far. The camera showed only darkness. She went forward ten, then twenty seconds, and let the video run; almost immediately, the absolute, spectral darkness disappeared, to be replaced by natural gloom, punctuated by faint swatches of light. Next she froze the image and played with the input frequency bands — turning down ultraviolet and blue, increasing infrared. As she did so, an image began to emerge — a vaguely T-shaped image represented by extreme cold in the infrared band. For a moment she adjusted the ratio of inputs until the image clarity was the best possible; then she scrolled back to before the moment when the emitters had been switched on, and let the video run.

At first there was darkness, as before, natural and patchy with light; then, like a shark emerging from deep waters, the T-shaped image began to form, bringing foul blackness wrapped about it like a cloak. A smudge, then a smudge with arms, became a looming giant, a vast, rotting creature with deep shadowed pits of eyes and mouth. The leering, trollish form more than filled the screen for a moment; then, something incredible happened. The emitters were switched on, and the grainy image faded and thinned; the monster seemed to split apart and at least a dozen vague forms emerged, like parasites issuing from the body of their host. The vile behemoth folded up and collapsed, as if punctured, shrinking as it fell –

– and as it fell, the cloudy frothing form resolved into that of a boy, a boy who glared back and forth from one of his adversaries to the other with a face of unalloyed hate. The boy went straight down through the floor and out of sight, leaving the other vague forms floating about with all the purposefulness of flakes of snow.

Milla quickly clicked back to the live feed, which now showed nothing, a void. Again she fiddled with the input bands until an image emerged. In the infrared band she could see a jumpy image of an open area, a distant far wall, a declining ceiling, and a very cold floor. Now the professor moved into view, somewhat below the camera's position, and she realized that what she had thought was the floor was actually water, water in a half-flooded basement, into which the professor was gingerly stepping. David, presumably, remained above, where the camera was –

There was a ghost watching her. She knew this with deadly, immediate certainty: but there had been no movement or sound to warn her, nothing but the grainy image on the computer screen and the ongoing throb of the car's engine. She looked from the old factory wall, to the wet-edged patches of ice and the brown dead weeds. Nothing was out of the ordinary. She peered up at the boarded-up windows of the factory next door in case her sense of foreboding was nothing more sinister than Drake peeping down – but she could not sense him there. Seeing nothing, Milla closed her eyes and listened. At first all she could hear was the uneven chugging of the car; then, gradually, more sounds emerged. She could hear a voice – someone ranting, not speaking in sentences but shouting insanely. No, she realized: not one insane voice, but two.

WANTS IT STOPPED, HE

THE CAR...

WANTS IT STOPPED, HE

THE CAR...

Milla opened her eyes and turned towards the front of the car. There was nothing there – there *was* something there... was there? There was *less* than nothing there, she realized: a folding, a pocket in the surface of the world, a secret window that gave a glimpse of another place – and another person. No – other *people*. She could see two indistinct forms near the car. They were grey, webby auras, only just visible against the faded brick background of the factory, shadows of shadows, nothing more. She knew at once that there was no life in the creatures to which these auras belonged. The auras were colourless, dead and flat, unlike those of living things, which sparkled vibrantly. The auras of the people around her did not really have colours, of course, she knew that well enough, but her mind thought of them as colours, and made them real. These auras were less *there* than those of living people – they were cobwebs and dust in a sunlit window. They moved forward, *through* the car, until they were standing *in* the bonnet.

She guessed that they meant to stop the engine, and that was a chilling thought, because it inferred intelligence (they knew the car was powering the emitters), purpose, and organisation (those ghostly snowflakes she had seen drifting around on the computer screen were co-operating against the ghost-hunters). Whatever they were doing, she did not want them here. Milla raised her left hand, palm out towards the two ghosts. As her grandmother had taught, she imagined her will pouring down her arm, out of her hand, a light shining on the shadows.

"Vexag," she said gently. She pushed against the two forms, and felt them resist, felt their wills push back against hers.

The car shuddered, lurched, and its steel heart skipped a beat.

"F'war vexag," she said again; this time it was an order. Angry sparks flared in the two auras like steel striking stone.

The force of her will was no more than the beat of a fly's wing; but these specks of dust hanging in the air were no match for her. Slowly, like a thinning pall of smoke, the auras spread out, merged, faded, and disappeared. The voices, too, had gone.

Then, just as the threat seemed to have been averted, the car's engine rattled once and died. In the near-silence that followed, Milla simply stood there, her arm outstretched like a statue. Eventually she was able to move, and hurried around to the driver's side of the car and clambered in. She turned the key to the off position, then forward again to the start position. The engine responded – but not as well as she had hoped. It coughed, choked, swallowed and began to drown in its own bile. Black smoke gathered in the air behind the car like a murder of crows. The old estate's engine would not start.

The professor started down the cellar steps, David dutifully trying to light his way with the torch from the top step. About six steps down, the stairway plunged into a dark lake of watery mud. "From the river," commented the professor calmly.

David said nothing. Some way off, his roaming torchlight picked out a cleaning-fluid drum, half-floating in the water, half-stuck in the murk. He set his emitter down at the top of the stairs.

At the sixth step down, the final dry one, the professor halted. He waved his little gadget around in a half circle. There was a signal, a weak one, from a dim, half-submerged recess some way to the left. Professor Fuller stepped gingerly into the water. He put the ghost-detector in his breast pocket and used both hands to raise his emitter above the level of the water as he waded down into it. "Light my way," he ordered.

David did not need to be told. His torchlight was feebly illuminating the professor's way already. He changed position slightly, and glanced down at the emitter to make sure that he didn't knock it down the steps.

"Professor," David blurted suddenly, "is this light meant to be off?" The top of the emitter was blank, dead. David flicked the switch a few times. Nothing happened.

"The car!" exclaimed Professor Fuller.

David could hear the car, far away, coughing painfully.

"Come on, Milla!" muttered the professor.

There was a faint sloshing noise from somewhere in the shadows, under the archway. After the noise came a noxious stink as disturbed gases bubbled to the surface of the water.

"Professor, we have to get out of here."

Professor Fuller turned back to face David. He took a pace back towards the concrete steps. In the distance, they could still hear Milla trying to start the car.

Milla was sitting in the driver's seat. She gave the car another rest, and then engaged the starter again, but still the car would not start. What had those ghosts done to it? Suddenly her foot felt very cold. Strange. Actually, it felt wet, icily wet. She looked down into the foot-well. There was a puddle of black down there that she hadn't noticed before. There must be some kind of oil leak, and the level of the liquid was rising. *That's a lot of oil*, thought Milla. It was up to her ankles now, soaking her shoes, and still the car wouldn't start.

The oil on her shoes would not go down well with her mother.

Suddenly the driver's door slammed closed. She immediately tried to open it again, but the door was jammed shut. Try as she might, she couldn't open it.

The car wouldn't start. The level of oil was rising. This was not oil. No car held this much oil. The window wouldn't wind down; behind her, the open hatch, too, slammed shut of its own accord. She leaned across to the passenger-side door, but it was stuck fast too.

The black stuff was up to her knees. She drew her legs up, and the black came with them, like treacle.

Milla lunged for the horn and leaned on it.

At the top of the cellar steps, David heard the spluttering engine noise replaced by an incessant note from the horn.

"She's in trouble," David said. The professor was wading back towards him. Further away, in the shadowy depths, something else was moving in the water. "Hurry, Professor!" called David. But the professor could only wade on, silent and dignified. David came halfway down the steps, shining his torchlight into the shadows. The batteries seemed to be going, but the fading torch beam was still strong enough to pick out faint reflections from something moving behind the professor.

David had once read about someone called Tollund man. He was a man who had been thrown into a peat bog, sacrificed immeasurable ages ago as an offering to pagan gods. Tollund man had been perfectly preserved by the acidity in the mud, and his remains, discovered by a pair of Belgian peat-cutters, were able to tell archaeologists much about ancient society. David remembered thinking at the time that, although incredibly well preserved (where were his *murderers* now?), Tollund man looked as if he had been made

– badly – from distressed leather. Something that looked exactly like Tollund man was closing in behind the professor now. Perhaps the creature was not exactly like Tollund man – for this wading monstrosity was much shorter than the professor, more like a Tollund teenager. And the Tollund teenager had a friend – there was another figure splashing out of the deeper water.

The Tollund boy quickly caught up with the professor and grabbed him. As they struggled, David could make out the boy's hair, hanging like matted seaweed over his twisted, leathery face. The professor swung the emitter, using it like a club, and the Tollund boy fell away for a moment. Behind them both, the second Tollund boy was wading nearer. The first Tollund boy was holding on to the professor, undaunted by repeated blows.

"Run, David!" gasped Professor Fuller.

David started to go. He got as far as the top of the stairs, at which point the blaring of the horn from the car outside ceased. He did not know whether this was a good sign or a bad one. As he wondered, he put down the torch so it lit the scene, then hurtled back down the steps, hung onto the railing, grabbed the professor's hand, and heaved as hard as he could.

The black fluid had reached Milla's chest. Wherever she touched it, it clung to her, coating her limbs in thick glue. She could see through what was still available to her of the window that the professor and David weren't coming. They should have heard her; they should have come running. She stopped pressing the horn. Milla pulled her legs back and stiffly kicked at the windscreen. In this reclined position, the stuff was up to her neck. The windscreen was tough. She kicked again, knees and feet together, greatly hampered by the rising slime. Just before her mouth and nose went under she took a last breath, determined never to breathe out. Then the oil was up to her eyes, and her sight was gone. She kicked, kicked, and kicked again. She could feel her strength waning.

Then, from nowhere, an image came into her mind. From somewhere above the car, looking down, she saw herself, locked in an empty car, making little kittenish taps on the windscreen with her feet. This, she suddenly realized, was a spiritual foe, not a physical one, and she was more than its equal. She kicked again, and this time she could have kicked down a brick wall. Everything that she was went into that blow, mental and physical knotted together into an immeasurable force. She kicked with all the strength she had, and all her will.

The windscreen fairly flew out of the car. There was a burst of light. The liquid had gone. It had never been. Gasping for breath, Milla turned the key in the ignition again.

The second Tollund boy had reached the foot of the stairs and had silently joined in the deadly game of tug of war, adding his pawing and pulling to that of the first. The professor was slipping back, slowly, but inexorably; David was slipping too, down into the water. With one hand on the railing and the other on the professor, he was being stretched to breaking point. Something would have to give soon – either he would let go of the railing or he would let go of the professor. One of the boys began gurgling with excitement. Perhaps he was trying to say something, but his long-disused tongue, after decades of rot, could not shape the words.

Somewhere, a long way away, the car engine was trying to start again. This time it caught. And that was when the pain started.

David felt as if he was being shredded, as if a whirlwind of razors was trying to skin him, pare his soul from his body. His grip on the railing was lost; he fell forwards, splashing into the murky water. One of the Tollund boys was pulling him under, and he did not have the strength to fight. Then, gradually, the pain eased; he was not being pulled under, but away; his blinking eyes could dimly see that he was being held, not by one of the Tollund boys, but by Professor Fuller.

"Okay?" demanded the professor.

David nodded weakly. He was dimly aware of the professor hurling his emitter towards the top of the steps, heard a clatter as it collided with the one standing up there.

"Come on," said the professor.

"What happened?" asked David weakly.

"You left your emitter switched on – and when the power came back on – we're lucky it didn't have time to build up a charge… then, it couldn't in the on position…"

David silently followed the chattering professor up the stairs. He felt sick and dizzy; with every movement it felt as if his soul was walking away, leaving his flesh and bone behind. Of the Tollund boys, there was no sign, just an occasional burst of foul marsh gas from the sludge behind them.

Milla was standing by the car waiting for them as they emerged into the brilliant sunshine. She looked scared and very relieved to see them. "What happened?" she asked. "Are you two okay?"

The professor surveyed the wreckage of his windscreen, and then wordlessly swept the remains off the car's bonnet. "It looks as if you have had your own tribulations," he commented at last.

"Sorry about the windscreen," apologized Milla. "There were two other ghosts – boys I think. Then there was fluid, black, and sticky. I was drowning –

the doors were all jammed shut –" Milla stifled a sob, and David went to her and put his right arm around her, although he was still trying, literally, to hold *himself* together.

The professor leaned against the side of the car, closed his eyes, and breathed deeply. "Two boys? I think we, too, may have had the pleasure of their acquaintance. Victims of our friend William Tipler, split apart from him and yet still his to control... it was a mistake to half-charge the emitters. We should have given it all we had."

"But Nathan –" began David.

"I'm sorry. Nathan may not be coming back. *We're* still alive. At the moment. I suggest it is better that we stay that way than risk all our lives trying to rescue a ghost who is ultimately going to fade away anyway."

David let himself sit down heavily on the cold concrete. Milla stood over him, clutching his good hand.

With an enormous effort, the professor pushed himself away from the car. His wet clothes had started to steam in the cold air. "I'm coming back, this time tomorrow. I'm going to use the emitters on full power, if I have the chance. I'm sorry, David. If you want to help me finish the job, then meet me here. If not, I'll understand. We must finish this ghost or others will die... but for now, I'm going to get dry and warm. I feel as if I could sleep for a week."

"I'm not losing him," mumbled David bitterly.

Milla enveloped him in a hug, which seemed to say: *You already have.*

David pushed her away, lurched to his feet, and walked a few unsteady paces back towards the factory. "I'm not leaving you, Nathan," he shouted, a burst of energy that almost finished him off. "Whatever it takes to get you back, I'll do it," he added, more quietly.

David did not know whether or not Nathan could hear him, but he guessed that others within the factory heard and comprehended his words. It was as much to them that he spoke as to his brother.

PART FOUR

*

THE SHADOWLAND

He knew that they were after him
To hunt him till he fell;
He turned and fled into the dim,
And after him came hell.

John Masefield

Chapter 24: Drawn into Shadow

David could not shake off the effects of the professor's anti-ghost ray. Every inch of his skin felt sore and chafed against his clothes as he moved; his stomach churned with nausea, and whenever his eyes strayed from the horizon, the world swayed, tilted, and began to spin, so that he had to grab something solid to keep himself upright. He did not even have the energy for a post-mortem with Milla, who was tired and shaken by her own experiences. When he got home, he went straight to his bedroom and fell on his bed, eyes shut against the spinning world. He tried to kick off his shoes, but his wet feet had swollen inside them and they were wedged on tight. He lacked the energy to sit up and untie them. As he lay down, the tiredness, dizziness, and nausea receded. After a few moments he opened his eyes — then immediately closed them again. His body felt better, but his vision had gone haywire. Everything looked grey and cobwebby, as distorted and out of focus as if he was looking through the bottom of a bottle.

He kept his eyes shut for a while, and then opened them again. Briefly. The visual disturbance was still there. He had no doubt at all that he was experiencing some strange hangover from being in the path of the professor's emitter. He fought against panic, willing his eyesight to restore itself, and promising whatever powers controlled such matters that — despite his brave words earlier — he would never go near a ghost ever again if only he could see properly once more.

Minutes passed, perhaps hours. He did not dare open his eyes. As he lay on his bed in self-imposed darkness, hope and despair chased each other's tails around and around, faster and faster. His heart was thumping, his breathing was ragged, and all his muscles were knotted. The relief that would come if he opened his eyes and all was well would be immediate and complete; but if, after all this time, his vision was still broken, would it not always be so? At last he could bear it no longer and looked at the world again. His heart sank; his vision was as bad as ever. Even up close – he raised his palm and scrutinized it – he could see very little. The universe he knew seemed to have shifted out of focus, to have retreated away from him.

David could not even see his own palm properly. He could see *through* it. At first he could not believe it, quite, but the evidence was indisputable. He could see through *everything* to a greater or lesser extent – he could actually see his hand relatively well compared to everything else in the world. He could see through the walls as if they were thick, dark glass; through the front wall he could see the leafless tree in the front garden frozen in an agonized pose. His mother's painting hung on the transparent ghost of the wall as if in mid-air. Instead of the usual faint blotches, it appeared now to be an entirely black canvas. He was sinking into his bed as if it was less substantial than before, spongier – less *there*. He moved across to the painting, the floor rubbery under his feet. It was as he had thought: the painting was black, utterly featureless.

I'm dead, he realized, and turned back to look at his bed, expecting to see his lifeless body there, but the rumpled bed was empty. No David there. Could it be – was this grotesque version of the world the same one that Nathan saw?

The bedroom door was there, but not entirely. Pushing it produced a strange sensation. He could both touch it, and push right through it if he chose – there was a degree of elasticity about matter in this world. If a light touch became a firm one, his hand went through, stretching the stuff of the door like caramel. He was unable to operate the door handle, which just warped and twisted as he tried to turn it. It was with some trepidation that he finally walked *through* the door, worrying about what would happen if he returned to normal half-way through. The stairs were soft and spongy, their lack of substance threatening to trip him at every step. Guy and Rebecca were in the kitchen. Rebecca was bustling about preparing a meal – lunch, or tea?

Even the Reads weren't entirely there, but they were nevertheless the most solid objects in the kitchen.

"Hello," said David. He expected the Reads to ignore him. His expectation was fulfilled. For a while he stood in the doorway, listening to the Reads' conversation, which was like listening to a fly buzzing in an upturned glass. The words were muffled and faint. At one point Guy walked out of the kitchen; he would have walked straight into (through?) David if he hadn't leapt to the side.

Rebecca Read stood at the cooker, stirring something on the hob. David walked up behind her and reached out to touch her bare neck. Rebecca's skin was burning hot, painfully so. David snatched his hand away. Rebecca shivered. She buzzed something to Guy (it might have been 'it's cold in here...').

David really *was* dead. But where was his body? He remembered falling onto his bed an unknown time before – not too long, it seemed, if Rebecca was preparing lunch. Unless that had been a dream. Maybe he had been dead for days – since the first time he had been in the Tipler factory. But that couldn't be. Just couldn't be.

Then, looking down the hall and through the semi-transparent front door, he realized that he was being watched. Two shadowy forms could vaguely be seen beyond the front door. They seemed to be watching him. He hurried down the hall and went *through* the door.

Two boys. They stood there silently and watched him emerge. These two were real enough – not half here and half somewhere else like the Reads.

"Are you ghosts?" asked David. There was something odd about these boys – about their clothes. They wore drainpipe trousers, bomber jackets and boots. They were of an age with David, he guessed, but were not wearing the kinds of clothes he or his friends would wear. They were of an age with him but not of a time with him...

The boys said nothing – they just stared at him.

David skirted around them, having the idea that Milla might be able to see him – the only plan he had was to get to her house. The boys moved sideways, aiming to cut him off, one in front and one behind.

"What do you want?" he snapped, and stopped moving.

The first boy spoke at last. "*He* sent us," he told David.

"We do as *he* wants," clarified the second.

The two boys had stopped moving, just as he had. David noticed something else, at his feet: the finely etched network of cracks between the paving slabs at the foot of the Reads' garden. The boys had not crossed the salt-line drawn by Professor Fuller even though it had long since washed away.

"We come from the dark place," smiled the first boy.

"Where the bones are," added the other.

"*Our* bones," they chorused. In that moment both youths were transformed: the bomber jackets and trousers became mere scraps of cloth; their faces caved in, eyes sinking behind swollen, tan lids; their hair thinned and plastered itself to their skulls like seaweed; their lips shrivelled back, revealing the foul peg-like remains of their teeth. They were the ghosts he had christened the Tollund boys.

"You're dead," David blurted.

"Join the club," said the second boy. His voice had decayed with his body and had developed a gravelly rattle.

David had a choice to make – he could wait here indefinitely behind the safety of the professor's salt-line, or make a dart for it and hope that he could outrun the Tollund boys. He ought to be able to, looking at their stick-thin legs and heavy boots; but he guessed that Newtonian physics might not apply to ghosts in the Shadowland.

After a brief period of contemplation David realized that it was inevitable that he would have to get past these two. He might as well try now. He darted for the gap between them. The two boys moved with alacrity to cut him off once more, one on either side. Both boys caught him up and grabbed him with their bony fingers before he had made it ten metres from the salt-line. But they couldn't stop him from running. They were light, insubstantial, like a collection of twigs, rags and paper. He ran with them for a little way as they pawed and hissed at him, then he decided to try to throw them off, which was far easier than he could have hoped. He was too strong for them – too dense, as if he was made of something different, steel against rotten sticks. He peeled one off him and threw it away, then did the same with the second; they flew through the air a long way, before landing in small disorganized heaps. Buzzing and rattling with fury, they struggled to their booted feet, but could only watch as he ran off.

"You're strong now," called the first boy.

"You'll be weak soon," added the second.

"Watch your back, Jack," the first boy threw after him. But then he was too far away to hear their rasping utterances, which were fading away in his wake.

David ran easily a while, and then he sprinted. He did not tire; he felt that he could sprint a marathon, and then sprint back. Nathan had always moved at amazing speed, which was another piece of evidence that he, too, was a ghost. Why then was he so much stronger than the Tollund boys? Was it because he had only just become a ghost ('You'll be weak soon,' the second Tollund boy had said)?

Cars sailed past him, ghost machines driven by oblivious spectres. He crossed the road, but misjudged his timing: one of the phantom vehicles smashed into him. It was like being hit by a deluge of water. He was swept along with the car – caught up in its insubstantial substance – for some distance before managing to scramble out onto the pavement. After that, he slowed his pace.

The Shadowland was a strange place. Although everything was partly transparent, the cumulative effect of layered objects was enough to attenuate his perception as distance increased, rather as a glass of sea water seems to be clear but one cannot see to the bottom of the sea. He could see, for instance, into some of the front rooms of the houses he walked past, but not, generally, much further into those houses. The sky and the ground had a similar, greyish appearance, which together with the limit of his vision gave the place a claustrophobic feel. Strangely, the houses were not as regular as in real life: they seemed to be twisted, bizarrely stretched, or too small. Even the roads were less regular than they should be. It was as if the world was made out of slightly melted transparent plastic. There was something else, too; barely noticeable at first, there was a definite nip of cold in the air.

He got as far as the pavement in front of Milla's house, and then found that he could go no further. There was no obstruction that he could see, but as he tried to move forwards, he found himself walking into an invisible, elastic wall. The harder he tried, the more it stretched. But eventually the tension in the wall would become great enough to throw him backwards. He tried calling Milla's name, staring up at her bedroom window like a hopeful spaniel whining to be taken for a walk. He had reached whatever protection Milla's grandmother had provided her house.

It was beginning to get noticeably colder. For some time David stood and considered his options. Could he make the professor aware of his presence? And what could either Milla or the professor do to help him anyway? As he stood there pondering his next move, a shadow emerged from within the house and approached him. It took a while for him to be sure that it was Milla and not one of her siblings. But it was her all right, and relief flooded through him. The opposite emotion seemed to be afflicting Milla. She stopped walking and visibly slumped. She had seen a ghost.

"Milla! Can you hear me?"

"No, David," she said faintly, "you can't be dead, you just can't be."

"I'm not dead! Can you hear me? I'm not dead! At least, I don't think I am."

Milla seemed to pull herself together. "If you can hear me, then follow. You may come in. I give you permission to enter."

David followed Milla back inside her house. At times he was struggling to keep up with her; at other times, she seemed to slow to a crawl. He tried to speak, but it was clear that she could not hear him, despite him being able to hear her much more clearly than he had been able to hear the Reads. Milla held the door open for him, rather needlessly; behind her, in the hall, stood a vague figure he took to be Milla's mother.

The figure buzzed something about being surprised to see Milla back so soon.

"Just remembered I've got to finish some homework," Milla explained, and went straight upstairs. David followed her to her bedroom; once inside, she closed the door behind them.

"Lotus flowers, wormwood powder, Devil's ears and sage..." Milla muttered, rooting through half-visible, shadowy drawers and boxes. Next she emptied her wardrobe, flinging everything within onto her bed; that done, she placed a candle on either side of the wardrobe's doorway.

David could only watch dumbly as Milla hurried about organising herbs and lighting the candles in the wardrobe. Suddenly he realized he was being addressed: "Get in!" Milla was saying, pointing him to the empty wardrobe. He did as he was told, and stood in the darkness of the wardrobe as Milla ran a fingernail around the door frame muttering *"Baxuwa apoara, fex bas jubs, baxuwa apoara, febar now kit ginar, baxuwa apoara, die ragua kiar xagus."*

Milla rubbed some of the herbs she had collected into her hands, threw some in the air, and crumbled others onto the candle flames, releasing a pungent aroma that David could somehow smell through the veil between worlds. Eventually Milla gestured for David to come back out of the wardrobe. He stepped over the magical threshold, emerged into the bedroom, and turned to look at Milla. She was as solid, and real, as anyone he had ever seen before. The floor was real, and so were the walls. He immediately felt warm again, as if he had come in from the cold to stand by a hearty fire. He was not dead.

"Thank you," he said simply, sagging with relief.

Milla, who was staring at him glassy-eyed, grabbed and held him. "The Shadowland is a dangerous place," she said. "You're cold… and wet…"

David had never felt so warm, or so welcome, even though he was still standing in soaking wet clothes. "I'm all right. Thanks to you."

"Don't ever do that to me again," said Milla.

"Do what?"

"I thought you were dead," she said.

"So did I," he said, trying to laugh. But it was not funny, and there were hot tears on his cheek.

"I'm going back," Milla said. She broke away from the hug and began to rifle through her furniture again.

"Back? Back where?"

"Strange," she said, hardly hearing him, "that doorway trick never worked till now. I guess I just didn't need it to work badly enough the other times I tried to reach the Shadowland. Anyway, now I can save Nathan," Milla said. She squeezed David's arm and darted back into the wardrobe.

"No, hang on," started David, but Milla had turned, said a word, and vanished before he could as much as move after her. "Milla! I know you can hear me! Come back!" he shouted. But Milla didn't. The wardrobe was empty and dark. He stepped back into it, but the doorway was again just a doorway into a wooden wardrobe, not a gateway to the Shadowland.

A deep sense of foreboding washed over him. He could not follow her —
but he knew she could not hope to face Tipler alone.

Chapter 25: The Stones of Hungry Hill

David sneaked out of Milla's house, wary of questions from her mum. As soon as he was out of sight of the house, he started sprinting towards the Tipler factory. As far as he could tell he was on the best route to intercept Milla, unless the path she took through the Shadowland went *through* houses rather than *around* them. After half a mile, David skidded to a halt, swept his shadow lens to his eye and did a three hundred and sixty degree search for Milla. There was no sign of her, so he ran on.

As he ran, David used Milla's mobile phone to call the professor.

"Professor," he gasped, when the old man finally picked up the phone, "it's Milla – she's stuck in the Shadowland."

"Stuck? How? How did she get in there in the first place?" asked the professor.

"She opened a door to let me out –"

"Let you out?"

"That emitter – it sent me into the Shadowland. It must have been the emitter… I want you to use the emitter to send me back so I –"

"Where are you?"

"On the way to Tipler's – I'm going to try to head her off. She thinks she can save Nathan…"

"I'll get there as fast as I can," snapped the professor, and hung up.

Rain gusted down fitfully, thin and chilly. As he ran, David realized that he did not have a coat. He remembered taking it off in his bedroom and collapsing on his bed – he was lucky that he even had his shoes on. He was already soaking wet and freezing cold from his dip in Tipler's cellar. If he had undressed when he had reached the Reads' place he would now be running along naked, he thought; he did not have enough humour left to be amused by that thought. His shoes, heavy with water, squelched noisily as he ran.

He stopped again, long enough to catch his breath and survey all directions with the shadow lens. Milla was nowhere to be seen. Was she ahead of him or behind him? Increasingly heavy-legged, David hurried on towards the factory. By the time he reached the deserted road in front of Tipler's, his pace had dropped to little more than a painful jog. He leaned against the wall of the factory yard, gasping for breath and steaming, and peered again through the shadow lens. He was facing the mausoleum-like abandoned factories; to left and right, the road he had run down was empty; behind him – well, behind him was the wall. Although the lens could see into the Shadowland, it did not enable him to see through solid objects. Rather, the lens seemed to bring Shadowland objects into view if they were in front of *real* objects. He would have to get a better view if he wanted to see whether Milla was already in the courtyard. He skirted the factory and went down the alley that separated it from the ruin where Drake was hiding out. Along with his bike, which was beginning to rust from exposure, his faithful (some might say treacherous) plank was still there. In seconds, despite a stabbing pain in his wrist as he dragged the plank back into position, he was high enough to see over the wall. Once more he peered through the lens...

Two ghosts stood in the courtyard. They seemed to be guarding the factory. At this range, he could make out little detail, but he had no doubt that he was looking at the two boys from the cellar, the same boys who had ambushed him in front of the Reads' house. Milla was walking into a trap. He had dealt with them easily enough – but what was it they had said? *You're strong now. You soon won't be.*

The grey sky was darkening further as, unseen behind the clouds, the weak winter sun slid down towards the horizon. He slithered off his plank and checked out the front of the factory. No Milla. There was only one thing to do – they would have to use those infernal emitters of the professor's to send him back into the Shadowland again. David found an old, rotten piece of cinderblock and wrote a brief message of warning on the wall with it in large, upper case letters. He wasn't sure whether or not Milla would be able to see it or read it.

He looked forlornly once more through his lens and began to walk up to the corner to wait for the professor.

Professor Fuller drove up ten minutes later. The battered old estate car, still missing its front windscreen, was running unevenly, its engine throbbing. "Get in," said the professor.

"But where are we going? Can't we use the emitters here?"

"The emitters are a weapon, not a surgical instrument. Standing in front of them is suicide. And even if it worked, and the emitter squeezed you into the Shadowland, how would you get back?"

David hadn't thought of that.

"Get in," ordered the professor. "I have an idea. We can talk on the way."

"The way where?"

"Hungry Hill."

"Never heard of it," said David, climbing into the car, "but I don't like the sound of it."

"Few have," said the professor, getting in the driver's side, "and they don't like the sound of it either." With a roar of loose gravel, he reversed the car out onto the road, and they were off. "You're soaked. There's an overcoat on the back seat."

David reached back for the heavy old overcoat. Under it, he noticed the professor's swords, wrapped tightly in a roll of silk.

"She went through into the Shadowland to save Nathan?" asked the professor.

"Yes."

"And the door..."

"Closed it behind her."

"Impetuous girl! How long ago?"

"Maybe half an hour."

"Then we must hurry," said the professor, and accelerated. A gale blew in through the gap where the windscreen should have been and whirled paper around the inside of the car. There was hardly any traffic on the southern edge of Fairfield, and what little there was thinned still further as the professor turned down narrow lanes with high hedges, gaunt trees, and only a few, solitary houses. "We have five minutes. Tell me what happened."

David related the events of the past short while, at times having to shout over the wind blowing through the car. At least the rain had stopped, which was one curse lifted. In front of them, the two windscreen wipers flapped uselessly in the breeze like the broken wings of a bird. At one point the professor asked David to get a map out of the glove box to confirm the right direction at an unsigned crossroads. The map quickly became damp and started to shred in the hurricane winds hurtling through the car. But the professor seemed to know where he was going again; he swung abruptly off the road onto a dirt track and raced along it, into a wooded area. The track curved around to the right, but straight ahead was a less-used track, this one roped off. A sign hung from a chain suspended between two posts: NO PUBLIC ACCESS. Professor Fuller drove straight through the chain and on up the narrow path. Bony trees overhung the path, ripping at the car as it passed; in the middle of the path, between the wheel-ruts, smaller plants swam in the unsteady headlights and were easily mown down by the rampaging car. The trees began to narrow in, leaning against the sides of the car, their branches lashing angrily through the open front of the vehicle at its two occupants. A flailing branch smashed one of the headlights, but still the professor ploughed on; he was only stopped a few hundred yards later by a medium-sized tree that had fallen diagonally across the ride.

It was now almost completely dark.

"Now what?" asked David.

"We walk."

The trees on either side of the car were pressing in so close that it was impossible for either of them to open their door more than an inch or two. "It's at times like these," said the professor, "that a windscreen is more of a hindrance than a help." He climbed out, and from the bonnet of the car asked David to pass out from the back seat his sword-roll, a pair of torches, a lantern, a bag of salt, and, unseen by David until now, a large, leather-bound book.

"What do you need the swords for?" asked David.

"I'd take the emitters too if I had a power supply. I really don't think you know quite what we're getting into."

"Then tell me."

"I'll do my best. As we walk. Come on." The professor was already past the obstructing tree and had started off up the track before David could even scramble out of the car and onto the bonnet. The old man had left one of the torches and the sword-roll behind him. "Bring those," he called over his shoulder.

David hurried to catch up, waiting for the professor to elaborate.

"We have to open a doorway to the Shadowland," said Fuller.

"We didn't need weapons last time."

"You think the Shadowland is empty? As soon as we open the gateway, every wandering entity for a hundred miles around will be homing in on us like moths to a hurricane lamp in the desert night."

David digested this news in silence. In the play of his torchlight, the fragile nets of spider webs seemed to be sprinkled with sparkling gems. Fog that gathered on overhanging branches became droplets of water and fell in a constant, gentle rain. As if they were forging upstream in a river, each fork of the path brought about a further narrowing of their road, until the wheel-ruts were long forgotten and the branches of the trees were snagging their shoulders. All was still except for the occasional startled woodpigeon flapping across their path and vanishing into the murk.

"I take it the entities you're talking about aren't friendly," said David at last.

"You take it right. The Shadowland is adjacent, subjacent and superjacent to innumerable corporeal universes. Not one of them, as far as I know, is a nice place to have a picnic. Creatures from these out-of-phase corporeal universes wander into the Shadowland and out again; ours is less… porous than most, thankfully. When a gate is opened between this universe and the Shadowland they can come through – and uncontrolled, may cause havoc."

The path had begun to incline. David noticed that the trees had changed – now they were tall pine trees, closely set, and the path had straightened as well as turned uphill. The only other trees were occasional birches, their trunks ghostly white amongst the ranks of gnarled grey-green pines. The ground became increasingly boggy, and the carpet of cushioning pine needles deadened the sound of their footsteps. Somewhere high above, where perhaps a few dregs of daylight remained to be used, unseen birds could be heard calling *chip* and *seep* to each other. This gentle music, the crack of occasional twigs underfoot and the brushing of pine needles on their clothes were the only sounds for a time.

"Nearly there," announced the professor suddenly.

Without warning the ground levelled off and the trees opened out. David, emerging into the clearing behind the professor, panned his torch around and gasped in surprise.

They had come upon a circle of standing stones. The circle itself was perhaps twenty metres across, and was dominated at its centre by a giant doorway made of three huge stones, two verticals and a lintel. A tree flanked each of the uprights, and David could see that one of the trees was still in leaf – a holly, he realized, while the other, larger tree was either a winter skeleton or dead. Somewhere above the doorway the two trees merged together into a single huge crown. Around this central feature were several low slabs, and forming the perimeter of the clearing was a series of pointed stones, some upright, some leaning crazily.

"What is this place?"

"It was made by the tree-folk. Before history was written. There is a legend – somewhat garbled by time – that the bravest of them would enter the Shadowland on one day each year, at dawn on midsummer's day, to hunt for the Tree of Life. To be the first to return with a leaf from the tree was a great honour. Most did not find the tree. Some did not return at all. At some point before written history, the Tree either died or its location was forgotten." While he was speaking, the professor moved up to the stones of the gateway and began making strange chalk marks on them, gesturing for David to cast a light on his work.

"There's a tree in the Shadowland?"

Fuller shrugged. "In legend, it is in leaf, flowers, and fruits in just one day a year, and was never to be found in the same place twice. Which may explain how it came to be lost. Now, to business. We will shortly have a way into the Shadowland. I will go in and get Milla. You will guard the entrance." He finished covering the stones with symbols and turned back to David. He pulled a gun out of his coat pocket. "Take this," the professor told him. "If anything comes out of that doorway except Milla or myself, I want you to shoot it. If it doesn't die, you must close the book and run."

David gingerly took the heavy black pistol.

"Say nothing for a moment," warned Fuller. "I have to charm the entry-way. Let us hope this works..." He began to read from the large book, illuminating the page with his torch: "*Psasenta. Fyrigia. Doronok...*"

David sat down on one of the slabs and set the gun down gently beside him. He waited until Fuller had at last stopped speaking, and then said: "I'll go. You do the shooting, if there's any to be done."

"I can't ask you to do that. There is great danger beyond."

"I can't... use this."

"It probably wouldn't work anyway," said the professor, with a gentle smile.

"I'm quicker than you. You guard the entrance. I'll get Milla."

They stared at each other for a long moment. "I know you would die for Milla or Nathan," said Fuller, "but this isn't about dying. It's about living."

"I'm coming back. We both are. Nathan – well, rescuing him may be impossible, but if it is possible, it can wait. It sounds like saving Milla can't wait."

"Then let me make something clear. I'd give my life for either of you. My star is falling in the west, while yours and Milla's have hardly risen over the eastern skyline... but if saving you might cost countless other lives, if something comes through that doorway that I cannot turn back, I will have no choice but to close the portal. If that happens you will be stranded and you will not last long. You must concentrate. If you hesitate, *you are lost*. If you deviate from your path, *you are lost*. Go. Run for all you are worth. Touch nothing, and let nothing touch you. Get Milla. Get back here. Time is everything. Remember that you are a creature of this world, not that. You are not compatible with it. You will burn like a supernova – but never forget this: the flux of energy in Shadowland is not as it is here. There are entities in Shadowland that might spend millennia in frozen sleep, waiting for the moment when a smattering of free energy might pass by…"

"If I don't get her, Milla isn't coming back, is she?"

"No."

"Thanks for your help," said David, and turned towards the portal.

Fuller grabbed him and hugged him.

There was no sign that the way between the stones was anything unusual. But David flinched as he stepped through anyway. One pace beyond, he turned back to look at the professor, who raised a hand in farewell, and then tapped his wrist. *Time*. Not for the first time that day, David ran.

Chapter 26: Journey into Darkness

Professor Fuller watched David until he was out of sight on the other side of the portal. Quietly, he said: "May all mercious things grant you Mercury's wings." For a few seconds he stood still, staring at the dark, stone-framed doorway; then he got to work.

The first thing he did was to make a circuit of the standing stone circle, drizzling a trail of salt behind him as he went and muttering words of warding under his breath, linking each of the perimeter stones to the next. Next he returned to his sword-roll and reverently unrolled it. Two blades were sheathed within. Each was a katana, but one was four inches or so longer than the other. Both had been made by the same swordsmith, and the guard stops of both bore the same decoration: lotus flowers and reeds. He picked up the slightly longer sword, and returned to the salt-line, dragging the tip of the blade along it for an entire circumference, carefully making a groove in the salt. That done, he took the old leather-bound book, which was still lying open, placed it carefully on one of the flat slabs within the circle, and laid his overcoat, neatly folded, beside it. Finally, he returned to his sword roll and knelt down on it, tying the silk cord that had secured the roll around his waist. He slotted his swords into the cord, the longer katana on the left, the shorter on the right. Then he closed his eyes, rested his palms on his knees, and waited, breathing slowly. He imagined his senses spreading beyond his body, as a spider's legs resting on her web widens the net of her perception Without seeing, he imagined the position of every feature, however small, within the arena he had made: fallen slabs, tussocks of unruly grass, a low branch of the oak tree flanking the doorway into the Shadowland.

For five minutes all within the stone circle was tranquil.

Then the professor's eyes snapped open. Something was moving on the other side of the doorway.

David was hurtling down the hill through the ghostly trees, not bothering to take the time to go around them; their faint essence in the Shadowland impeded him a little, but it was no worse than running through long grass. Sometimes he passed features other than trees, things that he guessed were either rooted in the Shadowland or in one of the other universes that abutted it: outcrops of rock, many metres tall, cracks and rents in the surface of the earth, or the crumbling remains of large sections of wall. The strange intrusions he passed were superposed on the spectral trees, but seemed either too close or too far away; their semi-transparency only added to the visual confusion, and trying to scrutinize them too closely hurt his eyes.

He headed down from Hungry Hill in the general direction of Fairfield, hoping that the closer to the city he got, the more markers he would find to guide him towards the Tipler factory. He was making good progress, running easily, tirelessly. The strangeness of his surroundings was slightly disturbing, but he was not afraid.

Then, out of the corner of his eye, he caught a glimpse of something deathly white in the trees beside him. A glance was enough to tell him that he was being tracked by something. The creature had long, skeletal legs and arms to match hanging from a thin, bow-chested body. There was something odd about its head. A second look told him that the creature's head was curiously flattened, with a protuberance where a mouth ought to be. There were no clothes on this creature. It was naked and bony, with skin white as parchment stretched painfully over a prominent rack of ribs. And it was following him – or at least, keeping pace with him.

David stopped running. The creature reacted instantly, freezing in place. It regarded him with the lifeless eyes of a shark.

"What are you?" called David.

There was a flash of movement to the left, another of the creatures arriving, drawing up short. The two creatures watched David motionlessly for a few moments. Then a third arrived, moving silently, lolloping along on two gangly legs, and squatted down into a hunched position to peer at him, extending one long forelimb for balance.

Nathan had made no mention of these creatures, although they had started to home in on David within moments of him entering the Shadowland this second time. And yet he had seen none on his first journey between worlds. Maybe the difference was because he was alive – Nathan only a ghost – and maybe they only came at night. They were keeping pace, not approaching too close: why? Were they waiting for the whole pack to assemble before they moved in for the kill? He started running again, and they moved with him; he stopped, and they drew to a halt also. There were now seven or eight of them. David took a step or two towards a cluster of three, who collectively backed away, keeping their distance. Strange. But there was no time to waste. He ran on.

He was in the open now, and the orange streetlights of Fairfield were visible far away like the raked embers of a bonfire.

For the first time, David became aware of the cold. Odd, feathery flakes of snow were drifting lazily out of the night sky. Those that hit him melted instantly and fairly sizzled out of existence, leaving behind them a cold burning sensation. This was no normal snow. It was *Shadowland* snow.

David ran on, as fleet as a gazelle, tracked by a dozen silent wraiths, as patient as wolves.

Professor Fuller watched motionlessly as a vague white shape approached the doorway between worlds. The dim, shadowy form gradually resolved into a barrel-chested torso, long, pitifully thin legs and stick-like arms. Its head was strangely flattened and had large black eyes as dead as buttons. There was a strange protuberance around the area where in a human a mouth would be. The creature approached the stone doorway nervously, moving its head to and fro to scan the other side of the portal with those flat blank eyes. It pushed through an elongated finger, then an emaciated, clawed foot as if testing bathwater.

The professor did not move an inch. His breathing was almost imperceptible.

The creature stepped over the threshold, and swivelled its head around once more apparently without noticing the professor. Then, casting garish shadows from the lantern light, it started to run towards the trees that fringed the stone circle. About halfway to the outside ring of standing stones, where the professor had laid his warding line, the creature began to scream. It stopped running, but the ear-splitting shriek continued; one delicate claw slapped down against the papery skin of its body as if some insect had bitten it. It seemed to be smoking. The wraith-like thing turned, looking back the way it had come, blackness spreading over its back. Smoke gathered, fizzing off its skin, which in another second erupted into flames. It took one step back towards its home, but then its legs gave way beneath it, brittle as dry burning twigs. The screaming stopped, and the creature ceased moving. It burned as fast as if it had been doused in liquid oxygen. The flames crackled on merrily for thirty seconds or so until all that was left of the weird Shadowland dweller was ash.

Other individuals of the same species had gathered behind the doorway, looking through nervously, unwilling to risk the same fate as the first. For a while they looked out into the real world making longing, wheedling hooting calls; then, as one, they scattered and disappeared. The professor could hear different sounds from the other side of the doorway: a faint crackling and rustling, punctuated by occasional popping noises. There was nothing yet visible beyond the doorway, but the sounds, whatever they belonged to, were growing.

David was speeding through the open ground on the outskirts of Fairfield. The only signs of the real world around him were the shadows of wintry hedge banks marking the borders of desolate farmland. Snow still fell in the Shadowland, and it was beginning to finely carpet the ground. The cold had become an almost physical thing, a biting, pinching, and nipping foe that, like the Shadowland wraiths, dogged his every step; his fingers, lips, nose and toes ached. But still David ran, his speed unflagging. His retinue of pallid monsters had not left him, but he was encouraged that their numbers were no longer growing.

Ahead, the road opened up; there was a translucent road sign on the left, and now a roundabout he recognized. From here to Tipler's was a ten minute walk in the real world; he estimated he could cover the distance in less than half that in the Shadowland.

Then he heard a furious roar from close by. The first thing he saw was a dozen of the wraith-like creatures, scattering like chaff in the wind; then he noticed something huge in their midst. From this distance, and in this poor light, the creature appeared vaguely human. It towered over the gaunt Shadowland entities, at least twice their height. It seemed to be lunging at the wraiths, trying to grab them, and bellowing angrily at its failure as the nimble creatures darted out of the way. Did these wraiths dog every traveller in the Shadowland? They seemed to be stalking this vast humanoid much as they were stalking David.

Whatever they were doing, he did not need to get involved. He would give them a wide berth, and perhaps even lose some of his pursuers if they decided to switch targets. David veered off the road, into the first housing estate on the sprawling edge of Fairfield. But it was too late. The creature, whatever it was, had spotted him.

"Human!" it shouted, and David was so shocked at both the roaring power of that voice and that the creature was able to speak English that he almost pulled up short. It was lumbering towards him, trying to cut him off. With it came its spectral attendants, unafraid that it might make another attempt to seize one of them. The closer it came, the more detail David could make out. Its height he estimated to be almost twice his, approaching three metres, but its mass must have been much more than twice his. The giant was reddish in colour. It was naked, and had a mop of black hair on top of its head, and was as muscular as a bodybuilder overdosed on steroids. "Human!" it called again. There was something odd in the way it shouted. Light gleamed faintly on a mouthful of irregular, sharpened teeth. "How did you get into this world?" it bellowed, still stamping towards him.

David did not reply. He swerved again, yet further out of his way, sprinting now directly away from the monster towards the heart of Fairfield. He tried to kick, to increase his pace, and was surprised to find that his legs could not respond. He was tiring at last. Nevertheless, a glance behind him told him that he was gaining on the giant and would soon be able to resume his course towards the Tipler factory. Moments later, he heard an expressive snarl from his wake, and guessed that the giant had called off his pursuit. David was just congratulating himself on an escape well made when he ran headfirst into a solid object.

For a moment David lost all sense of where he was and what he was doing there. The first thing he was aware of was that one of the emaciated wraths was stooping over him, its mouth-flap proboscis extended; he saw now that it was a hollow tube, toothed within and without, the teeth wickedly hooked like a dog rose's thorns. With immediate instinct, David lashed out, the back of his hand catching the creature on the side of its face. There was a loud crack and the wraith's head broke apart like an eggshell; it fell to the side and remained there unmoving as David scrambled to his feet. As he stood, he brushed against the thing he had collided with. It was with amazement that he realized he had charged into a tall stone column, as hard and real as anything in the real world. He moved on a little way, painfully stiff; there was movement behind, and he saw that the other wraiths were falling on their unfortunate comrade, their sucking mouths quickly finding points of purchase. As they fed, jostling for position, they gave a contented fluting noise.

As David turned away in disgust, he was confronted with yet another amazing sight. On this side of the column there was an open area covering a quarter of a circle, banked behind like an amphitheatre by giant stone steps. There were many figures in the open area. At first, David thought that he was looking at a crowd of ghosts; then he realized they were not ghosts, but statues. They numbered at least a hundred, all, as far as he could tell, statues of humans in a wide range of poses; some stood, others sat; some reclined, or lay as if dead. Most seemed to be looking at the column, and David turned to look at it again. Now that he was further from it, he could see it better. The column was perhaps ten metres tall; at its very top, only indistinctly visible, was what appeared to be a wrought-iron sculpture of a bush or perhaps a flower. Fascinated, he turned back to the statues and approached them. They seemed to be made out of solid ice, but the detail on them was fantastic; it was as if real people had turned to ice... as if they had looked upon the face of a glacial Medusa. He decided that it would be best not to look at that column again, at which so many of these statues, if statues they were, were staring. Were they made of ice, or was it glass, or some other crystal? He touched a statue of a bearded man with one careful fingertip. It was certainly cold enough to be made of ice.

In the background beyond the frozen people of the amphitheatre, David could see the shadowy forms of humans hurrying about in the real world. He was in Fairfield city centre now, in one of the open squares. The column had a real-world counterpart, a market post topped not with a flower but a cross. The two columns, the amphitheatre and the market square, the icy statues and the scurrying pedestrians… they occupied the same space, but somehow separately, like two facing pages of a closed book…

David realized that he was wasting time again, getting diverted from his path, while at the Tipler factory, who knew what perils were befalling Milla… he began to move on, but was startled by a voice at his shoulder.

"Have you seen the tree?"

David swung around. He was looking at the statue he had just touched — except that it was no longer a statue. It was a man of flesh and bone, in an old, full-length grey coat and with what looked like a harpoon slung over his shoulder. The man's attire had an old-fashioned feel about it: it was almost as if David was looking at an eighteenth-century sailor about to embark upon a whaling trip. "No, sorry," David told him, and backed up, careful not to collide with any of the other statues.

The man was looking around. "It's yet dark. Why are we two the only ones to have thawed? Why do the others not join us?"

"I'm sorry, I should never have touched you… it was an accident."

"It's not yet midsummer? How then come you to be here? Are you to search for the tree?" the man asked, following David. "Are you one of the Ephemerae?"

"I'm here to save someone," said David.

The man clasped his hands together. "Save *us*," he implored.

"Can't…"

The man fell to his knees, trying to grab David, who backed out of his way. "Save us, I beg…" he muttered. But his voice faded away into nothing, and he became immobile once more, one hand reaching out despairingly. His eyes were fixed fiercely on David; in a few seconds he was as transparent as glass again. David edged away, zigzagging through the frozen people until he was out the other side of the crowd. To left and right, wraiths appeared from nowhere and closed in on him, seemingly having finished devouring the dead individual. They gathered around, but still did not come in too near, perhaps even giving him a little more room out of newfound respect. He set off running again, but his legs were stiff, he was tired and cold, and could not go as fast as before. The wraiths kept up easily, loping along beside him, ever watchful, awaiting their moment.

Professor Fuller watched calmly as a second creature made its way out of the Shadowland. Unlike the wraith, whose ashes were still cooling nearby, this entity had no resemblance whatsoever to a human; indeed it would have been hard for a biologist to assign it to a phylum. There was something plant-like about it as well as something animal. It was short, but wide, and there was some degree of elasticity about its overall shape – it humped itself up to squeeze through the narrow stone doorway before puddling back into a wider form once again. It moved rather like a starfish, appearing to walk on millions of waving fingers. Tentacles of various kinds covered it; some, the ones that gave the creature its plant-like aspect, started off as thick as an arm and divided repeatedly until they were as fine as hairs. The professor wondered at the function of these: for tasting the air perhaps, or detecting vibrations in it, or were they some sort of external lung? Other forms of tentacles, mud-grey and provided with thick azure veins, had more predictable uses, for foraging or manipulation. There were at least two eyes – the professor could not be sure, owing to the apparent radial symmetry of the creature, whether there were any more on the side facing away from him – eyes that were large, black, oval saucers, adorned around their margins with spines and nodules. Plunging around in the morass of tentacles, smaller, eel-like creatures could be seen, although whether they were parasites, young, or simply using the larger creature as a habitat, the professor could not tell. The creature moved surprisingly quickly, tentacles brushing the ground in front as it came. Not far inside the doorway, it seemed to notice the professor sitting watching it, and swivelled its whole body so that the two great eyes were fixed upon him. A piping, fluting noise came from it, blown apparently through flaccid appendages that hung from its upper parts. The sound was complex, musical, dipping and rising in pitch. It seemed to be speaking.

"If that means 'I come in peace,' then I must apologize," replied the professor. "But this is no place for you. Return through the portal." He pointed back at the tree-lined doorway.

The creature did not move for a movement, regarding him unblinkingly. Then it moved off, away from him, but away from the doorway also, piping as it went. The professor leapt to his feet and moved quickly after it. He noticed that there was another eye, a smaller one, in the back of what might be described as the creature's head. Seeing him coming, it stopped moving and twisted its upper parts around fluidly so that the two big eyes were on him.

The professor stepped forward, drew his longer katana, and cut the creature somewhere below those expressionless eyes. The ease with which the blade entered the creature and passed out the other side threw him off balance; he straightened himself and prepared to hack at riposting tentacles. The counter-attack, though, never came; the creature seemed to be slowly deflating, oozing pus-like fluid through the gash the katana had opened in its front. The piping, musical speech died away to become a bubbling quiet, interrupted by the threshing of the wormy companions of the collapsing thing.

Professor Fuller stepped back, lowering his sword. Then he noticed that something strange was happening. The worms were growing. They were greedily consuming their former host, and as they devoured it, their bodies were ballooning in size with amazing rapidity. He raised his sword once again, and then strode forward, cutting indiscriminately at the writhing mass. He was able to kill these creatures with a blow, but now they were scattering, writhing away like maggots from a disturbed corpse. The professor pursued them, stamping and cutting; at one point one of them reared up as it was trodden on and, with a hitherto unseen mouth, bit him on the leg, but in moments the carnage was over and the last section of worm was flopping to a halt. A fetid stink hung in the air, like the smell released when a beachcomber turns over a pile of seaweed on the strandline.

The professor backed away, his face a grimace of distaste, wiping his shoes and katana on the dewy grass. Then he resumed his seat on the sword-roll, and put his right hand under his clothes to lay it on his heart. *Be calm*, he told himself, and breathed deeply. But he was not calm; his heart skipped, galloped, and fell over itself in its hurry to get wherever it was going. At times there was an empty pause of a second or more when it seemed to have given up beating altogether; at other times, the beats of his heart were so frequent that they ran together like a drum roll. *Be calm*, he said inwardly again, and he imagined his heart to be a giant clock in a high tower, whose huge gears and wheels moved with stately ease, as timeless as time itself.

Chapter 27: The Three Faces of William Tipler

David hurtled into the Tipler factory forecourt and skidded to a halt. The two Tollund boys were waiting for him. They had dressed themselves in their pretend-living forms, just as they had when he had first met them. Both looked up expectantly as David approached, and moved together to block his path to the factory itself. Behind them, the factory loomed into the grey sky, its outer surface as impenetrable and forbidding as it was in the real world, as if, like the stone column he had collided with earlier, it too had real substance here in Shadowland. The central door into the factory stood open, but it was too dark to see anything within. Huge, slow flakes of snow still settled out of the spectral sky, burning cold to the touch.

"Where is she?" demanded David.

The Tollund boys smiled. David was braced for them to become rotting corpses again, but for now at least, they did not. "Your friends not coming with you?" asked one of the boys. David glanced behind him. His accompanying wraiths were skulking in the shadowy background on the other side of the factory wall. They were too scared of what lurked within the factory to come any closer.

"Milla!" David shouted. His voice, muffled by the snow, fell into a cushioned silence.

Both boys found his shout inexplicably funny. Whatever they thought, he was not going to let them slow him down. David ran for the door through the gap between them. The boys moved swiftly, grabbing him before he could get past. As they did so, their transformation happened again, clothes shredding, living flesh becoming mummified skin and dead white bones. David tried to throw them off, expecting to cast them aside as easily as he had before; but this time the boys seemed to be more substantial, heavier, and they hung onto him fiercely with gappy teeth and broken nails. For a moment, the shock of their assault drove David back, but it was only for a moment. Nothing was going to stop him from saving Milla.

David shoved the right-hand boy away by main force, and then twisted in the grip of the other, succeeding in getting his right arm around the boy's neck before his friend could rejoin the fight. Keeping his headlock on the boy, he turned to face his companion, who was scrambling back towards them. David raised both feet in a kick at the oncoming boy, leaning his weight on the boy he had in the headlock, who collapsed under him. As they tumbled to the floor together, something strange and shocking happened: the raggy body of the boy split into pieces like the constituent parts of an old scarecrow and simply stopped moving. One of the Tollund boys was dead.

"You killed Paul," rattled the other Tollund boy, staring in disbelief.

"No," David, getting up, contradicted him, "*he* killed him." He stood, pointing at the factory. At his feet, the dead ghost was crumbling, reducing to a fine powder that mingled with the Shadowland snow and quickly evaporated. David ran for the door again, and this time the remaining Tollund boy made no move to stop him. The fight had gone out of him, and with it, the reason for his spirit to be there seemed to go too. As David ran past, he began to crumble just as his friend had done: his legs turned to dust, and his hollow torso collapsed soundlessly down into the snow. David barely had time to consider the disintegration of the two ghosts: in three paces, he was through the open doorway, and inside the Tipler factory once more.

There was no sign of Milla. Impenetrable darkness extended in all directions. "Milla!" he shouted once more, and his voice echoed hollowly in the void within the factory. There was no reply. He moved cautiously onwards. For a time he could see absolutely nothing. Then, ahead, a faint white glow began to develop. At first it seemed to form a strip at around waist height; then, as he got closer, he realized that he was looking at misty light falling from somewhere above and cascading onto a large stone block. Resting on the stone block, just as it had done in Tipler's vision of the vampire in the cellar, was a large, shiny coffin, its lid tightly closed. Was the ghost of William Tipler within? Where was Milla? David almost called out again, but he stifled his shout and moved on, picking his way carefully forwards. He passed the coffin, giving it a wide berth, and tiptoed into the darker unlit recesses of the factory. It was by now very cold, and growing colder all the time. He could feel his warmth, his energy, his very life force draining away by the moment, and could only guess at what condition Milla was in, if she was even still alive after all this time in the Shadowland. The inside of the factory was huge, impossibly so; it was as if William Tipler had distorted the space within to frustrate, disorient, and weaken his adversary. David knew that he could not outwait a creature with the patience of a crocodile; he would have to open the coffin and confront whatever awaited within. But just as he had made up his mind, a faint voice from the darkness startled him.

"David?" it was Milla's voice. She sounded tired, and a long way away. "Don't say anything," she added quickly, "and stay away from the coffin!"

Milla was still alive! He turned towards the sound of her voice, far away in the darkness, and waited for her to speak again so that he could find her. She had not found Nathan here – only the vengeful spirit of William Tipler. He moved quietly in the vague direction Milla's voice had come from; the further he moved from the coffin, the darker it became, until he was shuffling forward blindly, arms outstretched. Why didn't she speak?

"David!" Milla's voice hissed out of the darkness. There was an urgent note of warning in her voice – but she seemed, if anything, further away than before.

David froze. He looked around him, but there was nothing to be seen. Just a sea of impenetrable darkness, and a coffin on a stone platform, much nearer than it should have been... David's eyes swept twice past the coffin, washed in that ethereal light from above, before he noticed that the lid had silently opened. "William," David called desperately, "it doesn't have to be this way!"

"William, my dear," a crooning voice said quietly from behind him.

The gaunt wraiths were scattering from around the gloomy doorway again, chattering to one another in distress. Over the noise of the wraiths a threatening rattle could be heard, dry and gravelly like the shaken tail of a rattlesnake. Something new was approaching the portal between worlds.

The professor was still kneeling on his sword-roll, meditating, trying to settle his pulse. A small flower of pain was budding in his chest to add to the discomfort of his skipping heart. He disinterestedly considered the possibility that he might be dying. The threat of his own death did not alarm him: it saddened him. There was a poison in Fairfield that only he knew how to draw. The only two people he could pass his secret knowledge to were relying on him to keep their escape route open. He knew that the only chance he had was to disregard his own life, to reject the distinction between life and death. To treasure something is to protect it; to protect it is to fear its loss; to fear its loss is to lose objectivity. Clouded thinking could lose a battle before it had begun.

He focussed his attention on the Shadowland doorway. The wraiths were all gone, and the rattling noise had ceased, but an air of expectation was left in this apparent void. The new entity was not long in coming. At first all he could see was a gleam of white, an arch of bone; then, as it moved closer, the entire alien form became clear.

For how long, and through what realms it had travelled, it was impossible for him to guess. There was something of a scorpion about it in its legs, movement and armour plating, but in form it was more like a fantastic creature of legend, a centaur: it was supported on four legs, like a horse, but they were jointed like an arthropod's, and splayed out; there was a torso-like extension to its body rearing up at the front, somewhat like the humanoid part of a centaur, but there the resemblance ended. Its arms, waving about in front of it like antennae, were finger-thin, little more than folded, jointed spines. It had no neck, for its head was just a rounded ending to its torso. The head itself contained unblinking eyes that glittered in deep pools of shadow; a stout, sharp, horny beak could be seen set close below them. It came on in a jerky fashion, scuttling and then stopping, testing the air with those raptorial arms before advancing again.

Most bizarre perhaps of all the creature's strange features was its outer covering. It had partly enclosed itself in the long limb-bones and bleached, malformed skulls of its prey, which it had glued to every inch of its body to form grotesque protective armour.

The creature fixed its attention on the motionless professor as soon as it had squeezed through the doorway into the real world. For a time it did not move, watching him with those glassy eyes, but then it hurried forwards until it was almost upon him before stopping once more. It loomed over the professor, deadly arms extended above his head, for a few moments as still as he was. From this close position Professor Fuller, moving yet only his rheumy eyes, scanned every inch of the creature's bone-encased surface, hunting for gaps, weaknesses in that hideous armour. Amongst the adorning skulls of strange, alien creatures that it had killed was one that was clearly a human skull. A very small one. Seeing this, the professor's rein on his emotions slipped a little, and he twitched, almost pulling out his swords. He gathered himself in a split second and froze once more, but too late.

The bone-demon's spine-like arms snapped down like a spring-loaded trap closing. Quick as they were, the professor was quicker, drawing his longer sword and parrying both forelimbs before they could reach him. With his other hand, he drew his shorter sword and stabbed at a chink in the creature's armoured chest; he missed, only succeeding in chipping a bent limb-bone. Then the monster drew back its arms and tried to nail him again; this time he rolled out of the attack and riposted with a double cut at the creature's flank, but his swords skated harmlessly over its armour. After that, he ran, using the upright stones dotted about the circle as cover, pursued by the darting bone-demon, which was hissing at him in its rage. Even as it hunted him down, he was formulating a plan, working out where his weapons had the best chance of striking home, calculating which part of the landscape he could best use to his advantage. The weakness of any suit of armour comes from its moving parts, he reflected, dodging a flailing forelimb; a joint encased in armour cannot move, therefore joints must be vulnerable. Unfortunately, lethal spine-tipped arms and a stabbing beak protected these weak points. He would have to get close – but not *too* close. He was feeling light-headed, and breathing was becoming hard; the flower of pain in his chest was blooming. He would have to end this soon, if it was to end in his favour. He could not allow this creature to chase him down until he was exhausted.

A pair of upright stones that were close together gave him an idea. He worked his way towards them, going out of his way to conceal the fact that he was deliberately heading in a particular direction; the creature followed, darting after him, lunging, and then darting once more. He slipped between the two stones and awaited the creature's next move; whichever way it came for him, he had a chance to strike. He stabbed the longer katana into the ground and transferred the shorter blade to his right hand.

The creature came, not as he had hoped, over or between the stones, but around them, showing an unguessed-at intelligence. Its approach was clever, but its attack was predictable, both spine arms spearing down to transfix him so that its robust beak-like mouthparts could be deployed. The professor grabbed one of the spines as it came down, and stabbed home his sword where the limb joined the creature's torso. It went in easily, up to its rounded guard stop, but pain flashed into his left shoulder as the bone-demon's other spine struck home. The combatants reeled apart, the professor diving behind the stones, pulling away with him the sword, which brought with it a rush of red blood.

The professor pushed himself upright, concentrating on readying his defence; but the bone-demon was fleeing, scuttling towards the surrounding forest. He picked up his longer sword as he watched it go. With its injured forelimb hanging uselessly, it hurried to the outer ring of stones and stopped dead as if hitting an invisible wall. Confused, the creature shuffled about, trying to circumvent this unseen obstacle; but try as it might, there was no escape from the stone circle. After a minute or so, it gave up, and turned towards the professor once more. "Back the way you came," he told it, "if you want to live." The creature hissed loudly at him and waved its good arm threateningly. The professor raised both his swords, ignoring the searing pain in his left shoulder. The bone-encased monster moved forwards, but it was not coming towards him; instead, it gave him a wide berth, and cautiously carried on in the direction of the doorway through which it had come. Professor Fuller watched it go, turning to keep it in view as it passed him.

There seemed to be something else in the doorway, blocking the monster's path. For a moment he thought that David was back, but it soon became clear that he was not looking at a boy. This was something vastly larger, a huge reddish humanoid that had to bend double to get through the doorway.

"Hurry, David," whispered the professor.

By its stealthy approach the monster had crept to within a few metres of him; now, relishing David's terror, it stood still and waited for him to move. Its grotesquely oversized head loomed over him, its fanged mouth hanging open in an insane smile; a beard of blood dripped down its chin. It slowly raised its thin arms, eyes gleaming, flexing its claw-like hands. What he had thought in his vision of the monster were occult symbols covering every inch of its flesh turned out, this close, to be children's drawings, scribbles, and badly-formed writing. "William, my dear…" the creature murmured.

"I'm not William – you are," David said desperately. For a moment it was almost as if comprehension flickered in the monster's dead eyes, but that glimmer was immediately consumed by fury. The monster lunged for him, its jaws agape. David skipped backwards, almost tripping, and began to flee blindly. "Milla!" he shouted as he ran. "Where are you?"

"Over here," came a voice from David's right.

David stopped short and looked. He could see nothing. Behind him he could hear the jerky, lurching approach of the monster. "I can't…" he began, but Milla *was* there, as if she had somehow willed herself to be visible. She was tied or chained to a similar stone platform to the one the monster's coffin rested on. "Milla!" David called again, rushing to her side.

"I'm all right. Just get me out of here."

"I had thought of that," rejoined David.

"I just need to get at my pocket… but I can't move my arms."

"Hang on," David said, his hands feverishly skating over her bonds, trying to find a weak point.

"David," hissed Milla, pointing with her face over his shoulder.

The monster was closing in, stalking across the floor, its footsteps uneven. Panicking, David tore at the ropes binding Milla to the stone, but he was not making much of an impression upon them. He did not need to turn his head to see the monster's approach; Milla's expression painted him an exquisite portrait of what was looming over him.

"No time," he hissed, half-turning. The monster was upon him, and flailing with its clumsy hands it knocked him to the ground and bore down on him. Its mouth opened once more. A sewer-stink blast of vapour swept over him. Tipler's vampire fangs gleamed in the darkness like two wickedly curving daggers, and hung over him, poised to strike. There was no time to move as the fangs stabbed down; all David could do was interpose an arm between his face and the toothy knives. He flinched, bracing himself for searing pain; but instead of the fangs spearing through him, something incredible happened. As the fangs hit him, they shattered like crystal, bursting into a thousand fragments that exploded in all directions that scattered all over the floor. William Tipler was as brittle as the Tollund boys had been.

Tipler reeled back, holding his mouth, keening in pain; David went after him. This was no vampire, only a ghost, a mere shadow of the monster it was mimicking. A long-dead, scheming, evil ghost, but only that. And in this world, he was more than a match for a ghost. He lashed out at the confused monster, and his fist smashed its already bloody face. Tipler leapt back, screaming and weeping, but David would not let him go; he was on his feet and after him in a flash. He quickly closed in and attacked again, punching, kicking, and tearing. Pouring vile fluid, Tipler fell to his knees and tried to drag himself away, but David was not about to let him escape. He thought of all the evil Tipler had done him, thought of Nathan, of Milla, and of his own narrow escape, and he screamed at Tipler in fury as he rained blows upon his already shattered body.

At last the monster that William Tipler had become stopped moving. David had pulverized him utterly. He staggered away and fell to his knees, exhausted.

"Hurry," Milla said.

David looked up. Her face looked down on him from her position on the stone platform. He had to rouse himself for another effort. He staggered to his feet and began to pick at the ropes pinning her down, in a calmer, more systematic way than before.

"Thanks for coming to save me," Milla said.

David looked down on her and managed a smile. "Coming here was a crazy thing to do," he said. "How were you planning to get back?"

"Same way I got in. But how did *you* get in?"

"The professor's opened a doorway at a place called Hungry Hill. Speaking of which, we'd better hurry. He's worried about what things might be attracted to it."

"That's why you shut it behind you. Polka told me that a long time ago."

"He doesn't know how. He doesn't do magic very well. He's a scientist, you know." As he spoke, David suddenly noticed something. After he had killed the monster, the atmosphere within the factory had seemed to lighten, the enveloping darkness lifting a little; now, the light was waxing still further, almost as if the dawn was coming.

"Quickly," whispered Milla, having noticed the change too. She seemed to be looking at something somewhere behind him. There was something else in the factory with them. David stopped trying to free Milla and turned around to follow her horrified gaze.

It was a sight that David remembered well. Enormous, vague, the monster had gathered about itself the darkness in the factory like myriad tattered veils. The two fishlike eyes were the first feature visible on the surface of the creature as it approached. Here was the beast that had swallowed up the ghost of his brother. For a moment David's heart sank: he had thought the ghost of Tipler was finished, but it seemed that the battle had only just begun. Close on the heels of black despair, tinged with more than a colour or two of fear, came fury, joyful, red fury.

David balled his fists and went to meet William Tipler once more.

"David, wait, just get me out…"

"It's all right," he told Milla without turning around. "He doesn't scare me any more." Milla was saying something else, but he couldn't hear her. He was running, charging straight for the night-thing, the simulacrum of the Solvent Man, the Alchemist, with a mind only for tearing the vile creature to pieces one shadow at a time. As he neared the ghost, he ran through the chilly wisps of nightmare darkness that were swirling around it. It was not fully formed when he reached it, but he saw no reason to wait. He swung his fist as hard as he could, aiming at somewhere around Tipler's middle, but his punch met little resistance and his arm plunged straight into ice-cold, watery slime. Before he could draw back, his arm was in up to the elbow; as he pulled it back, the blackness clung to him like syrup, remaining attached to the ghost. He tried to free his hand by chopping down at the pseudopodium-like structure joining him to Tipler, but this only resulted in transferring some of the goo onto his other arm, further ensnaring him.

This, he suddenly realized with a terrible feeling of foolishness and despair, was like Brer Rabbit fighting the Tar Baby, a fight he could never win. He remembered the blazing form of Nathan gradually enveloped by the blackness; too late, he knew that running had been the better option. He punched at the ghost, kicked at it, and screamed at it. But it simply oozed out of the way of his physical attacks and flowed over him with gentle, tide-like inevitability. His leg got stuck in the ooze and he toppled onto the floor, bringing liquid night down with him. He saw a glimpse of Milla, who was still struggling to free her arms from the ropes that bound her. "Run," he shouted, "Run…" he could say no more because the blackness had flowed into his mouth. His eyes flinched shut as the gluey fluid crept over them; his last sight was of Milla shouting something at him, but he could not tell what because his ears were already covered.

Strange sensations swept over him. He seemed to be sinking into the liquid, which was impossible, because he was lying on the floor already. He kept his eyes clamped shut, but was choking, gagging on the liquid in his throat because he had automatically tried to take a breath. Something seemed to be tugging at his ankle. Something else jostled him. He opened his eyes, and was amazed to find that he could see. Indefinite shapes swam around him in the dark water, grey, humanoid forms that pawed at him and clutched at his arms and legs. These were ghosts Tipler had swallowed, David realized. Nathan would be here somewhere. He tried to call his brother's name, but could make no sound, only lost some more air. Then he noticed that above him in the water there was sparkling light – the surface? He struck up towards it, pulling free of the flailing hands of the ghosts, and broke through. The direction of *up* veered through a right angle in a moment; he had emerged out of the side of the monster and could see *below* him the floor of the factory. As quickly as he had emerged, the suffocating tentacles were drawing him in once more; he remembered Nathan's final emergence, his desperate pleas for David to run… still he could not breathe. Stars of false light twinkled in his eyes… was Milla running? He craned his neck to look, his only wish that she would be gone, that she had managed to free herself before she joined him in death…

Milla was free all right, but she was not running away. She was facing the ghost, pulling something out of her pockets – it looked like she was holding two handfuls of confetti. That was all he saw before he went under again, and once again the direction of *up* changed and he was sinking. As he faded, lights glimmered above him like sunlight playing on the waves… then came some real waves, and he was thrown up, sucked down, and whirled about as the cold dark sea became a stormy one. Then he was falling, and landed heavily on a hard floor. He coughed and choked, but could breathe once more; the foul liquid had gone, and he was back in the factory, lying on the floor. The first thing he saw was Milla, her arms wide, shouting; rolling over, he saw that something had happened to the ghost of Tipler. Its black surface was barely visible under a covering of glowing pieces of paper… no, not paper, but *petals*. They were what Milla had drawn from her pockets, the same lotus petals that she had used earlier to open the first door into the Shadowland. Tipler was screaming, shrinking, and disgorging one grey ghost after another, which as they emerged fell to the ground, rose, blinked dumbly, and simply stood, gawping around them. The shadowy form was now no larger than a normal man; as it shrank the lotus petals covered more of the surface, and quickly they joined together until they completely concealed it. More ghosts, opaque, waxy, and blank-faced were emerging, perhaps ten or twelve in all. As the last ghost emerged, the lotus petals lost their glow and began to blow away; there was nothing, only emptiness, underneath them.

For a time David could do nothing but lie on his back, gasping like a fish on the riverbank. Milla appeared above him, kneeling down to take his hand. "You saved me," coughed David. "Why didn't you say you had those petals in your pocket?"

"I tried," Milla said, and smiled. "You don't think I would have come all this way without a plan, do you?" She pulled him up into a sitting position. Around them, the ashen figures of Tipler's ghostly victims wandered to and fro, lost, unaware.

"That's Nathan," snapped David suddenly, spotting his brother among them. Milla helped David to his feet, and together they moved to intercept Nathan.

Nathan did not notice them as they approached; when they blocked his path, he tried to move around them. David grabbed his brother by the arm. Nathan was solid and cold; he was unresisting, and stood as placidly as a tethered sheep.

"Nathan, it's me, David," David said urgently, desperately seeking a flicker of recognition in the pale grey eyes of his dead brother, but finding none. Nathan was gone, as lost as all the other lonely ghosts that Tipler had once devoured and had now in his demise vomited up. David hugged Nathan; his brother was unresponsive. How long had he wished to be able to hold his brother! And here he was, able to grasp him as if he had never died, only for him to be as warm and aware as stone.

From somewhere in the shadows of the factory, a distraught howling could be heard. Both David and Milla looked for the source of the noise, and when a couple of ghosts had ambled out of the way, they could see what it was.

"Tipler!" hissed David. A pale, naked boy was curled up on the floor in the corner, crying his heart out. "Keep hold of Nathan," David ordered Milla, and stalked towards the boy, fiercely taut with anger. As he approached, he felt his steps becoming gluey, slowing, finally halting altogether – just as other, cooler steps emerged from his shadow and strode quickly ahead. He was advancing on William and he was standing still; William was a naked ghost curled up in the open and he was a well-dressed boy crouched behind a massive loom.

David pulled a metal case from his pocket and opened it. Within was a cold, reeking pad; the smell he so delighted in waxed as he took the pad from the case. He was smiling as he approached the boy, who was too frightened to move. He said not a word. He felt the worms rippling under his skin as, laughing silently, he reached down for the boy and pressed the pad to his face.

As William fell limp in his arms, he realized that a voice was calling him. His violent joy vanished as if he had been struck. William Tipler was still a few steps away, watching him out of the corner of his eye. The voice was calling him again.

"He'll get you," Tipler said, his voice that of a well-bred boy. "I've seen it all. You can't beat him. No-one can."

"And the grey one? In the coffin?"

Tipler smiled, then clacked his jaws maniacally, eyes shining insanely. "William, my dear," he said, his voice having become a sinister croon. His eyes refocused suddenly. "Why did you come back for her? Why?"

"That's what we do for those we love…"

"My father never came back for me…"

"He loved you. He was distraught about your death… that's why he killed himself…"

The calling was insistent, anguished, and it was growing fainter.

"He didn't kill himself," Tipler said, and bowed his head in shame. "I was angry! So angry! I waited for him and waited…"

"You must let go of your anger," David said, but he knew that his words were hollow.

Tipler knew it, too. "Anger! You are full of it! You hate me, you hate the one who took your brother… just as I hate my uncle. Bring me my uncle. Let me hear him say why he gave me to them. Let me hear him say sorry for what he did to my mother… bring him and I will leave all these other ghosts be."

"Is he still alive?"

"David! David!"

"I would know if he were dead. Find him for me. Go – quickly. Your friend needs you…"

Milla was in trouble. David ran, following the sound of her voice, and through the crowd of listless ghosts he finally saw her. She was on the floor, and Nathan was on top of her. She was desperately trying to fend him off, calling David as she fought. Nathan was crushing her with his arms and bearing down on her with his mouth agape.

"Nathan!" David shouted as he ran towards them. His brother paid him no heed. David reached them, grabbed Nathan by the shoulder and dragged him off Milla. Nathan wheeled on David, his eyes wild, his hands clutching. David tried to push him away, but his sunken-eyed, ghoulish brother would not be put off. After backing away for a while with his zombie-like sibling following, grabbing at him, David at last resorted to swinging his fist at his brother's head. Nathan fell in a heap, but quickly got up again and started back towards Milla, who was still lying on the floor.

"Nathan, no!" shouted David, and grabbed his brother by both shoulders.

"You're not yourself," he said, wrestling Nathan towards the stone platform where Milla had been tied up. "I'll come back for you, I promise," he said. He would get Milla safely out of the Shadowland, and then he would circle back in the real world to find Nathan. It would be like that first time in the cemetery – Nathan lost, bewildered, until contact with his brother reawakened him. Nathan was free of Tipler at least: David was so close to rescuing him that he could hardly believe it. Hope surged in him. He was finally about to repay a small part of his debt. But first he must get back to the real world. He managed to get Nathan at least partly tied down, and praying that his brother would not free himself and wander off before he could return for him, he ran back to the prone Milla. He grabbed her hand and pulled her up to a sitting position. "We've got to get out of here," he said tersely.

"What did he do to me?" she asked faintly.

"He was after your life force, energy, call it what you like. That's where ghosts get it from – people."

"He took too much," Milla said, her voice weak. She could barely stand. David put her left arm around his shoulder, and then put his right arm around her middle. He felt some of his earlier optimism evaporate as they started to move clumsily and agonizingly slowly towards the door of the factory. Some of the other ghosts seemed to notice them for the first time, staring at them blank-faced, and one or two even began to edge towards them. Luckily, none of the ghosts were between them and the door, and before any of the hungry spirits could intercept them they were staggering out of the Tipler factory.

They were met by a wall of cold as they stepped outside. The snow was by now ankle deep, and was still falling. "How far is it?" gasped Milla.

"Don't worry – we'll get there," David assured her, trying to sound more confident than he felt.

Chapter 28: The Way Back

The professor was gasping for breath. He hurried to the flat stone where his revolver and the open book of summoning were lying, snatched them both up, and carried on moving, out of sight of the doorway. He stationed himself behind the great stones of the portal, and, looking through, was able to watch the next intruder arrive. It was a vast, reddish humanoid, grossly muscled. As if born of the thinly misted air, its back loomed in front of the professor as it emerged on the other side of the doorway. It was laughing a deep cruel laugh as it straightened up to its full height, a bass-drum chuckle that brought a warning hiss from the bone-demon. The latter backed away, but too late: the crimson giant leapt forwards and seized it in his oversized hands. The fight between the two was brief and brutal, and ended with the bone-demon in pieces, smashed like kindling. The red demon carried on demolishing the remains of his opponent long after it was dead, pounding, tearing, and snapping, glorying in his immense strength.

The professor watched this display silently. He carefully stowed the open book on top of the stone lintel of the doorway, hidden from casual view by mildewed branches. He considered his options. This new demon was huge, strong, and ran deep with untameable ferocity, but it was flesh and blood. His weapons could bite, if he had the time to use them.

The colossal beast, having reduced his victim to a pulpy mass of meat and scattered fragments of bone, tried to leave the stone circle. He found the same problem as his predecessor: an invisible, impenetrable wall. He threw himself against it, pounded it with his great fists, bellowing in fury, but to no avail. Suddenly he stopped and turned around, looking about him with a cunning expression. He spat something, an expression that Professor Fuller could not catch. Then the demon began to stride back towards the portal, straight at the professor, who knew that he could not be seen; from the demon's perspective, the portal opened onto the Shadowland. It was as if the professor was looking out through a two-way mirror: he could see, but not be seen.

The demon was close now, and was peering at the portal intently, as if suspecting the presence of the professor. He stared at the portal for some time, and then decided to go around the back and look behind it. It was the professor's only chance: wait any longer, and he would be discovered, and the element of surprise would be lost. He stepped through the doorway and cut the demon across the back of its neck, striking down with all his remaining strength. The blow from the longer sword would have killed a human instantly, but this was no human. The sword lodged, stuck in sinew tough as wood; only as the demon turned to face his assailant did it come free.

The demon smiled with a mouthful of misshapen teeth as it saw who had attacked it. "Human," it laughed. Then it roared, trying to cow him with an explosion of sound.

The professor stood his ground, sword at the ready. If only I was ten years younger, he thought, I could win this. Blood eddied unevenly in his head, making him dizzy and blurring his vision. The pain in his heart had mingled with that in his wounded shoulder; redoubled, the aching pressure spread all down his left side.

The demon lunged, and the professor moved, too slowly… its next grab would have him… and then he had an idea. It was a ghost of a chance, but it was all he had. The professor jumped back, through the doorway, out of the real world and into the icy wastes of the Shadowland.

David took most of Milla's weight and led her through the gossamer curtain, the Shadowland equivalent of the brick wall that marked the perimeter of the courtyard. As soon as they emerged on the other side, the first of the pale wraiths reappeared. It was joined by another, and another; by the time they had taken a hundred paces, they were accompanied by at least a dozen of the things. As before, the wraiths followed at a constant distance, but this time they were bolder, much closer than they had been before. David ached for a rest; beside him, Milla was still moving her legs, but they were no longer taking any of her weight. "Keep going," he lied, "we're nearly there."

In truth they were still moving through the outskirts of Fairfield, and were only just approaching the roundabout where David had encountered the large red demon. They had saved time by avoiding the diversion he had been forced to take through the frozen people, but still had a great distance to cover, most of it uphill.

No longer did David feel superhuman; the battles with William Tipler and the sapping cold had taken nearly all of his energy, so that it was now an effort of will simply to keep walking. The cold bored into him from the snow-bound ground; it rained on his back like a fall of stones; it stabbed at him with icy knives until his heart seemed as cold as a fish's. They plodded on, legs stiff and numb. Still the burning cold snow filtered out of the grey Shadowland sky. Still the hollow-chested cooing monsters followed.

Milla had said nothing for some time. Suddenly she pitched forwards, pulling him over with her. The wraiths hooted excitedly and began to close in, but quickly backed away again when David lurched to his feet and waved his fists at them. He stooped to help Milla up, but she resisted his attempts to pull her to her feet.

"I can't," she said, "there's nothing left." She would not look at him.

"On my back," he ordered.

"You can't," she objected.

"GET ON MY BACK!" he screamed, and fell on his knees. With Milla's arms around his neck and her legs around his waist, he staggered to his feet once again, and started to walk.

He could see the woods now, the jumbled beautiful ghosts of a million trees. They had reached the foot of the hill. It had seemed only a short way from hill top to hill bottom when he had been running down; on his return, the little hill had become a mountain. David thought of nothing for a while except his footsteps. He took one step, then another, and then the next; each was harder than the last, each shorter, less sure. He told himself that they must be nearly there, willing it to be so. But his hopes were crushed when a landmark came into view on the right, one he remembered from his dash down the hill, a zigzag column of rock that in hopeful oblivion he had assumed that they had long since passed. They were still nearer the bottom of the hill than the top. At that sight, in that moment, he allowed himself to think for the first time that they might not make it back.

David could hardly move his legs. Despair began to weigh on him as heavily as the exhausted Milla. He could walk for eternity and never reach his destination. All his plans for rescuing Nathan had been snatched away from him again. His brother, should he escape the phantom snares he was caught in, would wander, empty and lost, for all eternity.

Milla was silent, a dead weight on his back. She might be unconscious for all he knew, but he did not have the breath to ask her. Around him the patient wraiths piped whooping music to one another, knowing their moment was close. He staggered twice, righting himself both times, but at last his legs gave way beneath him and down he went, his fall and Milla's cushioned by the deepening snow. Milla could barely move, and David could no longer lift her. He was physically spent, frozen, and for some reason he wanted to sleep, he was desperate to close his eyes and curl up in the snow, heedless of the murderous monsters waiting, longing for him finally to give up. Every inch of his body screamed at him, but he somehow got his numb feet under him once again. He could no longer lift Milla, but started to drag her behind him instead.

"Go – please," she murmured.

He said nothing, his teeth clenched. He kept a vice-like grip around one of her wrists, and went back to counting steps. At some point he lost count of steps. He was even a little confused as to where he was going, but it didn't matter. He knew that he must climb. All that mattered was that he placed one foot in front of the other, and repeated the movement over and over again. Once more he slipped, and the breath was knocked out of him. He got to his knees, and then to his feet, and started to drag Milla again, or tried to: he no longer had the strength to move her. The wraiths were coming in closer now, barely an arm's reach away, a crowd of them, their button-bright eyes shining. Milla was saying something, but at first he couldn't catch it.

"I said I'm not cold any more," she whispered. "You go on ahead."

A glimmer of anger warmed his heart: a flaring match, quickly dead. "You really don't know me if you think I'm ever going to give up on you," he snapped.

"Please," she begged quietly. He gazed at her, amazed: Milla was crying tears that quickly became beautiful crystals, tumbled down her cheeks, and fell, diamond hail lost in the Shadowland snow.

David gave up trying to drag Milla on and sank down on his knees beside her. He held her close, covering her with his own body. The leering wraiths inched closer, their toothed proboscises extended, until they were almost touching him. "Leave her alone!" he shouted, rearing up and swinging clenched fists at them, and they danced away a metre or two. But with this lunge went the last of his energy. The grey-white forms moved in again, keening gently, hypnotically. He no longer had the will to resist them. When the first proboscis latched onto him, there was a moment of pain, but only a moment; others joined their fellow, fastening onto him, and he almost revelled in the freedom of having finally given up. Other wraiths had got past his shielding body and had started feeding on Milla, too. His only hope was that she felt as little pain as he did.

Between the gorging wraiths he could see that the light was growing – surely it could not be dawn already? Maybe the dawn would scare them off, and bring with it a little warmth... but he quickly forgot that hope. It could not be dawn yet. He could have been in the Shadowland no more than an hour – and yet, the sky was definitely getting brighter, so much so that the wraiths were silhouetted against it. The light did not bother them in the slightest: they carried on feeding, jostling for the best position. David felt his eyes closing and no longer had the strength to keep them open. *If this is death*, he thought, *it's not so bad. Just like falling asleep after a long day...*

Suddenly the contented cooing noises the wraiths were making became hooting, screaming notes of panic. With a final monumental effort, David opened his eyes again. The circle of wraiths had opened; none of them were feeding any more. Something had disturbed their feast, but he could not see what, he could only blearily make out fleeing ash-grey forms. Then a hooting cry was cut short, and he looked that way; a wraith had just been torn in half by –

At first he thought it was a living firestorm, an inferno given human shape; then, as his eyes adjusted to the figure's brilliant aura, he realized that it was a boy, a boy of about his size. The boy, burning like a supernova, raged after the howling ghouls, scattering them in all directions. He caught several, tearing them to pieces like paper; others he caught glancing blows as they fled that were enough to break them like birds that had been struck by a speeding car. When there were no more of the wraiths within range, the boy turned to David and Milla, the golden illuminance that surrounded him dying away until only a faint glow was left.

"Nathan," gasped David. It was all he had the strength to say. His brother knelt down beside them and touched them both on the forehead with warm hands. David felt the warmth from his brother's hand suffuse his body, pushing away the aching cold, restoring his strength. Beneath him, Milla was stirring to life also.

"Come on," Nathan told them. "We have to get you out of here."

Professor Fuller quickly surveyed the Shadowland landscape. He could see a little way in all directions, but there was no sign of David; the only movement was of that of the wary wraiths backing out of his way. The demon followed him, slowly, cramped in the narrow doorway between the ancient stones. From this side, the Shadowland gateway was nothing more than a dark, irregular rectangle, a slash in the fabric of the world.

The demon was coming for him. "Kill me," the professor said, backing away, ready to sting the monster one last time with his katanas, "and the portal will close."

The demon laughed again, his mop of black hair shaking. "There will be other days, other doors, but not for you," he growled, and charged.

Professor Fuller stopped backing off and swung his sword at the onrushing giant; the impact of the blow jarred his wrists, and the sword once again stuck fast, this time in one of the monster's reaching forearms. It was hopeless, like hewing at a tree. He pulled out his other sword and swung that, but the demon batted it out of his hands, and it sailed off through the air. Then it swung a fist at him; the professor dodged most of the blow, but caught enough of it to be sent tumbling to the ground, half-stunned. He pulled out his old Webley revolver and fired it at the monster's chest, desperately pulling the trigger again and again until instead of an explosion only an apologetic click answered. The demon was undeterred by the volley of bullets. It advanced and stood over him, glaring down in hatred. Once again it opened its mouth to roar, but this time no explosion of sound came out; its chest foamed bloodily as air escaped through the bullet holes in it. The professor tried to scramble backwards, but his strength was fading; he thought he should head back to the portal, but could not be sure where exactly it was, lost as it was in all these shadows. The demon pressed him down, bending its head towards his, toothy mouth agape, eyes furious.

Then came an incongruous sound, distinct, like the snapping of a flag in the wind. The demon was falling, collapsing on top of him, a great, suffocating mass. But it had stopped moving. Its knotted muscles had relaxed. Suddenly it was moving once more, rearing away from him, but the professor quickly realized that it was not moving by its own volition. Standing behind it was a boy, one of the professor's swords in his right hand, easily dragging the demon's enormous weight away with his left hand. The boy was glowing from head to foot, suffused in golden light as if he had been woven out of a million sunbeams. He was smiling.

"Nathan Carraway, I presume," said the professor, and fell back, exhausted.

David and Milla stood by as Nathan rested his palm on the professor's forehead, imparting some of Milla's borrowed energy to the old man. Around them, the omnipresent ghouls were closing in again, this time daring each other to feed on the carcass of the red demon.

"Is he all right?" asked David.

The professor's eyes flickered open. "Of course he's all right," he snapped. He allowed Nathan to pull him to his feet. The professor was quite a sight: he was bruised and cut, and his clothes were stained with blood and gore. Still, he drew himself to his full height with dignity and even tried to straighten his collar. "We must leave this place," he said.

There was no disagreement from any of the others. The professor led the way out, followed by Milla, David and Nathan. Behind them, the wraiths had at last found their feast: they fell on the remains of the red demon, hooting with triumph.

"Good feeding tonight," David commented.

"I'm going to close the doorway," the professor told Nathan pointedly.

Nathan nodded. "It's all right," he said.

Professor Fuller reached stiffly up for the old book, drew it down from the lintel and snapped it shut.

"You're safe now," Nathan said to David.

"You mean *we're* safe now."

Nathan ignored him. "That was a crazy thing you did, coming after me," he said.

"Blame her," David told him, indicating Milla, who had sat down beside the professor on a flat stone and was gingerly examining his wounded shoulder, wincing at what she saw as she peeled back torn clothes. "And anyway, that's what we do, remember? Whatever it takes."

Nathan did not reply.

"So – was it you? Who got me out of the factory?" David asked, grinning.

Nathan smiled. "I was able to influence Tipler a little sometimes. But you came back! Why on earth did you come back?"

"Why do you think? Same reason you always come back for me. And what about in the hospital? Did you influence him then?"

"I don't know… I was trying to, but it was hard… maybe there was always something in him that was not pure evil… we had something in common that he recognized: the Solvent Man. I tried to show him that we have the same hatred for the Solvent Man that he does. Without that… maybe that encounter in the hospital would have turned out differently, and he wouldn't have got you out of the factory that first time."

"Listen. About the Solvent Man. We're getting closer to finding him. He's called the Alchemist, and when you look at him through the shadow lens, he's nothing but worms..."

"Dave, come here a minute," interrupted his brother. Nathan led him off a little way.

"What is it?" demanded David. A sinking feeling was growing rapidly in the pit of his stomach.

"You know I can't stay, don't you?" Nathan asked simply.

"Of course, you'll have to back through, back to how you were, I realize that... you can't go around glowing everywhere..." David looked at his brother's face, seeking reassurance. There was none to be found. Nathan was shaking his head.

"I have to go. I don't know where I'm going, but I have to find out."

David grabbed his arm. "You can't leave now – not when we're so close to catching your killer... with you back we'll nail him in no time..."

"I want you to drop it," Nathan said firmly. "Forget about it. It's too dangerous. And there's no point. You can't change the past, you can't... bring me back, however much you want to, however much I wish you could. People die. We have to let them go. Remember them forever. But let them go."

David could only clutch his brother tighter, voicelessly forbidding him to go.

"I've realized why I couldn't leave... it wasn't to find out what happened to me, or even to find out what happened to Mum and Dad... it wasn't my death I cared about, but your life, Dave. I couldn't leave you on your own." He looked away, towards where Milla and the professor were sitting. "You're not on your own any more."

David found his voice at last. "No," he said. His hoarse whisper rapidly grew to an anguished howl. "You're not leaving me. You don't know how long I've wanted you to be real so I could hold you again..."

"Me too. But it isn't realistic," Nathan said quietly. "Look where it ends up… look at Michael and his brother…"

"His brother!"

"Still-born twin."

"You never told me."

"I guessed – then some things I saw in Anna Andersen's bedroom confirmed it. Didn't think you'd go through with it if you knew," explained Nathan apologetically. "I'd better apologize to Milla for stealing some of her energy – she's going to be one powerful witch one day…"

David looked at his feet. His brother disentangled himself gently and moved over to Milla and Professor Fuller, speaking to them in quiet tones. David couldn't hear what was being said, but he didn't need to. Tears welled up in his eyes. For a moment he fought them as he always did, but this time there was no holding them back; this time the floodgates finally burst. He fell to his knees, sobbing openly.

Nathan returned, kneeling in front of him, holding him for the last time. "Demon hunting was fun, wasn't it?" he asked. "But you know what? Homework is more important."

David could say nothing, only nod dumbly in agreement.

"You'll see me again, I know it. Not too soon. But you will… this moment is one I will never forget… but it was not meant to last…" Nathan began to fade, dissolving into mist; the harder David held him, the less there was to hold, like sand falling through his fingers, until in a few moments his arms were tight against his own chest and Nathan was gone.

Chapter 29: A Ghost Hunter Calls

On the TV, a boy hurtled down a snowy slope on a toboggan, collided with another boy on a toboggan, and both were sent sprawling into the snow. A studio audience chortled with amusement at their misfortune.

An old man and an old woman were watching the TV, or rather they were allowing the noise of it to fill the room and fill a decadal void in their conversation. The old man had once been tall and strong; now arthritis had twisted his spine and wasted his legs. His ears had continued growing all his life and were now almost comically large. His hair was perhaps the only thing about him that retained any youth; although so thin that his scalp could be seen shining underneath, his hair still had streaks of dark pigment, an echo of its once almost black colour.

The old woman wore a blue apron with pockets at the front. Her hair, in contrast to her husband's, was as white as the snow outside; but her face was still firm and expressive, while his hung so slackly on his skull that it had hardly more life in it than a mask.

Christmas decorations, precariously erected a week earlier, hung all around them, gleaming as they were caught on draughts of air.

The silence between them, and the inane laughter on the TV, were interrupted by a sharp knock at the door.

"Carol singers," guessed the old woman.

"Carol singers?" muttered the old man. "Not how they did it in our day. Sing first, knock later, if at all – that's how we did it. Not any more –"

The knocking came again.

The old woman levered herself to her feet and padded to the front door in slippered feet. "Oh, cat, I do wish you'd get out from under my feet," she complained half-heartedly, as a small black feline darted ahead of her, guessing where she was going and hoping to be let out. The old woman opened the door, only a crack, careful not to let her pet out into the snow.

A cold-eyed boy stood on the doorstep. There was a grubby plaster cast on his left wrist. He did not start singing when she opened the door. "Mrs Horton?" he asked. "Could I have a word with Mr Horton? It's about the Tipler factory."

"That old place," grimaced Mrs Horton. "Hasn't it fallen down yet?"

"Not yet. Not quite," said the boy, with a half-smile. "They want to turn it into luxury flats."

"Luxury flats? That place is haunted, no-one's going to want to live there."

"Who is it?" called Mr Horton from the living room.

"Someone who wants to talk to you about the factory. They want to turn it into luxury flats."

"Don't leave them standing on the doorstep in this weather. Ask them in."

Mrs Horton made way for the boy, using her feet to shepherd the cat away from the door. When the door was closed, he wiped a little snow from his shoes on the doormat. Mr Horton twisted around awkwardly to look at the boy, keeping his walking stick balanced on the arm of his chair. If an expression was to be read on his face, it was disappointment: disappointment, perhaps, that his visitor was only a boy.

"Sorry to bother you this late…" the boy was saying, "only I wanted to ask you about the Tipler factory."

"Not the Tipler factory as you call it. It's our factory. My wife's a Tipler, you know."

"Your factory. Yes. They want to turn it into luxury flats."

"First I've heard of it. They send boys now, do they?"

"I'm not involved," the boy told him evenly.

There was a pause in the conversation, filled by waves of laughter coming from the TV. Mrs Horton spoke next. "Put that rubbish off, dear," she told her husband. To the boy, she asked: "Would you like a cup of tea, love? It's rotten cold out."

"Yes please," replied the boy, watching impassively as Mr Horton struggled with his arthritis-folded hands to press the correct button on the TV's remote control. Mrs Horton shuffled away towards the kitchen.

The boy noticed one of the photographs on the mantelpiece. A boy wearing a bomber jacket and drainpipe trousers smiled out at the camera. The photo was faded, bleached by years of sunlight. "Your grandson?" asked the boy innocently. He knew very well that he was looking at someone who had died thirty years before.

"Paul." The old man's tone hardened. "What exactly is it that you want?"

The boy smiled, but there was no warmth in his expression. "I want to talk about your factory – for a school history project."

"Long time ago, that was. I used to be the manager there before it closed down." Mr Horton's eyes seemed to glaze over, as if he was looking at the past. "Great shame it was. All the work went to the far east."

"That's not the only reason it closed, is it?" asked the boy, still standing in the centre of the room, refusing a seat.

"You mean William and his son. You know about them."

"I know *all* about them," said the boy, his tone harsh.

"If you know so much, what are you asking me for?" snapped the old man.

"You know whose ghost haunts the factory, and you know why. He's ready to make peace with you. We have a car outside. If you get your coat, and come with us, it will all be over in a little while."

"You're insane!" muttered the old man, his face draining of colour.

"Peace, Mr Horton. That's what I'm talking about. It's not too late for you... and William... even if it is for others," said the boy, looking at the photograph on the mantelpiece once more.

"I don't know what you're talking about. Get out –" the old man said. He grabbed his stick and raised it threateningly.

But the boy only laughed humourlessly in the face of this warning. "I know it's a long time ago — so let me refresh your memory. Unless you'd rather wait until your wife comes back with the tea?"

"Say your piece and go," said Mr Horton, sinking back submissively into his armchair.

"You were married to William's sister — still are — but you coveted his wife," began the boy, staring down at the old man, who averted his gaze. "You made your move one day at the Tiplers' country house, down by the lake. But it all went wrong, didn't it? She rejected you. I don't know what went through your mind in those fateful moments. Were you afraid of losing your job? Angry, humiliated? Whatever the reason, you, John Horton, manager of Tipler's textile factory pushed her, Amelia Tipler, the wife of its owner off the bank and held her under the cold water until she stopped moving. So much for your love of her."

The old man was rocking gently in his chair, staring into space.

The boy continued. "You didn't know it at the time, but you were seen. The boy, William Junior, had been playing in the woods. He heard his mother's screams, and saw you holding her under. You didn't know it at the time, but you guessed later, by the way he no longer dared to look you in the eye... he was always a little strange, was William, quiet and furtive. He probably would never have told anyone. But you saw a chance not to be missed when the Alchemist asked for him — there was great personal advancement at stake by toadying up to him. Somehow you separated William from his father. Then you arranged for him to meet the Alchemist in the factory after it had closed one night... have you any idea what happened to him then? And then what? Did they give him back to you once they had finished with him? Or did they throw him from the roof of the factory themselves? Then there was the father. Whether he jumped by himself, tortured by guilt — guilt that only belonged on your shoulders – or was pushed by the ghost of his son, you were responsible for his death too."

"A nice little story," muttered the old man hoarsely, when the boy had stopped speaking. "A nice little made-up story."

"I'm not finished. Would you like to hear about your grandson next?" asked the boy.

The old man's eyes flickered, meeting the boy's for an instant. Then he looked away, shaking his head.

"Paul and his friend Kevin. The year was nineteen eighty-seven. It was raining – it had been raining for weeks, but that day it came down harder than ever. They decided to shelter – they made the mistake of sheltering in *your* factory." The boy laid emphasis on that. *Your* factory. "I don't know exactly what happened. I do know that the ghost of the boy William had been growing stronger for years. All the kids knew the factory was haunted. But it had never been as haunted as it was that day. A relative of his enemy had come to visit – William was not about to let that opportunity slip. The bodies were never found – well, no-one knew where to look. Later, floods covered them with silt, and they lie there still, in the cellar of *your* factory, waiting for the developers to find them..."

Tears were running down the old man's sagging face.

"It isn't too late for you. If you come with us, make your peace with him – perhaps he, too, will find peace at last. The Alchemist took my brother too – after all these years he's still out there. You can help us track him down, stop him at last."

"The Alchemist? I don't know any Alchemist. I didn't have anything to do with any of it. Nothing!" The old man's denials were absolute, but the tears flowing down his face told a different tale.

Mrs Horton reappeared in the living room, carrying a teapot and cups on a tray. The first thing she noticed was her husband's silent agony. "John? What's the matter?" she asked, panicking.

John Horton ignored her. The arrival of his wife seemed to have galvanized his confidence. "Get out!" he shouted at the boy, his mouth thick with saliva. "I don't know where you get your ideas from, but I don't want you bringing them around here." So saying, the old man grabbed his walking stick and once more raised it in threat. It was an empty gesture, like a trapped wasp stinging the inside of a jar.

"It's all right," the boy said, nodding, not flinching at the old man's threatened attack. "I won't bother you again. I see that it is too late for you, after all." He turned towards the front door.

"My husband isn't well," Mrs Horton told the boy, following him to the door. Once again the little cat rose in her path. "Why are you disturbing him like this?"

The boy smiled faintly at her. "Don't worry. You won't be seeing me again." He walked down the garden path to the road, turned right at the end, and vanished into the evening darkness.

David climbed into the back seat of the estate car. Milla and Professor Fuller turned to look at him. "Well?" asked Milla.

"He's not coming," David said simply.

"We could drag him out by his ankles," Milla suggested.

David shook his head. "It's too late. He's too old. It was too long ago – I think he may even have convinced *himself* that he is innocent."

"Never mind," the professor said. "We have bigger fish to fry." He reached for the ignition but let it go again without starting the engine. He sat back with a heavy sigh. "But I am assuming too much. I'm assuming that you want to come with me, that you want to know the truth. And I should assume no such thing."

"Of course we want to know," David said stoutly.

"It is in your nature to want to know. But it is a heavy responsibility for me. The consequences could be lethal..."

Milla spoke up. "We've been there already. You have to tell us what you know."

"Forewarned is forearmed," David put in.

"You cannot un-know these things. Once you know you may wish you don't. Ignorance can be bliss. If I say nothing, you may never meet the demons I can show you... but if I tell you, if I show you, it is inevitable that you will.... Do you see?"

"I don't care," David said flatly.

"You can't dangle this in front of us all the time!" Milla said, sounding slightly exasperated. "Either tell us or stop talking about it."

"Please tell us."

"Wait! There's more. I may be able to do little more than show you the door. I don't know how much longer I have left. I fear not long. It is not fair to you two for me to just point you towards the battlefield and then say goodbye..."

"Who else will do it if not us?" David replied. "For myself I want nothing else. I fear nothing... I'm sorry... that sounds... but it's true. I want only revenge..."

"Is there nothing you have to live for beyond this?" demanded the professor.

"Nothing." Did he imagine it, or did Milla suddenly stiffen in the seat next to him?

"And you Milla?" the old man asked.

"This is something big, isn't it? It's something that affects a lot of people. This is more important than anything. It would be wrong to walk away."

There was a long silence. Snowflakes landed on the windscreen and slid down, melting as they went.

Abruptly the professor sighed. "All right – I'll show you. Though it condemn me to hell… I'll show you. But not today." The professor reached for the keys again, but did not start the engine. "Would you two mind walking home? I'm a little… tired."

David and Milla obediently got out and stood on the snowy pavement to watch the old white car drive away.

"He doesn't have long left," Milla said. "His aura is dark, like the sky before a thunderstorm."

"If we could only get him to register at a doctors'…"

"He won't. You know what he's like."

"He hasn't been the same since that night."

"None of us have," Milla rejoined.

David felt Milla take his hand. He immediately felt safe, and warm, and he knew that whatever happened, life was worth living.

"I want to tell you something," she said, and turned to face him. "Something happened to me last week in the Shadowland, when I got too cold. It's my eyes. I can still read. Up close anyway. But every day it's getting worse, and I don't think it's going to stop…"

"You're going blind?" David blurted, shocked.

"Don't tell me you haven't noticed that I'm getting clumsy. That I trip over things, read with my nose an inch from the paper, and cannot bear to cross the road on my own…"

"But I thought… I mean… this is all my fault!" David turned away and stamped off a few paces before wheeling back to grab Milla's hand once again.

"No. It isn't. It really isn't."

He stared into her eyes. "Can you still see me?"

Milla smiled at him – a cold smile, not her usual sunny version. "Yes. Not really. Not well. But I can see your soul."

"There'll be treatment..."

"I want you to kiss me," she said.

David was too stunned to speak.

"While I can still see you. I want you to kiss me."

"But... but I might be rubbish..."

"It won't matter," Milla said.

And she was right. It didn't.

To be continued in *The Factory of Souls*...

Coda: Justice for William Tipler

Mrs Horton listened with something approaching despair as her husband awkwardly hammered out numbers on their big-button telephone and ordered a taxi. He would not explain where he was going, nor why. He pulled on his huge overcoat and waited in his armchair, gripping his walking stick tightly.

"Why won't you tell me what's going on?" Mrs Horton was saying for the umpteenth time.

John Horton ignored her. At last, there came a toot-toot from the taxi outside. He pushed himself to his feet and began to shuffle to the door.

Mrs Horton blocked his path. "John! Where are you going?" she demanded.

John stopped and stared her straight in the eye. "I've always loved you, Lotty, I want you to know that… whatever else I've done, I've always loved you. What happened with William should never have happened."

"John! You're scaring me. What do you mean, what happened with William? What's going on? Is it something to do with that boy who just came round?" She stopped speaking suddenly, a long-buried memory resurfacing. "No! You didn't! You swore to me that you didn't… we agreed that we wouldn't give him to them…"

"I'm sorry. Goodbye," John told her, firmly but gently displacing her from his path.

"Wait! Wait, John, please! Let's talk about it first. You're too old," babbled Charlotte. "You can't go out at night in this weather!" She grabbed at her husband, but he shook her off. He was at the door now. Another toot-toot came from the impatient taxi driver. "Please John," she said, crying, "don't leave me."

But John Horton would not reply. He set off down the path to where the taxi waited, climbed in stiffly, and slammed the door shut behind him.

Charlotte slumped down on the hall floor. Her mouth worked wordlessly. She heard the taxi rev its engine, heard its gears shifting, wondered where her husband was going, and feared that she would never see him again.

Robbie Drake heard a car pull up nearby and looked up from his candlelit game of solitaire. This was a strange time for traffic to venture down the little dead end of Raglan Road. It was late, dark, and snow covered everything — even the leafless branches of the butterfly bushes in the abandoned factory he called home were decked in a ghoulishly festive blanket of white. He rose, taking care not to disturb his playing cards or the guttering candle lighting the game, and crept to the boarded-up front window. A taxi had pressed new tracks into the snow, and had drawn to a halt in front of the factory next door, the one Carraway reckoned was haunted.

For a moment Robbie wondered if it was perhaps Carraway himself on some strange late-night errand at the factory or even following up on his promise to return to visit and discuss their mutual enemy he called the "Solvent Man." But the figure that emerged from the back of the taxi was not that of Carraway: it was a stooped old man.

The taxi driver wound his window down to accept his fare. "Are you sure, Dad?" he asked, his voice loud in the crisp still. "There ain't nothin' around here."

Robbie watched as the old man pressed a much-folded banknote into the driver's palm. "Don't wait," he said.

"Suit yerself. But there ain't nothin' around here. What did you say this road was called?" the taxi driver asked.

"Raglan Road," said the old man, and backed away a few steps, waiting for the taxi to drive away.

"What do you want here, anyway?"

This time old man did not reply.

"Fair enough," the driver said, and gunned his engine. The taxi made a U-turn and roared off into the night, scattering snow in its wake.

The old man approached the gate of the Tipler factory. Robbie could have told him that it was locked, and that the only access was up a rotting plank propped against the side wall. After a few short, unsteady steps the old man was out of view, and Robbie had to relocate to a window giving a better vantage point. When he arrived at a suitable spy hole, he could see that the tall gate was already swinging open and the old man was entering the factory yard, shuffling through the snow. The fool was going to die of hypothermia. What was he planning to do, kip out here? Even with a sleeping bag in a pile of rubbish, Robbie was generally freezing cold all the time.

The factory gate swung closed behind the old man with an agonising creak.

Robbie Drake's sneer became a rictus of terror as he watched the gate swing closed of its own accord: the only person anywhere near it was the old man, and he was now standing in the middle of the yard, facing the old factory itself, clutching his wooden walking stick as if he was about to clout someone with it.

For a moment Robbie wondered whether the gate could have swung back on its own, just by the way it was hung. Maybe if Carraway hadn't mentioned a ghost he wouldn't have thought twice about it.

Suddenly the old man shouted aloud at the factory. "I don't owe you anything, not after Paul!"

Robbie relaxed a little. As long as there was madness around, there was less chance that there were actual ghosts. And there was plenty of madness around: Carraway shouting his dead brother's name, Carraway and a different old man going into the factory tooled up like the Ghostbusters, Carraway's friend Milla kicking out the old man's car windscreen because for some reason she couldn't remember how to open the door. Now this old boy was ranting about someone called Paul. The sooner someone knocked the place down, the better. Although then they might come for Robbie's home and knock that down, too. On balance perhaps it was better if they left it standing.

There was a screeching sound from the direction of the factory. Robbie flinched, imagining a screaming monster within; he finally identified the sound as someone pulling a nail out from one of the boards covering the lower windows and doors. He started breathing again.

One of the many boards fell away from the window it was protecting into the snow. Either there was someone inside, or –

The screeching came again, but it doubled and tripled in volume again and again until it seemed that all the demons of Hell were coming after the old man. One board after another fell from the front of the factory, flumping down into the snow one by one until the front of the factory was completely clear of them. But for the decay of time and vandalism, the factory looked again as it had sixty years before.

All the nails had been removed. All the boards had fallen from the front of the factory. The screeching had stopped. An eerie silence reigned once more.

Robbie could hardly breathe. The eye that was pressed to the crack in the boards was frozen, his chest was hurting, and he was beginning to see stars.

The old man gripped his stick tightly and resolutely shuffled on towards the factory.

Robbie wanted to scream at him not to go in, but he could not bring himself to utter a word. A moment later – before he had time to collect himself or do anything – the old man had entered the factory and was out of sight.

Suddenly Robbie knew without a doubt that if he didn't drag the old man out of the factory he wouldn't be coming out alive. Going in would be terrifying. Probably suicidal. Whatever the old man and the ghost had going on between them, they probably wouldn't thank Robbie Drake for trying to referee. He hesitated. He stared through the crack until his eye was scarcely able to blink and his neck was locked in place. He saw nothing. He heard nothing. But after a while he was sure the old man was not coming out again.

A sudden thought occurred to Robbie: *what would Carraway do?* Bloody obvious what Carraway would do. He'd be in there faster than a ferret down a rabbit hole. In his mind's eye he saw Carraway sprinting across the snow and into the factory on his next heroic (read stupid) quest. "I'm no hero like you, Carraway," Robbie said under his breath, "but anything you can do, I can damn well do it too." With that realisation, the spell was broken: Robbie Drake turned away from the window and ran down the concrete stairs. He was slowed up a little by having to duck under the iron sheeting of his makeshift door. The footing in the side alley was treacherous, with all sorts of junk hidden under the snow. He flipped over the plank, so that he could walk up the side with no snow on.

As Robbie walked up the plank, an empty window frame high up on the front of the factory banged open. He jumped and nearly lost his balance.

The old man was standing in the window. He was going to jump.

"Hey!" Robbie shouted, and started running forwards again. He dropped down inside the factory forecourt. But he was too late; as he watched, the old man stepped forwards, into space. He did not scream; he just fell limply, like a mannequin thrown out of a window to stand in for a falling person in an 80s TV show. There was a crunching thud at the end of that fall that probably broke every bone in the old man's body. Robbie forced himself to look; he forced himself to go closer; and finally he forced himself to kneel in the snow and check whether life had departed from the old man.

It had.

"Who are you?" asked a curious voice.

Robbie Drake turned to find himself confronted by a boy. The boy was small, and was dressed in long shorts and a white shirt. He was also semi-transparent, and seemed to be lit from within; little moonbeams gleamed around the seams of his clothes as he moved.

"Robbie." *Carraway is right, damn him*, Robbie thought. *There is a ghost. And I'm next on his menu. He's going to send me up to jump from the window now...*

But the boy only smiled. "Hello Robbie. I'm William. I'm going to go now. If you see your friend David, say hello for me. And cheer up, Robbie. Don't give up hope just yet. Your sister's still alive..."

"My sister!"

But the ghost said no more. It faded quickly, the way a shadow fades when the sun goes behind a cloud. In moments it had completely disappeared. Robbie found himself standing alone in the snow with the body of an old man and realized that he needed to get as far away from it as he could as fast as he could get there.

Your sister's still alive...

If there was a chance... the slightest chance... that the ghost was speaking the truth... that Becks was alive, and had somehow escaped...

Where would she go?

Robbie could only think of one place.

Home.

Afterword

The city of Fairfield and all the characters in it are fictional. In this story, Michael Andersen is possessed, but shows symptoms of severe autism. As David says, exorcism cannot cure autism. The reason I felt the need to spell that out in the story is that after writing *The Door into Shadow* I discovered that real people in the real world have been known to try exorcism to cure autism. One such notorious case resulted in the death of Terrance Cottrell, a boy of eight.

Autism is not caused by spirit possession. It cannot be cured by exorcism. Spirits do not exist except in our imaginations, which is also the only place that exorcism belongs.

The Factory of Souls:

The second book of the Shadowland Hexology

The ghost haunting the shell of the abandoned Tipler mill is finally at rest.

But the true monster at the rotten heart of Fairfield is still alive – if you can call a vampire alive. Mister Jack and his procurer the Alchemist have been terrorising the children of Fairfield for more than two hundred years. Week after week, year after year, children vanish in the night and are never heard from again.

And the rate of disappearances has suddenly increased. Unknown to David Carraway and his friends, Milla the young witch and Professor Fuller the aged expert on the occult, not all of the abducted children end up with Mister Jack's fangs fastened upon their throats. His secret cult the Red Guild are stockpiling living children at the Factory of Souls in preparation for a blasphemous ritual at which the elite of the city believe they will become gods.

There is only one enemy that the ancient vampire Mister Jack fears: sunlight. But with the Alchemist and the Red Guild around him, there is no chance that David and his friends can ever use this ally to defeat him. Their only hope of survival lies in avoiding Jack by night. Because the night time s his time.

With all the important people of Fairfield members of the Red Guild and hundreds of others employed by it, the odds are against David even finding out where the Factory of Souls is, let alone being able to free the captives held there before it is too late.

And there may be even more at stake than the lives of the missing children…

About the Author

Your author is usually called Jit even though his real name is Jonathan. He lives in Norwich, UK, with his darling wife and two (probably grown up by now) children. When not writing fiction, Jit is an entomologist, as well as a butler to three cats.

Farewell Clyde: missing in action since 2015

Welcome Scully: joined the family in 2016

Jitland.blogspot.co.uk

By the Same Author

Elsie Smith Vampyre Hunter

Edison Blue

The Shadowland Hexology:

The Door into Shadow

Coming soon:

The Factory of Souls

World's End

The Deepest Grave

Demon Hunter

The Tree of Life